THE STAKES WERE HIGH . . .
AND SHE WAS DESPERATE

Langdon had been in the saloon only a few seconds when he spotted prim Ivy Barton—now dressed in a daring scarlet gown—and heard someone refer to her as Miss Montana.

Nothing could have surprised him more, and at first he couldn't believe his own eyes and ears. Why, he wondered, would she be posing as someone else?

Unless she was involved in some sort of scam . . .

She had revealed nothing that would lead him to believe she was capable of that. Obviously, however, there was more to Ivy Barton than met the eye.

SWEET IVY'S GOLD

PAULA PAUL

HarperPaperbacks
A Division of HarperCollinsPublishers

This is a work of fiction. The characters, incidents, and dialogues are products of the author's imagination and are not to be construed as real. Any resemblance to actual events or persons, living or dead, is entirely coincidental.

HarperPaperbacks *A Division of* HarperCollins*Publishers*
10 East 53rd Street, New York, N.Y. 10022

Cover illustration by Jim Griffin

First printing: February 1993

Printed in the United States of America

HarperPaperbacks, HarperMonogram, and colophon are trademarks of HarperCollins*Publishers*

❖ 10 9 8 7 6 5 4 3 2 1

In memory of Julie.
Our memories of you will always be golden.

ACKNOWLEDGMENTS

I gratefully acknowledge the use of Marshall Sprague's *Money Mountain, The Story of Cripple Creek Gold* (University of Nebraska Press, 1953) in my research on Colorado gold mining. Although this story, conceived in my imagination, is based loosely on the history of Cripple Creek, Colorado, I have altered the facts considerably and thus have called my boomtown Eagleton instead.

I also wish to thank Kenneth, Timothy, and Kristen Paul, for encouraging me to gamble, and Madge Harrah and Dr. Terrisita McCarty for helping me stuff the aces up my sleeve.

1

1891

Hell would smell like the air during a thunderstorm, she thought. The way it smelled now, acrid and gaseous, while lightning was tearing open the sky in great electrical rifts. Maybe the storm was a sign. Another sign that she and Alex never should have left Tennessee.

Ivy Barton watched the turbulence through the windows of the train as it moved with a heavy, sensuous sway across the prairie. The storm had come in suddenly, wearing a yellow shroud, and then had begun to scream and slash. Now ice, secretly frozen somewhere in the hot summer sky, pounded the train with increasing racket and rage, piling up on the prairie like snowdrifts. Hell frozen over, she thought.

"Lord have mercy," she said half under her breath. Alex glanced toward her. "What? Speak up, Ivy."

"Look at that, Alex! They're big as hen's eggs." As

Ivy leaned forward to speak to her husband, who sat across from her, she caught the scent of liquor on his breath.

"God, they *are* big."

But Alex's attention was focused on something inside the train. When Ivy followed his gaze, she saw a tall, heavy-featured woman walking down the aisle, wearing a dress of emerald-green taffeta cut unfashionably low in front. A heavy film of perspiration made her large breasts look as if they were melting over her neckline. When the woman's gaze met hers, Ivy quickly turned away, but not quickly enough. The woman stopped beside her and spoke.

"Hot, ain't it?" She fanned herself with a garish handkerchief edged in emerald-green lace, wafting a sickly sweet scent of lilac water over Ivy. A layer of death-white powder had mixed with her sweat, making her florid face look as if it were coated with putty.

"Yes." Ivy spoke in the slow, taffy-candy idiom of the South, stretching the single syllable into two. She turned away from the woman to gaze once again at the storm. It was not that she wished to be rude; she only wished the woman would move away so that she wouldn't have to be rude. She had no idea what to say to someone so tawdry and coarse. Lord, how she wished the rain and hail would stop so she could open a window!

"Aft'noon, ma'am," Alex said. "Right pretty dress you're wearin'."

"Why, thank you, sir."

Ivy felt the woman's eyes on her again, but she refused to look up, and finally the woman moved down the aisle.

Alex was clearly enjoying every aspect of the trip,

including the unfortunate mix of fellow travelers. Ivy knew he had expected her to enjoy it, too. He'd said it was high time she experienced the marvels of modern transportation.

Ivy didn't care for such marvels. To her, the train was a raving mad mechanical beast that had filled up on all manner of unsavory people as it raced across the plains of Colorado, carrying her toward a frighteningly uncertain future.

It still seemed incredible to her that Alex could have done what he had done—sold their home outside of Nashville to buy the land in Colorado, sight unseen, after reading a newspaper advertisement. He'd done it without consulting her, and now here they were, racing across a frozen inferno.

As Alex saw it, they were headed toward the promised land. It was farmland he had bought, but farmland smack in the middle of Colorado gold country, the advertisement had said in its alluring prose. Ivy knew that only fools went looking for gold. Alex had sensed her discontent. "If we don't find gold, we'll have the land, and we can farm," he'd said.

She had wanted to cry out to him in fear and anger that he was no good at farming, that he had barely scratched out a living on their Tennessee farm, and it would be even worse in a place where the land was strange. She'd wanted to remind him that they'd likely have starved had she not grown a vegetable garden each year, kept a flock of chickens for eggs and a little meat occasionally, and taken in sewing.

But she had said nothing. It was best not to remind him of his failures; her own had been far more heinous. Two graves on the farm that now belonged to young Elijah Moore were dark reminders of her inadequacy. Although she was tortured every time she looked at the graves, she could not bear the thought of never seeing them again. Did they, like the land and the small house on the creek, now belong to Elijah? she wondered bleakly.

Ivy sensed Alex looking at her, and when she glanced at him, his smile broadened. It was a charming smile, even now, when it was a little loose and crooked from the effects of the liquor he'd sipped all afternoon out of the flask he kept in his hip pocket. Alex was a handsome man, blond and fair and still somewhat boyish looking at the age of thirty-five. He had kept his youthful look while she, at thirty-two, had lost hers.

Ivy reached to give Alex's hand a pat, as if to assure him that her unexpressed anger and despair had passed. It was a habit she had—shielding him, even from her own ill feelings. Yet it wasn't all one-sided. She knew he had done all he could to protect her from hurt as well.

Suddenly the air around them pulsated with light and sound as another lightning bolt struck the prairie. Ivy jerked herself upright and clutched the edge of her seat. The atmosphere inside the train was charged with tension.

A man slid onto the seat across the aisle from them. He was dressed like a gentleman, in a dark woolen suit with black riding boots and a wide-brimmed black hat. Ivy noted his square jaw and weathered face, very much in contrast with Alex's blond good looks. The man glanced at her and nodded, touching his hat, then turned to speak in a low tone to the elderly gent next to him. Ivy brought her hand up in a nervous gesture to the heavy auburn hair in a topknot under her small feathered toque. The man's gaze had left her oddly uncomfortable.

"Damn, it's a wild storm," Alex said, drawing her attention back to the window. Thunder roared like an angry giant. "Ivy, I think the train's slowin'."

It was raining harder than ever, and the hail that had blanketed the ground was melting rapidly under the steady downpour. The frozen hell now looked drenched and endless, stretching from horizon to horizon. Like a vast ocean? Ivy had never seen an ocean.

Something about the immensity of the prairie disturbed her. She shuddered and turned away from the window. Then, quickly, she had to clutch the edge of her seat again as the train lurched to a stop. Her hat slid forward, covering her eyes, and her cloth handbag tumbled from her lap, its contents spilling at her feet. She quickly pushed back her toque, then dropped to her knees to gather up her embroidery, an ivory comb, a handkerchief, and a small package of hairpins.

"These are yours, I believe." The bottle of camphor and wad of cotton that had tumbled out of the bag along with the other contents were being thrust toward her.

Ivy raised her eyes to meet the deep blue of those belonging to the man across the aisle. She grabbed the bottle and the cotton from him a little too abruptly to be polite, then lowered her eyes as she murmured her thanks. But before she'd averted her gaze, she'd detected a slight twitch of the man's mouth, as if he were amused, as if he knew the purpose of the camphor and cotton. She pushed them into her bag and turned to Alex, who was having trouble readjusting himself on his seat.

"Are you all right, madam?" the blue-eyed man asked.

"Yes, thank you." Ivy slid back onto her seat.

"Thank ye," Alex echoed, leaning forward to address the stranger. "My wife 'preciates you helpin' her with her belongin's." His speech was slurred by the liquor. Ivy let it pass that Alex thought he knew what she was feeling.

Instead of returning to his seat, the tall, blue-eyed man stepped closer to hers to allow the people crowding into the aisle to move past him. Many had left their seats to retrieve their scattered possessions, and several were trying to find out why the train had stopped.

Ivy felt the man's eyes on her, and she turned to see that he was still wearing his slightly amused smile.

"I'm Langdon Runnels," he said, extending his hand toward Alex.

Alex took the hand. "Alex Barton. And my wife, Ivy Barton."

At that moment Mr. Runnels was jostled from behind, and he fell forward, across Ivy, his shoulder striking her head and toppling her hat. The weight of him almost crushed her chest as he sprawled across her, his face in her lap. Ivy gasped and threw her hands up, not knowing whether she should move his head or avoid touching him.

Slowly he turned himself over, his head still cradled by her thighs. "My apologies," he said, looking up at her, seemingly no more embarrassed than if he had bumped her arm.

"You all right, Mr. Runnels?" Alex tried to rise but quickly sat down again.

"I'm fine," the man said, finally pulling himself upright. Once he was on his feet again, he retrieved Ivy's hat from the floor, gave it a quick brush with his fingertips, and handed it to her. "And you, madam?"

"Quite all right," Ivy answered stiffly.

"Why don't you join us?" Her husband sounded downright jovial.

Mr. Runnels grinned. "It seems I already have."

Alex laughed. Ivy was not amused.

"Are you traveling far?" Runnels asked, taking the seat next to her. She tried to inch away inconspicuously.

"We've come all the way from Tennessee," Alex said, oblivious of her unease.

"Then let me be the first to welcome you to Colorado." Runnels settled in, draping his arm across the back of Ivy's seat and stretching out his long legs. She stiffened at the unavoidable proximity to his leanly muscled frame.

"Thank ye. You the 'ficial welcome committee?" Alex asked. "A native of the state or somethin'?"

"No," Runnels answered, "but I've been here long enough."

"Well, I'm mighty pleased to meet a man who knows the country." Alex smiled amiably. "You in the gold minin' business by any chance?"

"Oh, I've owned a small claim or two."

"Have you now? Any luck?"

Runnels grinned. "I've come by a little gold." He pulled a sack of tobacco and a packet of papers from his pocket and rolled a smoke. "If not from the ground, then from the fools who bought my claims."

Alex laughed and in the next breath was telling their new companion how they had invested in land in Colorado in the heart of the gold country. Ivy stopped listening, not wanting to be reminded of how heartsick she felt.

The coarse woman in the green dress was once again in the aisle, taffeta rustling. "Why do you think we've stopped, Langdon?" she asked, stepping next to them. Before he could answer, she spotted the conductor, who had just entered the car. "You there! What's going on? Why are we stopped?"

"If you'll all take your seats, I have an announcement to make," the conductor answered, speaking to the crowd.

The woman sat down across the aisle on the seat Runnels had vacated.

"I'm afraid we've met with some bad luck," the conductor said when the passengers finally quieted down. "This downpour has washed out the tracks ahead, and—" A din of protests surged through the car. "Please, please." He raised his arms. "We've sent a man ahead on foot to telegraph the depot in Colorado Springs. The railroad will send another train out to transport all passengers to town." He slid his watch from his vest pocket. "I predict only a few more hours' delay." With a genial smile and a look of confidence, he snapped his watch shut and moved down the aisle toward the next car.

The passengers clamored their impatience and disappointment. Alex, however, was unperturbed. He continued to expound on their "investment." Mr. Runnels, equally unruffled, admitted he'd never heard of the town where Alex had bought land, but there were dozens of new communities sprouting up throughout the mountains all the time, he said.

Ivy let it all wash over her, trying not to dwell on

her worries. Tolerating the noisy, cramped, stifling railroad car was trouble enough. She fanned herself with her handkerchief and mopped at the damp ringlets of hair at the back of her neck, longing to open a window for some fresh air. It was still raining too hard, though. Perhaps if she could get near the door, some air would be seeping in from between the cars.

"Excuse me," she said, rising.

Mr. Runnels stood as she moved into the aisle. Alex made an attempt to stand as well but stumbled backward, knocking his hat askew. Ivy ignored him and made her way to the back of the train. It was not much cooler there, she discovered, but the stench of confined and sweating human bodies seemed slightly less offensive.

Two children on a nearby seat quarreled over who was to have the place nearest the window. The sight disturbed her, and she started back to her seat. Lord o' mercy. The woman in the low-cut green dress was moving toward her.

"Got so even the railroad ain't reliable, but what can a body do?" the woman asked as she drew near. She daubed the top of her breasts with her startling handkerchief. "Damned rain. I wish it would stop so we could get some air."

Ivy was so unaccustomed to hearing a woman swear that she could only stare at her without replying.

The woman didn't seem to notice Ivy's reaction. "Allow me to introduce myself. I'm Mrs. Montana McCrory." She thrust her hand forward as if she were a man.

Compelled to extend her own hand, Ivy murmured, "I'm Mrs. Alexander Barton."

Mrs. McCrory touched the tips of Ivy's fingers lightly in what she undoubtedly felt was a genteel manner. "Where you heading, honey?"

"I—I believe the place is called Green Valley, Colorado," Ivy said, doubly uncomfortable with the casual endearment.

"I'm on my way to Eagleton myself," Mrs. McCrory said. "Is Green Valley anywhere near there?"

"I'm sure I don't know," Ivy said, trying to look away. Mrs. McCrory's face was even more flushed, and the puttylike mixture of powder and sweat had begun to run, some of it settling into the large pores in her cheeks.

"Well, I'm goin' to take possession of a drinking establishment and gambling parlor in Eagleton," Mrs. McCrory said, forcing the conversation. Her eyes suddenly brimmed with tears. "My late husband left it to me." She used a corner of her lace-edged handkerchief to dab at her eyes. "Poor Tom. Died one night when we was—"

She glanced at Ivy and coughed nervously, twisting the handkerchief with her thick, pudgy fingers. "Weak heart. Too much excitement for him." She sighed, smiling reminiscently. "Oh, but it was good. Just because a man's older don't mean he can't—"

She coughed her nervous cough again. "We'd only been married three weeks," she said, tears filling her eyes once more. "I met him in Kansas City. We was plannin' on comin' out here together to run the Golden Palace. Tom said it was a good business in a nice little town that's just beginning to boom. But now Tom's gone, and it's up to me to do it all alone." Her voice broke, and she dabbed at her eyes again. "What's a lady to do?"

This woman was the owner of a saloon! Ivy had heard of such females, but she'd never expected to meet one. "I—I'm sorry," she said, desperately wishing the woman would move away.

"Ladies like us ain't used to runnin' a business. But you have to do what you have to do." She sighed again. "What's Green Valley like? This place you're goin' to—is it a boom town, too?"

Ivy hadn't allowed herself to think that Green Valley might be filled with saloons and rough and rowdy miners. If that was the case, then it wouldn't be at all like the quiet village of Byrneville, Tennessee, with only a post office, a general store, and a school where her father had once been the schoolmaster. She felt despair creep over her again.

"I've never been there, so I can't say," she said stiffly. "Please excuse me." She tried to move around the woman to make her way back to her seat, but people were suddenly crowding into the aisle. Evidently the rain had stopped, and everyone was eager to get out of the train.

Alex and Langdon Runnels found her at the exit. Mr. Runnels stepped out ahead of her, then offered his hand to help her from the train. She hesitated a moment before she placed her small, work-roughened hand into his. When she was safely down the step, he held her hand a heartbeat longer than was necessary, and his eyes met hers. Then Alex stumbled from the train, and they each took one of his arms to steady him. The liquor obviously had affected him more than even Ivy had realized, but he had a ready excuse.

"Damned altitude seems t' make me dizzy."

Passengers stood beside the stalled train as the

conductor pointed out the churning stream that had destroyed the tracks. It was rolling down what only a few hours ago had been a dry wash. Children raced across the prairie, delighting in the freedom. Then, like a swarm of earthbound insects, they zoomed toward the churning water.

Ivy tried to head them off, but she couldn't move, and her scream remained frozen in her throat. Tears welled in her eyes and slid down her cheeks.

"Miz Barton?" She knew she should respond, but she couldn't tear her eyes off the children. Then she saw the other women, the mothers, cautioning the little ones and turning them away from the water. For a moment she could not believe her eyes. The children had not fallen in. They were safe.

"Miz Barton?" Ivy recognized Mrs. McCrory's voice. "Miz Barton, are you all right?" Ivy turned slowly and looked into the flushed face of Montana McCrory. Alex's arm slid around her waist, steadying her.

"You want to sit down, Ivy?" he asked.

"No," she said quickly, embarrassed that Mrs. McCrory had seen her reaction. "No, I'll be just fine."

"I know how you feel," Mrs. McCrory said. "The air in this high country makes a lady weak. I feel a mite wobbly myself."

"Why don't you get back on the train," Alex said, taking Ivy's arm. "I'm afraid we're goin' t' be here for a spell."

"No, Alex, it's so hot, I don't want—"

"You think we will?" Mrs. McCrory interrupted. "Be here for a long time?" She seemed nervous, agitated. "I can't afford that."

"Beg pardon?" Alex said.

"Ever'thin' goes to hell when there's nobody around to keep things runnin' right. I got to get to my business in Eagleton."

"Your business?"

"A drinking establishment and gambling parlor. I inherited it from my late husband." She reached into the small valise she carried and pulled out a deck of cards. "It's too bad when a lady finds herself having to support herself," she said to Ivy with an apologetic smile. "Ah, well, if I can't get to my business, I might as well bring business to me." She slipped the playing cards from their box. "Gentlemen," she said to a group standing near the tracks. "Is there a sporting man among you? Or maybe two or three? Montana McCrory, here, owner of the Golden Palace, invites you for a pleasant diversion with a game of chance. How about you, Langdon? I never knew you to pass up a game."

Langdon Runnels, who had moved a short distance away, gave her an affirmative nod.

"If you mean poker, I'm ready," another man said. "And if you got any other games in mind, I'm ready for that, too."

"What's your name, mister?" she asked, ignoring his suggestive tone.

"Name's Bill Mott."

Mrs. McCrory scrutinized him, taking in his rough work clothes, his greasy hat and scuffed boots. "You got the means, Mr. Mott?" she asked.

"Damn right. Got a week's pay in my pocket, and I aim to double it."

"You're welcome to try." She set aside her valise and shuffled the cards. They made a slurping sound, like water falling through a hole.

"Let's have some of them trunks from the baggage cars brought down here to use as tables and chairs," Mrs. McCrory said. Several of the men hurried to comply with her wish.

Ivy sensed a change in Alex even before he dropped his hand from her waist. He looked at her half-apologetically as he made a move toward the makeshift table.

"Alex . . ."

He turned back to her and smiled. "It's all right," he said quietly. "Jus' a little diversion."

"But, Alex, we can't afford—"

"Don't worry," he said. "I don't aim t' do anything foolish. I know what I'm doin', and I know when to quit."

She watched in silent rage as he moved away from her. She could not count on his knowing when to quit. Under the best of circumstances he had no sense when it came to money; he had even less when he was drinking. He'd lost money at cards before or had simply spent it foolishly on things they neither needed nor could afford. Sometimes it had gone for trinkets for her, like the music box that played "Humoresque." He'd brought that home just two weeks ago. She'd thought of returning it and retrieving the money, but in the end she'd kept it for fear of hurting his feelings.

She saw him drain his flask as he sat down to the card game, and she nervously raised a hand to the high neck of her dress. She took some comfort in the tight fastening. Sewn into a ruffle of her camisole were a few bills. Thirteen years of living with Alex had taught her to keep something to fall back on. She'd held out a small amount from the proceeds of the sale of their household goods.

"Five-card draw," Ivy heard Mrs. McCrory say as she welcomed Alex to the table with a nod and flicked the cards from the tips of her fingers. The practiced movements belied Mrs. McCrory's claim that she was a novice at supporting herself.

Langdon Runnels, clearly an acquaintance of Mrs. McCrory's, seemed equally at ease at the gambling table, his long frame draped across one of the trunks that served as a chair.

"Haven't sat down at a game with you in months, Langdon," Mrs. McCrory said. "Don't get to Kansas City like you used to."

Ivy glanced at Alex again and saw him accept a drink from a bottle of liquor Bill Mott offered him. Since she didn't want to create a scene by insisting that he not play, she could only hope that he would keep his head. Forcing herself to walk away from the gambling, she found one of the extra trunks pulled from the baggage car. She sat down and withdrew her embroidery from her traveling bag, carefully working the cross-stitches and stealing glances at Alex.

Soon she was joined by other women, who also used the trunks and baggage pulled from the train as chairs on the wet prairie floor.

"Do you think we'll be here long, ma'am?" asked the young woman who sat next to her. She had introduced herself as Sylvie Ledbetter.

"Hard to tell, but the conductor seemed to think not." Ivy tied off a strand of blue thread and snipped it with her scissors, then picked up a skein of green to work into the design.

"Well, I do hope not," Sylvie said. "My Luther will be waiting for me in Colorado Springs, and I know he'll be worried. I haven't seen him in two weeks. It's the first time I've ever been away from him that long, but I just had to visit Mama down in Pueblo."

Ivy listened to Sylvie's talk, wondering if she had ever been so moonstruck about her own marriage. The truth was, she couldn't remember. Thirteen years was too long ago. She did remember, though, that she had dreamed of going away to school as her brother had done. Her father had not allowed it. Although an educator himself, he considered too much schooling a waste of time and money for a girl. Marriage had been expected of her, and Alex Barton, the most handsome, charming, and sought-after young man around Byrneville, had proposed. It was also expected of her that she love him, and so she had.

Sylvie was talking of children now, making Ivy think of her own girls, both dead now. Oh, God, why did she have to remember? After their accident less than a year ago, another child had been dead before it left her womb. God's punishment because she'd let the first two die, maybe. Or maybe it was crazy to think that. Sometimes she thought she really had gone a little crazy. Crazy from too much loss, too much grief. And there were times when she thought she deserved God's punishment.

She'd found a way to beat him at his own game, though. The midwife had told her about the cotton wads soaked in camphor and taught her how to attach a string to them to make them easy to remove afterward and how to mix a bit of lard with the camphor to keep it from being too drying. Such a practice was illegal, of course, but she'd taken no chances and never talked openly about the device, not even with Alex. She had told him it was to prevent infection.

She continued to listen to Sylvie while she worked at her embroidery, trying not to think of anything except the needlework. But her thoughts kept wandering back to Alex at his game. If he was still playing, did that mean he was winning? Or simply that he had not yet lost it all? She grew careless with her cross-stitches and began to find Sylvie's voice annoying. It was hard to tell what was going on in the game, since everyone talked low. Only Bill Mott's voice rose occasionally, whether in anger or delight, she couldn't tell.

A few of the women decided that it was time to eat, and they produced biscuits, fried chicken, salt-cured pork, and jars of beef from their food baskets. As they called to their children, Ivy found her own basket, filled with cornbread, boiled eggs, and buttermilk, and set it out with the communal picnic supper. Alex had complained of their unvaried fare, but it had been economical and filling, and Ivy had refused to spend their money in restaurants along the way. They'd need it to buy supplies, including a tent, and they'd need to hire a wagon to take them to their new land, where they would set up camp with the tent until a house could be built.

The picnic attracted the attention of the gamblers, and they stopped their game long enough to eat. Ivy watched Mrs. McCrory force her entire hand into a jar of meat to sop at the juices with a biscuit, then hold the morsel daintily between two fingers coated with the thick liquid.

Langdon Runnels hung back from the crowd, leaning against one of the railroad cars while he smoked.

Alex had been the last to leave the card table, taking a long drink from Bill Mott's bottle, then wiping his mouth on his sleeve before he stood to make his way on unsteady legs toward the food. Ivy watched him staggering about the makeshift table, spilling food and trying to excuse himself with silly jokes in thick-tongued, slurred speech.

She tried to urge him away from the crowd to save them both from embarrassment. "Come with me, Alex," she whispered. "Maybe it's not so hot in the train now. You could have a nap."

"Hell, I don't want t' sleep." Alex pulled away from her. "Not now. Not when my luck's due t' change."

"What do you mean, your luck is due to change?" Ivy whispered, alarmed. "You haven't lost all our money, have you?"

Alex laughed recklessly. "Jus' don' worry. You worry too much."

He made his weaving way back to the game. Ivy watched him a moment, her brow furrowed. Mr. Runnels had not rejoined the gamblers, but she didn't see where he had gone. She turned to help clear away the food, pretending not to notice the knowing looks the women gave her. She hated their pity, and she hated for Alex to look foolish in their eyes.

By the time the remaining food was stored away, the late-afternoon sun had inched closer to the horizon, turning the used-up rain clouds clustered there into liquid scarlet and the sky overhead burnished gold. Ivy strolled away from the crowd, walking toward the brilliant sunset, hoping that the train from Colorado Springs would be there soon, sparing her and Alex further embarrassment.

But she couldn't keep her thoughts on rescue; the

dramatic sunset bathing the prairie in color had captured her attention. The wash that had uprooted the tracks was only a sparkling trickle now, like a child whose tantrum had worn down into tears, and the the horizon was so red that it seemed about to explode into flames.

Twilight was not peaceful here, as it was in Tennessee, but intensely charged, making Ivy feel as if she were on the verge of discovering some great secret. She was uncertain how long she strolled across the open expanse, but she began to sense that she could walk forever. She stopped, staring, suddenly frightened by the idea of having no limitations.

Her heart pounding wildly, she turned back toward the train, which, in the distance, looked like a toy miniature. Then she saw a lone figure moving toward her with a long, slow stride. She knew even before she saw his face that it was Langdon Runnels. For a reason she couldn't explain, she wanted to walk to meet him. Yet she forced herself to stand still, waiting for him to reach her. He stopped a few yards away.

"Are you all right, Mrs. Barton?"

"Yes. Why wouldn't I be?"

"You looked . . . disturbed. Upset."

"Not at all," she answered, sounding deceptively calm. "I was merely enjoying the sunset."

He was silent for a moment before he spoke. "Come with me."

Their eyes held. "Why?" she asked.

"Your husband is asking for you. I told him I'd find you."

Ignoring his outstretched hand, Ivy gathered up her skirts and began walking toward the train. He touched her arm. "I'm afraid there's bad news," he said. She turned to him, startled. Had something happened to Alex? "The messenger came back saying that the depot in Colorado Springs can't send a train out until morning."

Ivy sighed. Another night in that cramped car. But at least Alex was all right.

As they neared the train, she could see the conductor directing passengers back inside for the night. Mr. Runnels held her arm as he handed her over to the conductor, but he did not follow her into the train.

"Where were you, Ivy?" Alex asked when she joined him at their seats.

"I took a walk. Just to get away from the crowd."

"You came back with Runnels. I saw you through the window."

"Yes, he said you were looking for me."

"I coulda come for you myself. I don't need another man to look after my wife."

"It's all right, Alex," Ivy whispered, hoping no one could overhear them and wishing, as she had each night since they'd begun their journey, that they could have afforded the privacy of a sleeping car. She reached for his hand and felt his fingers curl tightly around her own, the way a child's might. She held his hand for a long time, until she heard his breathing relax to the steady rhythm of sleep. Then she carefully slipped her fingers free and made her way out of the train and into the night.

2

He saw her as she stepped down from the passenger car, but he felt sure she hadn't seen him smoking in the shadows.

He had watched her all afternoon while he'd played cards. He'd noted the way she'd kept an eye on her husband. She'd been worried about his losing money, no doubt. And for good reason. Alex Barton was a foolish gambler.

Langdon had pegged Barton as an easy mark when he first saw him flashing a wad of bills in the station in Trinidad. Langdon had an eye for a sucker with money, and he'd looked forward to getting this one into a game of cards. He'd watched carefully to see which car he'd boarded, then he'd worked his way up to a seat next to him. As it turned out, it was his old friend, Montana McCrory, who got the game started, making things easier for him.

He hadn't known there'd be a wife, since he hadn't spotted her earlier. But even if he had known, it wouldn't have concerned him at the time. Now that he'd seen her, he had to admit that she was attractive in a homespun way. Not strikingly beautiful; she was a bit too buttoned up and prim.

It was her aloofness that intrigued him. He'd encountered such aloofness before, in the wives and daughters of the wealthy merchants and professionals in New York and Boston and Philadelphia when he'd moved from city to city looking for work in the dirty, sweltering factories that belonged to the husbands and fathers of those arrogant women.

He had seen it again when he'd abandoned the cities of the North for New Orleans. The women there were freer in spirit, looser in their attitudes, but still aloof when he, in his white apron, carried trays of food through the dining rooms or into private suites. The chilling attitude wordlessly pronounced that he was beneath them, that he, the son of a poor and ignorant West Virginia miner, was in fact not worthy even of notice unless he did something to displease them. God, how he had hated it.

He'd learned the ways of the world in New Orleans, although not before he'd been taken for a sucker more than once. He'd learned to protect himself by using other people before they used him. He learned how to be charming and how to be ruthless— sometimes in the same instant. He was quick of mind and clever with the cards, and he soon found that gambling was an ideal way to take a sucker.

His success at gambling got him noticed by rich men as well as by their ladies. The aloofness remained in some of the women even after they were obviously trying to seduce him, and he finally learned that it was a game, a charade. And he was an expert at gaming. Ever since that discovery, an attractive woman who held herself apart, remote and cool, was to him a challenge he felt compelled to accept.

As he had watched Mrs. Alexander Barton while he played cards with her husband, he'd noted the way she seemed to hold herself slightly apart even from the other women. He'd noted, too, the way she moved with an agile grace, punctuated with an occasional nervous flutter of her hand to her hair or to the buttons just above her bosom when she worried about how much her husband was losing. Langdon had managed to take almost all of that wad of bills Alex Barton had. But the woman had begun to make him edgy. So he'd left the game before the son of a bitch was completely broke and his poor little wife destitute. That was something he'd never done before, and he hoped it didn't mean he was going soft.

When he'd quit, Barton was still singing the sucker's song, saying that his luck was bound to change. And maybe it had. Langdon hadn't stuck around to see. He'd left him to Montana McCrory, as she called herself now. That woman was forever changing her name. Mathilda Susan Brawley was the name by which he'd first known her. Then it was Susan Brawley, and then Montana Brawley. She'd chosen that name, she'd said, after she'd seen a pretty picture of a place called Montana. Now it was Montana McCrory. Seems this time, though, the name change was because she'd gotten married since he'd last seen her in Kansas City.

Long after Langdon had left the game, he'd seen Alex Barton looking around for his wife, Ivy. That's when he had volunteered to walk out and fetch her, since Alex was too drunk to do it himself. He wasn't sure why he'd made the offer. Out of boredom, maybe. Or maybe just to see if he could penetrate that cool, standoffish shell. He had sensed that she was attracted to him, and along with that he'd sensed a vulnerability.

He continued to watch her from the shadows. She was the starched-and-buttoned kind all right, and, as he had observed earlier, not beautiful. Yet she was tall and slender with fine green eyes and luxurious hair. A little soft living would take that hard look from around her mouth, and a taste of happiness could make those eyes luminous. Something about her hard-bitten manner disturbed him. Was she hiding something?

"Evening, Mrs. Barton."

She turned quickly, startled.

He took one last draw from his smoke, threw it to the ground, and crushed it beneath his heel as he walked toward her. "Does your husband know you're out walking in the dark alone?"

"I'll be quite all right, I'm sure," she answered.

"You're sure?" he said in a mocking, teasing way. He watched her a moment. "Well, now that you're out here, I'm glad you came," he said. "That sky is something that ought to be shared with somebody." He raised his eyes to the ornate canopy above them. "I'd venture to say you never saw a sky that spectacular in Tennessee."

"Tennessee is quite different, yes," she said, her voice strained, tense.

"Why did you leave if you wanted so badly to stay?"

"What makes you think I wanted to stay?" she asked.

"Didn't you?"

"It was Alex's decision to come to Colorado. I am his wife, so of course I came with him. I am sure I can learn to be content once we get to farming."

"Your husband seems to be interested in the gold fields."

"We will farm," she said with firmness.

"Won't be easy farming in the Rockies. Hard winters, stubborn land—"

"Farming is always difficult, Mr. Runnels, but it is an honest way to make a living."

Langdon leaned against the passenger car, watching her, and she took a step toward him. What she said next surprised him at first. "Actually, I hoped I'd find you out here. I'd like to ask you something." Her voice had a ring of desperation. "I—I wanted to ask you about Colorado. You seem to be familiar with it. I was wondering what to expect. What kind of seed to buy, actually. I don't know what grows best here, but we know a little about raising cotton and corn. And tobacco, too, although not as much as we do—"

Langdon laughed. "You're not going to farm cotton or tobacco in Colorado," he said. "Growing season's too short. Wheat, maybe, if you're out on the plains. But livestock's your best bet. Beef cattle, sheep, or maybe a little dairy farming. Especially if this place you're going to is around Colorado Springs and Pikes Peak, like your husband said."

"Livestock's expensive," she said, more to herself than to him, "and we've never raised wheat. We'll have to learn, I suppose. . . ."

It was odd, he thought, that she, rather than her husband, should be the one asking about the farming. And it was odd, too, that they'd come all this way without knowing what crops they would raise. But he wasn't interested in talking about farming. Maybe Ivy Barton wasn't as intriguing as he'd thought. He was about to excuse himself and get back on the train to find Montana and perhaps a better diversion when Ivy Barton stopped him.

"I also wanted to find you to thank you," she said, "for coming to get me when Alex couldn't. I realize he was in no condition—I mean, Alex is really a very capable and intelligent person when he's not—"

She stopped and turned away from him, and he knew that in spite of her spouting off about the honesty of farming, she was not very honest with herself when it came to her feelings about her husband. He would bet that she was a lonely woman, too. Maybe that was what her hardness was covering. He placed both hands on her shoulders, turning her to face him.

"Your husband is a very lucky man to have such a thoughtful wife," he said, "but you ought to stop trying to cover for him, and you ought not to let him make you so unhappy."

She hesitated a moment before she spoke. "Mr. Runnels, I have no idea what you're getting at, but let me assure you that my happiness or unhappiness is no concern of yours." Her tone was haughty as she pulled away from him and moved toward the train door. "I bid you good night," she said coolly over her shoulder as she stepped into the car.

There was no doubt left in his mind now: he wanted her.

The train from Colorado Springs arrived by early morning. It had traveled backward on the track the entire distance so the engine would face the right direction going into the station. A work crew constructed a makeshift bridge for passengers to cross the chasm the tracks had once spanned.

As Ivy stood outside, waiting for the signal to board, she saw Mr. Runnels and Alex help load luggage into the baggage car. Just as Mr. Runnels stooped to pick up a large valise, his eyes caught hers and held them. She turned away abruptly.

It was the first she had seen of him since she'd left him outside the train the night before. She had not seen him reboard, and she had assumed he'd found another car. She had fallen asleep thinking of how his shirt had felt to her fingertips when she'd pushed away from him. Cool silk. She had not owned silk since she was a little girl and her mother had tied her hair with silk ribbons. She thought of it now, covetously.

In a little while the conductor called for all passengers to board the train. As it began its swaying trek across the prairie, Ivy noticed that Mrs. McCrory now sat across the aisle from her and Alex, where Mr. Runnels had been. Her formerly flushed face was a pale, sickly white, and she was no longer talkative and gregarious. Instead she fell into a fitful sleep, waking and starting, then dozing again, her head bobbing and her chin rolling along the tops of her voluptuous breasts.

Alex was sober but unusually nervous. He stared out the window, stood up to pace the aisle, then came back to sit beside Ivy again, to tell her stories about the rich strikes in the gold fields in Colorado he'd heard from fellow passengers.

"It's an exciting place, Ivy. There's fortunes to be

made if a man's willing to try. Why, they say there's been many a man who's started with nothing and ended a millionaire."

Ivy kept her eyes on her cross-stitch work. "We will clear the land for farming," she said.

"But, Ivy—"

"It is all we know. Perhaps you—we didn't do it well, but it is still all we know."

"But if times ever got so bad on the farm we couldn't make it—"

"We will make it." So Alex was finally waking up to his folly and beginning to worry about it, she thought. A fine time for that! She wouldn't let him know that she was fighting to hide her own fears. No sense in both of them working themselves into hysterics.

Alex turned away from her, staring wordlessly out the window, but she could still sense his edginess. His unease lasted until a young woman with two little girls boarded the train and sat nearby, diverting his attention. He soon moved onto the seat next to them and began entertaining the girls with a hand puppet he fashioned from his handkerchief.

Ivy watched him enjoying himself and smiled. She remembered how he had loved playing with his own daughters. He had never been any good at disciplining or helping them with their problems. He had simply loved them as one playmate loved another, and they had loved him in the same way. She remembered, too, how it had frightened him when they died. But she wouldn't think of that now, she told herself. She had to keep the memories at bay. Maybe one day she would stop using the cotton sponges and camphor, but not yet. It was too great a risk to love someone she could not protect enough.

Mrs. McCrory moaned in her sleep. Ivy glanced at her, and the woman woke with a start, clutching her stomach and moaning, "I got a god-awful pain in my gut!"

The man on the seat across from her leaned forward with a concerned look. "Madam, can I help you?"

"Not unless you can keep this train from swayin'," Mrs. McCrory answered. "It's makin' me bilious." The elderly man stared at her, obviously uncertain what to do. "Oh, Lordy!" Mrs. McCrory said. Holding her hand over her mouth, she stood up quickly and rushed down the aisle toward the ladies' lounge at the back of the car. When she emerged several minutes later, her face was even paler and she had to grip seat backs to steady herself as she walked.

"Them dry hoppers smell like crap," she mumbled, sliding onto her seat. She rested her head wearily against the back while she pressed her decidedly soiled handkerchief to her lips. She groaned and doubled over, clutching her stomach again. "Somethin' I et. Somethin' poisoned me."

The man across from her shifted uneasily. Alex, too, looked frightened as he whispered to Ivy, "What did the woman eat? Are we all going to get sick?"

"Try not to worry," Ivy said, giving him a reassuring smile. Then she noticed that Mrs. McCrory was motioning to her. Reluctantly Ivy stepped across the aisle and sat next to the restless, unhappy woman.

"What I need," Mrs. McCrory said in a hoarse whisper, with her lips next to Ivy's ear, "is a enema. But a lady can't see to them things herself. I know I can trust you to help me. When we get to Colorado Springs—"

"But, Mrs. McCrory, I'm sure there are others who are more—"

"You're a lady," Mrs. McCrory said, her pale lips tightening. "Being gently bred myself, I can see that. I put myself in your hands." She fell back against the seat again and was so quiet that Ivy thought she must have fainted. In a little while Ivy moved back to her own seat.

Alex, who had been watching her with a strange nervousness, excused himself from the young woman and her daughters and quickly rejoined Ivy. "What did she say?" he asked, sounding anxious. "What did the woman tell you?"

"Nothing important."

"By damn, I want to know what she said!" Alex insisted a little too loudly.

"Alex!" Ivy whispered, surprised at his outburst. "I do declare! Whatever has come over you?"

"Tell me what she said." Alex's demand was quieter this time, but he was growing more and more agitated.

Ivy leaned close to whisper, "She wants an enema."

Alex gave her a questioning look. "An enema?"

"Yes," Ivy said, "and I'm afraid she expects me to administer it."

"An enema? Is that all she said? She just asked you to give her an enema?"

"Shh, Alex! You don't have to let the whole train in on it."

He sputtered with laughter.

"It's not funny, Alex. The woman's sick. I'm sure you wouldn't find it so amusing if you'd been asked to—" She tightened her mouth, trying to suppress her own giggles.

"You're right. It's not funny." Alex turned his face to the window and shook with laughter.

His mirth proved short-lived, however. Within a few minutes he had fallen into a quiet, melancholy mood and simply gazed out the window while Ivy worked on her embroidery and listened to Mrs. McCrory's intermittent groans. By the time the train pulled into the Colorado Springs station four hours later, Mrs. McCrory was in such agony that she hardly seemed able to breathe without crying out. Alex had to help her from the coach.

"I'll get her into that hotel across the street," Ivy told him. "You see to our connections to Green Valley while I get her settled."

Alex wore a confused look, as if in spite of Ivy's instructions he still wasn't sure what he should do.

"Alex, please," Ivy said with exaggerated patience. "You must find out about the stagecoach to Green Valley. The advertisement said the stage leaves from Colorado Springs, remember?"

"What? Oh, yes. I'll see to it, and then I'll meet you at the hotel." He hesitated, looking uncertain. "Yes, of course," he said again, and this time turned to walk away.

Ivy frowned at his puzzling behavior, but she soon had to turn her attention to Mrs. McCrory, whose heavy weight leaning against her almost caused her to fall. She managed to get her across the street and into the hotel, where the woman collapsed onto a sofa in the lobby, still looking pale and drawn.

"You got to help me," she said weakly. "You got to get me that enema."

"Yes. Yes, in a moment," Ivy said. Nervously she clutched at the high collar of her dress as she tried to think what to do. She was used to handling illnesses without the aid of a doctor, but administering an enema to a perfect stranger surely was more than anyone could expect. She glanced toward the desk. "I'll get someone to call a doctor," she said. "A lady doesn't do that kind of thing without—without a doctor present. It's just not ladylike," she improvised, playing into Mrs. McCrory's charade.

"Yeah." Mrs. McCrory's voice was little more than a whisper. "Yeah, I knew that."

"I'll be right back," Ivy said, hurrying toward the desk, relieved that she had thought of a way to give responsibility for the woman to someone else.

Ivy had the desk clerk call a doctor while she signed Montana McCrory's name on the guest register. Then she had a bellboy help her get Mrs. McCrory to her room, where the woman immediately collapsed on the bed. The bellboy stood around awkwardly, and Ivy couldn't imagine why he wouldn't leave. Perhaps he thought he could help.

"There's nothing you can do," Ivy said to him. "I'll wait with her until the doctor arrives. You go on about your business."

The bellboy gave her a questioning look, then turned sullen and stormed out of the room. Ivy puzzled over his curious reaction a moment, then shrugged and turned back to Mrs. McCrory, who was thrashing about fitfully on the bed. She dampened a towel with water from the pitcher on the bureau and laid it across Mrs. McCrory's forehead. Then she pulled the room's one chair next to the bed to wait for the doctor to arrive.

The room was small and sparsely furnished with nothing more than the brass bed, the narrow oak bureau, and the simple ladder-back chair, but it seemed the height of luxury to Ivy after spending three days and nights in the cramped train. She thought with longing of spending the night in such a room.

That was out of the question, though. She and Alex would have to do whatever was necessary at the courthouse here in Colorado Springs to record the deed to their land and then take the stage out to find it. Their bed tonight would be a thin mattress of quilts spread upon the ground underneath the shelter of a tent—if they could afford a tent, and if they could find a place to buy one.

A knock at the door brought her to her feet. It would be the doctor. She could leave Mrs. McCrory in his hands and be on her way.

It was not the doctor but the bellboy again, bringing Mrs. McCrory's trunk. This time he didn't linger but barely pushed the trunk inside the door before he left, looking as sullen as before.

Mrs. McCrory began a convulsive retching, and Ivy hurried to pull the slop jar from under the bed. But it was only dry heaves that racked her body, and she fell back to mumbling incoherently in a feverish delirium.

"Miz Barton!" she called suddenly.

"I'm here, Mrs. McCrory. Please try to be calm," Ivy said.

"Miz Barton!" she said again. "Don't tell him my real name."

"I beg your pardon?"

"Mathilda." Her eyes glistened like marbles. "God-awful common. You tell the doc it's Montana. Just like I signed it."

"Please, Mrs. McCrory, I don't think you need to worry—"

"I don't want no common name. I give myself a fancy name, like a lady would have. Promise me. It's Montana, hear? Promise me."

"Of course, Mrs. McCrory—Montana. Yes, of course." What was taking the doctor so long? And Alex? He should be here by now. Would he be able to find her in the hotel once he got the stagecoach tickets? In her haste she had forgotten to leave her own name at the desk but had simply signed for Mrs. McCrory. She hoped Alex would remember the name.

In a little while Ivy heard another light tap at the door, but before she could get up to answer it, Alex opened it and stuck his head in.

"Ivy?" he called cautiously. "Is she all right?"

"I don't know. She's feverish and fitful. I wish the doctor would get here. We need to be on our way. Did you get the tickets to Green Valley?"

"No," Alex said. "I—I didn't get them yet. The stage doesn't leave until tomorrow afternoon. We'll have to spend the night. I could get us a room if—"

"A hotel room is expensive, Alex. Maybe you should try to hire someone with a wagon."

"I can't. I mean, I tried, and there weren't any available for hire."

"All right," Ivy said, knowing that he was waiting for her to take over, as he often did. "If we have no other choice but to spend the money to stay here, we'll have to make the best of it." A part of her felt secretly glad of the excuse to stay in the hotel, where she would have at least one night in a real bed. "It will give us more time to find the courthouse and to make sure we get the deed recorded," she said. "But you should have bought the tickets anyway. It would have saved time tomorrow."

"Ivy . . ." Alex gave her a strange look. "Ivy, I—"

"What is it?" Ivy asked, distracted again by Mrs. McCrory, who had awakened and lay with her fever-bright eyes fixed in a stare.

"Ivy, dear, I'm afraid I—I don't have—"

Ivy turned her head quickly toward him, suddenly knowing what he was trying to say. "You don't have any money to buy the tickets. You lost it gambling." Her voice was calm, belying her emotions.

Alex dropped his eyes contritely. "I'm sorry, Ivy. It was that damned Bill Mott. I thought I had him."

Ivy continued to stare at him, her face expressionless. That, she realized, was the reason for his nervousness earlier. And his angry outburst on the train must have been because he was afraid Mrs. McCrory was tattling to her about his losses. Slowly Ivy brought her hand up to rest on her bosom, and she felt the bills stitched into the ruffle of her camisole.

"How did you think we would survive, Alex?" she asked, her voice still quiet but with an edge like a cold, sharp blade.

Alex lowered his eyes again, as if he were a child receiving a scolding. Then he raised them slowly to look at her.

Ivy knew he was expecting her to bail them out. She had done it before, coming up with an extra dozen eggs to sell or finding someone who needed sewing done or who needed help with housework. She wondered if he had considered that she would have no eggs to sell now, nor would she know anyone who needed a dress made or help with a house. Did he know about the money she had sewn into her clothing? No, he had not thought of how she would do it; he had simply hoped that she would.

"All right," she said wearily. "Get us a room. Tell the clerk your wife will pay when we check out."

Alex gave her an uneasy, self-conscious smile as he turned to leave.

When he had gone, Ivy calculated the expense. The cost of a rented room, plus money for the stagecoach tickets, would take most of her cash, leaving very little for supplies. They would certainly have to do without a tent, and there would be only beans and flour for provisions. But maybe in time she could find a way to scrape some money together to buy seeds and by fall have food from a garden, unless winter came too early, as Mr. Runnels had hinted. Well, they could pray for the best, and once Alex was on the land, he would be away from the temptations of drink and cards. While she planted a garden, he could start splitting logs to build a cabin.

She had not expected to be starting over in a one-room cabin of split logs in the third decade of her life. For the briefest moment she pictured herself as she should be—settled in a two-story white frame house in Tennessee, surrounded by half-grown children. But she forced away the daydream and pressed her hand to the buttons at her bosom.

Mrs. McCrory groaned and clutched her abdomen again. Turning in the bed to look at Ivy, she tried to speak, but her eyes rolled to the top of her lids, and her thick, white-coated tongue seemed to stick to parched lips. She only uttered another groan. Ivy walked to the bedside and removed the damp towel, warm now from the woman's burning skin. She poured a basin of water and loosened the woman's bodice to bathe her throat and chest, trying to cool the fever.

The woman flung her arms about and tried again to speak in a hoarse, croaking voice. She was delirious and appeared to think that she was dealing cards for a poker game. When she returned for a moment to a lucid state, she clutched at Ivy's arm and spoke in short, gasping sentences.

"I—I got somethin' to say. Somethin' you got to do for me. If—if my time has come."

"Nonsense," Ivy said, her voice as crisp as starched linen. "You're not going to die from a stomachache. Just lie still, and the doctor will be here soon." She'd played this role before and knew her lines well, having coaxed Alex through more than one illness that he'd thought would be his last. Alex had developed an intense fear of death after the girls died. For Ivy, there was little fear. At times, when she thought about the girls, she thought she would welcome death.

"No. Listen to me. I'm god-awful sick in my gut," the woman insisted. "Say you'll do it for me. Say you'll help me."

"All right," Ivy relented, hoping that would calm the patient. "I'll try to help. What is it you want me to do?"

"I got nobody. No relatives. So I want that place in Eagleton—the Golden Palace—I want it to go to charity. And I want you to tell 'em Mrs. Tom McCrory done it. That's the way a lady would do it, ain't it? A lady would be generous and leave her holdings to charity if she had no family, wouldn't she?"

"Yes, I suppose so," Ivy said quietly, "but there's no need to worry about that now. By tomorrow you'll be opening for business. Now please try to rest until the doctor—"

"I want people to remember Montana McCrory. I want 'em to know I was a lady. Mathilda Brawley weren't no lady. She was a common whore. But I saved a nest egg with that whorin' money, and I put it in the bank. Signed my name Montana on the bank papers. That makes it legal, don't it?"

"I—I don't know. I—"

"And I married Tom McCrory legal and proper. Just like any lady would." She gave out a long, agonizing whine. "Oh, God." She was drenched with sweat. "If—if my time comes, promise me you'll see that it goes to charity, like a lady would."

"Please, you're going to be fine—"

There was another knock on the door, and Ivy hurried to open it to a small, balding man carrying a black bag.

"Dr. Davis," the man said. "I was called to room—"

"I got to have a enema," Mrs. McCrory croaked when she saw him. "I got to have a enema bad."

Dr. Davis stepped inside and set his bag on the bureau. "Ask one of the maids to bring me some water," he said, turning to Ivy.

Ivy nodded, grateful for the excuse to leave the room. She found a housemaid and gave her the doctor's instructions, then went down to the desk to ask for the room Alex had rented.

"Mr. Barton is in thirty-two," the desk clerk said. "Someone else just asked for that room. A cousin of the gentleman who rented it, I believe."

"A cousin?" Ivy asked, surprised.

"Yes, Mrs. McCrory. Said he was Mr. Barton's cousin."

Disturbed, Ivy turned away without bothering to correct the mistaken name. Why would anyone come visiting, claiming to be a cousin? Neither she nor Alex had relatives west of Nashville. She was still puzzling over it when she reached the room.

She opened the door and gasped at the sight that met her eyes. The room's one chair lay on its side against the wall. Quilts and sheets had been ripped from the bed and strewn about. The lamp was over-turned on the bureau, its globe broken, and oil dripped to the floor. Alex lay next to the bureau, his head resting in a small pool of blood.

"Oh, Lord have mercy!" Ivy cried, running to him. She dropped to her knees and picked up his head, cradling it in her arms and putting her face next to his. She was relieved to feel his warm, moist breath on her cheek. "Alex," she said, shaking him gently. "Alex, wake up! Who did this to you?"

His eyes fluttered, and he opened them slowly, staring at her as if he couldn't remember who she was.

"Alex! Tell me what happened," she pleaded.

He tried to raise himself but collapsed against her, moaning and clutching his head. "Is he still here?" he whispered.

"Who? Is who still here?"

"Oh, my God, Ivy, I didn't mean to—I—"

"You didn't mean to what? For heaven's sake, Alex, tell me what happened! Here, put your arm around me, and let me help you to the bed. Then you've got to explain this to me. Was it a thief? Someone who saw your money while we were on the train? I suppose he got mad when he couldn't find any money. I'll tell the hotel management. We'll see to it that—"

Alex struggled to stay on his feet. "We've got to get out of here."

"We will, tomorrow. But you need to get to bed now, and I'm going to get that doctor who's with Mrs. McCrory. He'll bandage your head."

"No!" he said angrily. "I'm not seeing any doctor. I said we're getting out of here."

Ivy looked at him, startled, but she quickly regained her composure. "Don't shout," she said calmly. She took his arm to lead him with gentle force toward the bed. "The thief's gone, and he won't be back, since you have no money."

"It wasn't a thief." Alex sank to the edge of the bed. He rested his elbows on his knees and held his head in both hands as if he were trying to keep it from tumbling from his body.

"If it wasn't someone out to steal your money, who was it?" Ivy asked, standing over him.

"Bill Mott."

"The man you played poker with? But what could he want? You said he'd already won all your money."

"I thought I had him, Ivy," Alex said. "I thought, back there on the prairie, that if I played just one more hand, I could win all my money back. And it was a good hand." Alex raised his head slowly and carefully to look at Ivy. "I had two pair, aces and queens. How many hands can beat that? How many chances in a thousand were there that Mott would have a full house?"

Ivy felt the blood drain from her face. She had no idea what aces and queens and a full house meant, except that it meant Alex was telling her something dreadful. "If you'd already lost all the money, what did you—" She gripped a bedpost to steady herself.

"The land." Her voice was barely more than a whisper. "Oh, no, Alex, you didn't—"

But she knew by the look on his face that she had guessed the truth. Alex had lost their land to Bill Mott. They were absolutely homeless now and practically penniless. What were they to do? How could they survive? The future now was more terrifyingly uncertain than she had ever dared imagine. But if Alex had lost the land to Mott, why had Mott come back looking for him? Suddenly she saw a glimmer of hope, and she grabbed at it like a cat swatting its paw at a stream of moonlight.

"The title! He didn't have the title to the land, did he? And he came here looking for it. But he didn't find it, did he? You still have it! That's what you meant when you said we've got to get out of here. Oh, Alex, that was so smart of you! And you're right, we've got to leave. Before he comes back." She hurried about the room, picking up Alex's hat and coat. She was about to pick up his valise when Alex stopped her.

"He'll be back," he said, "but not to look for the title." He reached into a hip pocket and brought out a crumpled piece of paper. He studied it a moment, then tossed it aside. "He brought it back to me. When he comes back, it will be to kill me. He woulda finished the job this time, but he heard a noise in the hall and got scared. He left through the window."

"What are you talking about?" Ivy asked. "I don't understand."

"We were swindled, Ivy. The title's no good."

"No good? But—"

"That's why Mott was so mad. He's already been to the courthouse. That's where he found out that the land sale was bogus. There's no such place as Green Valley, Colorado, Ivy." Alex dropped his head into his hands again.

"No!" Ivy protested. "That can't be. I don't believe—"

"It's true," Alex said without looking up. "There'd already been a passel of people there ahead of Mott asking for the same place. I'm not the only fool in the world." He raised his eyes. "Others have been cheated just like us. Paid good money for a piece of nothing."

Ivy felt a tightness in her chest, and she was barely able to breathe. "It's not true. It can't be true."

"It is true," Alex said. He picked up the bogus title, wadded it, and threw it angrily across the room. "Do you think Mott woulda brought the goddamned thing back and thrown it in my face if it was any good?"

Ivy walked across the room and picked up the paper. She straightened it slowly, then smoothed it against her breast. As she stared straight ahead, a bitter laugh escaped her throat, followed by another and another until her whole body shook with laughter and the crumpled paper dropped to the floor.

"What's wrong with you, Ivy? Stop it!" Alex sounded frightened. Ivy turned away from him as her hysterical laughter turned to sobs.

"We have no money. No home. What will we do?" she asked through her tears. Alex took a step toward her, and she spun around to face him, suddenly overcome with anger. "How could you be such a fool?" She stopped, and the words died in her throat when she realized what she was doing. "Oh, my God," she said. "Oh, my God, I'm sorry."

Neither of them spoke for a moment, and Alex

reached for her. "Ivy," he said, putting his arms around her. "My dear, sweet Ivy."

He held her until she felt the warm moisture against her temple. She saw that his head wound was bleeding again, the blood dripping down to saturate his shirt collar. She cried out and reached for a towel. "Here. Hold this against your head, and I'll go get that doctor. I hope he's still here."

"Oh, God, Ivy, what are we going to do? How are we going to survive?" Alex's voice cracked with despair.

"You'll get a job," Ivy said, slipping back into her reassuring role. She wiped her eyes with the backs of her hands and reached for another towel to dab Alex's blood off her temple. "I'll find one, too. We both will. But first you need a doctor." She threw down the towel and started for the door.

"How will you pay him?" Alex called out.

Ivy stopped, her hand on the doorknob. He was right. They had to conserve the small amount of money she had saved. Maybe the doctor would be kind enough at least to give her a bandage and some salve so she could dress the wound herself. She left without answering Alex. As she walked down the hall she took a deep breath to try to calm herself so she could think clearly. She knew she had to ask for more than a bandage. She also had to ask a favor of Montana McCrory, something she was loath to do. But she had to swallow her pride, since she could think of no other immediate solution to the problem Alex had created for them.

Mrs. McCrory should be feeling better by now, she reasoned, perhaps well enough to talk to her about a job in her new place in—where was it? Eagleton?

Mrs. McCrory had said it was a booming gold-mining town. If it had to be a boom town full of rowdy, disgusting miners, so be it. Ivy only prayed it would not be another fictitious place.

But what sort of job could there be for her in a gambling saloon? In a restaurant, she could be a cook. How hard could it be to increase a few recipes? Maybe there would be a restaurant in connection with the saloon. Or if there was no restaurant, she could be a seamstress for Mrs. McCrory. The woman certainly could use a bit more taste in the cut of her dresses. But what about Alex? What could he do? She hated to think of him sweeping floors and emptying spittoons. She would try to decide what he might be suited for, but there wasn't time now. She was in front of Mrs. McCrory's door, and she knew she had to knock or lose her courage. She had just raised her hand when the door opened and Dr. Davis met her face to face.

"Oh, I'm so glad you've returned," he said. "I was just about to come looking for you, and I had no idea how to find you, since I didn't get your name."

"You were looking for me?"

"Yes." The doctor lowered his voice. "I'm afraid I have bad news."

Ivy stared at him blankly.

"I'm sorry. There was nothing I could do."

Ivy was unable to speak at first, unable to accept what he was saying. "No!" she cried at last. "No! It was something she ate! You can't be telling me she's dead."

"It was appendicitis. The appendix had ruptured, and the poison had already spread. I'm afraid the enema was a mistake."

Ivy saw her last hope suddenly disappear. "But you're a doctor! You were supposed to know that! You were supposed to save her, not make mistakes!"

"I'm not some all-knowing god," the doctor said wearily. "I didn't know it was appendicitis. Just constipation, a stomachache, I thought. I did the best I could."

"Oh, no," Ivy whispered. "Oh, Lord, no."

"I'll need to get some information from someone," Dr. Davis said. "You apparently were close to her."

"Information?" Ivy was too stunned to think clearly. "What kind of information?"

"For the death certificate." Dr. Davis pulled a writing pad from his bag. "I'm afraid I don't even know her name. I was just summoned here for an emergency in room eleven." He took a pencil from a vest pocket. "Her name?"

Ivy felt her heart pound in her chest. "Her name?" Her mind raced as she glanced at the sheet-covered mound on the bed. "Her name was . . . Ivy Barton."

"Are you the next of kin?"

"No." Her voice shook. "I am—was—a friend of Mrs. Barton's. My name is Montana McCrory."

3

"My God, you'll never get away with it, Ivy."

"You must not call me Ivy!" She paced the floor in their hotel room. Alex rested in bed, wearing a bloodstained towel around his head. "Oh, Lord," she said, glancing anxiously toward the door, "when is that doctor going to get here? I never saw a man so slow. He said he'd be here as soon as he contacted the undertaker."

"The doctor's coming to see me?" Alex asked. "I told you we can't pay—"

"I'll take care of it, Alex, don't worry."

"But, Ivy—"

"I told you, I'm Montana." Lord, how she hated the name! It had a cheap, awkward sound. "Get used to it."

"It's crazy! Take over a gambling saloon? You don't know the first thing about it."

"It's the only chance we have. Our land is gone. How else will we live?"

Alex groaned and slid farther into the bed.

"We'll have to change your name, too," she said. "Just in case Bill Mott tries to find us."

"But taking over that saloon, Ivy, that makes us sound like criminals. I don't like it." He spoke to his wife's back as she continued to pace the room.

"We're not criminals," she said, turning to face him. "Mrs. McCrory said she wanted what she had to be turned over to charity, and we're charity cases now. We're desperate." She paced the floor again. "We just need to take a few simple . . . precautions, that's all." She seated herself on the edge of Alex's bed. "You will be . . . Mr. Miller," she said, giving him her maiden name, the first that came to her mind.

"Miller?" Alex pushed himself up in bed, wincing at the pain in his head.

"Yes," she said, "Mr. Miller. It will be easy for both of us to remember. "And you can still be Alex. Alex Miller, my—my brother!"

"Wait a minute. If I'm your brother—"

"She was married to someone named Tom McCrory, Alex. Everyone at this—this saloon we're going to will know that, so it's obvious that you can't pose as my husband."

"But he's dead. I could be your new husband."

"But only recently dead. Not even a woman like Montana McCrory would have taken another husband or even a lover without a decent period of mourning. Oh, Alex, please! Don't make it so difficult. Just play along for a little while, until we make enough money to get back to Tennessee."

"But a saloon? What will people think of you? I can't have my wife—"

"Don't think of me as your wife! And as for what others will think of me, let them think what they will. We'll only be there a short while. Just long enough to make enough money to get back to Tennessee, where we belong."

Alex fell silent, staring at her, his face drawn. She would have tried to reassure him further, but there was a knock at the door, and the new Montana stood quickly. "That will be the doctor," she said. "He's probably a quack, but at least he can manage to bandage your head. Just concentrate on being Alex Miller."

She smoothed her skirt, walked to the door, and opened it to Dr. Davis.

"I spoke to the undertaker on the telephone," the doctor said by way of greeting. "He'll be here shortly. Now let me have a look at your friend, Mr.—"

"Miller," she said quickly. "My brother, Mr. Miller."

"Your brother. Of course," Dr. Davis said wearily. He stepped to the bedside. "The result of a disagreement, I imagine," he said in the same tired voice as he removed the towel from Alex's head. He seemed to expect no reply, and he asked no further questions. "Head wound always makes a man bleed like a stuck pig," he said, squinting at the gash. "Doesn't look too serious." He used the end of the towel to remove a bit of dried blood. "You'll have a hell of a headache, though, if you don't already."

Ivy excused herself and stepped into the hall, then leaned against the closed door, breathing deeply and trying to adjust to the vast, unfamiliar wilderness into which she'd been thrust within the last hour. Feeling not at all certain of herself, she walked up the hall to the room where the woman she herself had named Ivy Barton lay dead.

As soon as she saw the sheet-covered mound in the bed, she wished she'd waited for the body to be removed. But there was too much to do and no time to wait. She forced herself to step into the room, and once inside, she closed the door and quickly unbuttoned her bodice. She slipped a finger under the stitching of her camisole and pulled at the threads to break them. After removing the bills she had sewn into the ruffle, she counted them. There would be enough, barely enough, to pay Dr. Davis and then the hotel bill.

Quickly she stuffed the money back into her bodice and rebuttoned it while her eyes searched the room. She spotted the trunk near the bed, but when she tried to open it, she discovered that it was locked. She found the key in the valise Mrs. McCrory had carried with her on the train. A shawl, some extra stockings, a corset, a deck of playing cards, and a roll of bills were in the valise along with the key. She stuffed the bills into her bodice with the other money.

When she opened the trunk, her eyes fell upon shimmering scarlet satin. Slowly she reached to touch it. Then she pulled the gown up and out of the trunk, letting it fall out to its full length. It had enormous puffed leg-o'-mutton sleeves, fitted from the elbow to the wrist and covered with black lace netting. It was cut very low in the front and filled in with more of the sheer netting. Wide black velvet ribbons fell from the shoulders to the bottom of the skirt, the edge of which was heavily embroidered with red on red.

She held the dress against her shoulders and turned toward the mirror. The brilliant color made her auburn hair look less red and more of a rich brown, but it brought out the rosiness of her cheeks. It made her look, she thought, like someone else.

She had never had a dress of such a vivid hue before. She remembered her mother, a demure woman of southern breeding, saying that a woman over thirty should never wear red. Turning away from the mirror, she dropped the dress on the chair and went back to the trunk.

A peacock green taffeta trimmed with violet ruching was on top of the stack now. Ivy pulled it out and saw beneath it a gown of old-rose satin and, beneath that, another of slate gray brocade with black velvet trim. The gowns were luxurious and daring, but Ivy would not allow herself to dawdle over them. Later she could sort them out, decide what to do with them. Now she had to find something. She tossed aside the gowns, then dug through a stack of accessories—silk fans, suede gloves, colored stockings, whimsical feathered headdresses too small to be called hats. Finally, at the bottom, atop the somewhat crushed ostrich plumes of a shiny pink wrapper, she saw a stack of papers.

Carefully she pulled the papers from the trunk and tilted them toward the light to read. The printed documents gave Mrs. Montana McCrory, widow of Tom McCrory, title to the property of the Golden Palace saloon in Eagleton, Colorado. She read the documents quickly, then laid them aside and turned back to the trunk. She stuffed all the clothing in and closed the lid. Clutching the documents to her chest, she walked toward the bed and looked down at the body.

The woman who lay there had been Mathilda Brawley. A whore, by her own admission. She had decided to become someone else—Montana McCrory, who she imagined was a lady of high breeding. The gold plating had been thin, and the brass underneath had shown through all too frequently. Now, though, in her death, she would have the identity of a lady at last.

"Good-bye, Ivy Barton," the new Montana whispered. She turned and walked swiftly into the hallway.

Dr. Davis was seated on the chair opposite Alex's bed when she returned to their room. He stood as soon as he saw her, his expectant look conveying not so much gentlemanliness as eagerness to be paid. She turned her back to him to pull the money from her bodice, then paid him and showed him the door. When he'd gone, she turned to Alex to tell him the rest of the plan.

"Where'd you get all that money?" he asked before she could speak.

"I saved it. Before we left Tennessee," she said evasively. Before he could ask anything further, she added, "We have to get you out of here before Bill Mott comes back. We'll both stay in Mrs. McCrory's room tonight."

"In her room? But you said she just died in there. I can't—"

"Here." She handed him his hat. "Put this on to cover your bandage, and I'll help you with your shoes. You have to go downstairs and tell them you're checking out. Pretend to be the bereaved husband."

"Check out? I don't understand. I thought you said—"

"Please, listen to me. You're going to tell them that since your wife has died, you can no longer bear to stay here, so you're checking out. To the hotel people you're still Alex Barton, remember? So tell them that you've asked Mrs. Montana McCrory, the woman who came in with your wife, to see to your wife's possessions and to have them shipped to you. Then you leave. That way, if Bill Mott comes back, they will tell him your wife died and you left town. But you come back in by the back stairs and you go to Mrs. McCrory's room. I'll wait for you there."

"I don't know, Ivy. I don't know if I can be that convincing."

"Of course you can, Alex. And don't call me Ivy."

"But what about you? The desk clerk saw you come in. How are you going to leave later if he thinks you're dead?"

"He doesn't think I'm dead. He thinks your wife is dead. Since Mrs. McCrory and I came in together, and I registered for her in her name, he thinks I'm Montana McCrory."

"Well, I don't know. . . ."

"Take this." She handed him some of the money she'd taken from Mrs. McCrory's valise. "Use that to pay for the room. That should be more than enough."

Alex stared at the money. "All right," he said reluctantly. "I'll check out of the hotel, and I'll look bereaved, and I'll come back in by the back stairs so I won't be noticed, but I won't stay in that room."

"There's no reason to worry about staying in that room," she said, gently leading him toward the door.

"A woman just died in there."

"The body will be gone by the time you get back, Alex. Please don't worry." He walked away from her slowly and reluctantly. "And hurry," she whispered, watching him go.

When he was out of sight, she walked up the hall to Mrs. McCrory's room to wait for his return. She was glad to see that the body had, in fact, already been removed. She found, however, that the empty, silent room did nothing to ease her edginess. She paced nervously, wondering what was taking Alex so long.

It was a full hour before he finally returned, smelling of liquor.

"Alex," she said. "You were gone so long. I was worried." She didn't bother to ask where he'd been, since it was obvious.

"No need to worry." He sounded tipsy. "You said yourself there was no need to worry." He removed his hat and tossed it onto the bureau, and she could see that blood had soaked through his bandage. He slumped onto the bed and propped himself against the headboard, then smiled at her a little crookedly. His face, she saw, was pale and drawn, and she knew that he was afraid. She suppressed the urge to berate him for staying out so long and for coming back drunk. The liquor, she knew, was a means to drive the fear away. She went to him and helped him remove his boots and then his clothes.

"I'll never be able to sleep a wink in this room," he said. "I can't sleep in a bed where a woman just died."

"Don't worry," she soothed him. "It will be all right."

Within minutes his breathing was deep and even, and he was sleeping soundly beside her. It was she who lay awake listening for Bill Mott and thinking of the woman she had become.

* * *

By early morning the woman who called herself Montana McCrory had checked out of the hotel. Alex had left earlier, using the back stairs. When they met at the train station, Montana had bought tickets for the two of them for Eagleton.

The trip was a long one. The train wound through valleys and labored up steep grades for hours. The scenery was spectacular, alternating between thick pine forests and steep cliffs of granite, some of which had been blasted away for the railroad. At times the train seemed to career dangerously on the edge of the world, threatening to fall off as it rounded a curve.

His bandage hidden beneath his hat, Alex looked pale and tired as the swaying motion of the train rocked him back and forth. Montana, beside him, was equally pale beneath the sprinkling of soot that had settled on her face from the train's smokestack. As they moved farther and farther away from Colorado Springs, she thought of the first Montana McCrory. There would be no funeral, but she had given the undertaker instructions and the funds to make it a decent burial. And Mrs. McCrory would have something else to compensate her: in a manner of speaking, she would be assured of a life after death.

Montana closed her eyes, trying to see herself in her new role. She had thrust herself into this part without rehearsal or preparation, but she willed herself to put away her fears and to believe that it was possible to do what she had to do. And why couldn't she do it? It was no more than running a business, she told herself. Hadn't she managed the business of running a home for years, and on a meager income? If there was more money to be concerned with, more money to be made, wouldn't that only make it easier?

The ride seemed endless before the train finally slowed and Montana saw, with a mixture of curiosity and apprehension, the valley the train was approaching. The barren expanse was dotted with buildings, a few rising to two or more floors but most of them one-story shacks. Several tents also were scattered along the muddy streets.

Montana and Alex gathered their possessions and got off the train.

"God," Alex said, "this is going to be a nightmare. How are we gonna pull this off? How did I ever let you talk me into this?"

"We had no choice."

"But you've got to act the part. Like a common— like a saloon owner! You can't hide behind your embroidery, you know."

"No," she said. "I can't hide. There is no place left for me to hide." She didn't know what made her say those words, but hearing them aloud left her more afraid than ever. She stood trembling for a moment until Alex took her arm.

"It's all right," he said. "I told you long ago, it's all right." He looked around. "Let's get to the Golden Palace."

They found a wagon for hire and paid the owner fifty cents to drive them and their trunks to the Golden Palace.

As the wagon rolled along a dusty, rutted street, they passed a tall wooden building with a sign pronouncing it the Portland Hotel, a brick structure bearing the name N. O. Johnson Department Store, a pharmacy, several small groceries, and a number of assay offices. The wagon had just turned down another street when the blare of a trombone made the horses start, and Montana almost fell from the seat. The driver managed to get the team of horses under control and pulled the wagon to the side of the street.

"What is it?" Alex asked. "What's going on?"

"It's the Central about to parade their new burlesque show down Baylor Avenue," he shouted over the drumbeat now begun in rhythm with the trombone. They could see the musicians stepping high in time to their music and behind them a row of women holding their skirts up and kicking while they sang "There'll Be a Hot Time in the Old Town Tonight."

Men and a few women poured out of the stores to watch, and other wagons and carriages pulled off the street to allow the parade to pass.

"Does this happen every day?" Montana asked.

"Nope. Just when a new show comes to town," the driver said. He waited, watching, until the parade was out of sight before he flicked the reins to urge the horses on again.

The street they now drove down was lined with mostly shabby false-front buildings: the Gold Dollar Saloon, the Lone Pine Drinking Establishment, the Okay Shaving and Bath House, New York Chop House, and Central Dance Hall. One place, called the Nolton, was larger and more stylish that the other saloons. Montana could see chandeliers hanging from high ceilings as the wagon lumbered past the open doors.

Finally the wagon pulled up in front of a rickety two-story frame building next to a vacant lot. The structure was badly in need of paint, a broken window on the top floor had been boarded over, and the balcony across the front had a deep sway in the middle. A weathered sign read GOLDEN PALACE. Montana stared at the building, a sinking feeling in her stomach. Alex reached into his hip pocket, pulled out a flask, and took a swallow of its contents.

"Help me down, Alex," Montana said, forcing herself into action. When she was on the ground, she turned to ask the driver to unload the trunks.

"Two bits more if I unload," said the sullen man.

"I'll pay your price," she answered sharply.

The driver pulled both trunks from the wagon none too carefully and stood waiting for his money. Montana took the cash from her traveling bag and paid him, then watched him roll down the street while she tried to gather enough courage to enter the Golden Palace. Finally she turned toward the building and, with great resolve, walked toward the door. Alex followed her.

The large room struck Montana as almost colorless. The floor, though swept, was made of bare wooden planks turned gray from ground-in dirt and grime. A few darker spots were scattered near the brass cuspidors along the b..r, where tobacco-stained spittle had missed the mark. The bar was made of mahogany so dark it was almost black. A mirror behind it reflected the colorless room and the row of bottles and glasses poised like statues of saints waiting mutely for prayers. A sign advertising fresh buttermilk for two cents was tacked to the frame of the mirror. The walls were almost the same undistinguished gray as the floor, as were the wooden tables and chairs spaced around the room. Three men, just as colorlessly dressed, sat at a table in a corner, sipping mugs of beer.

As Montana stepped inside, the trio stared at her, one of them holding his mug suspended between the table and his lips.

"Lookin' fer somebody?" one of the men asked at length. The dirty, uneven beard that covered his ruddy face gave him a grizzled look and made it impossible to determine his age.

"Yes, sir, I am." Montana's southern accent was even more pronounced, as it often was when she was nervous. "I wonder if I might see the—the person in charge here. The manager, maybe?"

The grizzled man shot a glance at Alex, then turned to look inquiringly at the other two men at the table, as if uncertain whether or not he should answer the lady.

"That would be Diana Pollard," said a man with a cleanshaven but pockmarked face. "Di!" he shouted over his shoulder without taking his eyes off Montana and Alex. "Di! Somebody here to see you."

He called twice more before a tall woman in a faded brown dress stepped inside the door. Her hair, a dark, rich brown streaked with gray at the temples, was pulled back severely from a well-sculptured face, the skin of which was tanned, showing that she never wore a bonnet when she was out in the sun. She held a large rock in one hand, and she looked annoyed.

"What are you bellerin' about, Norton? I told you if you want another drink you can get it your—" She stopped speaking when she saw Montana, and she stared at her, as dumbfounded as the men had been.

"This here lady wants to see you," the pockmarked man said.

Diana glanced at Alex, then gawked at Montana

again. "You wanted to see me?"

"Are you the person in charge?" Montana asked.

"Now, look, lady if you're one o' them temperance—"

"I'm Montana McCrory," she said, her voice a little unsteady.

Diana gave her a hard stare, and for a moment Montana felt frightened enough to turn and flee the Golden Palace. She heard Alex's nervous shuffling behind her. Quickly she set the valise she carried on a table, opened it, pulled out her documents, and shoved them toward the woman.

"I'm the new owner," she said.

Diana set down the rock she'd held and reached for the papers. She looked at them, then handed them back to Montana. "Tom's widow," she said almost reverently. But her eyes narrowed, and she studied Montana intently. "You come in from Kansas City?"

"Kansas City?" Then she remembered that was the place Montana McCrory was from. "Oh, yes, Kansas City. That's right." Montana rolled the papers nervously in her hand.

"You don't sound like Kansas City."

"Oh, well . . ."

"And you don't look like the woman Tom described."

"I don't? What did—"

"Said you had red hair."

Montana's hand flew to her head. She tried to speak again, but Diana interrupted.

"I'd call it auburn, but then Tom never did know shit from— 'Scuse me," she added quickly when she saw Montana's reaction to her crude expression. "He also said you had big—" Her eyes went to Montana's bosom, but she now seemed uncertain about how descriptive she should be.

"This is Alex Miller," Montana said quickly. She pulled Alex by the arm and thrust him toward Diana. "My brother. He'll be staying here with me."

"Yeah?" Diana eyed him suspiciously.

"Yes," Montana said. "We're very close, my brother and I, and I've asked him to help me run the business since—since Tom, my husband—"

"I'm the accountant," Alex said quickly.

Diana scrutinized both of them without speaking, and Montana felt increasingly uncomfortable. "Well!" she said, glancing uneasily at the three men in the corner, who were still staring at her. "Our trunks are out in front. I suppose we should have them brought in. Do you—do I have living quarters here? I mean, upstairs or—"

"There's two bedrooms upstairs that's decent, and a room off the kitchen in the back where I sleep," Diana said.

"Mr. Miller will be staying here as well, so—"

Diana folded her arms across her chest and narrowed her eyes as she continued to scrutinize Alex. "Ben! You and Norton and Phineas help Mr. Miller here get them trunks in," she called over her shoulder to the men at the table.

They jumped to do her bidding, and Alex followed them out. Montana watched them through the front window, then, aware that Diana's eyes were on her, she turned to face her.

"Are there always so few customers?" It was the only thing she could think to say to break the awkward silence.

Diana shrugged. "Business is slow this time of day. It'll pick up a little when the miners come in. But don't expect no stampede. This ain't the most popular place in town. But then, I reckon it ain't the worst, either. You get yourself dressed up and deal a little blackjack, a little faro, it'll bring 'em in. 'Least for a while. Outta curiosity, if nothin' else. But you're gonna have an uphill battle to bring this place outta debt. Up there, boys." She pointed to the stairs. "Put the lady's trunk in that room at the head of the stairs, and put Mr. Miller's in the one at the end."

Montana saw the look Alex gave her, but she turned back to Diana. "You say the place is in debt?"

"Tom didn't tell you? He's been havin' some trouble payin' his liquor bill. I kept tellin' him to serve food the way the Nolton and the Gold Dollar does, but he wouldn't listen."

"Serve food?"

"I say it's worth a try."

Montana nodded. Maybe it was going to work—if she could just get through the first few days. "How long before those miners start coming in?"

"Coupla hours, maybe."

"Then if you'll excuse me, I'll use that time to—to rest. It's been a long day." She forced a smile, then turned to follow her trunks up the stairs, very much aware that Diana's eyes followed her all the way and feeling more uncertain than she had ever felt in her life.

The men had just deposited the second trunk in the room that was to be Alex's. They doffed their hats awkwardly, then hurried down the stairs. Montana walked into her room, where Alex stood waiting.

He gave her a worried, unhappy look. "Separate bedrooms? My God, how far are we going to carry this?"

"Shh," she cautioned. "They'll hear you."

"Well, what if they do? Didn't you say it don't matter what people think?"

"Give me time, Alex." She dropped wearily to the edge of the bed. "I can only handle a little at a time. I certainly couldn't tell them I'd be sharing a bed with my brother."

"Well, I'll be damned if I'm going to sleep by myself."

"All right! All right!" Montana said, holding up her hands in a gesture that was half despair and half impatience. "You'll sleep in here with me, and no one need know the difference. But I've got something else to worry about now."

"You've got plenty to worry about."

She went to the valise and pulled out the deck of cards. "You've got to teach me to play cards."

"What?"

"Do you know anything about games called black-jack and faro?"

"Well, yes, but—"

"Then you have two hours to teach me."

"Two hours? My God! I can't—"

"Don't say you can't. You have to! You can't let me down this time." Suddenly she burst into tears, ashamed at her accusative tone. "Oh, Alex," she said, sobbing into her hands. "Maybe you're right." She forced herself to face him. "Maybe I shouldn't have gotten us into this."

Alex encircled her with his arms, pulling her close. "No, you were right," he said, stroking her hair. "This was the best we could do under the circumstances. And of course I won't let you down. Didn't I tell you that I'd always be here to help you?" He held her a moment longer. "All right," he said quietly, "I'll teach you what I can."

A little less than two hours later, Montana was still practicing and still trying to remember the rules, when they heard voices downstairs.

"They're here!" she said. "The customers are arriving. I'd better get down there." She stood up, smoothed her skirt, and tucked in a few strands of hair. "Alex, what's that term I'm supposed to remember for faro? Cat house?"

"Cat hop! God, Ivy, you haven't had to time to learn even the simplest things."

"I have to try it, anyway," she said, digging through her belongings for a hairbrush. "I have to make it work."

"Ivy," Alex said. "I—I know you blame me for this. . . ."

"No," she said, turning to face him. "No, I won't think of blame. How can *I*, of all people, cast stones?"

He looked at her with an expression she couldn't read.

"It's all right," she added quickly. "I'm not going to think about the past now. We've both got to think about the present. And we'll get through this. Just like we got through the other. But we have to work together, just as we did when—just as we always have. We must work to earn money to go back to Tennessee to buy more land. We've been given this opportunity, and we can't let it pass."

Alex breathed a shuddering sigh, and Montana noticed the blood soaking through his bandage again.

"Your head," she said. "Let me change the bandage, and then you should stay upstairs and rest."

"No. I'm going down with you. I'm not letting you go into that lions' den alone. Besides, I've got a good story made up to explain this bandage."

Montana laughed and kissed his head as she unwrapped the old dressing. "All right," she said, "we're in this together."

When she'd finished with his bandage, she started for the door, ready to go down to the saloon. But she hesitated, then turned to the look at the trunk sitting beside the bed. She walked to it, opened it, and slowly drew out the red satin gown. She stared at it for a few seconds, then, moving quickly, pulled needle and thread from her traveling bag and began sewing tucks into the bodice, taking it in to fit her smaller frame.

"What are you doing?" Alex asked. "You're not thinking of wearing that, are you? You'll look like a strumpet, a cheap—"

"I have to look the part," she said. She broke a thread with her teeth, reknotted it, and pulled it into another tuck.

Alex breathed another deep sigh, shook his head, and left the room wearing a worried expression.

Montana worked quickly, taking in seams with long stitches she knew would have to be redone later when there was more time. Within minutes she had knotted and broken the last thread. She pulled her gray gabardine over her head, then picked up the other dress, raised her arms, and let the scarlet satin settle onto her shoulders. She smoothed the skirt and fastened the tiny buttons hidden beneath the tucks. At last she stepped to the mirror mounted on the front of a wardrobe.

Her breath caught in her throat when she saw her image. The white curve of her breasts showing through the black netting above the low-cut bodice seemed uncommonly daring, and her first inclination

was to reach for her own dress again. But the severe
style and drab color of her gabardine suit would not
do for the role she had to play. She feared more than
ever that she would make a fool of herself, but she
wanted to go back to Tennessee, and she knew she
couldn't do that by taking in sewing and mopping
other people's floors. This was the only way, and
she'd do it because she had to.

Brush in hand, she pulled up her thick hair and
fastened it with celluloid pins in a roll at the back of
her head. She rummaged through the trunk and
found accessories to go with the gown—a comb of
black, scarlet-tipped bird's wings fashioned in a
V shape, red suede gloves, and a black silk fan. She
would not try the powder and rouge she had seen
among Mrs. McCrory's possessions. She would be
her own Montana McCrory, not a slim replica of the
tawdry original.

She took a deep breath, trying to prepare herself
as she walked to the stairs. When she was halfway
down she saw Diana, her brown dress now covered
with a fresh white apron, standing behind the bar.
She was holding two mugs of beer in each hand,
grasping them by the handles. When she spotted
Montana, the hardened look on her face changed to
one of surprise. For a moment Montana felt unsure
of herself. Perhaps she'd overdone it; perhaps she
should have stuck to her own frock after all. Then
Diana's expression softened, and Montana sensed
approval. But there was something more in Diana's
look, something Montana didn't understand, and she
remained frozen in place, her eyes locked with those
of the other woman.

Finally Diana tore her eyes away and set the beer

mugs on the bar with such force that the contents sloshed over her wrists. The gesture gained her the attention of everyone at the bar, and in the next instant she pointed to the stairway and shouted, "There she is! That's Miss Montana!"

Silence overtook the room, and Montana felt for a moment as if she would faint. Then a loud cheer rushed over her like a flood, and she felt an unfamiliar buoyancy as she floated down the last step, yards of scarlet satin billowing around her like voluptuous sails. She didn't remember walking to the bar, but suddenly she was there and reaching for Diana's outstretched hand. Diana led her around the room, introducing her to one customer after another. Somewhere in the fog of confusion, she sensed Alex standing at the end of the bar, looking pale and nervous.

"The faro table, ma'am." Diana's voice seemed to be coming from somewhere far away. "The faro table," she said again. Montana tried to smile, tried to overcome the odd feeling of otherworldliness that had swept over her. She took the deck of cards from Diana and looked at them, puzzled. Several men approached her. She saw their faces, their eyes looking at her. It was a moment before she realized that they expected her to deal. She glanced at Diana, who still watched her with that odd expression. She looked around for Alex, but she couldn't see him now; the crowd was pressing too close.

What was it Alex had told her? That the cards must be shuffled first. She slipped them from the box and broke them into two sections as Alex had instructed her. But it felt awkward, and they began slipping from her hands. Desperately she grasped the cards to her bosom, but several fell. Suddenly Alex was in front of her, a horrified expression on his face, and for one dreadful moment the room was as quiet as death.

In desperate reflex she threw the remaining cards into the air. "Gentlemen!" she said, her voice high-pitched and ringing with false gaiety. "Let the cards fall where they will, and let he who finds the highest card—the first to find a—an ace—let him win the prize. A—a free drink!"

"A drink with Montana McCrory!" She heard Diana's voice call as a sea of bodies washed about her feet, scrambling for cards.

A diminutive man in a tattered dusty hat stood up, waving a card. "The ace o' spades! The ace o' spades!" he called.

Shouts of protest and congratulations filled the room as everyone crowded around the little man. Diana held up his card, confirming that he had won. "It's the ace all right!" she cried. "Looks like you finally made a lucky strike, Clay Tuttle." She turned to Montana. "Take the table in the corner," she said, depositing Mr. Tuttle on her arm.

Montana made her way toward the table Diana had indicated, and as she passed Alex, she clutched his arm and leaned toward him. "You'll have to deal for me for a while until I get myself together." Her words were a desperate whisper.

"My God, Iv—Montana, they expect—"

"Do it, Alex!" she said sharply, and moved away from him, smiling down at Clay Tuttle.

Clay sat down across from her, looking as shy and uncomfortable as she felt. The rest of his clothing was as work-worn as his hat, which he had removed and now clutched with roughened but well-scrubbed hands.

The old Ivy remembered her mother, the gracious southern lady who had taught her daughter that the secret of the art of conversation was never to talk about oneself but to ask a few questions and allow others to talk.

"Mr. Tuttle," she said, giving him her warmest smile, "tell me what kind of work you do."

"Do a little prospectin' on the side, but mostly I'm a miner, ma'am. Down in the Lucky Lady."

"A miner! And just what, exactly, does a miner do?"

"Why, Miss Montana," he said, looking at her with surprise, "we're the ones that does the minin'."

"Of course," she said, feeling disconcerted and not a little foolish. "And how do you do that?"

Clay was busy explaining how finding telluride and sylvanite in rock was a sure sign of gold when Diana appeared carrying a tray. She set a whiskey in front of Clay.

"There's your usual, Clay," she said. "And you never told me what your usual was, ma'am, so I took the liberty of pourin' you a glass of buttermilk." She set a mug full of the white liquid in front of her.

"Thank you, Diana." She managed a smile. The woman's kindness made her nervous. Maybe she had guessed the truth. Maybe Diana knew she was more used to buttermilk than liquor, and maybe she would soon confront her with the truth. For now she wouldn't think about that, though. She would simply try to get through the moment at hand. And she would be grateful that at least the buttermilk would soothe her churning stomach.

If Diana was suspicious of anything, she didn't reveal it. She went about her business behind the bar without another glance toward Montana. Alex had moved to the faro table, and Clay seemed content to move on to a group of poker players at another table when Montana excused herself.

Still with nothing but her mother's training to fall back on, she moved about the room, greeting customer after customer, spending a few minutes with each as a hostess might do. It seemed to be working. The men seemed happy, buying drinks and laying down their money at the faro table. A few urged her to take over as dealer, and she laughed, promising that she would—later. Alex, she was thankful to see, was absorbed in the game and showed no signs of expecting her presence. In fact, he seemed to have all but forgotten her. He didn't even notice when a tipsy customer grabbed her to whirl her around the noisy, smoky room in rough time to his own discordant singing. Montana managed to pull herself free and was about to sink onto a chair near the back of the room, hoping to steal a few seconds to rest, when she heard Diana's voice calling her.

"Miz McCrory! Somebody here to see you. Says he's an old friend of yours."

Montana turned. Her knees went weak, and she had to grasp the edge of a table to steady herself. The man smiling at her over Diana's shoulder was Langdon Runnels.

4

He sensed her nervousness. He knew he could have put her at ease by calling her Montana, but he merely nodded and said, "Good evening, ma'am."

Letting his eyes sweep over her, he noted the way the dress accented her slender waist and the flare of her hips and revealed the curve of her breasts. The dress obviously belonged to Montana McCrory, but Ivy Barton had somehow made it fit her smaller frame, and, though a bit gaudy, it was flattering to her. She was more than merely pretty now, he realized. Now she was beautiful. He let his gaze linger on her breasts. He half expected her hand to flutter nervously to her bosom as it had during the poker game the day before, but she continued to grip the table behind her.

He had taken the train into Eagleton because he had decided to spend some time at a claim he had staked out nearby. He had to put in the hundred dollars' worth of labor the state required in order to hold the claim for another year. He believed the Honesty held the most potential of any claim he'd ever owned, but it was going to take time and money to develop it, and at the moment he was a little short of the latter. That was why he'd decided to pay a visit to Mathilda Susan Brawley, or Montana McCrory, as she was calling herself on the train. She had told him about her husband's death and that she was taking over an Eagleton gambling house. He had known a new owner, especially a female, would attract a lot of customers out of curiosity. There would be plenty of miners with money in their pockets, ready to lose it to his skill at the cards. When he found the Golden Palace and saw the crowd, he knew he'd been right about Montana attracting attention.

He'd been in the saloon only a few seconds when he spotted Ivy Barton, dressed in a daring gown, and he'd heard someone refer to her as Miss Montana. Nothing could have surprised him more, and at first he couldn't believe his own eyes and ears. Why, he wondered, would she be posing as someone else? Unless she was involved in some sort of swindle. She had revealed nothing that would lead him to believe she was capable of that. But there was obviously much more to Ivy Barton than met the eye. That made him all the more excited to have found her.

He had tried to make his way to her immediately, but Diana had intercepted him, asking him abruptly what he wanted. He'd thought she sounded a little belligerent, but then, Diana always sounded belligerent.

"I want to speak to Mrs. McCrory," he had told her. "I'm an old friend." She had given him a long, scrutinizing look, as if to remind him that she didn't like him and had never trusted him, but then she had plowed her way through the crowd with him in tow and brought him to Ivy. Now she stood by protectively.

He smiled at Ivy, enjoying his advantage.

She didn't return the smile, but she was doing a good job of hiding the fear that he knew must be there. She said coolly, "Good evening, sir."

He bowed slightly, the way he'd learned to among the gentry in New Orleans. "So nice to see you again," he said, ignoring the hovering Diana. He glanced toward Alex, who was busy at the faro table. "And how is your—"

"My brother is well, thank you," Montana said quickly.

"Your brother?"

"You were inquiring about Alex?"

Her eyes bored into him, and he saw a flicker of desperation. She was fighting for survival. He'd learned to spot the look at the gaming tables, and he'd learned how to use it to his advantage. There was no need to hurry, though. He was enjoying himself.

"So sorry to hear about the loss of your husband."

"Was there something you wished to see me about?" she asked, her voice sharp, nervous.

"Yes," he said, giving her his most charming smile. "There is." He glanced at the scowling Diana. "Perhaps we can talk about it in private?"

He saw Montana blanch and Diana move a menacing step closer to him.

"It's all right, Diana," Montana said, never taking her eyes off him. "Please go back to the bar. I'll speak to Mr. Runnels in private if he wishes."

Langdon gave her another smile and a nod. Across the room he saw Alex staring at them, the fear in his eyes even more obvious than Montana's. Langdon touched the brim of his hat in greeting. He saw Alex hesitate, holding a faro card in his hand as if he were unsure what to do. Then he was drawn into the game again by the impatient gamblers crowding around him.

When Diana had returned reluctantly to the bar, Langdon grasped Montana's elbow and steered her toward a corner table.

"You look a little pale," he said as he pulled out a chair for her. "Let me get you some whiskey."

"No, thank you. I never touch—"

"You never touch what? Liquor? Come now, isn't that rather odd for a saloon owner? If word gets around that you're a teetotaler, what's that going to do for your business?"

She stopped and, pulling her arm from his grasp, turned to face him. "What is it you want, Mr. Runnels?"

"Langdon," he said. "Please call me Langdon." There was a pause. "And what shall I call *you?*" he asked with peculiar emphasis.

Her mouth trembled almost imperceptibly. "Please, Mr. Runnels . . . Langdon. Tell me what you want." She glanced away nervously, and he saw her force a smile. He followed her gaze and saw Diana glowering at him.

Langdon gave the woman a polite nod, then turned his attention to helping Montana onto a chair. "I'm only concerned about your welfare," he said. "I want you to be able to have peace of mind." He settled onto the chair across from her.

"Peace of mind?" she asked.

"The peace of mind that comes with knowing you won't be betrayed."

Their gazes locked. "And what will that cost me, Mr. Runnels?"

"Cost?" he asked. "I thought we were friends. It seems so—so unfriendly to speak of costs. I'm only concerned that we are able to work out some . . . well, shall we say, *arrangement* for your peace of mind."

"And what, my *friend,* might that *arrangement* be?" A note of sarcasm had replaced the fear in her voice. That both surprised and, oddly, excited him.

"If I am to help you," he said, "I must understand what has happened."

"I can't talk about it now," she said, surveying the crowded room. "I'll explain later. After we close. I'll explain everything then. If you'll excuse me." She made as if to stand, but he placed a hand over hers, holding her back.

"I heard before I left the train that Alex lost the farm to Bill Mott," Langdon said. "Is that true? Does this . . . charade have something to do with that?"

She glanced at him nervously, then at a group of customers near their table.

One young man, still wearing his dusty miner's garb, grabbed her arm, pulling her toward him. "Nice to have a purty woman 'round for a change," he said. "You give the place some class, and I like class." He tried to kiss her on the lips and paw at her breasts while his companions laughed raucously and cheered him on. Langdon reached for the man, but in the same instant Diana was there.

"Keep your hands off her, you goddamned filthy son of a bitch." Though several inches shorter and considerably slighter than the burly young miner, she jerked him around to face her, shoved him against the table, and kneed him in the groin. The man groaned and doubled over.

A hush fell over the noisy room.

"I never meant nothin' by it, Di, honest," the miner wheezed.

Diana ignored him and stood, hands on her hips, her flinty gaze sweeping the crowd. "The same goes for the rest of you," she said. "There's a lady in the Golden Palace now, and she don't need none of your pawin' and slobberin' on her, or none of your filthy talk."

No one spoke for several seconds. The only sound was the distant tinkling of piano keys and riotous shouts from the Nolton a block away. Eventually a few of the men turned sheepishly back to their card games, speaking in low murmurs. Diana turned to Montana. "You need any more help, you call me," she said. She glared at Langdon.

"Thank you, Diana," Montana said. "I'm sure I'll be all right."

Diana let her gaze linger on Langdon before she turned and made her way back to the bar.

A smile played at Langdon's lips. "You suppose she would have done that for the other Montana?" he asked, reaching into his vest pocket for tobacco and papers and rolling a smoke.

Making her way through the room, obviously not happy that he was following, Montana didn't answer.

"By the way, where is she?" Langdon blew a cloud of smoke toward the ceiling.

"Dead," Montana answered as she smiled and nodded at a customer. "I hope you understand. I was desperate."

Langdon coughed, strangling on his cigarette smoke.

Montana glanced at him, and her eyes widened. "Oh, no, I didn't mean—It's not what you think."

Langdon raised an eyebrow. The situation was becoming more and more intriguing.

"You've scared Alex to death by showing up here," she said, turning away from him. Langdon followed her gaze and saw the look of fear frozen on the man's face. "I should go to him, I should—"

"And leave a paying customer?"

"Look at him. He's worried. I should go talk to him. After all, he's my—"

"Your brother, I believe you said."

She stared at her hands and seemed unable to speak.

"And your brother, I'm sure, doesn't need you at all. How fortunate that Mrs. McCrory is no longer married and can feel unencumbered about meeting me after closing."

She looked up. "Mr. Runnels, I have no intention of—"

"Go speak to your brother if you wish. Put him at ease. Tell him everything's all right, at least for the moment. I'll find a card game to occupy my time until closing. Then we'll talk. But first, tell me what happened to Ivy Barton."

Her eyes held his for a moment before she spoke. "She died of appendicitis. Ivy Barton is buried in Colorado Springs."

The news of Ivy Barton's demise had not seemed to affect Langdon Runnels. He had simply nodded as if her death had been expected, then turned away to find a card game. Montana watched him uneasily. What had made her think her luck would hold? Something was bound to happen to betray her. But she had thought it would be some mistake she made trying to run a business about which she knew nothing. She hadn't expected to be betrayed by someone who knew her true identity, least of all Langdon Runnels, one of the few people she'd spoken to on the journey. The chance of his showing up had been more than remote.

She certainly didn't like Mr. Runnels's manner, either—the way he had talked about an "arrangement" to assure her "peace of mind." He was clearly thinking of blackmail.

She looked back to Alex, who excused himself from the faro table and moved toward her. "What's he doing here?" he asked. She saw that the bandage around his head was dampened with sweat and a pink tinge of blood.

"I don't know," she said. "He wants to talk. After we close."

"God! He can ruin us if he—"

"Don't worry about it yet, Alex. We'll see what he says. I think he's willing to keep quiet for a price."

"A price? He's going to blackmail us? How much?"

"I don't know. Please try not to worry."

"I ought to go talk to him before it's too late. Before he starts blabbing to somebody and ruins us." He rubbed his forehead, and before she could stop him he moved away from her. Before he reached Langdon, however, he hesitated and seemed to change his mind, going instead to the bar. He took a full bottle of whiskey from the shelf behind it and made his way back to the faro table, eyeing Langdon uneasily. He paused halfway across the room to drink long and deep.

Montana was relieved that Alex had apparently lost his nerve. She wanted to talk to Langdon first, or at least be there to make certain Alex didn't say the wrong thing. Still feeling edgy, she went back to circulating among the customers and soon found herself helping Diana deliver drinks to the tables. She managed to stay busy and to avoid Langdon Runnels.

Suddenly she heard angry shouts from the crowd at the faro table.

"You're a goddamned cheat!" someone cried. "I coppered that stake. It's my money!"

"Who you callin' a cheat?" Alex shouted in return. "You coppered the ten, then moved your copper when you saw the nine come up."

Montana cried out when someone took a swing at Alex. She made her way through the crowd to his side. The man's fist grazed his jaw, and Alex staggered backward, only to lunge at the man who had hit him. Before Montana could reach him, Langdon was there.

"Hold on a minute," he said, one hand on each man's chest, pushing them apart. "What's the trouble here?"

"He's a cheat," the man said. "I won the bet, fair and square. It's my copper there on the nine."

"Here," Langdon said, picking up a stack of money. "Take your money, and no hard feelings."

The man gave him a surprised look, then quickly stuffed the bills into his shirt pocket.

"Who the hell are you?" another player asked.

"Mrs. McCrory's business partner," Langdon said. Montana saw him glance at her, then turn back to the crowd. "Now, if you gentlemen will excuse me, I'll put our faro dealer to bed. From the looks of his head, that's where he ought to be."

Alex started to protest, but Langdon spoke to him quietly, and Alex said no more. Montana had no doubt that whatever Langdon had said had been a threat. "What about the game?" someone shouted. "Who'll deal the faro for us?"

"Miss Montana," another said. "Montana can deal faro."

"The faro game is over," Langdon said. "Come back tomorrow. Montana will deal then."

"What's wrong with tonight?" a customer shouted.

"Give us time," Langdon said over his shoulder. "We're just getting started. The lady only got to town today. We haven't had time to get the business in full swing yet."

Montana watched him disappear up the stairs with Alex, worried at the thought of the two of them together. She didn't want Langdon to take even more advantage of him. He'd gone far enough, proclaiming himself a business partner. What else might he do with his blackmailing? But she couldn't follow them: there were still customers to deal with. Several more were leaving now that the faro game had ended; she had to stop the drain.

She did her best, bringing more beer and liquor to the tables. But her eyes kept moving to the stairs, watching for Langdon, and all the while the piano music and laughter from the other saloons along the street grew louder, luring her customers away.

"You didn't tell me you had a partner," Diana growled when she walked to the bar for two more beers.

"I . . . didn't think it necessary," Montana said stiffly.

"I like to know who I'm working for," Diana said as she drew the beer. "Maybe I don't want to work for no son of a bitch like Langdon Runnels."

Montana blanched at her language, but she managed to recover enough to ask, "You know him?"

"Well enough."

It occurred to her to ask what he was like, but she couldn't, she realized. She was supposed to know him well enough herself to have made him her business partner. "If you don't wish to work here, you're free to leave," she said, grasping the mugs Diana shoved toward her. When she tried to pick them up, Diana held on to them. For a moment their eyes locked.

"Who are you?" Diana asked.

Montana felt her mouth go dry. "I'm Montana McCrory, just like I told you."

"I don't give a damn what your name is. I mean, who are you?"

"I don't know what you—"

"You ain't never set foot in a saloon before."

Montana angrily tried to pull the mugs out of Diana's hands. "You don't know what you're talking about."

Diana held fast. "I know what I'm talking about all right. I just don't know why you did it."

Montana gave her a frightened look.

"You ain't the type to hook up with a man like Tom just because you fell in love with him. If you thought you was doin' it because he was rich, if you and your brother and that damned Runnels had some kinda swindle in mind, then you're wastin' your time. There's better places than this to steal."

Montana felt her heart pounding in her chest, but she narrowed her eyes at Diana. "We planned no scheme to get this place," she said, "but I have it now, and I intend to keep it. I have a marriage license, a will, and a title proving that I inherited the Golden Palace, and I can make anyone I want a business partner. And if you want to stay, you will not question my integrity again."

Diana's expression did not change, but finally she

nodded and said softly, "Yes, ma'am," relaxing her grip on the beer glasses and turning to straighten the bottles on the shelf behind the bar.

Montana carried the beer to her customers with a sinking feeling. Even more of the men had left. The music and laughter from the other saloons now seemed unnaturally loud. She set the mugs on the table and ran her sweating palms down her dress, glancing uneasily around the almost empty room. She saw Langdon descending the stairs, looking at her through a haze of smoke and wearing a hint of a smile on his lips.

She wanted to ask him about Alex, but his insolent look intimidated her, and she busied herself clearing glasses and bottles from the empty tables. The last three of her customers walked toward the door.

"Good night, gentlemen," she called.

Two of them turned and rather shyly tipped their hats.

"Please come again tomorrow," she said.

The men murmured an embarrassed response, then quickly left the Golden Palace.

She was now alone except for Langdon and Diana, who was wiping the bar with a damp cloth.

"Diana," she said, "why don't you leave it for tonight. We can finish cleaning in the morning."

Diana looked at her, then at Langdon. Wordlessly she tossed the cloth into a basin of water, took off her apron, flung it across the bar, and walked to her room at the back. Montana watched until she slammed the door behind her. Then she turned to face Langdon.

"You have a lot of nerve, announcing that you're my business partner."

Langdon laughed. "*I* have a lot of nerve? I'm not the one posing as somebody else."

"Shh! For goodness' sake, keep your voice down."

"'Goodness' sake'? Now that's a charming expression."

"All right, let's stop playing games," Montana said. "You're blackmailing us. You've made yourself our business partner. What else do you want? And what did you do to Alex?"

"Whoa! One thing at a time. First of all, I did nothing to Alex except put him to bed. But we had a long talk first. He told me about losing the land to Bill Mott, about Montana McCrory dying. He said that before she died, she asked you to take over her business. Said you were afraid of the idea at first, but you gave in because the two of you were desperate. Said you thought it best to use her name. Damned foolish of you, I say."

His expression was bland, and Montana forced herself not to blink. Perhaps if she was careful to allow neither her voice nor manner to reveal anything, he would decide that there was no potential for blackmail.

"Yes," she said. Her heart pounded like a hammer. "Alex is right. I was reluctant, but it was what she wanted, and we *were* desperate. I'm sure you can see that I had no other choice but to comply with her wishes." Montana managed a smile. "She was rather strange, you know. Eccentric. Had this farfetched idea that if I used her name, took over her identity, it would give her a form of immortality." She picked up her skirt and turned toward the stairs. "Now, if you'll excuse me, I've had a rather busy—"

He grabbed her arm. "Why don't you tell me the real story," he said.

Once again they were face to face, and she was forced to look into his eyes. His once bland expression had hardened; his eyes were like cold blue slate, and his hand, grasping just above her wrist, made her arm hurt. Her heart was pounding even harder now, making her breath come in short, shallow gasps.

"Alex told you the truth," she said.

"Then why are you so scared?"

"I don't know what you're talking about. Mercy, I'm not scared." She tried to laugh, to sound amused, but her voice was choked.

He relaxed his grip slightly but still held her arm. "You don't expect me to *believe* that wild tale, do you? Montana McCrory was a common whore who didn't have enough imagination to come up with a crazy idea about immortality."

"Oh, but you're wrong," Montana said. She tried to wrench her arm free, but Langdon tightened his grip again. "She had enough imagination to invent her name. Her real name was Mathilda Brawley, but she said that wasn't stylish enough. She had the wild idea that Montana was a name fit for a lady. And she was no common whore. She wanted to improve herself, to be a lady, to offer help to someone who needed it, even on her deathbed." Montana was surprised at how quickly these embellishments of the truth came to her tongue.

"And you agreed to everything she asked? To take over her identity completely?" Langdon dropped her arm, and his eyes seemed to have grown even colder.

"I couldn't see that I had a choice. I had to—" He was looking at her as if he could read her mind. She couldn't speak. She found it difficult even to breathe.

"You're lying, of course," he said, quite emotionless. "You were desperate, yes, but the idea to take over her name and her business was yours, not hers." He smiled at her. "It was pretty damned smart of you. Diana said there's a lady in the Golden Palace now." He picked up her hand and kissed it, bowing low, mocking her gallantly. "And the lady," he said, reaching for her face, holding her chin, forcing her to look into his eyes, "needs my help. Because she's scared. Very scared."

Her mind raced. She had to get rid of him. Get him out of her and Alex's lives so he couldn't harm them.

"No," she said. "I don't need anything from you."

He cocked his head slightly, then took another draw on his cigarette before he dropped his hand from her chin. "All right," he said, squinting through the smoke. "Then I'll bid you good-bye, Mrs. Barton."

He turned his back to her and walked with steady confidence toward the door. He had called her Mrs. Barton, not Montana—a subtle hint that the truth he knew could hurt her. But he didn't know the whole truth. And perhaps his not knowing could hurt them even more now. She hesitated, uncertain what to do.

"Wait!" she called to him just as he reached the front door. He stopped but did not turn around. "You're right," she said, fighting to keep her voice from shaking. "I'm scared. Scared for Alex."

He pivoted slowly to face her. "Are you always so protective of Alex?" He sounded ridiculing.

"It's Bill Mott," she said, ignoring his attitude. "He tried to kill Alex. I think he'll try again if he finds him."

Langdon walked toward her. "Is that what that bandage on Alex's head is all about? He told me it was an accident. Said he fell from a wagon."

"It was no accident," Montana said. "It was Bill Mott."

"But why?"

"The deed to the land he won from Alex was bogus."

"What?"

"There's no such place as Green Valley, Colorado. Alex wasted all our money on something that didn't exist."

Langdon laughed. "Another swindle! God, a man can make more mining for suckers than he can mining for gold."

"It's not funny, Mr. Runnels." Montana twisted her hands nervously and fought back her anger. "Bill Mott thought Alex was trying to cheat him. That's why he came to our room in Colorado Springs and tried to kill him. He would have finished the job if he hadn't heard a noise outside the room and gotten scared and run away. He meant to come back, but we left before he got the chance. I—I'm afraid he'll try again. That's one reason we're using other names."

Montana felt tears welling in her eyes, and she turned her back to Langdon. "The other reason is just like Alex told you. We're desperate. And, yes, you're right. Mrs. McCrory didn't ask me to take over her business." She forced herself to face him again. "The only thing she said was that she wanted everything to go to charity. I'm afraid Alex and I are in need of charity, Mr. Runnels. I could think of nothing else to do except try to make a living as Montana McCrory."

Langdon studied her face, but he didn't speak. His silence made her nervous.

"Alex is not—not trained for any trade," she stammered. Still Langdon said nothing. "It's up to me," she said. "Of course, I have no training, either, but I thought I could—" She knew she was babbling, and she felt foolish. Langdon still stared at her silently, still wearing his utterly bland expression. "You told those men you were my business partner. That was your blackmail, I know," she blurted. "But can't you see it will ruin us? Diana says the Golden Palace has debts, that it's barely possible to keep from going under. If we have to give you part of the profits—" She stopped again, realizing that she was about to grovel. She raised her eyes to meet his, and her expression hardened. She wouldn't beg. She would stand her ground, keep her pride intact. "Now you know the whole truth. I hope you understand why it's not possible to make you a partner. You can see we can't afford it. I also hope you won't betray us."

Langdon said nothing for a very long moment. He propped a foot on one of the chairs and rested his arm casually on his knee. "May not be me that betrays you," he said.

"What do you mean?"

"You'll probably tip your own hand," he said. "If you haven't already. You don't know a damn thing about running a saloon or playing cards."

"I'll have to learn." She turned away from him and began clearing glasses and bottles from one of the tables.

Suddenly Langdon was behind her, and he took her arm, forcing her to face him. "That's why you need a partner," he said.

"I just told you, I can't afford—"

"You can't afford not to," he said. "Let me show you how to do it."

"And the cost?"

"Equal partners. Fifty-fifty."

She tried to jerk away. "I just told you, I can't afford it."

"You can't do it without me," he said, forcing her to look at him.

"But fifty-fifty . . . it won't be enough for either of us."

"Do you think I'd make the offer if I thought it wouldn't be enough?" He dropped her arm and grinned, his manner self-assured, even cocky.

Montana observed him, her thoughts churning. "You would teach me?" she asked at last. "You wouldn't just take it over for yourself?"

"I'm a fair man."

Montana laughed, a short, cynical sound. "I reckon you are an opportunist, Mr. Runnels. You are exploitative, and I suspect you are downright greedy. You are all those things, but you are not, it strikes me, fair."

Langdon moved toward her and took the glasses she held. "You may be right," he said, wearing his self-assured smile. "And those are all the things you'll need to learn from me if you're going to make it as a businesswoman." He set the glasses on the table. "And it's never too soon or too late to start learning," he said as he led her toward the door.

"What do you mean?" she asked.

"I mean that you are going to begin your lessons in how to be Montana McCrory, gambling parlor and saloon owner, tonight."

Montana glanced toward the stairs that led to the room where Alex was asleep, the room where she should be. "We could start tomorrow morning," she said. "You could teach me to gamble. Alex tried. There just wasn't enough time. But I'm sure that with a little more effort I could—"

"I can give you the two most important lessons you'll need to be a successful gambler right now. First, you'll never win big if you're not willing to take big chances, and second, watch the other fellow for a sign of weakness and then take advantage of whatever his weakness is. There's more to running this business than knowing how to gamble, though," he said, persisting in moving her toward the door. "There's a whole other world out there. A world that sells pleasure in many different forms. It's your competition, Montana. You need to know what it is. You need to learn from it."

She held back. "You can't mean now."

"Why not?" He glanced around the empty room. "What else do you have to do?" Montana's gaze moved to the stairway again. "Ivy Barton could go to bed with her husband," Langdon said. "But Montana McCrory would come with me."

Myrtle Avenue at night was even uglier than it had been in the daylight. Electric lights from the saloons and dance halls washed out the dusty gray boardwalk and the false-fronted pine shacks, turning the street a garish white. The sound of a band gurgled from the nearby Central Dance Hall, accompanied unharmoniously by the Nolton's piano and by a whining pump organ somewhere farther up the street. Laughter, shouts, and the squeals of female voices threatened to drown out the music. People milled along the boardwalk, the men in the rough work clothes of miners and prospectors, the women in starched frills and laces. Some even wore scandalously short gowns that showed not only the ankles but the calves of their black-stockinged legs.

Langdon took her arm and led her through the crowd to the Gold Dollar Saloon. Inside, a piano player churned out ragtime, and three young women cavorted with customers in what passed for dance steps. Other customers crowded around a large table in the center of the room.

"Billiards," Langdon said, pointing to the table.

"And what's that thing?" Montana asked, staring at an odd contraption in the corner.

"Roulette," Langdon said.

"The men seem to like it," she said, noting the crowd around it. "Perhaps I should get one."

"Come on," he said, "I'll show you how it works." He led her to the wheel and explained the principle of betting on the numbers and colors. "Place a bet," he said. "You can never fully understand anything until you've tried it firsthand."

She stared at him. Around them people cheered and shouted, urging the wheel to do their bidding. "Of course not," she said. "I have no money to waste on gambling."

He looked at her, amused. "And no inclination to enjoy yourself, either, do you?"

"I'm here to learn, not for pleasure," she said primly.

"Certainly," he said, his tone somewhat sarcastic. "You're a very wise woman, of course."

She tried to ignore his sarcasm. "That wheel device," she said. "Is it expensive?"

"Several hundred dollars, I would imagine."

"Then I'll have to keep it in mind as a future investment." She glanced around the room again. "The girls," she said. "Are they customers?"

"No," Langdon said. "They work here. They're part of the attraction."

"Then I could hire one or two to dance with the customers. I'd have to make certain they were the right sort, who—"

"Oh, you can buy them, just like a roulette wheel or a piano, and then sell them each night to your customers."

"Mr. Runnels," she said icily, "I hardly think it's necessary to speak in such vulgar terms."

"Come on," he said curtly, taking her arm again. "There's plenty more to show you."

They walked outside again, but this time Langdon led her across the street to a row of two-story clapboard structures. "The parlor houses," he said. "This one's called the Parisian. Would you like to go inside?"

She looked at him, unable to speak.

"Of course not," he said. "The lady of the Golden Palace wouldn't be caught in such a place, would she? That is, not unless she wants to hire a few of the girls. Oh, don't look so shocked. Where do you think you'll find your employees?"

"Mr. Runnels, I didn't come with you to be insulted."

"No insult intended, madam," he said, linking her arm through his. "And I asked you before to call me Langdon. There," he said when they'd walked a few steps. "There's what passes for an opium den in Eagleton." He pointed to a tiny shack in the alley between the parlor house and the High Grade Saloon. "And there, across the street, is Pearl DuVal's, the fanciest parlor house in town."

He led her farther down the street toward a row of shacks. Montana could see women, some of them dressed only in flimsy wrappers, standing in front of the houses.

"Hey, mister," one of them called to Langdon. "Come on inside. Two bits a tumble." She opened her wrapper slightly, revealing a sagging, wrinkled breast. Seeing Montana, she smiled lewdly. "You can come along, too, honey. For another quarter we'll make it a threesome."

Montana turned away quickly, and Langdon made no reply except to tip his hat to the woman.

"Mr. Runnels—Langdon," Montana said. "I don't know what your object is in—"

"They come here and set up business in these one-room cribs when they're too old or too ugly to work in the parlor houses," Langdon said, ignoring her protest. "The men who don't have the money for the expensive ones—sometimes up to a hundred dollars a night—can come here. It's all part of the competition for the men's dollars, Montana. They're after the same thing you're after."

"You've made your point," she said. "I've seen quite enough."

"Have you? You haven't seen the dance halls yet. We'll stop at the Central. There's a burlesque show there."

"A burlesque show indeed! I certainly will not go."

Langdon turned to look at her, half questioning, half accusing. Montana bit her lip and allowed him to lead her toward the Central Dance Hall.

The two-story frame structure, one of the largest on the street, boasted double doors pushed wide in invitation.

An ethereal blue-gray haze engulfed the room, and customers moved through the cloud like boisterous angels. Some danced to the music of a very loud trio of piano, trombone, and drum, playing on a stage. More people crowded around the long bar at one end of the room.

Montana felt light-headed and disoriented as Langdon led her into the swirl of smoke and humanity, and involuntarily she tightened her grip on his arm. Langdon's fingers encircled the hand she'd placed on his arm as he guided her to the bar. "Two beers," he said, and placed two nickels on the bar.

When the bartender brought the foamy brew, Langdon handed Montana a mug and raised his to hers in a toast. But she didn't drink when he did. She couldn't stop thinking of herself as a married woman, for whom it would be improper to drink beer in a saloon with a man who was not her husband.

The music grew even livelier, and Montana saw that everyone's attention was turned toward the stage. A row of women had joined the band, the same women she had seen in the street parade. They were raising their dresses even higher than they had before, showing flesh-colored stockings and kicking their feet, clad in fancy low-cut slippers, as high as their heads. Montana gasped involuntarily at the daring show of legs and crotch. Without knowing she'd done it, she took a swallow of the beer.

By the time the dancers finished their bawdy number, raising their skirts in back to show plump, rounded bottoms covered with nothing but cotton drawers, Montana was pale and the glass of beer drained.

Loud cheering followed as the dancers ran off the stage and into the audience to find dancing partners while the band struck up a waltz. Montana felt a tug at her arm and turned to see a grizzled miner grinning at her and holding a quarter between two grimy fingers. She stared at the man, puzzled, until Langdon pulled her toward him.

"Sorry, mister," he said. "But I've already paid for this one." He took Montana into his arms and glided with her across the floor. Montana was startled, and she felt awkward. She hadn't danced since she was a child, when her father would guide her steps while her mother played the organ.

"That man," she said. "Was he offering to pay me?"

"Yes. He thought you were one of the taxi dancers."

"The what?"

"One of the dance hall girls. They dance with the customers for a quarter a dance." Langdon looked down at her.

"He thought I was selling dances?"

"Among other things."

Montana was nettled at the way he seemed to be enjoying himself at her expense. "Why are you doing this to me?"

"Have I shocked the lady?" he asked in a voice so gravely mocking that her cheeks flamed with anger.

"Of course you have," she said, "and you've done it purposely. Why? Do you find some perverse pleasure in it? Does it make you feel more the worldly man-about-town to shock the poor country wife?"

He stopped and dropped his arms. "So that's what you are? The poor country wife? I thought this little tour of ours might bring out the truth. We both had to know whether you could pull it off. And you've just told me. You're a poor country wife. One who has broken the law by stealing property from a dead woman. In that case, maybe I can't help you after all."

Montana tried to speak but found that she could not. They stood utterly still in the middle of the dance floor, looking at each other in silence. Then Montana raised her left hand to rest on Langdon's shoulder and placed her right hand in his. They began to dance, turning around and around in whirling circles until she grew dizzy. But she was determined not to miss a step.

5

Alex eased himself to a sitting position in bed and glanced at his wife lying beside him, motionless except for the deep, rhythmical breathing of sleep. He had never known her to sleep late, until the day after they arrived at the Golden Palace, three months ago now. Always before, on the farm in Tennessee, she had been the first one out of bed in the morning, and she'd always awakened him with a steaming cup of coffee. But she had always gone to bed early on the farm. These days she was up until well after the saloon closed every night, working on the books or practicing her card game.

He wished he had that coffee now. Maybe it would help ease the pain that cut through his head each time he moved, reminding him that he'd had a little too much liquor the night before. Since Montana was showing no signs of awakening, it looked as though he'd have to get the coffee for himself again. It was almost as if, when she'd started calling herself Montana McCrory, she really had become a different person.

He smiled to himself at that thought. Of course she was not a different person. She would always be his sweet Ivy, who loved him. He loved her, too, of course, more than she could ever know. He was truly sorry that her life had been so hard and so full of sadness. He'd always wanted to give her the kind of life she deserved, and he would someday, he told himself. It really wasn't entirely his fault that things hadn't worked out well on the farm. Now, though, he felt he'd been given a second chance—a chance to make it up to her and to make her life easier.

Life had been hard for him on the farm, too, but the worst of it had been the loss of both the girls. That had been almost more than he could take. He'd had to find ways to dull the pain and to keep from thinking about it. Sometimes he found it in liquor, or in cards, and a few times in a woman he had met in Nashville when he had gone there to sell their crops. She had been young and fresh and full of laughter, but, best of all, she had never known his two little daughters and, therefore, could never remind him of them.

Things were going to be different now, though, he told himself. Moving to Colorado, even losing the land, was going to prove to be the best thing that had ever happened to them. Here in this new place there would be nothing to remind them of the past. They'd both have a new life.

He glanced at his wife again and felt content. She was very clever to have thought of the plan to rescue them from the brink of disaster. And, in the end, she had been understanding about his mistake with the land, just as he'd known she would be. Didn't that prove she was his same sweet Ivy?

None of it had been his fault, he believed. It couldn't be his fault, because he could not possibly have known about the land fraud. The whole business had been completely out of his hands, and his wife had understood that.

He could smile now when he thought of Bill Mott winning that worthless piece of paper. It had served him right, the bastard. He still shuddered when he remembered how close Mott had come to getting revenge. Mott would never find them now, though, and that was another reason he had to be grateful to his wife. The scheme she'd come up with to change her name and become Montana McCrory had not only saved them from poverty but had saved his life. It was as if, as far as Bill Mott was concerned, Alex and Ivy Barton had disappeared from the earth.

Another good thing about her scheme for survival was that it was turning out to be more than survival. It was providing a damned enjoyable way to live. Naturally Montana was always saying they had to be careful to make ends meet, always talking about debts the saloon owed, but that was just her way. She was a born worrier. As for himself, he saw no reason to worry. What they had was certainly a lot better than trying to scrape out a living on a dirt-poor farm in Tennessee.

He never wanted to go back to Tennessee. He didn't want to go back to those graves. Even if the graves weren't there to haunt him, he didn't want to go back to farming. They could do much better with the saloon. He was sure of it. What could be easier than playing cards every night and having a few drinks with the customers to keep them happy and relaxed?

Of course that damned Diana could be a pain in the ass. He didn't like the way she was always scowling at him, always insisting that he sit down with her to go over the books she'd kept. He didn't know a damned thing about keeping books. He wished now he'd never told anyone he was an accountant. It had seemed another way to make their scheme work at the time. It might look odd if he didn't at least make a show of being an accountant, but he'd get around to that eventually. For now, however, he was content to leave the business end of things to Montana and Diana and Langdon.

He'd been resentful of Langdon Runnels at first. Didn't like his blackmailing. But even that had turned out all right. Not only was it insurance that he wouldn't spread the word about their true identities, but he had proved to be pretty good at the business. The two of them together had gotten Montana to dealing faro and poker and running a blackjack table in no time.

They'd had to work out sleeping arrangements for him, so they'd put him in the bedroom next door. They'd told Diana he was sharing a room with Alex. Alex smiled to himself. At least the old bitch didn't seem the type to snoop around upstairs where things were none of her business.

He glanced down at Montana again, still sleeping soundly beside him. Her face looked younger when she was relaxed. The tiny lines around her eyes and the hardness that had begun to show around her mouth after the children died all but disappeared while she slept. He noticed, too, how small her body looked under that mound of quilts. She wasn't small, really. She was almost as tall as he, although she had always been a bit thin. She was almost as strong as he was, too. Stronger, in some ways—the ways that required strength of will. Sometimes that strength frightened him a little. There was nothing frightening about her now, though. Now she looked soft and vulnerable.

He shifted his weight as his desire began to heighten, and he reached to touch her arm, which was outside the covers. Slowly he slid his hand up to her breast. She stirred slightly as he fondled her, but she didn't awaken.

She'd been a little peeved with him the night before because he'd drunk too much. He hadn't meant to. He was having a good time, and it just happened before he realized it. Maybe he ought to do something to make sure she was in a good mood this morning. He couldn't think what would please her. If only he had some coffee to clear his head. That bitch Diana was sure to have it ready now. She would have been up for hours. The woman never seemed to sleep. He decided to go downstairs for the coffee. He'd bring some up for Ivy, too. Maybe she'd like that. But he must remember to think of her as Montana, not Ivy.

Pushing the covers back carefully so that he wouldn't awaken her, he struggled to get out of bed. The pain in his head was hammering away, but he tried to ignore it as he pulled on his trousers. To add to his misery, he was shivering from the cold. It was damned hard to get used to the Colorado weather. It was never this cold in October in Tennessee. He reached for a stick of wood, then opened the door to the stove and shoved it inside, making more noise than he'd intended. The sound awakened Montana. She raised herself up on one arm and looked at him, her face still flushed from sleep.

"Alex?" She sounded groggy. "Is something wrong?"

He smiled at her, noticing that her white cotton nightgown had come untied at the top. "Nothing's wrong," he said. He walked toward the bed, his hand on the top button of his trousers. "I was just going down to get you some coffee. But now that you're awake—"

"Coffee? Good Lord, is it morning? I thought it was the middle of the night, and you were up because you were sick." She threw back the covers and swung her legs over the edge of the bed. "I've got to talk to Langdon this morning."

"Can't it wait?" Alex asked. "I wanted to—"

"We have to go over the books with Diana. I want to see if there's any way we can afford that roulette wheel and some other things I have in mind," she said as if she hadn't heard him. She reached for her drawers, which were lying on a chair beside the bed, pulled them on under her nightgown, then took the nightgown off over her head. Alex caught only a glimpse of her full breasts and the soft roundness of her stomach before she picked up her corset and encased herself within it.

"Langdon says there's a chance we can borrow the money from the bank here in Eagleton," she said as she walked on bare feet to the stove and pushed at the burning log with a poker. The corset hugged her figure, emphasizing her curves and pushing her breasts alluringly over the top.

Langdon! He was damned tired of hearing about Langdon. "I don't know about borrowing the money," Alex said. "You always said yourself that it's dangerous to go into debt."

Montana had pulled on her dress and was smoothing it over her hips. "But Langdon seems to think that if our profits are up enough, we can—"

"Damn Langdon!"

Montana was busy at the bureau, but she turned her head to look at him. "Now, Alex, hush. There's no need to get riled. After all, he *is* our business partner." She had spoken quietly, they way she sometimes used to do when the children were misbehaving.

"Don't forget, *Montana,* I'm your husband. That gives me a say in the business, too, even if it is in your name." He had meant to sound cold and equally reprimanding by putting sarcastic emphasis on her name, but he knew he'd sounded only whining and petulant.

"Of course you are, Alex. Have you seen my hairbrush?"

"Here," he said, taking it from the washstand and handing it to her. He watched her as she brushed her hair and braided it into a thick coil at the back of her head. He could take her now, and she would not resist. She would submit to him as a wife should. But he would sense, as he had at times before, that it gave her no pleasure. Anyway, his desire had waned; now that she was fully awake she had become Montana again, a strong, forceful woman who filled him with uncertainty and a little fear. When she remembered the children she would become vulnerable again. But he wouldn't remind her just now. For the moment he needed her strength as much as he feared it.

She smiled at him as she accepted the brush. "Thank you, Alex," she said. "And don't worry about our getting into debt. Langdon and I won't take any undue chances."

Langdon again! The way she relied on him made Alex feel weak and unimportant, just the way he'd felt as a boy. He'd had two brothers and two sisters, and all of them, even the girls, had managed to outshine him with their work on the farm. They were either stronger or more clever with the livestock or had more perseverance for the long hours of drudgery in the fields. None of them seemed to mind the awful silence of their home life, either, their cold, taciturn father exacting obedience the way he exacted hard work. Alex alone had longed for happy conversation, for levity, for pleasure. He longed for love, too, but everyone, even his mother, seemed too tired or too uninterested to give it. There was always the farm and the work it required. Pleasure, it seemed, was the forbidden fruit, and he'd never been able to get enough of it. At least in the pursuit of it, he could forget that he had never quite measured up.

He knew he measured up when it came to the opposite sex, though. Women had always liked him. He could have had his pick of any of them around Byrneville, and he had chosen the prettiest and smartest girl in the county. He watched her now as she moved from the bureau to the chair and pulled her skirt above her knees to put on her stockings and shoes. He noted the way her legs parted, and for a moment, when he thought of what was between those legs, desire stirred in him again. At the same time, he noticed her hands as she laced her shoes. They were darkened by too many hours in the sun and roughened by too much work. Those hands symbolized his failure to provide his wife the kind of life she deserved, another sign that he didn't measure up. He turned away from her and, without a word, left the room.

He was restless all morning. After breakfast he went into the tiny office off the kitchen with Montana, Langdon, and Diana so they could go over the receipts for the past evening and balance them against money owed to the liquor suppliers, the grocer, the utilities company. It was tedious and boring, and he would have left if it wouldn't have looked to everyone as if he were shirking his responsibilities.

"I know money is tight," Montana said, "but I still think it's time to consider hiring the others." She seemed to be speaking to Diana and Langdon, and Alex knew he had let his mind wander enough to miss part of the conversation.

"No," Langdon said. "It's too early. We can't afford it yet. You're already thinking of buying that roulette wheel and a piano. Buy the piano first, before you hire the girls. Don't try to do too much too soon."

"Aren't you the one who told me you can't win if you don't take chances?"

"Of course I did. But there's a difference between taking chances and being foolish."

"And who decides when it's a reasonable chance and when it's foolishness?"

Alex found himself turning his head back and forth, glancing first at Montana and then at Langdon. He sensed a tension between them that he hadn't noticed before.

They looked at each other, their gazes locked. "I

am saying," Langdon said in a carefully measured cadence, "that it is foolish to take this chance. I say no girls for the Golden Palace. Not yet."

Girls? They were thinking of hiring girls to work in the Golden Palace? Alex's interest was piqued.

Montana and Langdon still looked at each other as if there were no one else in the room. "No?" Montana asked. "You say no? You made it clear to me what my competition is in Eagleton. Didn't you say that if I—we are to succeed, we have to meet that competition? Doesn't that competition include the girls who work at the Nolton and the Central and the Gold Dollar and all the other dance halls and saloons?"

"Langdon's right," Diana said. Her voice startled Alex. He had managed to forget she was there. "Now's not the time to hire 'em. Maybe the time will never come. You're askin' for trouble when you hire women to work in a saloon."

"Diana," Montana said, "I know what you must be thinking, but—"

"I don't think you do," Diana said. "I don't think you know anythin' about it." Alex noticed that she seemed unusually agitated. "They'll have men in their rooms. The Ladies' Club will be accusin' you of runnin' a brothel."

"Well, of course I won't be running a brothel." Montana sounded shocked. "There'll be rules. I'll have the upstairs remodeled so they'll have rooms next to mine. I'll be able to see that they follow the rules."

"Montana's right," Alex said, deciding to speak his piece at last. "It will help business. And things will work out if we see that they follow the rules."

Diana suddenly turned her cold gaze on him. For a moment no one spoke, and Alex began to feel embarrassed, as if he'd had no right to voice his opinion.

"All right," Montana said, breaking the awkward silence. "We've all had our say. I reckon now is not the time to make a decision after all. We'll all of us think it over some more. Now, Diana," she said, turning to her, "we still have those other accounts to go over. Let's have a look at them."

Diana pulled out another book and opened it, and the long, tedious discussions began again. Alex's head began to hurt even more, and he longed for a drink to numb the pain. He sat at the table as long as he could, until the sheer boredom was more than he could tolerate.

"Did you notice the sugar bin this morning, Montana?" he asked.

She was absorbed in her work and barely acknowledged that he had spoken.

"It's low," he said. "I could hardly scrape up a teaspoonful for my coffee."

"I'll do the shopping this afternoon, Alex," she said absently.

"Oh, but you're so busy. Let me do it for you."

"Well, if you don't mind," she said, glancing up at him at last.

"Of course not," he said. "I'll just get my hat."

The N. O. Johnson Department Store, built of brick, was the finest building in town. There was another N. O. Johnson's in Colorado Springs, Alex had heard, but people said the merchandise in the Eagleton branch was just as fancy as anything to be found in the original. Alex had to walk by the store on his way to the Pikes Peak Grocery. He often looked at the display window when he passed, admiring the finery for sale. One day, he told himself, he would be able to afford a fancy dress for Montana. He had often dreamed of buying her nice things. There'd never been enough money when they lived in Tennessee. At least he had a little cash in his pocket now, though still not enough for one of the fancy dresses.

As he glanced in the window, it wasn't a dress that caught his eye, but a man's vest. It was made of fine satin brocade in a rich brown shade. It was, Alex was certain, the nicest garment he'd ever seen. His fingers fairly ached to touch it, and the thought of it buttoned across his chest made him shiver with expectant pleasure.

Within a few minutes he was standing in front of a three-sectioned mirror, admiring the way the vest fit him. He had never had on such a garment before and had wanted only to see how it would look on him. But now that he was wearing it, he was certain it was perfect for him. Maybe, he thought, just maybe he should buy it. After all, a man ought to look his best for the sake of the business. And it wasn't as if Montana were doing without. She had all those nice things that had belonged to the other woman.

In a little while he had convinced himself that he had to own it, and he asked the clerk to charge the vest to the Golden Palace.

Since it was almost noon when he left the store, he decided to take a detour by way of the Central Dance Hall. The Central served lunch every day at its long bar as a way of attracting customers during an otherwise slack time, just as Diana and Montana had begun to do at the Golden Palace. Alex had been to the Central several times both for lunch as well as for drinks, and although he'd felt a twinge of disloyalty at first for patronizing the competition, he'd soon overcome his qualms, and now he kept going back for the same reason everyone else did—he liked the company. Montana was right about girls attracting customers.

At the bar, he asked for a beer and the lunch, which today was ham, red-eye gravy, and biscuits. He had drunk the beer and was waiting for the lunch when he saw Lida Armstrong smiling at him from across the room. Alex returned her smile. He had bought a few dances from her over the past few weeks. He'd bought dances from some of the other girls as well, and that was another thing he'd felt guilty about at first. He'd quickly convinced himself there was no need for guilt, however, since all he was buying was dances. Of the girls he'd danced with, Lida was his favorite. She was not skinny like some of the others. Instead her figure was generous, leaning toward plump, and very feminine and curvaceous. She had a lovely round face with a delicious-looking bow mouth, which Alex liked very much. Her fine, fair hair reminded him of a halo.

She seemed to like him, too, and although he knew it was her job to be friendly with the customers so they would buy dances and drinks at the bar, he had noticed how, no matter how crowded the Central might be, she always managed to work her way next to him every time he came in.

He watched as she got up from the table where she'd been sitting with two other customers. As she walked toward the bar to join him, he admired the way her hips swayed and her invitingly rounded stomach undulated beneath her shiny taffeta dress.

"Alex!" she exclaimed when she reached his side. "Where have you been? It's been ages since I've seen you." She stood no more than a foot away from him, tilting her head to look up into his face.

"I've been busy, Lida," Alex said, signaling the bartender for two more beers.

"Yeah, I hear things are pickin' up over at the Palace. You shouldn't let your sister work you so hard, though. It keeps you away from me too much." Lida giggled and touched the end of his nose with the tip of her finger. Alex caught her finger in his hand and bit it lightly. Lida squealed and giggled again. "I mean it," she said. "You hardly ever get away to come over here anymore. You shouldn't let her do you that way. It's not like she's your mother or your wife, you know."

"What do you know about what a man should and shouldn't do?" Alex teased as he picked up one of the beers and handed it to her. "You're nothing but a slip of a girl."

"I don't know about that," Lida said, inching closer to him so that her breasts brushed his arm. "I'll bet I'm as much woman as you're ever likely to see."

Alex laughed. "My, but you're a saucy little wench, aren't you?"

Lida giggled again and moved away from him. She took a sip of her beer. "Just what do you do over there at the Palace all the time?" she asked, setting down the glass.

"I'm the accountant," Alex said. He noticed that her upper lip was moist with beer. "And I help Montana with her business decisions," he added. "We were just talking today about hiring some more help. Maybe even some girls."

"Taxi dancers?" Lida asked, brightening. "Like me?"

"Maybe."

Lida's eyes took on a shrewd glint. "It takes a bigger place than the Golden Palace for a girl to make any money. I can make twenty dollars on a good night here," she said. She turned her back to the bar and rested her elbows on the top so that her breasts were thrust forward.

Alex gazed at her breasts and wondered if her thighs were as milky white as the tops of those generous globes. He wondered, too, if the delta of hair between those thighs would be fair and golden like the hair on her head, or dark, to add a tantalizing contrast. He cleared his throat and forced himself to look into Lida's eyes. "Just give us time. The Golden Palace will be as big as any place in town."

Lida sniggered. "That old Golden Palace has been so rundown for so long, I'll bet those rooms upstairs aren't fit to live in. How're you gonna hire any girls if you can't offer 'em a decent place to live?"

"Why, the business is doing right good. Growing. We're gonna fix the place up. Remodel the rooms upstairs."

Lida cocked her head in a coy manner. "Do you suppose they'll be as nice as the one I have here above the Central?" She took her elbows from the bar and leaned toward him again.

"I wouldn't be surprised," Alex said. He tried to concentrate on the lunch the bartender had set before him.

"Bet they wouldn't." Lida leaned even closer until her breasts rested on Alex's arm. "But how you gonna know unless you see my room for yourself?"

Alex's throat suddenly felt dry in spite of the two

beers he'd just consumed. He put down his fork, which had been halfway between his plate and his mouth, with a piece of ham on it.

"Come on," Lida said, taking his hand and holding it close to her bosom. "I'll show you."

"Lida, I don't think I—"

"Don't be afraid. I'm just going to show you my room."

"I'm not afraid."

"Good. Come on, then." Her little mouth curled up at the corners in an enticing smile. She walked away from him, swishing her hips and turning back once to look over her shoulder. Alex hesitated, then laid a few coins on the bar beside his full lunch plate and followed her.

Lida walked ahead of him, up the stairs and down the hallway. Alex felt slightly dizzy, and he wondered whether it was the two beers he'd had on an empty stomach or the fact that he felt as if he were being sucked into a vortex of foolishness. But what he was doing wasn't foolish, he told himself. He would only have a look at her room, and then he could advise Montana on what any girls she hired would be likely to expect.

Lida stopped at a door, turned to smile at him again, and beckoned him with her dimpled hand. "Come, Alex," she said softly, and opened the door wide.

As Alex stepped into the room, the first thing that struck him was the ordinariness of it, despite her bragging about how nice it was. The floor was bare except for a braided rug beside the bed. Filmy curtains hung at the one window, and the poster bed was covered with a faded and slightly frayed quilt. Along with the bed, there was a gasoline heating stove, a wardrobe, a dressing screen, and a table with a mirror. The top of the table was covered with jars and bottles, the contents of which he had no inkling. The dark wooden wardrobe, its doors half-open, revealed frocks crammed inside in disarray. Lida, seeing him eye her messy closet, closed its doors and leaned back against them, once again thrusting her breasts forward.

"You look kinda nervous, Alex," she said. "Stop worrying. I'm not gonna bite you." She giggled again. "That is, not unless you want me to."

Alex managed a smile and ran a finger under his damp collar. "I'm not nervous. Why should I be nervous? I'm only here to see what kind of accommodations the girls we'll hire might expect."

"Oh, I'm sure you can make things very accommodating," Lida said, walking toward him. Her voice had lost all traces of girlish giggling and now sounded low and throaty. She put her hands on his chest, running them over the soft satin brocade. "You look so nice," she said. "This is a new vest, isn't it? I noticed it first thing when you came in."

"I'm glad you like it."

She kept one of her hands on his chest while the other reached for his hat. She pulled it off his head and threw it across the room, then ran both hands through his thick blond hair. "I never saw such beautiful hair on a man before," she murmured, her lips close to his ear.

Alex caught her hands in his. "Lida, I—I don't think you should—"

"Oh!" Lida cried. She sounded hurt, and she backed away from him. "You think I'm too forward, don't you? You must think I'm a brazen hussy. I only meant to give you a compliment." Her little mouth quivered, and her eyes brimmed with tears.

"Oh, no," Alex said quickly. "I don't think that at all, and I do appreciate the compliment. I didn't mean—"

Lida turned her back to him. "It's just that I like you so much," she said, still sounding hurt. She walked to the bed and sat down on it, then looked up at him. "I thought you liked me, too."

"Of course I do!" Alex took a step toward her. "I think you're a very nice girl. I like the way you're always so happy and so friendly."

"You do?" She sounded pleased and wiped away a tear with the tip of a finger.

"Yes," Alex said. "I do."

"Well, I think being happy is important, don't you? I mean, I think being happy is the most important thing in life because there's plenty in life that's just pure drudgery."

Alex smiled at her words. "You know, I feel the same way," he said. "And I think you're really very wise for such a young woman."

The compliment obviously pleased her. "It makes me think twice when I consider what a woman has in store for her," she said, encouraged by his response. "Like my mother. She worked hard on the farm and worked hard in the house, and all the time tendin' to a flock of kids, and with a new one comin' 'round just about every year. At least until my pa run off, finally, and gave her some relief. But by then she was near worn out. I saw her livin' that way, and I says to myself, Lida, you don't want that. You want to be free. Free as a bird to fly away and to get as much fun out of life as you can before you get old and haggard and it's too late. And there's nothing wrong with that, is there? As long as you don't hurt anybody?"

What she had said about her mother made him think of Ivy and the way she'd worked so hard on the farm. She still worked hard. But surely the pleasures of life had not been quite so elusive to her. Surely he had provided some for her. He could not bear to think otherwise.

Suddenly he was aware of Lida's silence, and he realized she was waiting for him to respond. When he could think of nothing to say, she cocked her head and spoke softly. "Do you think I'm pretty, Alex?"

"You're more than pretty," he answered.

She smiled and held her hand out to him. He stepped toward her and took her hand and let her pull him down to sit beside her on the bed. "How can a person be more than pretty?" she asked.

"You're beautiful, Lida," he said. "You're so beautiful and fresh and young, you make a man forget everything else."

She giggled again. "Really, Alex? Am I making you forget everything else right now?"

She was so close that he could feel her breath on his cheek, and he could see her little mouth like a full, ripe berry waiting to be consumed. In the next instant his mouth was on it, tasting, sucking, savoring its elixir. She moaned and clutched his shoulders, then pulled him down until they were side by side on the bed. They lay that way, kissing, for several moments. When his hands moved to touch the curve of her soft young breasts at the top of her low-cut dress, she did not stop him. Neither did she stop him when he released the buttons on her bodice, nor when he found the laces of her chemise. He loosened the strings, and her ample breasts were freed to fill his hand and to respond with tightening nipples to his fondling and caressing.

In only a short time they were both naked, the frayed quilt tangled at their feet. "Oh, Alex," Lida whispered, "we're both free. Free as birds to fly away to pleasure."

For the moment he believed her. He was free. There was no one else to consider. No one to be hurt. There was only he and the woman whose firm buttocks he cupped as she rolled on top of him. There was only this moment when she moved downward and teased him with what she had to offer until finally he turned her over and thrust himself into a warm, moist vortex.

It was not until later that it occurred to him that Lida might expect to be paid. She was, after all, a taxi dancer, and it was common knowledge that some of the girls got paid for more than dancing. The realization left him feeling chagrined. He had been foolish to let her seduce him with her pretty words and body. He finished buttoning his new vest and turned toward her. "Lida," he said. He reached for his hat and held it awkwardly in front of him.

She looked up at him, fastening her bodice. Her hair fell in wispy tendrils about her face, giving her the look of a mussed child.

"Lida," he began again uncomfortably. "I—uh—I don't know how much you—well, what I'm trying to say is—"

She was looking at him still, her expression questioning, and then her soft mouth began to quiver. "Oh!" she cried. "Oh, you think I would—" She sat on the bed, holding her face in her hands.

He hurried to her and sat beside her. "Lida," he said, feeling miserable. "I didn't mean to insult you. I just wasn't sure. I mean—"

She turned to look at him. "I *like* you, Alex. I knew from the first time I saw you that you were special. And I thought you liked me, too, just a little, at least."

"I do like you. Of course I do. Very much."

"I'm a taxi dancer, but you mustn't think I'm wicked," she said, her mouth forming a perfect bow in its pout.

"Oh, no, of course not."

"I don't do it for money." She looked at him shyly. "But I don't make much in the dance hall, so if a friend offers a little to help me out . . ."

"Lida, I just don't know how much—"

She began to cry and buried her face in her hands again. "I didn't mean it to come out that way. Just because I—what I mean is, I'm not a wicked whore, I just—"

"Of course you're not," he said, feeling wretched as he stroked her arm.

"I would like to see you again, Alex," she said, dropping her hands from her face. "I'd like to be your girl."

He was caught off guard again. "I—I could see you again every once in a while, maybe."

"That would be wonderful," she said, smiling at him through her tears. "I've never had a *real* beau before. Especially not a businessman like you. You're really special, Alex. I'll bet you're the kind of man who likes to take really good care of his girl."

He grasped her chin and brought her face toward him. He kissed her on the mouth and pushed her gently back on the bed.

6

"You're going into the mountains to do what?" Montana had stopped sweeping the board-walk in front of the Golden Palace to glare at Langdon. She was bundled into a heavy coat and had a woolen scarf wrapped around her head as protection against the wind.

"Work a claim. Up on Squaw Mountain. Got to take advantage of the good weather while I can." He stuffed supplies into his saddlebags.

"How long will you be gone?"

"A few days. A week. Maybe longer." He turned to her and grinned. "You gonna miss me?" He knew the mild flirtation was a way to keep her off balance, but he didn't know for sure why he felt he had to do that. Thus far he had managed to stay away from her except to talk business. No sense in risking trouble, he'd decided. He'd needed to keep things on an even keel while he concentrated on making money to work his claim.

"No! Of course not." Her too quick response

amused and secretly pleased him. He turned back to packing his saddlebags, but he sensed her gaze on him. "I reckon I don't have to remind you that you're my business partner," she added. Her voice was strained and her words deliberately measured. "If any decisions have to be made—"

"I trust your judgment. I know you can manage." He checked the cinch, then walked around to the other side of the horse to fasten the saddlebag. He'd meant what he said. She was new at running a business, but he was counting on her naturally frugal nature to help her keep her head, just as it had after her first unwise impulse to hire the girls had passed.

"Of course," she said stiffly.

"You really *do* hate to see me go, don't you?" he asked.

"Don't be silly." She went back to sweeping the walk. "It's just that I don't understand such foolishness," she said without looking up.

"Foolishness? You call it foolishness?"

"Yes, I do." She dared to look at him again.

"Then a lot of your customers are fools," he said with a shrug.

"Maybe they are." She wielded her broom with extra force. "It doesn't make sense. They could use all that energy to work at honest jobs to make a comfortable living and stop looking for an easy way to get rich."

"Oh, it's not just any old way to get rich," Langdon said. "It's *gold* we're all looking for. Gold that's usually too soft to be much good for anything. Gold that hasn't got much of any value that makes sense. It's all in the way gold makes a body *feel*. Maybe that's why you don't understand it."

She stopped her sweeping for a beat but refused to

look at him. He dropped his saddle cinch and walked to her, putting his hands on her arms, forcing her to face him. "Maybe you don't understand it because somewhere along the line you stopped letting yourself feel things," he said.

Her eyes met his for a moment. Then she tried to jerk away from him, but he held her fast. "What makes you so afraid?" he asked.

"Afraid?" She laughed, a brittle sound. "It's not fear you see in me, Mr. Runnels. It's plain, common prudence."

He held her gaze a moment longer, then dropped his hands from her arms. "That's what I'm counting on," he said as he turned aside and mounted his horse. He rode away, and when he looked back, she was no longer in front of the saloon.

He wondered, as he rode, if she knew that Alex was being unfaithful to her. He'd seen him at the Central dancing with the girls and more than once heading for the back stairs with the plump one called Lida. If Montana didn't know about it, it was partly her own fault. She closed her eyes to the truth so she wouldn't have to admit she didn't feel anything for Alex, at least not what a woman was supposed to feel for her husband. She ought to have left him long ago. A divorce now would be awkward, of course. That would mean admitting she hadn't been married to Tom McCrory in the first place.

If it hadn't been for Montana's loyalty to her undeserving husband and her damned respectability, he might have already seduced her. Then he could have gotten her out of his head and could get on with his life. He had to remind himself that seducing her wasn't important. Working the claim was important.

He'd filed the claim a year ago, and he'd given it the name Honesty, because this one, he'd felt sure at the time, was not going to fool him as some of the others had, the ones he'd either abandoned or sold for a few hundred dollars. He'd staked the Honesty out carefully, using what he'd learned from books on metallurgy. There was a granite ledge on Squaw Mountain that attracted him. He'd studied it, compared it with descriptions in some of his books, and finally figured out that the ledge had to mark the outer edge of an ancient volcano. Good-size veins were often found at the perimeters of volcanos, his books said. Those violent eruptions, when the bowels of the earth began to churn around, squeezed gold into cracks and fissures. The Honesty was on that granite ledge, and he'd started sinking a shaft along the face of it. If he could find the right crack, or vein, it might mean a rich deposit of gold. So far the assays had been poor, but he still had a gut feeling something was there. Unfortunately, the last time he'd worked the claim, he'd used up his grubstake before he'd found the gold.

With no promising assays to show the banks, he hadn't been able to borrow any more money. That's when he'd decided to go to Pueblo. He knew a sawmill operator there, an old Cajun he'd met in New Orleans who'd moved west. He could count on him for the money, but he hadn't expected the interest to be so high. With the exorbitant interest to pay, he'd had to settle for a smaller principal. Montana McCrory and her Golden Palace had come along just in time to give him the chance he needed. True, the profits weren't what he'd hoped, but it was more than he'd had before.

It was almost an hour's ride to the Honesty, and it was half an hour after that before he had his horse unpacked and his crude tent set up to shelter his supplies in case the weather turned damp while he was down in the shaft.

As he lowered himself into the hole he had blasted out months ago, he thought of his father. He could never go down a shaft without thinking of the man. His father had spent most of his life in the entrails of the earth, mining coal in West Virginia, and the darkness of that occupation seemed to have colored his soul. He must have had a taste of hell down there and was forever afraid of descending farther into it. But instead of seeking light and hope, he'd found a dark and vengeful god as taxing and unmerciful as the company boss.

Langdon remembered how his mother had tried to keep the darkness from overtaking them all—himself, his two younger brothers, and one baby sister. She had filled their life with music. Her rich, warm voice was like an angel's. And she'd played the fiddle—soft, melancholy melodies that overwhelmed him with such feeling that he thought he would burst, or airy, fanciful jigs that set his heart and his feet to dancing. He had wanted to play the violin, too, but he had been awkward at it, and that made him love his mother's music all the more. He loved the way she could dissolve the darkness with the music and with her own light. She was careful, though, to make certain her fiddle was hidden away and her songs were silenced by the time her husband came home from the mines, weary and covered with darkness.

He remembered the time, when he was no more than twelve years old, she had sung late into the day and then, when she'd realized the hour, had sent him to slide the fiddle under the bed while she'd hurried to peel potatoes to boil for their supper. He had been careless, though, and had left the violin on top of the bed when he got distracted by a ruckus outside the window. One of the dogs had treed a 'possum, and Langdon had run outside to join his brothers, who were clamoring for Mama to get there with the gun.

She had come out in time to shoot the creature, and they'd all been delighted at the prospect of meat with the potatoes that night. Their joy had been cut short, though, when Papa had come home and found the fiddle on the bed in the back room of the two-room house.

He'd picked it up by the neck and, holding it like a club, brought into the front room that served as kitchen and living room. "What's this a-doin' here?" he'd asked in his West Virginia twang.

Langdon remembered the stricken look on his mother's face and the silence that followed.

"You been a-playin' this thang?" he asked, his eyes blazing with the fires of damnation.

"Lang, I—"

"You promised me," he accused. "You promised me the night you was saved that you would put away the instrument of the devil."

Mama glanced quickly at the three boys, huddled, terrified, in the corner. "I—I reckon I did," she said. "But I prayed about it, and it come to me that the Lord don't count it as the devil's instrument if a body don't use it thataway."

"It come to you, did it?" His eyes flared with black anger, and his voice was so loud it woke the baby, who had been sleeping in her homemade cradle in the corner. "So the Lord comes down and speaks to you now, does he? What does he say? 'Don't pay no heed to your husband'? Is that what he says, woman?"

"'Course not, Lang. I never meant that."

"Well, your husband told you to do away with this thang," he said, raising the violin above his head. Langdon heard his mother's intake of breath. "It's the instrument of the devil, just like the preacher said. It leads the mind astray from the service of the Lord." At the word *Lord,* his father brought the fiddle down against the edge of the table, breaking it in two. The three boys cringed and the baby howled at the awful sound.

His mother had never been the same after that, and he had never heard her sing again, except for once when she had thought she was alone in the woods. It wasn't really singing then, but more of a mournful keening, a sound so sad and strange that he could bear to listen for only a little while before he turned and ran all the way home. The sound had reminded him that he had failed to protect her from his father.

He had left home at the age of fourteen, determined to make enough money to take her away. By the time he had returned three years later, she was dead. His father had died a few months before, coughing the bloody phlegm of the black lung and wondering why his careful attention to all the rules of life he'd thought so important had not saved him.

Langdon had stood over his mother's grave, crying, because there was no way now, ever, to bring back the music. His purpose now was to force himself not to remember any of it, and to think only of gold and its power.

As Langdon rode away, Montana opened the door of the Golden Palace a crack and followed him with her eyes. When she thought she saw him turn back to look, she closed the door quickly, not wanting him to know that she was watching. She leaned against the door, seething with anger. He had no business telling her what she felt or didn't feel. He had no business running off like that, either. She'd never run the saloon on her own except for the first night, and that night had been a disaster. How dare he leave her now when she was still unsure of herself? If he was to be a partner, as he had so cleverly managed to make himself, she certainly expected him to live up to his half of the responsibilities.

She went to the kitchen, threw the broom carelessly behind the door, and reached for the mop, surprised at her own anger. Why should she be angry? It didn't matter whether Langdon Runnels thought her capable of feeling things or not. And as for running the saloon, of course she could make it on her own. She'd learned how to deal the cards and play the games. Now it was only a matter of perfecting her skills. She didn't need him anymore.

The broom fell at her feet, and she kicked it out of her way. Maybe she didn't need him, but he was still shirking his responsibility. There was still work to do. The place didn't get mopped and cleaned by itself, for one thing. And there was plenty more to do besides. Even Alex was busy out in back splitting wood.

She paused, listening, but she didn't hear the sound of the ax hitting the logs. Throwing aside her mop, she headed for the door. The ax, she saw, was stuck in a large stump. The wood had been split. Alex had finished his work and gone off somewhere. Probably to the Central. She knew he frequented the place. She hadn't let it bother her before, but now the thought of it made her irritable.

She turned around and stalked through the kitchen, not completely understanding her fury. As she passed the open doorway leading to Diana's quarters, she saw Diana sitting at a table, a lighted candle in front of her, a slightly curved brass tube at her lips. She was blowing through it at something she held with forceps in the flame.

"Lord o' mercy, Diana, what on earth—"

Diana moved the tube away from her mouth. "What? Oh, I was just testin' this ore. Thought I'd do it while I was sittin' down to rest my back."

"What do you mean, you're testing ore?" Montana stepped into the room.

"You do it with a blowpipe, see?" Diana blew through the pipe again, making the candle flame glow brighter as it danced across the rough stone she held with the forceps. "If it melts, then it's gold. If it don't, then it's iron pyrite or maybe copper. Like this here rock." She threw down the piece and picked up another with her forceps.

"Where did it come from?" Montana asked, her tone sharp and impatient.

Diana glanced at her, obviously surprised at the anger in her voice. "Picked it up in the mountains last Monday on my day off."

"You were out prospecting?" she asked, incredulous.

"Yes, ma'am." Diana gave her a questioning look.

"Well, I suppose it's none of my business if you're as big a fool as the rest of this town on your day off, but it *is* my business what you do when you're working for me." She saw Diana's eyes widen at her outburst, but she couldn't stop. "Now put that contraption away and get to work."

Diana pushed away from the table and stood up. The cane-bottom chair she'd been sitting in toppled backward and clattered to the floor. "Now, wait just a damned minute—"

"No, you wait. There's plenty of work to do around here, and there's no point in Alex and me doing it all. He's chopped the wood, and I've started the cleaning. And if you please, you can stop that disgusting swearing."

Diana blanched. "All right," she said quietly. Her lips had turned so pale that they almost disappeared. "All right," she said again, her eyes burning into Montana's. "I'll try to watch my language, but I won't take your carping at me about not doing my work just because your man disappeared."

Montana felt her mouth go dry. "My what?"

"Don't try to lie to me. I know there's somethin' goin' on. I see the way you act around him."

Had she guessed that Alex was not her brother? "I—I don't know what you're talking about."

"I said don't try to lie to me. I ain't blind, and I ain't no fool, even if maybe old Tom McCrory was. Why'd you marry Tom, anyway, if you was in love with Langdon?"

Montana was shocked, and before she realized it, her hand flew out and struck Diana hard across the face. Diana grabbed her wrist, and, momentarily still, both women stared into each other's eyes.

Montana felt suddenly overwhelmed by what had happened. "Oh, my Lord, Diana," she said, her voice barely more than a whisper. "I've never done anything like that before. I—I don't know what's come over me."

Diana dropped her wrist. "I shouldn't have accused you," she said.

"No," Montana said. "No, you shouldn't have. Because you're wrong, of course. I care nothing for Langdon Runnels. But you are correct about my being uneasy that he's gone. I have come to depend upon him for . . . certain business decisions, and, as you know, to help me sharpen my gambling skills. I'm afraid I did lie to Mr. McCrory—to Tom—about my business experience. But it was because I didn't want to—to lose him, you see."

"You don't have to say nothin'. I got mad because you was takin' things out on me," Diana said. "But I still had no right. I reckon what I'm tryin' to say is, I'm sorry."

"You don't have to say it," Montana said, reaching to embrace Diana. "We both lost our temper. We both made a mistake. I want you to know that I need you. As much as I need Alex or Langdon. Maybe more."

Diana stiffened as Montana's arms went around her, and Montana sensed an indefinable change in her. When their embrace ended, she saw that for a brief moment Diana's gray eyes lost their coldness, and her hard mouth softened.

"All right," Diana said, her voice unsteady. She turned away. "But you quit takin' it out on me just because Langdon rides off, and you let me decide when I'm gonna sit down. Especially after I just spent the mornin' choppin' wood."

Montana was stunned. "You're the one who—you mean Alex didn't—"

"I knew you wanted it done right away," she said gruffly. There was another moment of awkward silence before Diana spoke again. "I reckon you're right about one thing. I got no business lollin' around in here. We both have work to do." She moved past Montana quickly and left the room.

Montana felt chagrined at the false accusation she'd made, and that Diana seemed intent upon keeping her distance throughout the rest of the day only made her feel worse. As evening approached, her embarrassment over the scene she'd caused was replaced with nervousness about getting through the night's work without Langdon.

She didn't think her nervousness showed until Diana came to her blackjack table and set a glass of buttermilk next to her. She had never done that before except for the first night.

"Don't worry," Diana said without looking at her. "You don't need Langdon. You know what you're doin' now."

She turned away before Montana could respond, and Montana felt a little uneasy as she watched Diana move back to the bar. Diana's keen eyes and senses had caught everything, including her dependence on Langdon. But she was wrong to think she felt anything else for him. That couldn't be possible. Montana shuffled the cards and willed herself not to think about it.

"Blackjack," she called to two customers who walked by. "Place your bets."

She caught Diana looking at her once during the evening, but the woman quickly averted her eyes and busied herself with customers for the remainder of the evening. At closing time she cleaned the bar quickly and left for her room without saying good night.

Business hadn't been particularly heavy that evening, and with Alex at the roulette wheel while she dealt blackjack, they'd had no problem handling the customers without Langdon. That, however, Montana thought as she walked up the stairs to her room, was no cause to celebrate. They had managed to bring in more business over the past several months, and they'd even managed to milk a small profit, but once she split it with Langdon, it was too small. It provided them a means of support, but nothing left over to get them back to Tennessee, which, she reminded herself, was her goal.

She unfastened the buttons at the front of the mauve silk dress she had salvaged from Mrs. McCrory's trunk and made over for herself. Once again she could hear music and laughter coming from the other saloons and dance halls along Myrtle Avenue. She walked to the window to close it so the noise wouldn't awaken Alex. He had come upstairs to bed ahead of her, and he was now sound asleep.

As she glanced out the window at people coming and going from the saloons and parlor houses below her, she remembered Langdon telling her she had to compete with all that to survive. He had also warned her about moving too fast. But she could also move too slowly, she thought as she took the pins from her hair. The other businesses had what the customers wanted. Even Alex frequented the competition sometimes. Maybe she couldn't blame him for being like everyone else.

She put on her nightgown and got into bed beside her husband, and she thought of Langdon. What was he doing tonight? Was he really in the mountains on some foolish pursuit for gold? Or was he in another town somewhere? With a woman, perhaps? It didn't matter, she told herself, turning on her back. It shouldn't matter at all whether he was hunting gold or women. She had other things to think about. She had the Golden Palace and getting back to Tennessee to think about.

She stared into the darkness, listening to the sounds of Myrtle Avenue, and she knew what she had to do. She would trust her own judgment, and tomorrow she would take another step toward luring more customers into the Golden Palace.

The next morning she put an advertisement in the *Eagleton Prospector,* asking young women interested in working as taxi dancers and barmaids at the Golden Palace to come by for interviews with Montana McCrory. Later that afternoon while Diana worked in the kitchen, she cleaned a thick collection of cobwebs and dust from the abandoned upstairs room. The window would have to be repaired, and she'd need furniture, but with a little work it would do as living quarters for taxi dancers.

When the paper came out on Monday, Langdon still had not returned, and Diana had taken her usual day off. She had left before Montana came downstairs. Presumably she was in the mountains looking for more rocks to burn in her candle flame. There was only Montana and Alex at the Golden Palace, and shortly after the last of the lunchtime customers left, even Alex was gone. Montana was working on the account books at a table in the back of the saloon when someone entered and asked for Montana McCrory.

"I'm Mrs. McCrory," she said, looking up at a slightly overripe young woman.

The girlish creature smiled and nervously brushed a wisp of light hair away from her face, trying to tuck it under her large feathered hat. She removed a dark coat to reveal a pink dress with a wide lace yolk that emphasized the glow of her young skin and uncommonly wide blue eyes. "I'm here about the advertisement in the paper," she said. She removed her gloves and held them tightly in her plump, dimpled hands. "My name is Lida Armstrong."

"Have a seat, please, Miss Armstrong," Montana said, indicating the chair across from her. "Have you ever worked in a saloon before?"

"Oh, yes, ma'am, I have. But only the best sort, of course, like the Central, where I work now."

Montana's eyes widened. "You're one of the taxi dancers at the Central?"

"Yes, ma'am."

"And you want to leave there to work for the Golden Palace?"

"Yes, ma'am, I do."

"May I ask why?"

"Why, I—" The young woman hesitated. "Oh, it's not what you think. I mean, I'm not in any kind of trouble or about to get fired or anything. I know you're thinking the Central is bigger and I won't make as much money at the Golden Palace. It's just that, well, I want a change, that's all. I thought it might be nice to work for—for a lady."

"I see."

"And I'm a good dancer. You'll see. Why, some of my customers will follow me here, I'm sure. If you give me the same cut, ten cents out of every quarter, I know I'll make just the same as I do at the Central. There won't be as much competition from other girls."

"Ten cents out of every quarter?"

"That's the going rate, ma'am."

Montana heard the front door open, and she glanced up to see Alex enter. "Over here, Alex," she called from where she sat with Lida. "I want you to meet somebody. . . . Alex, Miss Lida Armstrong."

Alex stopped halfway across the room, staring at Lida, and for a moment Montana thought he was going to turn around and leave. She frowned, puzzled at his strange behavior. Then it occurred to her that since he frequented the Central, maybe he knew the girl. He was surprised, no doubt, to see her in the Golden Palace.

"Do you two know each other?" Montana asked.

Lida smiled, and her eyes lit up, but before she could say anything Alex spoke. "No, we haven't met. I'm Alex B—Alex Miller, Mrs. McCrory's brother," he said rather stiffly.

Lida nodded and looked away. She seemed terribly shy for a taxi dancer.

"I was just interviewing Miss Armstrong about coming to work for us," Montana said. "She tells me she has experience, and she's looking for a change. Do you have any questions you'd like to ask her?"

"No," Alex said uneasily. His obvious embarrassment surprised her. She'd never seen him act shy in front of women before. Usually he was anything but shy, and he had a way of charming with his easy, open manner. He didn't speak at all during the rest of the interview, however.

"I think she's perfect," Montana said when Lida had left.

"No!" Alex said.

Montana was surprised that he seemed so adamant. "I don't see why not," she said. "She's very pretty. She doesn't appear brash and, well, indelicate or immoral, and yet she has experience as a taxi dancer. Says she works at the Central. Are you sure you've never met her over there?"

"No, of course not. Why do you ask?" Alex pushed back from the table and walked to the roulette wheel. He seemed oddly interested in examining it.

"I just thought you might have," Montana said. "I thought she acted like she recognized you."

"Well, I might have seen her there. I don't remember. I spend most of my time talking to the customers. That's important, you know, because they're usually our customers, too."

"If you don't know her," Montana said, walking toward him, "then why are you so against hiring her?"

"She just doesn't seem right, that's all. Besides, you don't know anything about her background. Aren't you supposed to ask about her other jobs, her education?"

"We're not hiring her to teach school, Alex. She's going to dance with customers in a saloon."

"But why is she so anxious to leave the Central? Maybe she doesn't get along well with people. You ought to check that out before you make a decision."

"Well, she seemed very pleasant. I can't imagine her not getting along. And she is rather pretty, you have to admit."

"I still say no."

"But, Alex, I don't see—"

He turned toward her suddenly, his face flushed. "Damn it, Ivy, why'd you bother to ask for my opinion if you don't want to listen to me?"

She stared at him, stunned. He had just called her Ivy—something he hadn't done for months. In spite of the fact that she knew no one else was in the room, she glanced around uneasily.

Alex paled. "Oh, God," he said. His voice was

barely more than a whisper.

"It's all right," she said quietly, and reached to touch his arm. "I don't think anyone heard. And don't worry. We can talk about it later."

"No!" he said. His response surprised her. "I—I think we should talk about it now." He was still very pale, and she wondered if he was ill.

"Alex, it's not important."

"What's not important? My opinion? It's just Langdon's opinion that's important, is that it?"

"Of course not," she said, unable to hide her astonishment at his behavior.

"You never ask for my opinion when you have to make a decision. I never know what the hell is going on."

"You seemed uninterested. You don't even seem to be listening when we're making most of the decisions. I didn't want to bother you with things you're not interested in."

"Well, I am interested, and I say no. Do you accept that, or do you have to check it out with Langdon?"

A moment passed, and neither of them spoke.

"Of course I don't have to check with Langdon," she said. "If you think this young woman is unsuitable, I'll find another."

Tension seemed to drain from Alex. He kept his eyes locked on hers for a moment, and then he said something very odd, she thought, considering the circumstances. "I've always loved you," he said quietly, almost timidly. "And I always will."

7

"*You could have* talked her into hiring me if you'd really wanted to," Lida said. She had her back to Alex, and she was pouting. He was trying to console her. He had no intention of doing anything else. In fact, he had resolved never to go to her room again, and he would have stuck to his resolve, except that he'd seen she was upset and he was afraid she was going to make a scene in the Central.

"Now, Lida, I don't know what I could have done."

"You pretended you didn't know me! Are you ashamed of me?" She turned to face him, her eyes blazing with hurt and anger.

"Of course not, I—"

"Did you even try to put in a word for me?"

"I don't understand why you want to quit your job here," he said evasively. "Every girl who comes to town tries to get a job at the Central. You can make more money here than you ever could at the Palace."

"Don't you really know?" Her accusing tone made him uncomfortable.

"Well, I—"

"So I can be near you, Alex. That's why I wanted to work at the Golden Palace. Even if it would be for less money. I thought you'd understand. I thought you'd want that, too." Her voice trembled, and he could see that she was going to cry. Her tears always touched him.

"Ah, come on, Lida," he said, putting his arms around her. "It would never work out. We might get caught if we—you know. . . ."

She snuggled closer, rubbing her breasts seductively across his chest. "Maybe it wouldn't matter," she said.

"What do you mean?"

"I mean it wouldn't matter if we got caught doing it if we was married."

He dropped his arms suddenly, and there was a moment of awful silence. "Lida . . ."

"What's the matter?" she asked when she saw his face. "I love you, Alex. I thought you loved me."

"Well, I thought . . ."

"You thought what?" Her voice had become shrill. "That I was just a common whore you could have a romp with and then forget?"

"Lida, of course I didn't mean—"

"There hasn't been anybody else since I met you, Alex. Because I never met anyone like you before. I don't want anybody but you." She sat on the edge of the bed and looked up at him. "I need you," she said, her eyes brimming.

He sat beside her and put his arms around her again. "Oh, Lida . . ." He liked it when she said she needed him.

"And you need me, too, don't you?" She felt so soft, so helpless, in his arms.

"Of course I do." His voice was soothing. She responded by wrapping her arms around him.

"Then why can't we be together?" she asked.

"We can," he said, easing her down.

She turned her face away from his kisses. "When?"

"Soon."

"How? At the Golden Palace? The money doesn't matter. You make enough—"

"No, not that," he said as his hands began to explore her.

"Then how?" Her voice was breathy. He knew she was having trouble concentrating.

"Don't worry," he said. "I'll think of something."

"Don't stop," she whispered. "Please don't stop."

Diana hefted the pick above her head and chipped away at the granite, digging a shallow tunnel. Last summer she had followed a float trail, bits of gold-bearing rock in the stream, to this spot and had staked out a claim. She'd found nothing promising yet, and if she didn't soon, she was going to let the claim go. She wasn't sure it was worth the hundred dollars a year in improvements the state required for her to keep it.

She lifted the pick again and dropped it against solid rock, feeling it stretch the muscles in her shoulders and jar the bones in her spine. She was not an unusually large woman, nor did she have extraordinary physical strength. Months of swinging a pick and working a claim had increased her stamina more than her brawn. But she pushed herself to swing harder and harder and to take the tunnel farther into the mountain, welcoming the numbing exhaustion it brought her as much as she would have welcomed the gold she sought. She was aware that people thought prospecting unsuitable for a woman. She knew, too, that if she ever found a strike, the old superstition about it being bad luck for a woman to enter a mine might hinder her in developing it. Still, she kept at it.

She needed the exhaustion to help her sleep, and she needed it even more now that Montana McCrory had taken over the Palace. Montana was an enigma— part vulnerable, part tough, unsure of herself at times and too cocksure at others. She had finally admitted that she'd never run a saloon before, but Diana had guessed that long ago. She didn't seem at all like the kind of woman Tom would marry, either. He'd always been attracted to the overripe, overpainted tawdry floozies that she herself knew all too well. Montana was just the opposite—a lady. The kind who made a person feel—well, she wouldn't think about that.

In spite of her high-tone manner, it was obvious that she hadn't had an easy life. And she was hiding something in her past. At one point Diana had thought it was some kind of swindle she'd worked on Tom while she was in love with Langdon. Now she was convinced that wasn't the case, and she regretted the quarrel they'd had over it. Whatever there was in Montana's past that she was trying to hide, it was none of her business, Diana thought. She, of all people, knew that sometimes a body had reasons for holding back the truth.

She took an extra hard swing at the wall of granite in front of her. Best that she didn't think of Montana McCrory at all. It was hard not to, though. For one thing, it was difficult not to remember that for all her obvious intelligence, Montana could also be foolish.

Foolish for letting her no-'count brother hang on like that. Foolish, too, for hiring two women while she herself was in the mountains working her claim.

The women, Anna and Dovie, were fresh out of the parlor houses and looking for a way to strike out on their own, so they wouldn't have to share their proceeds with a madam or a pimp. Everybody knew that. Everybody except Montana McCrory. She was as naive as a member of the Ladies' Club.

Diana knew Anna and Dovie's kind all too well. She'd grown up among the likes of them. What little growing up she'd done, at least. Sometimes it seemed to her that she'd been born full grown. Certainly she had no memory of a happy, carefree childhood. She'd been born in a parlor house, the daughter of a woman who resented her for being another mouth to feed, for having ruined her figure, for being in the way when she had men in her room. By the time she was seven, she was left more or less on her own, looked after only occasionally by her mother and sporadically by the other women. One in particular took an interest in her more regularly than the others. That was Velma Eden, who watched her with strange, brooding eyes and sometimes fed her and often let her sleep in her bed when she had no customers.

By the time she was fourteen, though, Diana had her own bed. She looked eighteen, and she had joined the profession. She never told anyone how painful, revolting, and terrifying it was to her. She was afraid of being laughed at, afraid of not being able to make a living. Her terror reached its zenith the day she was beaten by one of her customers, beaten so badly that she almost died.

It was Velma Eden who took her in and washed her wounds and nursed her back to health. It was Velma who lay beside her as she slept a healing sleep, and

Velma who, over time, once her nightmares had subsided, began to show her a new and gentler way to love.

In time she left Velma and the parlor house, knowing she would never be the same again. One kind of love she associated with bruises and open wounds and a mother who was never there. Another kind she associated with gentleness and healing, until eventually she learned that it was also to be associated with shame.

She had learned early that hard labor was her best escape from both the shame and the yearning. But most of the time men refused to hire her for that kind of work because of her sex. When they did, she was expected to provide more than an honest day's work. She'd settled for jobs as scullery maid and scrubwoman until Tom McCrory hired her to help run his saloon. It provided her with a living and gave her a chance at least once a week to be alone in the mountains. Everything had seemed satisfactory until Tom's widow came on the scene.

Montana was only three or four years younger than she and, Diana could tell, as used to hard work as she herself was. Maybe she had thought she could use Tom as a way to escape the hard work. But Diana wouldn't judge her too harshly. She well knew that being a woman too often meant either using or being used. Why Montana had come with her brother as extra baggage was a little hard to figure out, though. But that, Diana told herself, was also none of her business. Neither was Langdon Runnels. She'd always been leery of him because of his reputation as a slick operator. He used people, too, but in a more dangerous way, she thought.

What *was* her business, though, were Anna and Dovie. They stood for all that had meant fear and hate and pain and loneliness to her. They were going to cause trouble for Montana. Diana feared they would, in effect, turn the Golden Palace into a parlor house, and Montana would be seen as the madam, whether it was the actual truth or not.

Diana had thought she needed the job at the Golden Palace to make a living, but, she told herself now as she took one last angry swing at the granite walls of the tunnel she had dug, she didn't need any of what was happening. The way she saw it, the only thing left for her to do was give her notice as soon as possible.

At the end of the day, Diana drove her wagon past the front door of the Golden Palace, and she saw that the crowd seemed unusually large for a Monday night. She had always taken Mondays off because business was at its lowest point that day. The news of a new gold strike south of town had brought a new horde to Eagleton, though, and she supposed word had gotten around about Anna and Dovie. Montana and Alex would probably be having a hard time handling the extra business, since Langdon was still off working his claim.

Diana drove her wagon around to the back to unload her equipment and get to her quarters without passing through the saloon. It didn't matter how busy they were or how much trouble they were having; it was no longer her concern. She had resolved to quit.

The noise of the crowd and the sound of the player piano Montana had bought the day after she hired the girls drifted through the thin wall that separated Diana's room from the rest of the saloon, and once she had everything unloaded, she couldn't resist having a look. Alex was behind the bar and, from the looks of things, was making a mess of it. Chances were he'd drunk up half the profits, too. The damn fool couldn't leave the liquor alone. Rumor had it he couldn't leave the women alone, either.

Montana, across the room dealing blackjack, glanced up from her cards. Diana tried to close the door quickly before Montana saw her, but it was too late. Montana laid the cards aside, excused herself, and headed for Diana's room. She knocked on the door lightly, and Diana, seeing she had no choice, asked her to come in.

Montana's face was flushed, and her eyes shone like a child's at Christmas. "Just look at the crowds," she said. "Isn't it grand? I'm going to pay for that piano in two weeks if this keeps up, and in no time we'll have enough money to go back to—to do whatever we want." She smiled nervously and then impulsively placed a hand on Diana's arm. "I'm glad I saw you just now," she said. "I want to reassure you that the girls are working out just fine."

"I want to talk to you about that, Montana. I wanted to tell you that I—"

"I understand," she interrupted. "I understand that you were concerned about the way things would look if I hired the girls. I know their reputations. I haven't spent all my life in the woods. But I want to assure you—"

"Montana, I—"

"—that I have given strict rules to the girls. I have told them this is not a parlor house, and that I expect them to be taxi dancers only."

Diana stared at her, speechless. If she thought all she had to do was tell the girls to behave themselves, Montana was even more naive than she'd realized.

"I'll need you to help me oversee them, of course," Montana continued. "I don't suppose Alex will be much good at that. Or Langdon, either," she added bitterly, "particularly if he's going to be disappearing into the mountains all the time." Her tone told Diana more than words.

"I won't be either," Diana said.

"What?" Montana seemed distracted, and she glanced over her shoulder toward the crowd in the saloon.

"I won't be overseeing the girls either."

"Well, of course I didn't mean you were to start tonight. I know you're tired after a day in the mountains. You get some rest, and Alex and I can—"

"I mean not ever."

Montana looked stunned.

Diana tried to speak but found she could not. There was something in Montana's eyes. Something frightened and desperate.

"Diana," she said. Her mood had lost its effervescence, and her voice trembled slightly, but she was forcing herself to appear calm. "I must make a go of this saloon. You won't understand this, but I absolutely must make money here. Hiring the women will help ensure that I do. I know you were against it on moral grounds, and I fully understand your concern. But, please, let's not quarrel about it. I have done all I can to assure you that the girls will not be women of the half-world."

The use of the affected expression triggered a response in Diana, but not the usual scornful amusement at a prissy women who couldn't call a whore a whore. To hear Montana use the phrase seemed unaccountably sad, as if there were far more she wasn't facing up to than that the world was full of whores.

She hesitated, staring into those cool, light eyes she had come to know so well but that seemed to be hiding something she could not know. "I got no reason to quarrel, Montana. I know you do what you have to do, but so do I. And I can't stand by and see you get hurt by this."

"Why, that's very kind of you," Montana said, obviously touched, "but I don't see how I could possibly be hurt."

"I'm quitting. Let's just leave it at that."

There was a moment of stunned silence. "I cannot run the saloon without you, Diana," Montana said finally. "Not yet. I beg you to stay with me. For just a while longer, at least." Her eyes were bright with emotion.

There was another long pause, and Diana's brain was awhirl with confusion, with a desire both to stay and to flee. But she knew she was losing a battle with herself. "All right," she said. "I'll stay. For a little while."

Montana's eyes were locked with Diana's, but then her gaze faltered, and she gave a brief nod and turned away. Why? Diana wondered, feeling a moment of panic. Had she seen too much?

Diana watched her walk back to the blackjack table and pick up her cards. She was tired, and she longed to fall into bed and rest her aching muscles in a deep, dreamless sleep. But she could not turn away. It was as if the woman had cast a spell on her. That was foolish, she knew. She didn't believe in spells or any such romantic drivel. It was her own weakness that drew her to the woman. She knew that and deplored it and felt shamed by it. But she could not deny it.

She continued to watch as customers surrounded Montana, men from the established mines like the Lucky Lady and the Freedom, and the usual scruffy crowd of prospectors and fortune-hunters. But since word was out about a new strike, more people from all parts of the country were coming in. Now the Midland Railway was advertising Eagleton as far away as Chicago and San Francisco, calling it the richest gold camp in Colorado, where assays averaged over a hundred dollars a ton and ran as high as five thousand. The figures were exaggerated, of course, and the same advertisements claimed that the only way to reach the camp was by the Colorado Midland Railway.

There were plenty of new customers. Business at the Golden Palace would have grown steadily even without the women. But something was driving Montana. She wanted money, and she wanted it quickly, like the prospectors who hoped to strike it rich overnight—the kind Montana so frequently criticized.

The crowd around her had grown noisier. A shout was followed by a roar of raucous laughter. The excitement attracted even more of a crowd. Diana also moved closer. Montana was dealing for Dynamite Finley, a prospector who spent most of his time around Squaw Mountain, where he had a claim, coming to town only every three months or so when he needed supplies and an odd job as a handyman or a carpenter's helper to make the money for another grubstake.

Dynamite, whose real name was Joseph, had earned his moniker not only because of his liberal and sometimes injudicious use of explosives to blow away the side of a mountain, but also because he tended to blast his way through everything he did. When he rode his wagon into town, it was usually with his mule at a dead run and with boards and nails from the rickety contraption flying in all directions. When he entered a dance hall, the girls were said to brace themselves for bruised feet and extreme exhaustion. But he was generous with his money and was known to double or even triple the going rate for a dance or a tumble upstairs with a favorite.

His sexual prowess was legendary, and Diana had heard that the girls actually fought over him. Whatever he had that appealed to them wasn't immediately obvious. He was a short, stocky man in his mid-forties who wore wire-rimmed glasses and a dirty nautical cap over his sandy-colored hair. Tonight, several days' growth of beard made him look older than his years. As Diana elbowed her way through the crowd and got closer to the blackjack table, she saw the chips representing the money he had won piled high in front of him. He was going for more, trying for the magic count of twenty-one with the cards Montana dealt him.

"He's bet it all," Harold McCloud, a miner from the Lucky Lady, told Diana.

Judging by the number of chips in front of Finley, it would mean a substantial loss for the house if he won. Such a high bet was unusual at a blackjack table, where methodical thinkers generally built their winnings slowly and quit when the losses started. But Dynamite Finley never did anything in an orthodox manner. Even his claim, the Molly Maloney, which he'd named for some woman in his past, was located in a spot no one else would consider because the rock formations weren't right for gold.

Diana glanced at Montana. For all she had at stake, those cool green eyes showed no sign of concern, and her hands were steady as she dealt. She gave Dynamite a face card, and he signaled that he would stand. The other players, their bets small, had already been dealt their cards. Dynamite squirmed on his chair, a look of such agitated excitement on his face that it seemed at any minute he would explode.

It was time for Montana to deal her own hand. She had a six showing and one card down. The crowd at the table grew quiet. As Diana glanced around, she saw Langdon Runnels watching.

So he had returned. Diana knew Montana had thought he was gone for good. If she distrusted him that much, maybe now that he was back, she'd find a way to dissolve the partnership and get rid of him. And good riddance. Montana didn't need another man around. It was Diana she'd said she needed, not Langdon or Alex. If she could get rid of the brother as well, all the better.

Montana had not seen Langdon yet, and she had by now dealt herself a three. Diana's mind raced. Montana now had nine showing. If she had a face card down, that meant she would have nineteen; the chances of busting if she took another card were overwhelming. But she apparently felt the chance to beat Dynamite was worth it. She dealt herself another card, a four. She turned her hold card up: the queen of hearts. With a count of twenty-three, she had gone bust. Dynamite Finley turned up another face card, showing that he had twenty, and he roared with excitement. The crowd around him boisterously congratulated him.

Diana's eyes never left Montana. Dynamite Finley's wild bet had just broken the house at blackjack, a highly unlikely feat, but Montana didn't falter. She placed the chips representing winnings in front of each of the players, her face showing nothing but a mysterious smile. Two of the four players picked up their chips to cash in. Diana held her breath. If Dynamite raked his chips into that dirty hat of his to be cashed in, it would likely spell the end of the Golden Palace. But he heard the sound of Montana shuffling the cards, and he turned around to place a bet before the cards fell. His bet was another wild one, half his stash.

When the cards were dealt, he and Montana both came up with nineteen. Dynamite roared again, this time with a string of obscenities, because a tie meant the game went to Montana. But he was laughing, too, as heartily as he had when he'd won the previous hand, and he was enjoying the attention he was getting.

Diana rubbed a forearm across her brow to remove the sweat that had gathered there. If Montana had lost that hand, she could not have met her losses. She was gambling worthless wooden chips against thousands of dollars, but even knowing what was at stake, she had kept calm, played with deliberateness, and by some miracle had won part of it back. The losses were still heavy, but at least they wouldn't wipe her out. Diana expected her to excuse herself now and leave the unpredictable Dynamite Finley to find another way to have his fun. But she didn't get up. She was dealing the cards again, and again Dynamite lost.

Now losing more often than he was winning, he grew cautious and began betting smaller amounts. The crowd around him lost interest and drifted off to other amusements, and his roars of triumph or defeat were subdued. Montana had stood the test with icy calm. Diana saw her glance in her direction, and she responded with a smile and a nod, happy to share this moment of triumph with her, happy to let her know she'd been watching all along. Then she turned to go back to her room.

Before she had advanced more than a few steps she heard another shout from the thinning crowd around the blackjack table.

"Ol' Dynamite's goin' for broke!" someone cried.

Diana turned to see Dynamite waving a paper over his head, then he slammed it down on the table in a dramatic gesture. "The Mary Maloney against two hundred dollars!" Dynamite bellowed.

"What a crazy old bastard," Clay Tuttle said. "He's bettin' the thing he's devoted the whole damn past two years to."

For the briefest moment Diana saw Montana's expression lose its practiced coolness, but when she spoke, her voice was calm. "Mr. Finley, are you sure you want to do this? You have a great deal tied up in that claim, I'm told.

It would be a mighty big gamble to risk it all." Her southern accent had become more pronounced.

Dynamite laughed harder than ever. "Hell, lady," he said, "there ain't no gamble like the one I took when I sold my fish market in Galveston to sink the money into a gold claim. It's purt' near starved me out."

"Well, now, why would I want to gamble two hundred dollars against something that worthless?" Montana asked.

"Oh, it ain't worthless. There's gold there all right, for them that's got the stayin' power to find it," Dynamite said.

"And you've lost your staying power, Mr. Finley?" Montana shuffled the cards easily and gave Dynamite her usual charming smile, but Diana knew she wanted him to quit. Montana McCrory would have no use for a gold claim. She thought it was all foolishness.

"I'm givin' the Mary Maloney one more chance to put a little money in my pocket. Either I win the pot with her at stake, or I lose it and call it worth it for the fun I've had tonight," Dynamite said. He glanced around him, obviously pleased that he was attracting a crowd again.

"Give the man a chance to win back what he come in with!" someone shouted.

"I got two dollars says he'll bust!" another one cried.

The crowd grew noisy again, and Dynamite was reveling in the attention. With more and more voices urging that the bet be accepted, Montana quietly shuffled the cards and then stacked two hundred dollars' worth of chips in the center of the table.

Montana dealt a card facedown, first to Dynamite, then to herself, then took a quick look at her card, all with a deftness Diana knew had been missing only a few months earlier. Hours of practice with Langdon had sharpened her skills as well as her confidence. With the same easy grace, she dealt another card, faceup, to Dynamite, a four of hearts, and then placed the six of spades on her card.

"Hit me," Dynamite said. When the queen of clubs fell in front of him, he held up a hand to signal that he would stay.

Montana dealt herself a five on top of her six, then with a slow and easy movement turned up her hold card to reveal a ten for an even twenty-one. A shout went up from the crowd around the table.

"Well, I'll be damned!" Dynamite cried when he saw the twenty-one. He flipped over his six of hearts to show a count of twenty. "The Mary Maloney ain't changed her ways," he said. "She's been a near miss from the start. She seduced me like a goddamned whore and tried to take me for all I was worth, but, by God, I got one last night o' pleasure outta her tonight."

"Hey, Dynamite, come on, I'll buy you a drink," cried someone in the crowd. Dynamite let himself be led away to the bar while he continued to curse the Mary Maloney.

Diana saw Montana glance in her direction, her eyes shining with surprised delight. Obviously she was happy that she was still there, that she had not gone to her room. Diana responded with a shy smile. Montana stood and excused herself, telling the other players gathered around her table that she was taking a break.

As Montana advanced toward her, her face aglow, Diana could not keep her heart from singing. But in the next second she knew it was not she Montana was walking toward, but someone behind her. She turned—and saw that it was for Langdon Runnels that Montana's eyes shone.

8

Montana walked toward Langdon, her eyes never leaving his. Her pulse had quickened at the sight of him, and she knew, in spite of her wish to deny it, that she had missed him. She wondered if he was equally glad to see her; the odd look on his face was difficult to read.

As soon as they met, he spoke. "That was some game you played. What would you have done if he'd quit when he was ahead and broken the house?"

She had expected a compliment, but the tightening muscle in his jaw and the flame in his eyes let her know he was angry. "He didn't break the house," she said evenly. "I won. That's what's important."

His jaw tightened even more. "That wasn't just your money you were risking. It was mine as well."

She laughed to cover her hurt and anger. "You told me once that the only way to win was to be willing to take risks. You also told me not to show fear, even when things get rough. Is it getting too rough for you now?" She clenched her fists to keep her hands from trembling, but she no longer thought of controlling her anger.

He blanched. "Let's go upstairs where we can discuss this in private," he said.

She felt her face flush. "I hardly think a bedroom would be advisable—"

"All right, damn it, we'll talk in the kitchen." He placed a hand on her shoulder and turned her toward the kitchen, directing her steps as if she had no will of her own.

It was hard to imagine that only a few minutes earlier she had been so glad to see him that her pulse had raced. Now the memory made her feel foolish. When the kitchen door closed behind them, she spun to face him.

"I don't see that we have anything to talk about, unless you've changed your mind about staying on as a partner."

"I haven't changed my mind about anything. It's you who's changed," he said, pointing a finger at her accusingly. "The farm wife gets a taste of power and independence, and it goes to her head. I'm gone a few days, and I come back to find you've gone crazy."

"I don't know what you mean. I've done nothing crazy."

"I saw those two floozies out there. You went ahead and hired them without my approval, and then you risk everything at the damned blackjack table."

"Mr. Runnels," she said acidly, "I don't understand why you are so angry, when all I did were the things you taught me to do. You told me I was going to have to compete with places like the Nolton and the Central, so I hired the girls to do that, and it's paying off. You saw the crowds. And as for the game, you taught me to have nerves of steel when I'm gambling. I'll admit I didn't win big tonight, but I at least broke even, and I gave the customers a little excitement. That'll keep them coming back."

"You had no way of knowing you were going to break even! You could have lost it all!"

"That's the name of the game," she said angrily, advancing a step toward him. "It's called gambling! Nothing's certain. You taught me that! And when you left you told me you trusted my judgment."

"Good God, Montana, I might have said that, but I didn't expect—"

"You didn't expect me actually to *use* my judgment, is that it?"

"At the very least, I didn't expect you to break an agreement," he said. "Like hiring those girls. We agreed to wait."

"We *agreed* to nothing of the kind. You simply assumed I'd do your bidding. Are all major decisions to be left to you? I think you expected the little farm wife, as you so condescendingly put it, to be entirely dependent upon you. In fact, you counted on it, didn't you? Don't think I don't know what you were doing when you maneuvered your way into this partnership. You're used to using people, Mr. Runnels," she said angrily, "and you're a despicable blackmailer."

"And pretending to be the owner of this saloon is much more honorable, is it?"

She shot him a burning glance. "You don't understand. I—we—"

"I do understand," he said. "I understand all too well that you wanted something bad—just as bad as I do— and you were willing to forget some of your high-and-mighty morals to get it. So let's not get down to judging each other's motives. And as for business decisions, since I *am* a partner, you will not make them without my consent. Is *that* understood, Mrs. Barton?"

She stared at him for a moment, fighting for control. The threat was there again. He could expose her if he wished. "Quite understood, Mr. Runnels," she said finally. He walked to the door and grasped the doorknob. "I expect you to be here when they need to be made," she added with cold deliberateness. "Is *that* understood?"

He hesitated, but he didn't answer, and he didn't turn around. When he had left, closing the door behind him, the room blurred, and tears spilled over the rims of her eyes. But she dried her eyes quickly, then smoothed her skirt and walked back into the saloon.

She'd been there only a few minutes when Alex spotted her and moved from behind the bar to join her. "Where've you been?" he asked. "I've been looking all over for you."

"I went into the kitchen for a few minutes. Is everything all right out here?"

"Everything's fine." Alex's eyes were unusually bright, and this time it didn't seem to be liquor making them that way. "This has been some night."

"What do you mean?"

"It's not every night you win a gold mine."

Montana laughed and squeezed his arm affectionately. "It's not a gold mine, Alex. It's just a claim. A worthless claim."

"Well, no need to look on the dark side. Dynamite Finley believed in it for two years, they say."

"And see where it got him."

"We ought to have a look at it," Alex said.

"It's all the way out on Squaw Mountain," Montana said.

"Isn't that where Langdon's claim is?"

"Maybe. I don't know." Montana's eyes swept the room, looking for Dovie and Anna to make certain they were dancing with the customers. She was hardly aware that Alex was still speaking. "I'm sorry, Alex, what did you say?"

"I said, maybe we could get Langdon to take us up there, since he knows his way around. The weather's warm enough now. We could rent a buggy."

"Alex . . ."

"It would be fun. We need an outing. We haven't done anything like that since we got here."

She shook her head. "There's so much work to do, I don't see how we'd have time."

"It would do you good. It would do both of us good. We could go some morning, have a nice ride, maybe a picnic, and be back by the time business picks up at night."

"I'll think about it," she said, trying not to see how much he looked like their daughter Susan when she would ask for something she wanted badly. "I'll think about an outing, at least, even if we don't go all the way up to Squaw Mountain." She glanced at the bar. "Look, Alex, you've got customers waiting. And I've got to get back to my blackjack table."

She started to walk away, but Alex called to her. "There's something else," he said to her back. "I want to change the name of the claim. I want to name it the Sweet Ivy."

By noon several weeks later, Alex was beginning to get a headache, and he knew it was from the boredom of trying to concentrate on the invoices spread on the table in front of him. He had promised Montana he'd help her, and he had tried. It wasn't that he couldn't perform the task. The work was simple enough; he had only to add the total amount of the invoices, then arrange them in order of their due dates. He knew Montana had given him the task precisely because it *was* simple. That was demeaning, but it was hard to say whether knowing that was any worse than the boredom. All he was sure of was that he was miserable. Montana seemed oblivious of his misery as she sat across from him with her ledger, entering numbers into it for God only knew what reason.

Upstairs, something bumped and clattered as it hit the floor. A gauzy curtain of dust descended with solemn piety from the ceiling.

Montana glanced up, scowling. "What on earth are those women doing?"

"Anna's fixing up their room," Alex said. "Moving furniture around, I guess. I saw Dovie leave a while ago to buy some stuff they needed." The girls had taken over the spare bedroom next to Montana's, and he and Langdon had moved to the attic. That arrangement hadn't been as inconvenient as he had thought it would be. It was still possible to sneak into Montana's bedroom, and the illicit feeling made it all the more exciting for him.

"I see no need for her to be so noisy," Montana said. "I can't concentrate with that racket." There was another loud thump, and bits of plaster sifted downward to settle on the ledger. "Diana!" she called. "Diana, tell that woman to stop that nonsense!" She blew vigorously at the film of plaster covering her tallies. "Oh, my Lord," she cried angrily as she stood up and shook the dust from her skirt. "Diana!"

"I'll tell her," Diana said, hurrying upstairs. Montana grabbed the ledger and moved to another table, still scowling.

She'd been in a particularly bad mood recently, and it was hard to tell why. Back in Tennessee, Alex remembered, she would sometimes get cross when there was no money and she was having trouble making ends meet. But that was not the problem now. The Golden Palace was prospering. They had done the right thing by hiring those girls, despite what Langdon and Diana said. Montana had even mentioned the possibility of being able to return to Tennessee in a few months with enough money to buy a small parcel of land.

He didn't know how he was going to tell her that he didn't want to do that. She would say it was better to go back to what they had always known, and that she didn't want to spend the rest of her life living a lie. Being Alex Miller and Montana McCrory no longer seemed like such a bad thing to him, and after a while it had come to seem more true than the truth itself.

She had also had her cranky spells when she was pregnant, he remembered, although he didn't think she was pregnant now. At least he hoped not. There was a time when he would have warmed to the thought of having another child. Another girl. One who would sit on his lap and call him Daddy and love him unquestioningly. But that would be awkward now.

As he tried once again to concentrate on the invoices, he glanced frequently out the front window. The sky was a deep azure, and he knew the air would be crisp. It would be a good time for a stroll down Myrtle Avenue to the Central.

But he wouldn't go to the Central, he thought, forcing himself to add a column of figures. He couldn't go running off to the Central and to Lida every time he got bored or down in the dumps. He didn't want to hurt Lida, but he was going to have to find a way of breaking it off with her. It just wasn't right for him to betray his wife like that. He liked Lida, of course. He liked her very much. She was so sweet and pliable, so voluptuous and giving, so . . . Maybe he would see her a few more times, just to make the break a little easier for her. When the time did come, there was no denying that he was going to miss her.

He heard the front door open, and he looked up to see Langdon enter. Montana glanced up briefly, then returned to her ledger. The relationship between the two of them had seemed strained recently. At first Alex had thought it was because Montana had hired the girls against Langdon's advice. But now he supposed it was all due to Montana's ill humor. Maybe she'd been working too hard. He ought to see that she got away occasionally. She'd promised weeks ago that she'd think about an outing, but he knew she'd probably never get around to doing anything about it. If they were going to have any fun, it was up to him.

"Say, Langdon," Alex said, putting down his pen and stretching his arms above his head to relax his tense muscles. Langdon, whose eyes had been on Montana, turned to look at him. "You know, we never took that ride up to the claim like we talked about," Alex said. "You said you know where it is, and I was thinking this week might be a good time."

Langdon glanced at Montana again, then shifted his gaze back to Alex. "I don't know," he said. "It gets muddy up there in the spring."

"But not so bad we can't make it. I see 'em going up there every day." Alex stood and moved toward Montana's table. "And it would perk us up to have a ride in that fresh spring air. What do you say, Montana? I bet there's lots of wildflowers up on Squaw Mountain. Besides, I'd sure like to have a look at that claim."

"I have a lot of work to do, Alex. I don't have time to go running off like that."

"Nonsense." He put a hand on her shoulder. "You need a day off. It'd make you feel better. Remember how we used to take off for a picnic in the spring when we were kids?"

She gave him a tentative smile. "I remember."

"We could take along dry wood to build a fire. Maybe make some coffee to go with our sandwiches. It'd be fun."

"Well, I don't know. . . ."

"There's no reason not to."

"The saloon can't run itself."

"Diana will be here."

"Well . . ."

"Come on. It'll do you good."

"Well, I guess Diana could handle things for a little while."

"Sure she could. What do you say, Langdon?"

Langdon shrugged. "It's all right with me. I'll get you as close as I can in the wagon, but you may have to walk part of the way. Better wear boots to get through the mud."

"Then it's settled. We'll go. The three of us, so Langdon can show us the way. We'll make it next Tuesday. And don't worry. Diana can handle it." He bent to kiss Montana on the temple. "It'll do you good, you'll see."

She reached to clasp his hand affectionately but briefly before she turned her attention to Langdon.

He had placed a piece of paper in front of her and was telling her about the gasoline heaters he had ordered for the upstairs rooms, explaining how the liquid fuel was more cost-efficient than burning wood. Their manner, as they discussed the mundane business, was unquestionably tense.

Alex turned away, bored once again and dreading going back to his invoices. He saw Diana coming down the stairs. She had obviously succeeded in stopping the rambunctious activity upstairs, and now without a word she disappeared into the kitchen.

She had hardly closed the door before Anna appeared on the stairs. Dark-haired and dark-eyed, tall and athletic, she had proved popular with the customers and seemed never to tire of dancing. Her movements now, Alex noticed, were catlike—languid, sinuous stretches down the steps. She was wearing a wrapper sashed demurely closed across her front. The absence of petticoats made it cling to her long body like a luxurious second skin. She stopped when she reached the bottom of the stairs, and, leaning against the rail, she looked at him with her dark, slanty eyes.

"Could I get somebody to give me a hand?" she asked. "I need to move a heavy trunk, and if you want me to be quiet about it, I'll need help lifting it."

Langdon and Montana glanced up from their work, but neither made a move to help her. "I can help, I guess," Alex said, trying not to appear too eager for the excuse to get away from the invoices. "Just show me what you need done," he said, making his way toward the stairs.

Anna led him to the room at the end of the hallway. "There," she said, pointing to a large trunk in the middle of the floor. "I'd move it myself—just push it across the floor like I did the wardrobe closet—but the bitch came up here and told me I was making too much noise."

Alex grinned. "How'd you know her name was Bitch?"

Anna looked at him. An ambiguous smile crept across her lips, but she said nothing.

"That's what I call her," Alex said. "I think her face would crack if she smiled. Damned cantankerous old maid. Come to think of it, I'll bet that's what's wrong with her."

"What?" Anna was watching him with her odd slanting eyes as she slouched against one of the bedposts.

"She needs a man," he said, and smiled wickedly. "Maybe if I could find her one, she wouldn't be in such a bad mood all the time."

There was a brief silence while Anna continued to look at him, her expression not quite a smile but something that made him feel she might be secretly laughing at him. "I doubt if that would help," she said, moving with languid grace toward the trunk.

Alex laughed uneasily. "You're probably right." He picked up one end of the trunk while Anna hefted the other. "She's probably just naturally an old bitch."

When they had the trunk in place, Anna sat on the floor next to it. She unfastened the latches and reached inside, bringing out a small cotton pouch and a packet of thin brown papers. "Just what do you do here at the Golden Palace when you're not tending bar?" she asked as she sifted tobacco from the pouch into one of the papers.

"I—uh, I'm the accountant," Alex said, watching her with fascination. Until coming to Eagleton, he had never seen a woman smoke, and although he saw some of the girls at the Central smoking cigarettes occasionally, it still astonished him. "And I'm one of the partners," he added as an afterthought, although he knew it wasn't technically true. Only Montana McCrory's name had been on the title initially, and then they'd had papers drawn up making Langdon a partner. He ought to insist that he be listed as a partner, too, he thought. He'd just never gotten around to it.

"I see," Anna said. She struck a match on the floor and held it to the cigarette in her mouth, then settled back against the trunk, stretching her long legs in front of her and blowing a hazy cloud toward the ceiling. The wrapper she was wearing parted, and Alex could see a bare leg all the way above her knee, with fine dark hairs lying sleekly against the skin.

"I know I been tendin' bar since you came, but that was only because Diana was away. I'm not really a bartender. I'm an accountant. And I run the roulette wheel." He knew he was babbling, but he couldn't seem to help himself. "I just help out at the bar sometimes."

"For the old bitch," Anna said, smiling up at him.

"Yes," Alex said, and laughed. "For the old bitch."

Anna watched him for a moment, still smiling. "Here," she said, extending her cigarette toward him. "Would you like some?"

"What?"

"Don't you smoke?"

"Well, yes, sometimes, but I—"

"Take some."

"Well, sure. All right." He took the cigarette from her, put it in his mouth, and drew from it, inhaling its sweet, pungent gases.

"Come on," she said, patting the floor beside her.

"Sit down."

Alex hesitated a moment, then sat beside her. She took the cigarette from him, drew on it, then handed it back to him. Her eyes, so large yet slanted, were beguiling to him, and he kept his own eyes locked with hers as he took the cigarette. He smoked it again, still watching her.

"That's a very unusual tobacco," he said. "Kind of sweet. Like pipe tobacco."

"Do you like it?" she asked.

"Oh, yes, it's very nice."

She settled back again, resting her head against the trunk.

"Where are you from, Anna?" Alex asked.

"I've lived a lot of places. Denver was the last. San Francisco was the best. I'm going back there."

"Not too soon, I hope."

She turned toward him again and reached across him for the cigarette he held in his right hand. "I'll be around for a while."

Alex found that there was something very sensuous and exciting about sharing a smoke with her. After a while Anna put out the cigarette and stood up with an easy, liquid movement.

"Thank you, Alex, for helping me," she said in her throaty voice.

He gave her a smile to acknowledge her thanks. He hated to see the moment end. It meant he would have to go back to those damned invoices. Nevertheless he got to his feet, and he had started for the door when Anna called him back. He turned to look at her.

"There's something else you could do for me, if you don't mind."

"Of course."

"Would you hang the curtains for me?" She pointed to the white lace curtains she had threaded over a rod and laid on her bed.

"Oh, sure," he said, glad of any excuse to keep him from the invoices. He pulled the dressing table stool to the window, then picked up the curtains and stood on the stool. "I'll need a hammer," he said. "Looks like this nail that's supposed to hold the rod up is about to pull out of the wall."

"I don't have a hammer," she said. "You'll have to use my shoe."

"I could go down and get one from the kitchen. It—My God, Anna—"

She had placed her hands on his buttocks and was sliding them slowly around to the front. He gasped when she began unbuttoning his trousers.

"It's all right, Alex," she said in her sultry voice. The curtains fell from his hands. He tried to step down from the stool, but Anna stopped him. "There's no need for that," she said, holding his hips. She slid his trousers down while she moved around to the front. Alex felt his heart stop beating.

"Oh, my God, Anna. What you're doing is unnatural—it's—Oh, my God!"

Tuesday morning, Montana dutifully prepared for the picnic, but she did it with a sense of dread. Being with Langdon was bound to be awkward, considering their strained relationship, and even if that were not the case, she had plenty to do at the saloon. Diana had gotten sullen when she'd heard about the outing. Montana knew she didn't like being left alone with the saloon now that business was booming. But she also sensed Diana's disapproval at her going into the mountains with Langdon, even though her "brother" would be along as chaperon. Diana was overly protective of her, oddly puritanical at times. But she was also good to her and the only friend she'd made since she arrived in Eagleton. Montana had long since resigned herself to the cool treatment she received from the townswomen she met on the streets and in the stores.

In spite of her dread and Diana's disapproval, Montana was determined to go through with the picnic, mostly because Alex had been looking forward to it with such enthusiasm. She packed a lunch while Langdon was busy hitching a horse to the buggy he had borrowed. Alex seemed to have disappeared. He'd been awfully busy lately helping Dovie and Anna get their room fixed up. She'd have to remind him not to allow the girls to take advantage of him.

"We'd best get started so we'll have plenty of time. It can be mighty cool up there once the sun gets low," Langdon said, coming into the kitchen through the back door. There was no enthusiasm in his voice.

"I'll go look for Alex," she said equally joylessly.

She pushed open the door to the saloon and saw Alex walking toward her stiffly with slow, measured steps, moving as if he were in pain.

"Alex, what's wrong?" she asked anxiously.

"It's my back," he said. "I'm afraid I've strained it. Anna had me moving her damned wardrobe closet again. She can't seem to make up her mind where she wants it. Oh, don't look so worried," he said, reaching for Montana's hand when he saw her face. "It's nothing serious."

"But we must get you to bed. I'll fix you a mustard plaster. We'll call off the picnic. It wouldn't do for you to go bouncing over rough roads in a buggy."

"Oh, no, please," Alex said, holding up his hands in protest. "I won't have you calling off the picnic because of me. You and Langdon go."

"Certainly not! You need me here."

"Please, Montana, if I thought I'd made you miss it, I'd feel even worse."

"But you shouldn't. I don't want to go if you're not along, and especially if you're not well."

"I insist, my dear," he said, pushing her toward the door. He gave Langdon a pleading look. "See that she has a good time, won't you? She's been working too hard, and she deserves it."

Langdon took her arm. "I'll do my best," he said. Montana shot him a quick glance and noticed that his eyes had lost some of their coldness.

"Alex," she said, turning back to him. "I can't leave you like this. You really must have that mustard plaster."

"Nonsense. All a mustard plaster does is smell bad. I just need a day in bed, that's all."

"But, Alex—"

"Go on, please. I insist. I want you to have a good time."

Langdon grasped her arm firmly and led her toward the door. "Alex is right," he said. "It will do you good."

In the next moment they were out the door and he was helping her into the buggy. She looked over her shoulder to see Alex standing in the doorway, smiling and waving to her. Then he clutched at his back with his right hand and turned around slowly.

Montana sat stiffly on the seat, her eyes straight ahead. "This is ridiculous," she said. "Neither of us wants to go on this picnic. I don't know why you insisted."

"Who says neither of us wants to go?" Langdon asked as he picked up the reins.

She gave him a look of surprise. "Just a minute ago you were acting like you were going to your own funeral."

"That was before I knew it would only be the two of us."

"Now, wait a minute! If you think—"

"Don't get so riled up. There's nothing wrong with an innocent little picnic. And Alex is right. It will do us both good."

"It's not proper, and you know it."

"What's improper about a gentleman taking a lady out for a drive in the country? It's done all the time."

"But Alex—"

"What about Alex?" Langdon asked as he flicked the reins. "I'd say by the way he's acting, he doesn't see anything wrong with it. I dare say he was more than happy to stay home."

"What are you getting at?"

"Nothing. Just relax and enjoy the trip, and don't tell me you think you shouldn't go without your husband. Remember the game you're playing, Montana."

"There's no point in this," she insisted. "I was only doing it for Alex."

"Alex be damned," Langdon said. "It's time you did something for yourself."

"For myself?" she cried. "I have no interest whatsoever in seeing that worthless claim. That was Alex's folly."

"Whatever you say," Langdon said, urging the horse to a fast trot. "We won't go to your claim if you don't want to. We'll just take a ride out in the country. Alex is right about one thing. You do need to get away from this place."

"And you seem hell-bent to get away," Montana said, gripping the sides of the buggy seat. "Do you have to drive so fast?"

"Any way you like it, madam," Langdon said, slowing the horse. "I'll drive you through town slow and easy and show you off to every envious man"—he tipped his hat to a middle-aged matron, who tossed her head haughtily at Montana—"and woman we meet."

Montana's cheeks burned at the woman's rebuff, but she held her head high as they drove through the town.

Away from the city limits, they moved along a winding trail that hugged a rugged granite cliffside, then passed through aspen pregnant with buds, and pine trees black green against an intensely blue sky. Montana began to relax somewhat, and she found herself enjoying the scenery. She had spent almost their entire time in Eagleton in the Golden Palace, venturing into the shabby mining town only on errands. She had not known it would be so beautiful in the country in the spring.

After a while Langdon pulled the horse to a halt in a meadow. "I want to show you something," he said, holding his hand out for hers. She allowed him to help her down, but he didn't let go of her hand, leading her instead toward a stream that splashed over rocks and fallen timber.

"There," he said, pointing to a rock protrusion. "What I want to show you is only a short way up, where the stream takes a bend."

After walking a ways, he stopped to pick up a grayish rock and thrust it toward her. Montana looked at it. "It's quartz," he said. "See that other type of rock over there?" He picked up a differently shaded stone and handed it to her. It felt as light as a piece of rotten wood. "That's float," he said. He looked upstream, squinting against the sun. "It broke off an outcrop somewhere up there. These are the kinds of rocks that mean gold," he explained, turning back to her. "If a person could find the outcrop where that float came from, it might contain gold."

"That's just it," Montana said. "It *might* contain gold, and chances are it won't. Ask Dynamite Finley. He spent a fortune looking for it, and so have hundreds like him."

"Oh, it's a gamble all right," Langdon said. "Just like everything else." He squatted beside the creek and reached for a handful of sand and gravel on its shallow bottom. He let the icy water drain from his fingers like a sieve, leaving only the heaviest grains in his palm. Then he stood, showing her the gritty contents.

"See that?" He pointed to some shiny specks. "That's placer gold. Not enough here to wash or to pan, but that gold has washed off a vein somewhere up there," he said, indicating the mountains above them. "It's in a crack in the ground, just waiting to be discovered. Can you see the stake to the left of the two pine trees? That's my claim. The Honesty. That rich vein could be there."

"That's just a dream," Montana said.

"Tell that to Lem Bailey. He owns the Freedom mine. Or try telling it to Ira Griffith of the Lucky Lady. They started out poor prospectors. Eagleton gold made them millionaires."

"And that brings all the other suckers in," Montana said, "thinking they're going to be millionaires, too. But it only happens to a lucky few."

"Don't you know what it's like to dream that you

could be one of the lucky few?"

"I have no time or inclination to dream," she said stiffly.

"That's too bad."

She turned toward him. "Is it? I've found nothing bad at all in embracing practicality and doing away with dreams."

Langdon reached for her, grasping her arms. "What did it to you?" he asked. "What killed the dreams you must have had once? What turned you into this hard and bitter woman? Was it Alex?"

She tried to jerk free of his grasp. "You are quite out of line—"

"No!" he said, still holding her. "If he is the cause, then he ought to be shot. A beautiful woman like you deserves more than a bitter, hard life."

"Deserving has nothing to do with one's lot in life," she said coldly. "And anyway, I am quite content with my life."

Langdon dropped his hands from her arms. "In spite of the fact that you're not living it in Tennessee?"

He had caught her off guard. She had temporarily forgotten about Tennessee. "It is because I know that we will soon be able to return to Tennessee that I am content," she lied. There were times now when she actually dreaded the thought of returning to their meager life there, especially since the Golden Palace had begun to prosper. But she couldn't let herself be seduced by that.

"*We* will return to Tennessee? What makes you so sure Alex wants to go? He seems more than happy to be in Colorado."

She turned away from him, unable to think of a suitable response. He was right, of course. Alex would be even more reluctant to leave than she was. But he would leave. She would be able to make him see the wisdom in it. Tennessee was, after all, where they belonged.

"He is just as eager as I am," she said.

"You're deceiving yourself, Montana. Not only about Alex, but about yourself. You don't belong in Tennessee. Ivy Barton is dead, and you are Montana McCrory."

"You have a way of reminding me that Mrs. Barton is not dead when it suits your purposes," she said coldly.

"Montana, I—"

"But you're quite right," she said. "I don't want to forget who I am. I want to end this charade, and I must return to Tennessee."

"Why must you?"

"I don't like living this lie, and surely you must understand that I'm tired of the constant threat that you will expose us," she said, struggling to keep her voice steady.

"My God, woman, can't you see that I have as much to lose now as you do if you tip your hand?"

She studied his face. It had not occurred to her that he had become as dependent on the charade as she and Alex were, and she found it odd and out of character that he would admit it. The show of vulnerability touched her momentarily, but she pushed the feeling aside. It didn't matter, she told herself. She could not forget who she was and where she belonged. "We have to leave." Her voice shook. "As soon as possible."

"You don't want to go," he said.

"I do!"

"No," he said. He reached for her again. "You don't." He was very close. One arm went around her, pulling her to him. He kissed her, and to her surprise and shame, it was a moment before she turned away.

"You've no right. . . ."

His hand was on the back of her neck, his thumb stroking her jaw, then he moved it to caress her lower lip. She felt disoriented, vaguely aware that he was pulling her toward him again and that she wasn't resisting. Then his mouth was on hers once more, his arms tightening. Her own arms clung involuntarily to his broad back while the kiss, slow, gentle, potent, grew deeper, hungrier, intemperate. She began to feel frightened, not of him, but of herself, of the hunger she felt, the need to respond. Tugging free of him, she tried to turn away, but he pulled her back, forcing her to face him.

"Don't try to walk away," he said roughly. "Don't try to deny you felt something, too."

"No! No, you're wrong!"

He dropped his arms and let her back away. "I'm beginning to think that the reason you're so good at this little game of deceit you're playing is because you're so practiced at it," he said. "You're very good at deceiving yourself."

"I never deceive myself," she said. "I know what I want—what I must do. I have no choice but to go back to Tennessee."

"Why?" he asked angrily. "Why? Just give me one good reason."

"There is plenty of reason," she said heatedly. "My children's graves—"

She saw the look on Langdon's face, and she was horrified at what she had said. She had never meant to mention the girls. The past was none of his business. But in her agitated state, it had slipped out. She turned away from him, trembling as she fought back tears.

She felt his hands grasp her shoulders gently and turn her around. "I didn't know," he said. "But I understand now."

"No!" she said, her voice harsh. "You couldn't possibly understand."

"But I do," he said. "More than you know. I understand how it makes you afraid to love when you lose the people you love the most."

She dared to look at him, and she wondered for a moment if it were true, if he really did understand. She wondered, too, if she was afraid to love. But, no, she loved Alex, didn't she? For some reason she couldn't be sure at the moment that she did, and she was finding it difficult to concentrate as Langdon pulled her closer to him.

"Langdon . . ."

"Don't be afraid," he said as he stroked her hair.

She was unable to speak anymore as he brought her close, holding her, nothing more. She clung to him again, but only briefly, before she pulled away.

"Montana," he said, holding her hands in his, restraining her gently. "There's nothing for you in Tennessee. Let the dead rest. And let yourself live. Don't deceive yourself any longer. You don't love him."

Montana felt a moment of fear that what he said might be true. But of course it wasn't. She did love Alex. He had stood beside her when she'd needed him most. She could not forget that. She raised her eyes to meet Langdon's, and she said evenly, "I love Alex more than life itself."

9

The air on the hot Tennessee day was thick with humidity and with the heavy, sweet smell of the honeysuckle that grew on the fence near the house. Susan and Elizabeth were cross from the heat.

"Let's go to the creek, Mama," Elizabeth said. "We could wade in the shallow part."

"Not now, Beth. I have work to do. And so do you two. Y'all get busy and finish with that corn."

"Oh, Mama, couldn't we stop for just a while?" Susan said with a little whine. "We been gathering this old corn all day."

"You can stop when the work's done, Susan."

"But, Mama," Elizabeth said, "it's so hot."

"Hush up, girls, and get busy."

They went back to the small plot of corn to work, fussy and grumbling. Ivy watched them go, then glanced toward the cotton field in the distance. Alex walked behind the mule, guiding the plow. He had come in late the night before, staggering and reeking of liquor. He'd spent every penny of the money she'd saved for supplies. It had angered her, but she had said little, not wanting to make a scene with the girls asleep nearby. She had hoped he'd sense her anger in her stony silence, but he had shown no signs that he did.

She'd made no attempt at keeping the girls quiet that morning, in spite of the fact that she knew his head would be pounding with a hangover. Aware of his queasy stomach, she had cooked greasy ham and runny eggs for breakfast and sent him to the field, insisting that the cotton had to be plowed again to keep the weeds from choking out the plants before the harvest.

It gave her some satisfaction to watch him now, moving slowly and carefully, with obvious discomfort. She finally turned to select the plumpest and most choice ears of corn from the pile the girls had brought in. When her basket was full, she set it aside, went to the pump, washed her face and hands, then unbuttoned her dress and bathed under her arms. Hurrying back into the house, she went to the bedroom and pulled the gray muslin dress over her head, changing into a clean one of faded blue print that was frayed at the collar and cuffs. Susan and Elizabeth were just coming in with another basket of corn when she finished combing her hair.

"Where you goin', Mama?" Elizabeth asked. "How come you put on your Sunday dress?"

"I have business in Byrneville, girls, but I'll be back before suppertime."

"Can we put on our Sunday dresses, too?" Susan asked.

"No," Ivy said. "You're not going with me. I can walk faster if I go alone, and I want to be back in time to cook supper."

Susan and Beth both looked stricken. "How come we can't go?" Susan said.

"I just told you how come. Mercy, you're big enough to be by yourselves for a little while. I want you to stay here and finish up with that corn. It's got to be gathered now while the ears are tender and sweet."

"Mama, please," Elizabeth said, and at the same time Susan insisted loudly, "It's not right, you leavin' us here alone."

"Hush now, both of you. Your papa's just a holler away in the cotton field. You girls go on now and get busy. I'll be back as soon as I can." Ivy motioned with her hands, shooing them out.

"Oh, Mama, you're so mean!" Susan cried petulantly on her way out of the house. Ivy ignored the remark as she tied on her bonnet and wiped the dust off her shoes. She knew the girls were watching her when she left the house, carrying the bushel of corn.

She had worked at a furious pace all morning to get her work done early enough to walk the four miles to the store and back again before supper. She had decided during the night that she would go. She had decided while she lay in bed beside Alex as he slept off the drunk that had cost precious money they couldn't spare.

As she walked along the dirt path, the brilliance of midafternoon filtered through maple leaves and fell upon her in splotches, bringing a new dampness to her underarms and between her breasts. But she thought nothing of it. Her thoughts ran to pale lavender. She had seen it three weeks earlier in Ezra Byrne's store, dotted with tiny pink roses and beckoning her. She prayed that the bolt of cloth would still be there. She would trade the bushel of corn for the cloth, and she would have a new dress—her first in more than three years.

When she had first seen the lavender fabric, she had forced all thoughts of it from her mind, knowing they couldn't afford it. But in her anger last night, she had summoned the memory back. There had been enough left on the bolt for one dress. And it would be hers. It had to be hers. If Alex could spend money foolishly, so could she. It would mean he wouldn't have the new boots he needed, and he would have no sugar for his coffee—perhaps not even coffee, no luxuries at all for a while—but she wouldn't let that bother her. It was time she took some thought for herself.

She made the walk in a little more than an hour, and when she opened the front screen door, she saw that no one was inside except Ezra Byrne dozing behind the counter, a fly swatter stuck between his folded arms and his large belly. The creaking of the screen door awakened him with a start, turning a snore into a snort.

"How do, Miz Barton," he said, recovering but without bothering to get up.

Ivy nodded her greeting, and her eyes went to the counter where he kept the bolts of cloth. The lavender-and-rose print was still there. She gave Ezra Byrne the corn, and he calculated the price—enough for the fabric.

She picked up the bolt of crisp new cotton, running her hands over it slowly. She hesitated a moment, then put the cloth back on the table. Maybe she was justified in begrudging Alex his new boots and his coffee, but she considered that perhaps she should use the money to buy cloth for the girls' dresses. But they'd each had a dress last year, she reasoned, and she'd left the seams wide enough to let them out this year.

She picked up the bolt of cloth again but didn't move toward the counter. She was wondering now if she should take the money home and save it for emergencies. But Alex, she told herself, would only create an emergency, finding some excuse that meant he had to have the money. He could very well gamble it away or get drunk again. Her anger flared once more, and she could think of nothing except sweet lavender revenge. She took the bolt of cloth to Ezra Byrne, told him the length she wanted, then bought two sticks of licorice for the girls.

Ivy started her walk home, and after a while she began to walk faster. The girls would be growing restless, and Alex would soon be in from the field for supper.

As she approached the house, she saw the mule in the pen behind the barn. Alex was already home. He had probably come in early to nurse his hangover. She opened the door, ready to confront him, but she stopped short when she saw him kneeling beside the bed.

On the bed lay Susan and Elizabeth. They were dressed only in their shifts, and their hair was matted and tangled and damp. She couldn't understand what it meant. Why were her children not dressed? Why was their hair damp? Why weren't they running to greet her and ask her what she'd brought them? She tried to run to them but found she could not move.

Alex glanced up at her. He looked dazed and pale, and his voice sounded strange. "They were in the creek."

She heard a scream then, her own, she thought, and a voice, which also must have been her own, crying, "No! No!" She ran to the bed and touched Susan's face. It was waxy and cold, not Susan's face at all, and the lifeless hand that fell limply across Elizabeth's budding chest was not hers. "No!" Ivy cried again. She tried to gather Elizabeth to her bosom, but she was so cold. She whirled to face Alex. "I never allowed them to go to the creek! They didn't go there! Oh, my God—Susan! Beth!" She turned back to Alex. "They were afraid of the water. They didn't go in! They didn't!"

"You never allowed them," Alex said. "But they weren't afraid. It was you who was afraid. They wanted—they thought I—"

"They can't swim! You know that! You should have watched them," she heard herself saying. "You should have seen that they didn't go. They can't swim!"

"Ivy, I'm so sorry. I didn't know—"

"You could have watched them!" Ivy screamed, as if her screaming and denying would bring them back. "You could see them while you worked—you could see them! I only went to the store. You could see them gathering the corn. In plain sight! Oh, my God!" she moaned.

"You went to the store? You didn't see them go to the creek?"

"Oh, God, Alex, I was mad at you. Crazy mad. I had to leave. I—"

"You didn't see—"

"I told you, I went to the store. How did this happen? Tell me! Tell me everything!" She felt somehow that if she knew the sequence of bizarre events, every detail of how her precious daughters had tumbled to their deaths—were they playing? Had one tried to rescue the other?—if she could make sense of it, Susan and Elizabeth would awaken and tell her it was all a mistake.

"I . . . don't know," Alex said. She could see that he was trembling. "I—I worked until time to quit for supper." His voice sounded odd, and he turned his face away from her as if his grief were too much for her to see. "And then I couldn't find them. I couldn't find you."

"No!" Ivy said again, wanting to deny what he was saying. Wanting to deny that she had ever left. She turned to the bed and called their names, scolding them, shaking them, desperate to awaken them.

"Susan! Elizabeth! Get up!" She shook them again, shook their limp, lifeless bodies, and she heard Alex's frightened voice telling her to stop. Finally he grasped her shoulders and forced her away from the bed. He tried to hold her while her body shook with sobs, but she pushed him away. "Tell me," she said. "Tell me what happened!"

Alex didn't seem able to speak at first, but she kept insisting until at last he began.

"I went through the house," he said in the trembling voice of agony. "I went outside. I hollered for you. For the girls. The woods, I thought. The wild blackberries. But they're not ripe. All green and hard." He had grown pale. "I went to the creek. They—they couldn't swim. I saw—I saw them. It was too late. Already too late, Ivy. You believe me, don't you? It was too goddamned late!" He sank to the floor, sobbing convulsively.

Seeing him hysterical with grief had a strangely calming effect on her. She had to comfort him, to soothe him. She sat on the bed next to her children and reached for him, cradling his head in her lap, stroking his hair while he sobbed uncontrollably. The anger she'd felt a few hours earlier seemed misplaced now, unimportant in the face of utter despair.

She heard a sound then, a strange, unearthly moan, and didn't realize for a moment that it was coming from inside her, seeping from her very soul as she rocked back and forth, still cradling Alex's head.

"I shouldn't have done it," she cried. "It was wrong of me. 'Vengeance is mine,' saith the Lord." Alex raised his head, and she saw the stunned look on his face. "I did it," she whispered. "I left them because I wanted revenge against you. And God has punished me for my sin."

"What are you talking about?"

She told him, then, how she had plotted her vengeance and how she had not wanted the girls to slow her down in her rush for the sweet taste of revenge.

She was sobbing when she finished her story, but her confession had a sobering effect on Alex. He was silent while the sobs racked her body. Finally he took her in his arms and pulled her to her feet.

"It's all right, Ivy," he said. "You resented what I did. You wanted to get even. I understand, and I'm sorry for what I did. I never meant to upset you. I just had a little too much to drink—it happened before I knew it. I never meant to—It was a mistake—I—"

"Oh, God, Alex, how can I bear to live? Elizabeth . . . Susan!"

She had truly not wanted to live. From that moment the will to go on had begun to slip away, and it seemed that she moved about in a half-life, hardly remembering anything, not even the funeral. At some point she had taken to her bed and willed herself to die, but Alex would not allow it. "You have to forgive yourself," he had said. "You have to get through this. And I'll help you, Ivy. I'll help you. I'll always be here for you."

He had stood by her through the dark months that followed, not letting her give up, trying to offer her hope. When his own despair overcame him, he sought refuge in liquor, but he always emerged to help her, to coax her through her despair, to urge her to stop blaming herself. She could not have made it without him. He understood. He forgave. He had said he would always be there for her, no matter what. And he had said that he loved her.

Still, sometimes late at night when he thought she was asleep, she would hear him sobbing and asking, "Why, Ivy? Why? Why weren't you here?"

And even when he was quiet, or when he was not around, she could hear another voice—Susan repeating again and again, *"Mama, you're so mean!"*

Now, in Eagleton, Colorado, Montana could close her eyes and remember the feel of Langdon's mouth on hers. She could once again experience the desire it had awakened in her, and she could almost forget the horror of the past. But that only brought her more shame. She should have stopped him. She should not have enjoyed it. She was married to Alex. She knew of no way to redeem herself of this new shame except by willing herself not to think of Langdon. Instead she would concentrate on her work; she would begin by trying to balance a ledger, and she would think only of returning to Tennessee.

It was impossible not to think of him, though, and she was finding it impossible to work on the ledger. She had to find another way to stay busy. She would do the shopping for the kitchen. As she buttoned her coat, she noted how shabby it looked. Its frayed collar and cuffs and carefully mended elbows, incongruous over the handsome green dress, showed its years of wear in Tennessee as well as their first winter in Colorado.

She picked up her gloves, pulling them on as she walked down the stairs. When she reached the bottom, she glanced around for Langdon but saw only Anna, who stared back at her with an expression that was somehow disturbing, as if she knew too much, as if she knew how much Montana had wanted Langdon to be there. She turned away quickly to walk out of the saloon, but Anna called out to her.

Montana turned and watched the woman move toward her with her slow, languid walk.

"If you're going to the drugstore, I wonder if you'd pick up a few things for me." She handed her a list.

"Of course," Montana said. She took the slip of paper and left quickly, not quite sure why Anna made her so uncomfortable.

The drugstore was next to the department store on Baylor Avenue, a reasonable distance from the saloons and parlor houses and one-girl cribs of Myrtle Avenue, so that local housewives would not feel uncomfortable as they shopped. Montana couldn't fault the townswomen for distancing themselves from what they called the "sin district." A short time ago she would have felt the same way.

The walk in the crisp air lifted her spirits, and she stopped in front of the department store display window to admire a cape with a fur collar. On an impulse, she stepped inside and asked the clerk to let her see it. When he handed it to her, she wrapped it around herself, nestling her chin in the warmth of the fur. She saw in the mirror that it looked good on her. But then the reflection seemed to change, and she saw not the soft woolen cloak, but a dress of rose-printed lavender cotton. She tore off the cloak, flung it at the startled clerk, and hurried out of the store. She would wear her old coat, shabby as it was. She didn't deserve a new one.

She made her way up Baylor Avenue to the grocery and then doubled back to Adams's Drugstore to buy the items on Anna's list. Mr. Adams was busy with a number of customers, so she sat at one of the four small tables in the center of the room to have a phosphate. While she sipped it, a little girl approached her and stood staring at the lovely, fizzy drink in the tall stemmed glass.

The child was around the age Susan had been when she died. Montana had seen that same expression on both her girls when they yearned for a stick candy or any number of things in Byrneville's general store. She wanted to turn away from the child, to shut out the awful pain of the memory, but she found that she could not. She trembled as she pushed the drink aside.

"Would you like to have one?" she asked.

The girl's face was transformed by a wide smile, which very quickly faded.

"Oh, I'm afraid I shouldn't. I would be scolded," she said.

Montana smiled. "I understand," she said. She reached into her reticule and produced a penny. "But surely a piece of penny candy won't get you a scolding." Montana stood and walked to the counter to hand the clerk the coin, then offered the jar to the girl to select a piece.

The girl beamed. "Oh, thank you," she said as she selected a sticky red candy. Her voice had the soft, high pitch that sometimes still haunted Montana in her dreams.

"Nora!" The sound was bitter and harsh and came from somewhere behind her. Montana turned to see a tall, fleshy woman in the long black habit and veil of a nun. Her eyes were cold as they glared at the frightened child. "You are not a common beggar," she said, snatching the candy and tossing it into a cuspidor. "You do not ask for things from strangers." She took the girl's hand and pulled her away roughly.

"She didn't ask—I offered," Montana said to the nun's back as she dragged the child away. "And so that I am not a stranger, let me introduce myself. I am Montana—"

"I know who you are," the nun said, whirling to face her. "And I know what you are." Her hard mouth formed the words slowly, deliberately. "Isn't it enough that you corrupt the menfolk without stooping to the children as well?" She turned around again, giving the girl a harsh shove. The little girl stumbled but caught herself and hurried off with the nun.

Montana watched, stunned. She had been shunned by other women since coming to Eagleton as Montana McCrory, saloon owner, but never before had she been insulted openly.

"Don't let her get under your skin." She turned at the raspy voice to see a woman with blond curls piled high on her head and a smartly tailored cream-and-black taffeta dress hugging feminine curves. "I'm Pearl DuVal." She smiled, showing dazzling white teeth framed by ruby red lips. "And you're Montana McCrory," she added before Montana had recovered sufficiently to reply. "*I* know who you are, too."

"And do you also know *what* I am?" Montana asked, her voice edged with defensive anger.

Pearl laughed. "I told you, don't let the old biddy get to you. That was Sister Mary Frances. She has the guts to call herself a Sister of Mercy. She and the other nuns run the hospital and orphanage over on the east side of town."

"I didn't know there was an orphanage."

"It's not much of one. But since the sisters run the hospital, they sometimes get stuck with a kid when a woman dies. There's usually half a dozen or so living over there."

She studied Montana's face for a moment. "Hey, don't look so upset. You can't make it your problem. Besides, the kids don't usually stay there forever. Eventually they get sent off to Denver or somewhere. To what, I don't know, but at least they're away from the old battle-ax."

"There must be people here who would take those children."

Pearl gave a short, harsh laugh. "Could be, but if you're thinking of trying it yourself, forget it. Sister Mary Frances has her idea of what makes a fit mother, and you and me ain't in the running," Pearl said. "You have a saloon, I run a parlor house." Pearl took a pair of gloves from a small reticule. "And let's make sure we keep it that way," she added, working her long, slender fingers into the gloves.

"I'm afraid I don't understand."

"Don't you?" Pearl looked at Montana.

"No, I—"

"What I'm saying is, I won't be selling drinks at my place, and I don't expect you to sell whores at yours." Montana was shocked at her crudeness, but Pearl didn't seem to notice. She went back to working her gloves on as she spoke. "You've been quite the attraction here in Eagleton with your highfalutin ladylike ways. You ain't got a bad business head on your shoulders, either, bringing in those girls just before the novelty of all the rest wears off. But you can take what I said as fair warning. You make sure you ain't selling nothing except dances, and you and me will get along just fine."

"Miss DuVal," Montana said, pulling herself up straight, "I certainly don't need you to tell me how to run my business, but I can assure you that I will never be in competition with you. After all, whatever I sell will always be of the *highest* quality." She met Pearl's gaze meaningfully, then turned away.

Mr. Adams, Montana saw, was now free of customers. She walked to his counter to give him her order. "A bottle of iodine, a box of bicarbonate of soda, and an ounce of cocaine powders, please." When the order was filled she paid him two dollars and seventy cents and left the store, aware of Pearl DuVal's eyes following her.

Alex had told himself after the day he'd spent with Anna while Langdon and Montana were in the mountains that he would not go to the woman again. It was simply too risky, bedding her in the Golden Palace. He never knew when Montana might come upstairs and hear them or even see him coming out of Anna's room. It would hurt Montana terribly to find out, and he never wanted to hurt her. He loved her too deeply for that. But Anna kept inviting him back, and with each visit becoming more and more erotic, he found his promise hard to honor.

He'd been with Anna the night before and had been too exhausted and too hung over to get up early to help with the chores. He was up now, though, and as he worked in the storage area, arranging the casks of beer that had just arrived, he tried to strengthen his resolve. It was difficult, though, because he kept remembering the way she excited him with her rough play, her blatantly carnal acts that gave him such strange pleasure, and the things she had taught him that only a few months ago he had not even imagined any woman would do. Afterward he'd often join her with her hashish, and recently they'd begun smoking her opium pipe.

He began to wonder where she was now. He had thought he'd heard her voice in the saloon, but when he'd come inside, only Dovie was there. He found the girl pleasant, though not as pretty as Lida or as exciting as Anna, but before he had a chance to speak with her, she, too, drifted upstairs. Maybe that was just as well. The last time he'd spent any time talking with Dovie, it had made Anna violently angry. It had surprised him, the way she had screamed and cried and thrown things around in her room and even tried to hit him with one of her heavy metal curling irons. She'd worked herself into such a rage that she'd had to take four of her laudanum tablets to calm herself. She'd slept for hours afterward and had awakened in an eerily docile mood.

"Alex?" He looked up to see Montana entering the saloon.

"Here," he said, waving to her from the back. He walked toward her, kissed her lightly on the cheek, and helped her remove her wrap. "You ought to buy a new coat," he said. "This one's so worn."

"I don't need a new coat," she said, her words sharp and bitter.

"Well, you deserve one," he said affectionately. "I always wanted to dress my love in the finest."

"Alex!" she whispered. "If anyone hears you talk like that—what will they think?"

He had forgotten their roles for a moment, but now that she'd reminded him, once again the thought of making illicit love to her excited him. What would she say if he asked her to steal upstairs with him right now?

"Alex, dear, I wonder if you would do me a favor," Montana asked. Her expression told him her thoughts were nowhere near the same as his. She handed him a small package. "I picked some things up for Anna. Would you mind taking them up to her room for me?"

Alex hesitated, remembering his resolve, but within

seconds he was reaching for the packet. "Of course," he said. He turned toward the stairs, telling himself he would stay only long enough to deliver the package.

He wasn't sure that Anna would be in her room, but if she was, she was probably hitting the pipe. He toyed with the idea of joining her. He had come to look forward to the floating, lethargic feeling the pipe gave him, especially after a stint of physical labor such as he'd just done. But he didn't enjoy the hangover it gave him. Like the one he'd had this morning. He hadn't been able to get out of bed until almost eleven.

He wouldn't stay this time, he told himself. He was no dope fiend, even if Anna was. He'd just deliver the packet, then maybe he'd take a walk over to the Central. It had been days since he'd been there, and the truth was he missed Lida and her soft, vulnerable sweetness.

He approached Anna's door and started to knock but hesitated when he heard her voice. It sounded odd, slow, and muffled, as it did when she was on the pipe. But who was she talking to? Dovie? He'd never known Anna to smoke her opium when Dovie was around. If she had a man in there, Montana would be furious. He listened a moment and heard another voice—Dovie's, he concluded. The two of them must be up to some private woman talk, he decided. He started to turn away, but before he had taken the first step, Dovie opened the door.

Anna's voice floated toward him. "Alex, is that you?"

"Yes, it's me."

He could see her lying on her bed. She raised an arm and waved him toward her. "Come here."

Alex took a step inside the room.

"She's acting strange," Dovie whispered. "She's been kind of draggy all morning. Then she just played out completely awhile ago. Says she needs her tonic."

"Did you bring it?" Anna asked.

"What?" Alex asked, forgetting for a moment why he had come.

"The powders from the drugstore."

"Oh! Oh, yes. I guess so. Is that what Montana sent up?"

"Let me have it," Anna said, sitting up and reaching for the package. She unwrapped it, throwing the paper and string to the floor and letting the three items fall into her lap. "Oh, yes," she said. "The bicarbonate to help me live through that damned Diana's cooking, the iodine for my infected corns, and the powders for my nerves."

Alex watched as she opened the tin, took a pinch between her fingers, and sniffed it as he had seen other women do with snuff. Then she leaned back on her pillow. "Here, try some," she said, handing it to Dovie.

"Well, I have been feeling tired lately," Dovie said. "And it's sure to be a long night tonight. A good tonic will keep me going." She reached for the tin. "But sniffing's not refined, Anna. All the ladies are taking it as a tonic. Do you have any wine to mix it in?"

"No, I don't have any wine to mix it in," Anna said, mocking her.

Dovie turned away in a huff, reached for a drinking glass, and poured water into it from a pitcher. She dropped in a pinch of the powder, stirring with her finger, then she began to sip it.

"Give some to Alex," Anna said.

"Oh, no, I really have to be going," Alex said, holding up his hands and trying to back away.

"Come on. Try some," Dovie said. "You'll feel wonderful!"

"Take some, Alex," Anna said. "You've been working hard this morning. You must be tired."

"Well, I am a little, but—"

"Just a pinch, and you won't be tired anymore. It'll make you feel soooo good."

"Well, maybe just a little."

He took a pinch and sniffed it as Anna had done. At her insistence, he sat down on the bed beside her while Dovie wound up the gramophone. Before long he began to feel quite energetic, and the music, it seemed, made him cheerful. He began dancing with Dovie, heedless of how jealous it might make Anna. But he need not have worried. Anna was soon up, dancing along with them. He was holding them both, one in each arm, and it seemed he had never danced better in his life. He felt as if he could dance all day and all night and could not possibly miss a step.

When Dovie stumbled and fell backward on the bed, pulling him with her, it was not a misstep, because it was all done in perfect rhythm to the music and with what seemed to him uncommon grace. Anna floated on top of him with equal lightness and grace and kissed him. He had never had such a kiss, nor had he ever felt such sexual power rising within him. He clasped her close and felt her moving rhythmically on top of him. When she pulled away to unfasten his belt, he heard her deep, throaty laugh and saw that she was looking at Dovie. He followed her gaze and saw Dovie unbuttoning her blouse. Anna moved aside, and Dovie moved on top of him.

An hour later the three of them lay naked in bed. He'd had them both, and the sensation each time had been heightened beyond his belief. Now, thanks to Anna's ingenuity, he was about to have them both at the same time.

10

Langdon pushed the handle down to detonate the round of dynamite he had set in the hole he was digging on his Honesty claim. The expolosion sent a heavy cloud of dirt and rock flying into the air, and the sound bounced off the sides of mountains and canyon walls like a slowly dying stutter. In the past few weeks he'd managed to get down another twenty feet, but he still hadn't found anything.

It was becoming more and more difficult to keep his mind on the claim. He was still thinking about Montana. Ever since that day in the mountains, he'd had an even harder time than usual keeping his mind off her. And that had been months ago. She had been lying, of course, when she'd told him she loved Alex. Not lying just to him, but to herself as well, and he still couldn't figure out why. He didn't know why he was even trying to figure it out. Why couldn't he just accept the good luck that had come his way and stop thinking about her? After all, he had what had turned out to be the perfect setup—half interest in a prospering gambling parlor and plenty of time to work his claim.

After the cloud of dust settled, Langdon picked up his ladder and bucket to go down into the hole he'd blasted out. Now came the hard part of bringing up the rocks and dirt loosened by the blast. Working this damned claim was getting tiresome. The best he'd been able to assay was thirty dollars a ton. That wouldn't even buy his dynamite.

He loaded his bucket, brought it to the top, emptied it beside the shaft, and he was still thinking about Montana. There was a mystery about her that both frustrated and attracted him—something she was hiding deep within her. It added to that air of distance and aloofness he'd noticed in her from the first.

He remembered how he'd wanted her when he'd first become aware of that cool, standoffish air. He still wanted her, but not with such ruthlessness. He didn't want to hurt her. It was possible, he thought as he dumped another bucketful of rocks next to the shaft opening, that he was falling in love with her. He had even dreamed of going away with her, of selling the Golden Palace and taking the money, then leaving behind the Honesty and Alex and everything else and starting over somewhere together. He wondered, as he started to descend into the shaft again, if he would have felt that way if she was still Ivy Barton, the Tennessee farm wife with nothing to her name, instead of Montana McCrory, who had more assets at the moment than he had and who was a damned smart woman, capable of making even more. As much as he hated to admit it, hiring the girls had been a smart business move. But he still thought—no, he *knew*—that eventually they were going to cause trouble.

* * *

"Tell her I want more money or I'm leaving. I'm going to work for Johnny Nolton, and I'm taking Dovie with me." Anna's voice was harsh, and her lips were a thin red slash across her pale face. Her hair had come loose from the pins and drooped to her shoulders like a dull brown rag.

"I told you, Anna, we're paying you as much as you'd make at the Central or the Nolton or anywhere else. We can't afford to pay you more." Alex knew he sounded whining, but he couldn't seem to stop it. Anna was getting on his nerves. She'd been at him for three days now, nagging him to ask Montana to pay her more. Recently Anna's moods had gotten nastier and nastier.

"I don't give a damn what you're paying. I said I want more! All you have to do is ask that goddamned sister of yours."

"I told you, I can't—"

"And don't tell me you can't!" she said, flying into a rage. Alex dodged the glass vial she picked up from her bureau to throw at him. "She's your sister, isn't she? All you have to do is go in and ask her."

"Take it easy, Anna," Alex said, edging toward the door. "Let me go down to the drugstore and buy you some of your powders. We'll share them. Have a few laughs. Then you'll feel better."

Anna shot him an angry glance. "I'm not sharing anything with you until you talk to your sister. And I mean *nothing*. No more fucking with me and Dovie. No more nothin'."

"Don't get so upset. I told you yesterday, Montana's been awful busy lately."

"So what? She's always busy."

Anna was looking around for something else to throw at him. Alex had hoped to God she'd be in one of her easy, lethargic moods when he came up to her room today. The way she was when she was hitting the pipe. But she'd been avoiding the opium dens over the past several weeks, preferring to stay in her room and take her powders. He liked the cocaine better himself, but recently Anna had been turning the wild energy it produced into something less pleasant than the marathon sex he'd come to associate with the wonderful white powder.

"Well, I've been busy, too, you know. I don't always have time to talk to Montana. This place doesn't run by itself."

Anna laughed, a cruel, bitter sound. "You've been busy doin' what? Fuckin' Lida Armstrong? That vacant-headed child over at the Central? What would little Lida think if she knew you'd been screwin' me and Dovie?"

"You leave Lida out of this."

Anna took a menacing step toward him. "So! You're not even going to try to deny it, are you?"

She was bullying him, and it made him angry. Nobody had a right to bully him. He ought to fire her straight off.

"I heard it over at Jake's," she said. "Laura Bitwell was laughing about the way you sneak around to bed Lida just like the married men do. Who you hidin' from, Alex? You scared o' little ol' Anna?"

Her tone had changed from frothing anger to cold menace, but she was still bullying him, and he was coming to detest that more and more by the minute.

"It's none of your business what I do or who I do it with," he said. His mind was working fast. He couldn't fire her and risk her going to Montana. But he knew he shouldn't let her get by with pushing him around.

Anna's face showed a flicker of surprise that he dared to talk back to her, and then she laughed, a low growl in her throat. "Oh, Alex," she said, walking toward him slowly, her hips swaying provocatively, "you're just trying to make me jealous." She wore a seductive smile, and one side of the wrapper she wore slipped down, revealing a well-shaped shoulder as well as a breast almost to the nipple.

Alex knew the wrapper had not slipped accidentally. He knew she had done it for him. Her mood had changed again. But maybe not so unpredictably this time. Maybe he really was learning to control her. And it wasn't so hard after all. Women liked for a man to put his foot down and show them who was boss.

She slid her hand between his legs and fondled him gently. He swayed toward her, feeling himself pulsating and swelling in her hand. He lowered his face to meet her lips, which were slightly parted and still wearing the seductive smile.

Suddenly he pulled back, writhing and groaning, trying to escape the iron-vise grip of her hand.

"None of my business, you say? It damned sure is my business. Anything you do is my business, because you belong to me. You understand that?" she asked, squeezing harder.

He tried to answer but could only nod desperately. He felt his knees go weak, and for a moment he thought he was going to faint.

"You belong to me to use until I'm through with you. See that you remember it," she said, letting go at last. "No more Lida Armstrong. You're my property." Alex managed only a hoarse groan. "And you tell your goddamned sister I want that raise."

Alex nodded and fumbled behind him for the door-knob. He found it and opened the door and limped out like a wounded dog. Slumping against the door and trembling with fear, he felt a wave of nausea pass over him at the thought of nothing but the flimsy wooden door separating him from the crazy and cruel Anna. But he still felt too weak to run. He knew he was going to have to find a way to get rid of her. But as he leaned his head against the door and closed his eyes, in spite of himself he shivered with pleasure, remembering the things she had done to him and taught him to do to her and Dovie. As the pain began to ease, he realized that even the way she had squeezed his balls just now had given him a perverse kind of pleasure.

He felt himself growing hard again, and with it came a new surge of pain that brought him back to his senses. He was going to stick to his first resolve, he told himself as he pushed away from the door and made his way down the hall. He was going to get rid of Anna. They could always hire someone else. Montana was paying top money now. And he was not going to get involved with whomever they hired, he promised himself. He wasn't going to risk hurting his wife any-more. She was all he needed anyway, he told himself.

By the time he was halfway down the hall, he was remembering Lida and her sweet, childlike volup-tuousness, and he knew he would miss that, too. He would miss her blind trust and the fact that she thought he was wonderful, as much as he would miss Anna's exotic cruelty.

His resolve might have weakened completely if he hadn't caught a glimpse of his wife through the open door to her room. She was seated at her dressing table, her back to him. At first he thought she was doing her endless bookkeeping, and the sight of her working like that filled him with guilt. He took a step inside the room. She heard him and turned around. It was then that he saw it was not an invoice she held in her hand but the tintype of the girls she had pulled from one of her trunks.

"Ivy, don't—"

"No," she whispered, protesting his use of the old name. But there was no anger, no fire, in her voice.

"Montana," he said, correcting himself. "You can't do this to yourself."

"I'm all right," she said, turning away from him.

But not before he had seen the tears in her eyes. He went to her and put his hands on her shoulders. "You have to forget. We both do."

"How can I forget? They were my children."

"Of course. What I mean is, we have to put it all behind us, stop thinking about going back." He waited for her protest, a stiffening of her shoulders, maybe. But she said nothing. He saw only that the tears were now streaming down her face.

"I don't know, Alex. I don't know what to think. It hurts sometimes, remembering the girls. But it would be worse not remembering them."

"No, no. You mustn't think about it. You must let me help you forget," he said, sliding his hands around to cup her breasts. She needed him. And as long as she needed him, she could forgive him.

Anna turned away from the door and pulled her wrapper over her shoulder and breasts with a quick, jerky movement. Then, running her fingers through her hair, she went to her trunk and rummaged through it, looking for her vial of laudanum. She remembered that there were only a few drops left, but it would have to do until she could get to Jake's, the little house behind one of the saloons, where she could go for a hit on the pipe in the company of others or where she could buy the opium to take home for her own pipe. If she could find the laudanum now, maybe there would be at least enough to take away the edge of her nervousness.

Dovie told her it was the cocaine powders that made her feel this way, but Dovie was a nagging bitch, good only for a few laughs and an erotic diversion now and then. It wasn't the cocaine that made her edgy now; it was that Alex and the Golden Palace weren't giving her what she wanted the way she'd thought they would.

What she wanted was money. Plenty of it. So she could leave the backwoods boom towns and get back to San Francisco in style. She never should have left in the first place. She knew that now, but she'd been young and foolish and looking for new kinds of excitement and pleasure, and she'd let herself be lured away by the promise of all that. All that as well as the promise of money to burn if she came to the gold fields of Colorado. She'd learned the hard way that all the excitement and pleasure ceased to be new after a while, and the money had to be earned by hard work—harder than anything she'd ever had to do in San Francisco. She was tired of it now. Tired of the rough miners and the country hicks.

Alex Miller was just another country hick, but she'd decided soon after she met him that he was going to be her ticket back to San Francisco. She would have taken a higher-paying job at the Central or at Johnny Nolton's if she hadn't seen Alex and realized quickly that she could use him. He had told her he was part owner of the Golden Palace, and she could see that he was horny as hell, unlike Johnny Nolton, who was happily married, or Titus Rogers over at the Central, who was too old to care. She figured she could use Alex Miller to get more money and eventually maybe even a share of the profits in the Golden Palace.

He was proving a little more difficult than she'd expected, however. She could get him to promise her anything, but he had a way of forgetting that promise as soon as he'd had his fill of her. Even if he was part owner of the Golden Palace, which she had reason to doubt now, he had very little say in the business. It was his sister and Langdon Runnels who made all the decisions. Neither of those two were as easy to manipulate.

She found the laudanum vial at last, but it was bone dry. Angry, she threw it to the floor and searched through her trunk for something to wear. She would have to go to Jake's.

She heard voices as she neared Montana's room on her way down the hall. One was male, and the thought that Montana McCrory would have a man in her room piqued her curiosity.

She shouldn't be surprised, she supposed. She'd seen the way Montana and Langdon Runnels looked at each other. What she couldn't figure out was why they worked so hard at concealing their feelings. Unless it was the fact that Montana was widowed and felt some obligation to what polite society called a suitable period of mourning. But it had been over a year since her husband died, and besides, a woman who ran a gambling saloon wasn't polite society. So if she was playing around with that idea, it was just another way for her to put on airs, like insisting that there would be no sex sold in her establishment.

She'd seen the way Montana looked at her and Dovie, too. Like she thought she was dealing with trash and had to see to their morals. Like she thought she was better than them. What would be delicious, Anna thought, would be to catch her with her man. That would show the hypocrite bitch who was trash.

Anna took a step toward the partially closed door and saw, through the narrow opening, the male figure standing behind Montana, and she saw the hands reach around to caress her breasts. Then he bent to kiss her on the neck, and she saw his face reflected in the mirror on the dressing table. Alex's face! Montana's brother!

Anna stepped back quickly when she saw Alex pulling Montana to her feet, but she still saw him kiss her full on the mouth. She flattened herself against the wall when he moved toward the door. The door closed softly, and Anna could hardly keep from laughing. Montana and Alex! Brother and sister! It was the last thing she had expected. Why, to think that bitch was acting so high and mighty, while all the time she was fucking her brother!

A satisfied smile parted her lips as she walked down the hall. She had just what she needed to get what she wanted out of Alex and Montana.

Anna appeared for work as usual that night, and Alex knew as soon as he saw her that she'd been hitting the pipe. She staggered as she came down the stairs and then sagged onto a chair at one of the tables. When Clay Tuttle asked her to dance, she hissed an obscenity at him. Alex glanced around quickly to see if Montana had heard, but she was across the room, dealing blackjack. He made his way to Anna.

"I heard what you said to Clay." He glared at her. "We can't have you talking to the customers like that. And we can't have you drunk on opium when you're at work."

"Just what do you think you can do about it?" The sound of her defiance was heavy and thick from the drug.

"I can fire you, that's what," Alex said, buoyant with confidence from his afternoon with Montana, certain she would never believe any of Anna's vile accusations.

Anna smiled and stood up. "You can't do a goddamned thing to me, you little bastard, because I've got you by the balls. By this time tomorrow, I'll have 'em roasted and served to me on a silver platter." With that, she laughed in his face and turned away, weaving and staggering up the stairs.

Alex watched her go, fighting back anger that she had dared to insult him. Well, he would deal with her tomorrow. For now it was just as well that she had left the saloon, since she was in no shape to dance with the customers.

Anna did not show herself again the rest of the night, and Alex heard Dovie making an excuse for her to Montana. Tomorrow, when there was more time, he would tell Montana that Anna was a dope fiend and they had to get rid of her.

The evening passed uneventfully until Alex saw the pimply-faced youth who emptied cuspidors at the Central standing outside the door and signaling to him. When he went to the door, the boy handed him a note. Alex looked around nervously to see that no one was looking, then took it and read it quickly. It was from Lida, telling him she had to see him tonight and that it was urgent. Alex crumpled the note and threw it into the gutter.

"Tell her I can't come," he said. "Tell her I'm busy working." The last thing he needed was to go to Lida. He had to hold to his resolve not to hurt Montana.

"She told me not to leave until you said you'd come," the boy said. "She said I was to stay here until I made you understand that it's mighty important, and that you had to promise to come tonight."

"I told you, I can't. I'm busy." Alex turned aside to enter the Golden Palace again, but the boy followed him.

"She said I was to stay with you until you come with me," he insisted. "She said it was important. She said I wasn't to take no for an answer."

Alex made another nervous survey of the room to make certain no one saw him, then he hurried out of the saloon, pushing the boy in front of him. "All right," he said in a hushed tone. "I'll go with you, but we've got to make this fast before anybody notices I'm gone."

The boy led the way past the garish lights of the other saloons along Myrtle Avenue to the back entrance of the Central Dance Hall. Alex climbed the back steps and knocked quietly on Lida's door. She opened it immediately and smiled at the boy, handing him a coin.

"Come in, Alex," she said, pulling him inside. Warmth from the gasoline heater surrounded him, made thicker and heavier by the cloying sweetness of Lida's toilet water.

"What is it that's so urgent?" he asked, agitated. "I got to get back to work before I'm missed."

"It's all right," she said, running her hands up his

chest and encircling his neck. "I just wanted you to know right away. I couldn't wait until morning."

"You wanted me to know what?"

"That I'm pregnant."

Alex felt his heart fall to his stomach. "Are you sure?"

"I saw the doctor this afternoon." She dropped her arms from around his neck when she saw his stricken expression. "I thought you'd be happy."

"Lida, I—"

"It's yours," she said, near tears. "If you're thinking there's any doubt about that, you're wrong. I haven't been with anybody else."

"It's not that, it's just that I—I didn't expect—"

"But you are happy, aren't you?" she asked, hopeful again. "I knew you would be. We can get married right away."

"Married? My God, Lida, I can't."

The blood drained from her face, and she stared at him a moment before she began to cry. "You can't let me be disgraced! You can't let our child grow up a bastard! You have to help me. How can I make a living if I'm pregnant and can't work?"

She cried so bitterly and hard that he thought she would be sick. He put his arms around her and spoke to her soothingly. "It's all right," he said. "I won't let you be disgraced. I won't let you raise a bastard."

"You'll marry me, then?" she asked through her tears.

"I don't know. I—"

"You have to!" she wailed again. "You have to marry me."

"Yes. Yes," he said in desperation, willing to say anything to calm her. "Yes, I'll—we'll work something out. We'll talk about it tomorrow. I have to get back to work now."

"But you will marry me."

"Tomorrow, Lida," he said, easing his way out. "We'll talk about it tomorrow."

He was sweating and near sick to his stomach by the time he got back to the Golden Palace. No one seemed to have noticed he'd gone, and somehow he made it through until closing time. But he was consumed with worry as he made his way up the stairs to the attic room he shared with Langdon. He no longer spent every night with Montana, since it was so late when she came to bed, and tonight he certainly needed to be alone. He lay awake, staring into the darkness and trying to think of a way out of the mess he'd gotten himself into. There were people who could do some kind of operation on a woman and get rid of a baby. Abortion, it was called. But it was an evil thing, illegal and dangerous. Women often died afterward, he'd heard. He hated the thought of having either the abortion or Lida's death on his conscience.

He was still awake when Langdon got into the bed across the room, and it wasn't until dawn that he had woven together a solution. He'd tell Lida he was already married to a woman in Chicago. That seemed a distant enough place that she wouldn't be able to check up on him. He would tell her that his wife was insane and in an asylum. He would tell Lida that while he loved her very much, he could not divorce his poor wife. Lida would understand, he was sure. He was also sure that she would not want to raise an illegitimate child, and then the abortion would be her decision, and he wouldn't have to have it on his conscience.

In spite of the fact that he'd thought of a plan, when morning came, he still dreaded the confrontation. Before he went to the Central, he stopped by Dick

Shaw's High Grade Saloon for fortification and spent the rest of the morning and part of the afternoon there.

Montana felt the blood drain from her face and her heart thudding wildly in her chest at the words Anna had just spoken.

"How dare you accuse me of such a thing? And with my—my brother!"

Anna laughed and leaned back in her chair, throwing her arm across the top in a casual gesture that made her look like a defiant boy. She had come into Montana's office unbidden, sat herself down, and relayed with chilling arrogance what she had seen.

"Don't play the high-and-mighty queen with me, little sister. I saw you. With my own eyes. Yesterday. At about three o'clock in the afternoon. You was in your room, and he come up behind you, like this." Anna stood and walked behind Montana, bringing her hands around to cup her breasts. Montana pushed her aside quickly, and Anna laughed. "I saw him kiss you," she said, going back to her chair. "Then he took you to bed and put it to you, little sister. I saw it all."

Montana struggled to stay calm, but her mind raced, trying to remember. Had they left the door open? Surely not. They were always so careful. Surely the woman was lying. But how could she know she had been crying and that Alex was comforting her? How could she know that she had gone to bed, dutifully, with her husband?

"You are mistaken," she said. "My brother often stops by my room to discuss business, but I won't have you accusing—"

"I saw it and you know it, and I'm telling you

you're going to pay for what I saw."

"And I'm telling you to get out." Montana did not raise her voice, but there was no mistaking the cold, dangerous chill in her eyes.

Anna laughed again, but this time the sound was less arrogant. "Do you know what you're saying? If you kick me out, I'll spread this story all over town. Do you know what that will do to you? And I'm not talking about just the ladies' sewing circles and the church folks. I'm talking about your customers. They'll avoid you like the plague."

Montana stood suddenly. The chair she'd been sitting on toppled over, shuddering as it hit the floor. "I said get out. It doesn't matter what you say. No one will believe your filthy lies."

Anna's eyes showed a flicker of emotion. "I'll ruin you," she said. Then she laughed. "Does Langdon Runnels know he's not the only one gettin' it?"

"Mr. Runnels, of all people, will know you're lying." Montana was acutely grateful for the alibi Anna had just unwittingly suggested. "He was the one in my room yesterday."

"Like hell it was Runnels!"

"He will attest to it, and my brother will assure anyone who asks that he was not there. And if you're not out of the Golden Palace in fifteen minutes, I'll personally throw you out. I don't ever want to see you again or hear any more of your filthy lies."

"You bitch," Anna said, rising to her feet. "You're the one who's lying. I happen to know Langdon is off in the mountains digging for gold. And I know what I saw."

"Fifteen minutes," Montana said coldly.

Anna moved toward the door, but before she left she turned back, her eyes blazing. "You can kick me out, but you're still going to pay, little sister."

When Anna had slammed the door behind her, Montana braced herself against her desk and tried with desperation to collect her thoughts.

The woman had seen something, undoubtedly, and she was just ruthless enough to spread the story. Would people believe her? She sank onto her chair and put her head in her hands. No matter what people might or might not believe, the fact remained that she and Alex had to be more careful. It would be best if they abstained completely. For now, though, she had to find Alex, to warn him about what to expect, and to tell him to stick with her on the alibi she'd made up about being with Langdon.

She left her office and walked into the saloon. A few customers sat at the tables, and Diana was behind the bar, but Alex was nowhere in sight.

Alex had drunk enough whiskey to make his gait a little unsteady as he left the High Grade Saloon and approached the Central Dance Hall, but he wasn't so drunk that he forgot to look around cautiously to make certain no one was watching before he walked to the back entrance and headed up the stairs, just as he had done a number of times in the past. He knocked on Lida's door softly. No answer. That was sure as hell strange. He knew she was in there; he could hear her shuffling around. He knocked again. At last she came to the door. He could see that she'd been crying, and she looked sullen.

"Hello, Lida." He gave her his most charming smile. She didn't smile back, and he thought for a minute she was going to shut the door in his face, but she stepped aside, wordlessly inviting him in.

The room was as stifling as it had been the night before. "What took you so long?" she asked over her shoulder.

"I had important work to do this morning," he said, noticing the spot where the white flesh of her shoulders met her equally white and inviting neck.

"I'll just bet you did."

He had never known her to be sarcastic before. This was going to be even harder than he had thought. "Lida . . ." He reached to touch her arm, but she jerked away.

"You came here to tell me something," she said. "You're going to tell me when we can get married."

Alex opened his mouth to speak, but no words would come. Now was not the time to lose his nerve. He forced himself to say something. "I—I came to tell you something, yes. And the first thing I have to tell you is that I—I love you."

She whirled toward him. "You mean that?"

"Of course I do," he said.

"You're drunk, and I don't believe you," she said, turning away again.

"Lida—"

"You had to get drunk so you'd have the courage to tell me you can't marry me because there's someone else."

Alex put his arms around her from behind and held her close to his chest. "There's no one else I love the way I love you, Lida."

"But you're sleeping with someone else."

"Of course I'm not sleeping with anyone else." He moved one hand to fondle her breasts while the other slid downward to massage her stomach, then lower.

Lida caught her breath, leaning against him and

grinding her buttocks against his groin. "You're going to marry me, then? We can live in your room at the Palace until the baby is born and—"

"Lida, as much as I want that, too, I can't."

"What?" She pulled away from him suddenly and faced him, and this time he saw unmistakable anger in her face.

"I can't, Lida. You see, I'm—"

"It's not that you can't!" she screamed. "It's that you won't! And I know why. Don't think I don't know. It's that whore you're sleeping with."

"What?"

"Montana. You're sleeping with that whore Montana. Your own sister!"

Alex raised his hand and struck her face, sending her staggering backward. No one called his darling Ivy a whore or accused her of vile things. Not even soft and inviting Lida.

Lida stumbled to regain her balance, a hand against her red-marked cheek. Then she hurled herself toward him in a rage, pounding his chest with her plump fists, crying and screaming hysterically. "All the time you were making love to me, you were doing it to her, too, you dirty, filthy—"

"Stop it, Lida! Stop it! You're hysterical. You know what you said isn't true, and if you dare repeat it again, I'll—"

"But it is true!" Lida screamed. "She saw it with her own eyes. She told me."

"Who told you? What are you talking about?"

"Tell him, Anna! Tell him what you saw!" Lida screamed to the dressing screen she kept in a corner of the room.

Anna emerged like a stretching cat from behind

the screen. Her lips were tight with anger and malice. "It's true, Alex. I saw it all. You ought to be more careful about closing the door."

"You goddamned liar! I'll—" He lunged for her, but she backed away, and he stumbled.

"Oh, no, Alex, it's not a lie. I told your sister, and she knows it's no lie. Only she didn't think anyone would believe me. She was wrong, though, wasn't she? Lida believed me. And so will everyone else. I'm going to ruin you both, Alex."

"You're crazy, Anna. What do you hope to gain from this?" He felt sick and suddenly cold sober.

"Satisfaction. Your sister wasn't smart enough to give me the money I wanted, so I have to settle for the satisfaction of seeing you ruined."

"Why, you—" He reached for again and this time grabbed her arm.

"You certainly didn't think I was fucking you for the fun of it, did you?" she asked, trying to wrench her arm free.

Alex held her even tighter. "Tell Lida it's a lie!" he demanded.

Anna kicked at him and twisted her body, trying to free herself. He shoved her hard against the wall, and as she tried to keep her balance, one of her feet caught the edge of the gasoline stove and tipped it over. Suddenly a river of flame spread across the wooden floor. Alex heard both Lida and Anna scream, and he saw Lida try to skirt around the tributaries of fire rushing out in all directions across the dry wooden floor planks. A wave of flame washed against the posts of Lida's bed and in the next instant poured itself over it. Lida and Anna both screamed again as a cloud of gray smoke exploded from the bed.

Alex saw the two women dancing about, trying frantically to find a way past the flames. Smoke burned his eyes and filled his lungs, but he had seen a pathway out. The fire was surging like a tidal wave up the wall behind the bed, but it had not yet touched the wall opposite the bed. If he took both their hands and guided them, they might make it to the door.

In a split second he saw a solution to the problems each had created. If he reached for neither hand and inched his way alone along the wall . . . The moment passed in the blink of an eye, and he reached, but with his right hand only, grasping Lida's arm. Out of the corner of his eye he saw Anna's hand flailing for him. He made no attempt to reach her as he moved away, pulling Lida along with him. Anna tried to follow, but he knocked over a chair, blocking her way, willing himself not to hear her screams.

With more strength than he knew he had, he kicked the door down and pushed Lida ahead of him into the hallway. She was screaming, too, and he saw scarlet ribbons of flame leaping from her dress to her hair and face. He forced her to the floor and rolled her over and over on the faded carpet until the flames were smothered.

The hallway was filling with smoke, and the other girls who had been in their rooms were pushing their way out. Alex picked Lida up in his arms and ran with the others toward the stairs. Behind him he heard the sound of a burning rafter crashing to the floor in Lida's room and, along with the crash, a scream like that of a dying cat.

11

Smoke burned his eyes and his lungs, and he was vaguely aware of pain in his hands as well as the press of other bodies trying to push past him down the back stairway. He was first out the door, with Lida unconscious in his arms. He tried to take in great gulps of the fresh air, but the effort made him weak. Just as he was about to fall, someone caught him and relieved him of the heavy weight of Lida.

"Fire," Alex managed to gasp.

"The others are trapped!" someone screamed. It must have been one of the girls, but Alex could not be sure. The last thing he remembered before a swirling darkness overcame him was the sight of embers from the blazing building floating across the street.

Anna's threat weighed heavily on Montana, and she had searched for Alex so together they could decide what to do, how seriously it must be taken.

But Alex was nowhere to be found, and she tried to think it through alone, tried to remain calm.

She heard the shouts in the street but thought little of it—just someone getting an early start on a good time, she assumed. Then she heard the fire engine clanging, and she stood up from her desk and hurried to the front of the saloon. Diana ran from behind the bar, and the two of them met at the entrance. The air was choked with smoke, and they could see arms of flame flailing outward from a building down the street. The fire engine, pulled by two draft horses, had stopped in front. Men jumped down from the engine, taking hoses and ropes with them.

"It's the Central!" Diana cried.

"Look!" Montana shouted, pointing to the High Grade Saloon across the street from the dance hall. Embers had already ignited the saloon's dry, wooden-shingled roof.

"It's spreading north," Diana shouted. "If the wind don't die down, we'll be—"

Suddenly the roof of a small clapboard house across a vacant lot from the High Grade exploded. "It's going east, too," Montana said, "toward the miners' houses. "Come on!" She picked up her skirts and ran toward the residential section. "We've got to help those people get out of there!" She stopped and turned to Diana. "Wait! Go back inside and tell Dovie to come downstairs. She could be trapped up there if it spreads over here. Anna left earlier, so don't worry about her. I looked for Alex upstairs, but I didn't find him. Check again! Make sure he's not there!"

Diana turned back to the Golden Palace, and Montana ran toward the Central. She saw the faces of the women at the open windows of their living quarters above the dance hall, and she could hear their frantic cries for help. Firemen were throwing ropes to the windows, and some of the girls had managed to grab them and were now climbing down. Other firemen were sending heavy streams of water onto the building from the tank at the back of the wagon.

"The High Grade's as good as gone, and the Butte Opera House will be next!" someone shouted.

"We got to get the water hose up the hill. Got to connect it directly to the reservoir," another voice cried.

Montana grabbed the arm of one of the men in the crowd. "Get down to the freight company," she said. "Tell them to bring the freight wagons to load those people's furnishings in. We've got to get them out before it's too late."

Montana worked beside others for what seemed like hours, moving children and armloads of household goods into wagons that pulled it all up the hill to the city reservoir, which was upwind of the fire. By then the blaze had consumed six of the one-girl cribs on Myrtle Avenue and was raging toward Pearl DuVal's parlor house. People were saying the whole town soon would be burning.

After a while Montana saw that Diana had joined the crowd of volunteers trying to evacuate homes and buildings in the path of the fire. Her sleeves were rolled to her elbows, and her face was streaked with soot as she lifted a small girl into a wagon. Montana had spotted Dovie in one of the wagons rolling toward the reservoir, but she'd seen nothing of Alex, and she tried to make her way toward Diana to ask if she had seen him.

A woman stopped her, however, and asked her to help move a sewing machine into one of the wagons. Montana recognized the townswoman who had snubbed her weeks earlier when she was with Langdon. The woman, who held a child in her arms while another clung to her skirt, also realized whom she had asked for help, and her face, already pale with fear, blanched even more.

"Take the children to the wagon," Montana said. "I'll see that your sewing machine is loaded."

The woman nodded and wordlessly turned away with her two youngsters. Montana tried to push the sewing machine toward the wagon, and finally a man walking by offered to help her. "Hell of a blaze," he said. "Heard it started in the Central, in one of the girls' rooms. Said she was in there with her lover."

"Musta been quite a romp," another man said. "Heard they got so wild they kicked over the stove."

A deafening roar interrupted the gossip as a large building burst into flames.

"The Portland Hotel!" one of the men shouted. "By God, I was in there myself just a little while ago."

Half an hour later the Portland had not ceased raging, and when the roof collapsed it sent embers flying to the tops of nearby houses and stores that almost immediately burst into flames. By now the whole town swarmed like a mass of startled insects, with everyone trying to rescue as much as possible from the burning structures.

The task was becoming more and more difficult. Montana saw building after building consumed before anything could be saved. There had been deaths and tragic injuries, too. She'd heard that the Sisters of Mercy Hospital was full.

Still, she searched the crowds for Alex, her fear growing that he might be among the injured or dead. But she could not allow herself to believe that. She had to believe that he was somewhere in the mass of people at the top of the hill near the reservoir or in the human chain that slogged back and forth saving household goods. She had lost sight of Diana now, too, and so had lost her opportunity to ask if she had seen Alex. She did ask about him of everyone else she saw, but no one claimed to have seen him.

Within a few hours word was out that one of the wealthy mine owners had hired the railroad to send a train from Colorado Springs loaded with supplies to aid the scores of homeless. With fifty miles of mountainous terrain to cross, it would be hours before the train arrived.

When Montana stopped to catch her breath and to wipe the black soot from her face with her forearm, she saw, from the top of the hill, that the blaze had now reached the Pikes Peak Grocery. That meant it was inching northward, toward the Golden Palace. The fire was still several blocks from her saloon, though; it could be stopped before it reached there. But she wasn't going to take any chances. She had to get down there, to try to remove what she could while there was still time.

She'd gotten only a few steps down the hill when she saw Langdon, his face and shirt streaked with smoke and sweat. Their gazes locked for a moment before either of them spoke. "I thought you were in the mountains," she said at last, her voice thready. "Working your claim."

"I was. I saw the smoke."

She nodded. "Have you seen Alex?"

Before Langdon could answer, a deafening blast filled the valley, and a column of smoke billowed some distance from the main body of the fire. "They must have dynamited those shacks over on Third Street. That ought to keep the fire from reaching the hospital," he said.

"Langdon!" someone shouted from behind them. "Over here. We need your help!" Langdon and Montana turned to see a group of men trying to right an overturned cart that had been loaded with furniture.

"Go up to the top of the hill," Langdon said as he turned away. "You look like you need a rest. How long you been at this, anyway?"

"Since noon, but I—"

"Langdon!" someone shouted again, and he hurried away before she could say any more.

Montana turned her eyes back to the town. What she saw horrified her. The roof of the Eagleton Harness Shop was burning, and only a vacant lot separated it from the Golden Palace.

Forgetting her fatigue and her aching limbs, she ran down the hill toward the Palace. When she reached the front door, she could see Diana in the back, stuffing papers from the desk into a pillowcase.

"Diana!" Though hoarse with fatigue, her voice conveyed the relief she felt at seeing her. She paused, gasping for breath and steadying herself against one of the tables.

Diana glanced at her, alarmed. "I thought you was up on the hill with the others."

"Have you seen Alex?" Montana gasped.

"No. He wasn't upstairs when I went up for Dovie. She's already at the top of the hill. That's where you ought to be. It's not safe here."

"Then why are you here?"

Diana picked up another handful of papers and stuffed them into the pillowcase. "I thought I ought to get as much out as I could. I already got some of the barrels of whiskey and the new roulette wheel. Borrowed a wagon to put the stuff in. It's in the back." She opened another drawer and dumped its contents into the pillowcase. "I got all the cash Alex hadn't already took to the bank. Just thought I'd get these papers, too. Figured you'd need them."

"I'm going to need you worse, Diana!" Montana cried. "Go on. Get out of here!"

A strange and gentle crackling sound drew their eyes upward. "It's here!" Diana whispered.

Montana raced to Diana's side and took her hand, pulling her toward the door as the crackling became a roar. "Alex!" Montana screamed, hesitating before they reached the door. "He may be up there!"

"No!" Diana said. "I told you, I looked. And you looked, too. Besides, even he would have better sense than to stay up there."

"But he might have come back to look for me. I've got to make sure." She broke away, running toward the stairs.

"He's not there!" Diana shouted from the doorway. "I looked. I looked in your room, too." Her words were lost in the roar of the fire on the roof.

The smoke was so thick at the top of the stairs, Montana had difficulty seeing, and she had to grope along the walls to find her way. She went to her room first, calling for Alex, but there was no answer. She turned away just as a portion of the ceiling crashed to the floor. She tried to make it to Anna and Dovie's room, but smoke burned her eyes and lungs, and she dropped to the floor.

She heard someone shouting downstairs. "Where's Montana?" the voice called. "Is she in there? God-damn it, is she in there?"

Montana tried to answer, but she could manage only a rasping cough. She inched her way to the landing, and she could see, through the smoke, a figure moving up the stairs. By the time he reached the top, he was crawling on his hands and knees to stay as close to the floor as possible, where the smoke was less dense. She saw that it was Langdon and reached out for him. He pulled her toward him, then stood and awkwardly picked her up, carrying her down the stairs and outside. Neither of them could speak for a while, coughing and gagging from the smoke. Finally Montana made a move toward the building.

"Alex," she said. "I couldn't be sure he wasn't up there. I couldn't see. The smoke—" A fit of coughing interrupted her.

"Alex isn't up there," Langdon said angrily.

"But I haven't seen him all day. He wasn't at the reservoir or with any of the volunteers."

"Alex is at the hospital," Langdon said, still sounding angry. "Don't worry, he'll be all right," he added when he saw the fear on her face. "Just burned his hands, swallowed a little smoke."

"But how—"

"He—he was burned rescuing someone," Langdon said quickly. He shot a glance toward Diana, as if the two of them knew something they were trying to hide from her.

"Must have happened early," Montana said. She was still gasping for breath. "He must have joined the volunteers right at the beginning."

"Yeah," Langdon said. He turned his gaze toward the fire. "We've got to get out of here."

He urged Montana toward the wagon and helped her onto the seat, then swung himself up beside her. Diana was already aboard and had picked up the reins.

Montana turned back to look at the burning saloon. "It's gone," she said, her voice oddly flat and devoid of emotion. "One more time, all I have is gone."

"No," Diana said. "It ain't all gone. Just the building. We'll find a way to start over. You'll see."

Montana turned to Diana. "I can't expect you to stay," she said. "We'll have to rebuild. There'll be no money to pay you. Not for a while, at least."

"I'll stay," Diana said gruffly. "Long as you do." She flicked the reins across the backs of the horses and started the wagon rolling.

"I want to see him," Montana said.

Without a word or so much as glance at either Montana or Langdon, Diana turned the horses toward the hospital.

In spite of the flurry of activity inside, the Sisters of Mercy Hospital looked peaceful as they approached. It was still a safe distance from the fire. As the wagon drew closer, Montana saw the windows flooded with light from oil lamps, since the electricity had been cut off by the fire. Silhouettes of nuns moved through rooms full of patients.

"We'll wait here," Diana said when she had pulled the wagon to a stop. It sounded like a command, but Langdon obviously chose to ignore it.

He got down from the wagon and escorted Montana inside. He stayed with her as she picked her way through the crowds of bandaged patients lining the hallways, asking each nurse she saw about Alex Miller.

No one seemed to know for certain whether he was among the patients. The day had been too hectic to remember names. Finally, though, Montana found someone who did remember.

"Mr. Miller? Of course. He's here."

"Is he all right?"

The nun pulled bandages and salves from a shelf, placing them on a tray. "Some burns on his hands," she said, still busy looking for bandages. "There'll be some scars, but he'll heal." She turned away, carrying her tray of supplies down the hall.

"Where is he? Can I see him?" Montana called to her.

"You're his sister, aren't you?" the nun asked, turning to face her. She gave her a long, scrutinizing look.

Montana was aware for the first time of how she must look, her hair disheveled and her face and dress streaked with soot. "Yes," she said. "I'm his sister."

The nun nodded. "I thought so." She seemed to hesitate before she added, "I expect he'd appreciate a visit from a relative. Must have a lot on his conscience."

"I beg your pardon?"

"Talk is, your brother was the one started this mess," the nun said, her lips growing tight. "It was him that was in the room with his girlfriend whoopin' it up when they kicked over the stove."

Montana felt suddenly too weak to stand, and she grasped the edge of a table to steady herself. Langdon made a move toward her but stopped short. The nun didn't seem to notice. She simply nodded toward one of the rooms. "He's in there. He's been asking to see the young woman, but she's got burns just about all over her body. We gave her laudanum to make her sleep."

"Are you sure Alex is—"

"I told you, Mr. Miller's fine. He was lucky. It's a wonder they both weren't burned worse than they were." The nun gave Montana a professional frown. "You all right, miss? You look pale."

"Yes," Montana managed to say. "I'm fine."

"Go on in to see your brother," she said with a grim expression. She nodded again toward the room. "He'd probably appreciate seeing a friendly face."

Montana watched the nurse disappear into a room down the hall, then she stared at the closed door that led to Alex. She was aware of Langdon close by her side now. "Did you know?" she asked.

"I heard the rumors."

"And you didn't tell me."

"What purpose would it have served?"

She kept her eyes on the door for several seconds, then she turned away.

"You're not going in to see him?"

She didn't answer but kept walking toward the entrance to the hospital. She couldn't see Alex now. Not when she was so angry and confused. What could she say to him? How would she know what she was supposed to feel? There was just too much to sort through. Way too much.

Langdon followed her to the wagon, where Diana waited. Diana didn't inquire about Alex. She merely flicked the reins and headed the horses up the hill.

Montana sat in silence, numbed by exhaustion, confusion, and rage. Then the horror of the scene around her forced her thoughts in another direction. The fire had destroyed more than half the town. It had now subsided to a few remnant flames and scattered plumes of smoke rising toward the darkening sky. The wind, which had whipped the blaze all afternoon, had finally calmed. Looting had begun along the rows of burned-out houses, and a committee of vigilantes walked the streets, trying to control it.

The wagon moved past the town's three churches, already filled with homeless families for the night. There would be no room for the threesome there. Diana headed the wagon up the hill toward the reservoir, where a large crowd who couldn't find room in the churches waited, shivering in the cold night air and milling around in a subdued silence, turning their eyes frequently toward the pass, over which the relief train from Colorado Springs would travel.

Diana had hardly stopped the wagon when the crowd exploded into shouts and whistles as the glow of the train's lights were spotted several miles away. The three of them silently watched the Special race down the slope into town, looking like a moving display of holiday fireworks as the fireboxes spewed coals and the wheels spun out circles of glowing sparks from the brakes.

As soon as the train stopped, the crowd erupted into a torrent of activity. More carts were sent to join freight wagons already waiting to receive goods from the train. Someone shouted for Langdon to help unload the supplies. Montana was asked to help distribute food and blankets and tents. She was grateful for the task. It might keep her mind off Alex and the fire and the Golden Palace.

Later, as it neared midnight, she stood wrapped in a blanket, leaning against a wagon wheel. Among all the supplies she had distributed, the blanket was the only thing she had managed to get for herself. She had taken her turn at the public washstands that had been set up and had removed at least some of the soot and dirt from her face. She rested now in the light of a lantern, grateful for the growing numbness her exhaustion had brought, when she saw Langdon moving out of the shadows toward her.

"Are you all right?" he asked.

"I'm fine."

"I'm sorry you had to hear that Alex—"

"I said I'm fine."

He studied her face. "Had anything to eat?"

"No."

"Neither have I. But I got a couple of cans of beans and a box of crackers, and I have a tent."

She hesitated only a moment, then let him lead her away. He had warmed the beans and boiled coffee on a campfire outside the tent, and he brought them inside, where she sat on a flimsy cot. He settled across from her on a stack of blankets, eating his own plate of beans. They ate without speaking, the only sounds the scrape of forks against tin plates and the subdued murmur of others outside. Langdon had already doused the campfire, and the only light came from a small lantern in a corner of the tent, its soft glow sending long shadows swaying across the canvas.

Montana was the first to break the silence. "The whole town must have known," she said, raising her eyes to look at him. "Was I too busy to see? How long has it been going on?"

"Long enough for the whole town to know," he said without looking at her, intent on his food.

She turned her gaze to the closed flap of the tent.

"Does it matter to you?" Langdon asked, looking at her now.

She turned to face him. "I'm his wife."

"Does it matter?" he asked again. "Be honest with yourself for once, Montana."

She looked at him for a long moment. "I am being honest with myself," she said at last. "Why do you think I came to your tent?"

Her words startled him. Their eyes met and locked, his questioning, hers saying yes.

"Montana, are you sure?"

"I'm sure."

There was another brief silence while Langdon's mind raced. He had connived for this moment since he'd met her. How could he now be so completely unprepared for her submission?

"I don't want you to have regrets. I don't want to think you're only doing it to get back at him for what he did," he said.

"Don't examine me too closely," she said, lowering her eyes.

"Why are you afraid of that? Are you afraid I won't like what I see? Is it that you don't like what you yourself see?"

"Don't confuse me, Langdon. Don't—"

"Don't use me for revenge."

She looked up at him. "I need you. Isn't that enough?"

Something in her voice—vulnerability—caught him, and he reached, involuntarily, he thought, to touch her face. She caught his hand and held it, more a self-protecting gesture than an act of tenderness. "I'll never seek revenge against him again. I wouldn't use anyone for that." She looked at him a moment, then stood up and moved away from him. "I'm being brazen. I didn't mean—"

"Montana—"

"You told me once I should think of myself more," she said, turning back to him, troubled, agonizing. "You said I should think of what I want. Can't you see I don't know how? Can't you see I'm not good at this?"

Langdon was up and beside her, his hands on her shoulders, turning her around. They were very close. He could hear her breath coming in shallow gasps, feel it on his face. His inclination was to kiss her, but he resisted, knowing he must not rush her now. Slowly, wordlessly, he reached a hand to her hair and pulled away, one by one, the few celluloid pins that remained. The dark mass reflected highlights of red gold in the lantern light as it tumbled to her shoulders. He combed it with his fingers and brought a strand to his lips, watching her. Her eyes held his until he dropped the strand of hair and pushed the mass of it back, moving his mouth toward hers.

Her lips were tight at first, but they parted slightly, opening a small, warm wetness to him. He felt the pleasure of exploring her with his tongue, of tasting the sweet dampness, and he felt her hands move to his back, resting there with feathery lightness at first. Her lips seemed to grow fuller under his and her mouth more inviting, pulling him in with little sucking movements, inviting him to explore deeper. Then she tilted her head back, exposing her throat to him, and he claimed it with kisses and delicate bites.

"I need you, Montana," he whispered. "As I've never needed a woman before."

She tried to speak, but the pulse beating in her throat kept her from it. She felt his hand there, fumbling with a button. He pulled away from her then and held her only with his eyes while he unfastened the first button, and then the second one, and the next and the next, slowly and carefully, without so much as touching her until they were all undone.

Her chemise, damp with sweat, clung to her bosom, revealing her taut nipples. He untied the laces, freeing her breasts, and she in turn reached for his shirt and unbuttoned it, then pushed it down over his shoulders. His skin was dark and his chest sculpted with muscles. A mass of black hair spread across the expanse and thinned to a line that ran toward his groin. Montana felt her face grow warm and felt the pulsating in her throat again. She wanted to run. Wanted to stay. Didn't know what she might have done had he not pulled her toward him, pressing his chest against her heaving breasts while his mouth claimed hers again. Then, with great care, he brought her down with him on the narrow cot.

"I've wanted this for so long," he whispered.

She tried to tell him she'd wanted the same, but his mouth was on hers, preventing her from speaking.

His hands pulled at her skirt, inching it up, fingers finding the top of her underwear, inching it down, until she was free of it and he could slide his hands underneath her and touch bare thighs and buttocks. Her skirt gathered in bunched folds at her waist, leaving her exposed, naked, and her chemise had fallen away, leaving her breasts bare.

He raised himself above her only long enough to unbutton his trousers, and she felt a moment of shock, a moment of hesitancy, of wanting to turn back when the weight and heat of his penis fell against her. He moved away from her for a moment to free himself of his trousers.

In the next instant he was reaching for her, parting her legs, and she knew the moment of turning back had passed. He moved on top of her, covering her. And suddenly he was inside.

A sharp intake of breath. A whispered "Oh, my Lord!"

She heard his voice, too, small, deep sounds. She felt him shift, as if to penetrate deeper, and felt the flimsy cot start to buckle. He dropped a leg to the floor for balance and shifted his weight, pulling away for a moment, reaching for her to move her to the floor.

For one brief moment, for the blink of an eye, he looked at her, seeing her there, her dress pulled up, legs spread, exposed to him, waiting, yielding, and a vision of her that first day on the prairie flashed in his mind. He picked her up, moved her to the floor, and entered her again with a groan of pleasure. And he knew, as she did, that they had both known since that very first day that this moment was coming.

12

Langdon awoke first and lay watching Montana sleep in the bed they had made for themselves on the floor of the tent. Her hair was draped along her bare shoulders, and her face was relaxed and peaceful. She was beautiful, he thought, and it now seemed odd that he had thought her little more than plain when he'd first seen her on the train.

He had known that someday this moment would come, when he would have her in his bed, but he had not expected to be in love with her when it happened.

It had frightened him when Diana told him Montana had gone into the Golden Palace to look for Alex, and he would have gone through the fires of hell to save her. He wanted just as badly to save her now from Alex. She was destroying herself by staying with him, the way his mother had destroyed herself by staying with his father. He had wanted to save his mother, but he had been too young to know how, and then, when he was older, it had been too late. It wasn't too late for

Montana, though. He could take her away. They could move to Colorado Springs, and he would still be close enough to work the Honesty now and then. Or if she wanted, he'd sell the claim, and they could find another gold field somewhere. Alaska, maybe, or Canada.

She stirred slightly, then her eyes opened slowly. When she saw him she smiled, a lazy, sleepy smile, and touched his face with her fingertips. He caught her hand and kissed it, then pulled her toward him. She protested at first, whispered, "No, I mustn't," but he held her for a moment, stroking her hair, kissing her, coaxing her until she responded, and they made love again.

Afterward he held her in his arms, their bodies pressed together, warming each other against the crisp autumn morning. Her head was resting on his shoulder, and he couldn't see her face. "Come away with me," he whispered. She didn't answer, but he felt her stiffen slightly. "Come away with me," he said again.

"I can't," she whispered. "You know that."

"No," he said. "I don't know that. And neither do you. You don't love Alex. Don't lie to yourself about that."

"I told you last night. He *is* my husband." She pulled away from him and sat up. Her hair tumbled over her shoulders and curled at the tops of her bare breasts, and he thought he had never seen anything more lovely or more desirable. She reached for her dress, but before she could pull it over her head, he took it from her and turned her around to face him.

"I love you, Montana. I want you with me. Tell me, if you can, that you don't love me."

She tried to look away, but he grasped her chin, turning her face toward him. "Yes." Her voice trembled. "Yes, God forgive me, I do love you. I have for a long time. But I am married! I am Alex Barton's wife."

He dropped his hand from her face. "Ivy Barton was his wife. You told me yourself, she died. Ivy Barton no longer exists."

"Langdon, please. Don't make it harder for me."

"It doesn't seem to me that I'm the one who's making it hard for you," he said sharply. "You're doing it to yourself. Why? Why did you even come to me last night if you knew you weren't going to leave him?"

"Oh, Langdon!" Her eyes were bright, as if she might be about to cry. "I told you the truth last night. I needed you. And I told you the truth when I said I loved you. I'm not sorry for that or for anything that has happened. But that's all we can have, just that one moment. Please try to understand. I don't have the courage for more than that."

"Courage? Is that what it takes to leave someone you don't love? Even if he is your husband, that doesn't mean you owe him your life."

She turned away again and picked up her dress. "I owe him more than you know."

"Don't you owe yourself some happiness?"

"I can't explain it to you, Langdon," she said, buttoning her dress, refusing to look at him. "You would never understand."

"I understand that he's hurting you, and I can't stand by and let it happen. I can't let him trap you." She began to gather up her things, still refusing to look at him. Langdon felt an agonizing twist in his gut. He took her arm and turned her around, forcing her to face him. "He's already trapped you, hasn't he? How? What does he hold over you?"

He saw her lips tremble and something cloud her eyes. Was it fear? Or deep, crippling sadness? "We are bound together," she said evenly. "When I need-

ed him most, he promised he would never leave me.
And now, if he needs me—"

"What binds you together?" he demanded. "What
happened to make you think you needed him?"

"I told you, you would never understand." She took
a step away from him, turning her back to him. "There
are things between a husband and wife—families."

"Families! You were never a family," he said.
"He's used you, tried to drain you—"

"We were a family!" she cried, whirling to face
him. "We had two daughters! They—" She buried her
face in her hands.

"Montana," he said gently, and touched her arm,
but she flinched under his touch and ran from the tent.

A short time later Montana pulled a wagon up in
front of the hospital and sat, gathering the strength to
go inside. She knew she should have gone to Alex earlier. She knew what the nun had said was right: Alex
would need her. Why hadn't she gone to him? Why
hadn't she at least given him the chance to explain?

She was afraid she knew the answer. She hadn't
wanted an explanation. She had wanted Langdon, and
Alex's infidelity had given her the excuse. He had been
weak. He had been unfaithful. He had wronged her.
But she had been weak and wrong once, too, and Alex
had stood by her. She had to do the same for him.

She found him sitting up in bed in a ward filled with
men. Both hands were bandaged, and he was being fed
by a nun, to whom he was being predictably charming.
The young nun chatted happily with him and occasionally stopped feeding him to laugh at one of his jokes or
to dab at his mouth with a white linen napkin.

Montana stood at the door watching the two. When Alex noticed her, he held her gaze for a long, uncertain moment. The young nun, seeing his attention diverted, turned to look, too. When she saw Montana she put down the fork and napkin, picked up the tray, and walked toward the door.

Alex waited silently, his eyes still on her. When she walked toward him, he reached a bandaged hand to her. She touched it but was afraid to grasp it, afraid to cause him pain. Leaning over him, she gave him a sisterly kiss on the cheek.

"I knew you would come," he said quietly.

Now that she was closer she noticed the drawn look on his face and knew that he was suffering. "Your hands," she said. "They must be causing you pain."

He shrugged. "Some. But I'm told they'll heal right well. There'll be some scarring, they say, but I should be able to use them just like always."

"The young woman didn't fare so well, I am told." Montana worked hard at keeping her face and voice expressionless, but her heart was pounding wildly.

Alex was silent for several seconds, his eyes searching hers. "I saved her life," he said at last. "I found her and brought her out of the fire."

"You must not lie to me, Alex."

"It's true," he said, whispering so that others in the ward would not hear. "I brought her out, but not before her clothes caught fire. I picked her up, and I rolled her on the rug in the hall."

"You were in her room when it happened? Were you . . . romping, like they said? Or quarreling? A lovers' quarrel?" Montana kept her voice low and firm, and she would not let him escape her gaze.

Alex leaned back wearily on the pillows propped

behind his back. "Yes," he murmured, sounding distraught. "Yes, it's true. I was in her room. And we quarreled. She said something about you. Accused you of—of indecent things, and I struck her. She must have hit the stove and knocked it over." He stopped speaking and looked at Montana, waiting for her response. But she said nothing. She merely stared at him, also waiting.

"I have told you the truth. I swear it. I was in her room. Nothing happened between us, I swear to you. I—I admit I went up there with the intention of—" He had begun to sweat, and his face had grown pale. "I was tempted. I know it's wrong. But you must believe, I have never done anything like that before. I was tempted because we have not—you have been so busy that it's so seldom we—I am a man, Iv—Montana. I have needs." He brought one of his bandaged hands to his forehead to wipe at it, then winced at the pain. "My God, I know you will never understand this, but—"

"I understand, Alex." He glanced at her, obviously surprised. "I understand about needs. And I understand about weakness. God made us all weak."

Alex reached for her, touching her awkwardly with one of his bandaged hands. "You must not punish yourself," he whispered. "I know what you're thinking about. But you mustn't do that. What happened to the girls is past."

"Oh, Alex, I—" Her voice trembled. She had not been thinking of the girls, but of what she had done with Langdon. She could not be sorry for what she had done out of love, but now that Alex had reminded her of the girls, she no longer felt strong.

"Don't, Montana. Please don't think about it. Think about running the Palace. I'll be out of here soon, and—"

"It's gone, Alex."

"What?"

"The Golden Palace burned, like most of the rest of the town."

"My God, I heard it spread, but I didn't know— What about Diana and—"

"Diana and Dovie are all right, but I haven't seen Anna. She left. Before the fire. I had to fire her, Alex. She accused us of awful things, and now I'm afraid she might be—"

"You mustn't worry," Alex said, interrupting her. "I heard there were crowds of refugees at the top of the hill. She may be there."

"I don't think so. I would have seen her when we—when I went up there last night. Oh, God! She says she saw us together. If she spreads a rumor that you and I—" She looked around nervously at the others in the ward, but they all seemed oblivious of her and Alex. "Oh, Alex, it could ruin us."

Suddenly she was filled with fear. "You said that girl you were visiting said something awful about me. Had she heard Anna's story?" She leaned closer to whisper to him. "That you and I were lovers? Brother and sister. Was that it?"

"No, of course not," Alex said. She could see that he had started to sweat again. "She called you a—a whore, that's all. She hadn't heard any rumor. Neither had I. It was Anna that started it, you say? You were right to fire her, then."

"She saw us," Montana whispered. "When I was crying and you came into my room and we—"

"But if she died in the fire—"

"Oh, God, Alex, I never wanted that."

"Of course you didn't. But don't worry. If she died, it

. . . was an accident. Nothing you or I or anyone could do about it. Everything will be all right, I'm sure."

"But we can't be certain. She could still try to spread the rumor if she—if she's alive. I did what I could. I made up a lie. I told her it was Langdon who was in my room. It was all I could think of."

Alex smiled. "You were right to do that," he said. "I'll back you up if it comes to that. But it won't, I tell you. You mustn't worry about a silly rumor." He shifted his weight in the bed, holding his bandaged hands away from his body. "There's plenty more to worry about. The Golden Palace, for one thing. Did you save anything at all?"

"Diana managed to save a little. The roulette wheel. Some of the beer kegs and whiskey barrels. And she got the money from the safe and the papers. And, thank God, there's a little money in the bank. Maybe enough to pay a few creditors."

"Now, you see?" Alex said, brightening. "Things don't look so bad for us. It's a sign. A sign everything's going to be all right. I heard some of the others have already started over. People coming in this morning said they're setting up businesses under tents. Those that had insurance are already planning to rebuild, they say. We'll start over, too."

"It won't be easy. There was no insurance for us."

"But we'll do it, won't we, Montana? We'll stick it out together. Just like always when times get tough for us."

She looked at him, thinking of Langdon, but knowing there was no use trying to untangle the cord that bound her to Alex. "Yes, Alex," she said finally. "Just like always."

* * *

Diana was sifting through the ashes at the Golden Palace when Montana drove the wagon up to the site. Langdon was loading supplies onto a packhorse. She let him help her down, and they stood facing each other for a moment, neither of them speaking. Then she glanced at the horse.

"You're leaving," she said.

"Yes."

"Back to the mountains, so soon. We could use your help—"

"I won't be coming back," he said.

There was a moment of silence. "I see."

"I can't stand by and watch you destroy yourself." He looked at her, and she knew he was waiting for her to say she would come with him. There was another silence before she spoke again.

"You'll have some money coming to you. Your share of what's left."

His eyes held hers for a second before he went back to loading his supplies. "When you get it figured out, leave it at the Batteas Assay Office. I'll trust you to be honest with me, at least on that count." He mounted his horse and rode away without so much as looking back. She watched him go until he disappeared in the haze of smoke that still hung over the valley.

Alex leaned back on the pillows after Montana had left, feeling slightly sick to his stomach. He didn't like deceiving her, but he reasoned that it would have hurt her worse if she knew the whole truth. It was not as if what he had told her was a complete lie, he decided. After all, nothing sexual had happened between Lida and him yesterday when he was in her room, and it was also true that he had hit her because she'd insulted Montana. So in a way what he had told her *was* the truth, he rationalized—his own safe version of the truth.

He took a deep, shuddering breath, grateful to have gotten through the encounter with Montana with as little damage done as possible. He had been uncertain how to handle it, for fear that she would leave him. He couldn't bear to lose her. What would he do without her? Things were going to be all right now, though. He was sure of it. Why, in no time Montana would have the Palace going again, and they would be back on their feet, living the good life. He believed that she had been happy running the Golden Palace, and he certainly knew he had been happy with the life they'd had. Anna wouldn't be there with her nasty rumors, and that would make things even better.

It was too bad about Anna, of course, but what could he have done? What other choice was there? What he had done, he had done for his sweet Ivy as much as for himself.

Now all he had to worry about was Lida. He still hadn't been allowed to see her, but it no longer seemed so urgent. The only thing that seemed urgent now was his need to sleep.

A few minutes later a nun's voice brought him out of his slumber. It wasn't the young one, the one with the wide, luminous eyes and the wonderfully comforting and caressing hands. It was an older woman with a stern face and heavy jowls that hung like fleshy curtains over the edges of her wimple.

"Mr. Miller!" The crisp, authoritative voice resounded in his head. "Mr. Miller," the nun said again. "Miss Armstrong is asking for you."

"What?" Alex asked, still a little confused.

"The young woman who came in when you did. Miss Armstrong. She's asking for you, and we think it advisable that you see her."

"Now? I was sleeping. The doctor said I should get plenty of—"

"The *doctor* asked me to wake you," the nun said, her voice growing even more stern. "The young woman is quite upset, and in her condition that's not good. She's asking for you, and the doctor says we are to humor her. Come along now."

The nun was pulling him out of bed by the forearm. When he was standing, she insisted that he be fully dressed before he walked to the opposite end of the hall, where the women's wards were located. Since dressing himself with his bandaged hands was an impossibility, he had to suffer, embarrassed, through the nun's ministrations as she buttoned his shirt and trousers. He was sure that her bland, professional attitude only thinly veiled a disgusted sneer.

He heard the low, mournful keening as he reached the doorway to the women's ward. As he stepped inside, he saw several nuns and the doctor hovering over one of the beds—the one from which the crying came. One of the nurses looked up and, recognizing him, beckoned him. As he drew nearer, the figure in the bed called out his name. The poor, miserable creature with the raw and oozing face could not be Lida. Not his beautiful, plump, pretty Lida. He saw tears in her eyes and a bandaged hand reach toward him. He hesitated, thinking for a moment that he would turn away and go back to his room so that he would not embarrass himself and everyone else by being sick, but the stern old nun had him by the arm and was forcing him forward.

"Here he is, Miss Lida," one of the other nurses

said. "Now, didn't we tell you he would come? You must hush now. Calm yourself."

Lida said nothing but continued to stare at him and reach for him. At least she had stopped crying. She glanced at the doctor and said something unintelligible.

The doctor nodded and turned to the nurses. "Come along," he said. "We'll give them a few minutes. But not long," he added, looking back at Lida. "You must get plenty of rest."

When they had all gone, Alex walked cautiously toward the bed. Lida's face, he saw as he drew nearer, had been burned worse on the right side.

"Alex," she said, beginning to cry again. "What will happen to me?" It was obviously painful for her to speak, even with only minimal movement of her mouth, making her words ill-formed and distorted.

Alex could not answer her.

"You do love me, don't you, Alex?"

"Yes, yes, of course," he managed to say. Impulsively he reached for her hand, but it was a futile gesture, since hers were bandaged, as were his. He dropped his own, and the movement caused a nauseating ache.

"What about Anna? All those things she said about you and her, and about you and your sister, too. She said—"

"Anna was lying, Lida. She wanted to get back at me because I wouldn't buy opium for her. She was a dope fiend. Just a crazy dope fiend. She told filthy lies about me and my sister, and about me and her, too."

It was several seconds before Lida spoke again. "Am I ugly, Alex?" she asked at last, almost in a whisper.

"Oh, no! No, of course not. You will always be beautiful to me," he lied.

She saw the lie in his eyes and began to cry. "They say

I'll live," she said. "That's the worst part. What will become of me? And of my baby? No one will want me. What will become of me?" She started her keening again.

"You'll be all right," he said.

"The—the baby needs a father," she said.

Alex felt weak, and nausea was overwhelming him.

"I *won't* be all right!" she cried. "You're lying to me. I'll be all alone now. With a baby. You're the only one who can help me, Alex. You have to help me!"

"Of course. Of course I will," he said to please her so he could get away. He could not bear to stay another minute.

"You'll really help me?" she asked, calming some.

"I will do whatever I can," he said.

"You'll marry me?"

"Yes. Yes, of course," he said, desperate to leave the room. "I'll marry you. As soon as you're well enough."

"Alex, it must be soon. The baby—"

"Yes, soon. It will be soon. We'll talk about it later. When you feel better. But you mustn't tell anyone."

"Not tell anyone? Why not? I don't understand."

"It's because—because, like I tried to tell you, I have a . . . sick wife . . . in Chicago. She's in an asylum."

"You can divorce her. You must, Alex!"

"It takes time to work those things out. I'll do all I can, but you must promise me you won't speak of this to anybody. If my sister finds out—"

"Why would your sister care? You're a grown man. You can do what you want."

"Sure I can. It's just that I think I should tell her first."

Lida looked at him silently for another long moment. "You're very close, aren't you?"

"I reckon you could say that."

"I like that. It was wrong of Anna to mistake that for

the awful thing she accused you of. And it was wrong of me to listen to her. I shouldn't have doubted you, Alex."

Alex smiled and tried to pat her hand. "Rest now. The doctor said you must rest."

"A proper wedding? You promise?"

"I promise. Yes, I promise. Please, I—we must both rest. I'm very tired." He started to lean across her to kiss her cheek, but he caught the putrid scent of her seared flesh and had to turn away quickly to keep from retching. He could feel Lida's haunted eyes on his back as he left the room.

13

Montana finished sweeping up the last of the previous night's trash from the rough plank floor of the two-room shanty that now served as the Golden Palace. It had been six months since the fire, and after she'd paid Langdon his share of the assets, it had taken all that was left to rebuild even on such a small scale. There had been nothing remaining for operating expenses, and when she'd gone to the bank for a loan, they'd turned her down. Even though she was the money-maker, it was only when Alex, a man, went with her and placed his signature on the note that a small loan was granted.

Now they were faced with paying the money back in monthly installments. That was proving difficult, and the strain was showing on her. She had gotten sick with exhaustion during the last six months and had spent part of the time in bed, which put her farther behind. Now the lines in her face were a little more pronounced, and by the end of each day her shoulders were a bit stooped.

As Montana swept the debris into a neat pile, she could see several of the other saloons from her front window. Many of the owners, taking advantage of insurance money, had rebuilt on a grander scale than before the fire. New businesses were coming in, too, the owners counting on recent gold strikes to bring in more people. In spite of the latest boom, it had been a dreary six months for Montana and Alex. They had been concerned only with survival, saving funds to return to Tennessee long since forgotten.

Daily business wasn't providing enough to keep up the loan payments. As had been the case when she first took over the Golden Palace a year and a half ago, Montana was finding it hard to meet her competition because she had nothing special to offer. The piano had burned in the fire, and there was no money to replace it. Dovie was now working at the new Central Dance Hall; the Palace could no longer pay her. Having long since abandoned her own claim, Diana was spending most of her time in the mountains exploring the Sweet Ivy. There was no money to pay her and little work for her in the saloon. Anna had never shown up after the fire, and it was generally accepted that hers had been one of the charred, unidentifiable bodies found in the ashes of the Central. One of the customers, in fact, had said he'd seen her walking up the front stairs shortly before the fire.

One rumor had it that she was an opium addict and was going to one of the upstairs rooms to hit the pipe with another dope smoker. Montana had smelled the pungent burning odor coming from Anna's room, but she had supposed it was from the cigarettes she smoked. She had never suspected dope. And she was certain the most likely reason for Anna to be at the Central was to look for another job, since she had just been fired. Montana hadn't mentioned that to anyone, however, since she didn't want to explain why she had let her go. Not even Langdon knew Anna had been fired.

She tried not to think of Langdon, tried to ignore the ache in her soul when she couldn't keep the thoughts out, but he was there, invading her mind, her heart, making her yearn for him.

He had been into town once to pick up his share of the money she'd left at the assay office, but she had never known when. Perhaps their parting had been easier for him. He had to be going to Florissant or Colorado Springs rather than Eagleton for supplies, since she never saw him. Maybe he had abandoned his claim altogether and had moved on to someplace where she would never see him again.

There were times when the memory of their night in the tent would come floating back to her, and she would feel a wrenching sadness, knowing it could never happen again. She never felt regret, though. Never the feeling that she had sinned. She knew what sin was—it was to retaliate wrong for wrong and to allow those you loved most in the world to be destroyed in the process. She had not sinned with Langdon, but it could never happen again, so he'd been right to leave, in spite of the fact that it had left her emotionally empty and put her and Alex in a financial bind.

She couldn't fill the void Langdon had left, but recently she had stumbled upon a possible way of at least alleviating some of their money problems. She had said nothing to Alex of the plan she had devised after overhearing talk among her customers. Neither had she said anything about the man who had come into the saloon the previous night, seeking her out to talk to her about an option on the Sweet Ivy claim. They were to talk again later today. She knew that Alex had his heart set on finding gold in the Sweet Ivy, and he wouldn't want the option sold. He still wouldn't face the fact that the Sweet Ivy was worthless, even though he knew Dynamite Finley had spent months of work and a fortune trying to find gold there.

Since there was little for Diana to do at the Palace, she had offered to work the claim for a share of whatever gold she found. She had spent months at the worthless old claim, sinking a shaft and pounding at the rocks. So far she'd found mostly iron pyrite, or fool's gold, and barely enough gold-bearing telluride to buy the supplies she needed to stay in the mountains.

Harold Compton, who wanted to discuss an option on the claim, said he was a representative of a mining syndicate in San Francisco. He'd been attracted to Eagleton by the latest gold strikes. Montana wasn't about to tell him the Sweet Ivy was worthless and a long distance from the recent strikes. Anyway, she supposed a big syndicate had the money to take a risk, and she hoped he would offer at least two thousand dollars for the option. That was more money than she'd ever dreamed of, but she knew options sometimes went for that much and more. If Compton would take an option, she would have funds to pay Diana again.

She picked up her broom and walked to the bar, where Alex was wordlessly polishing glasses and dusting bottles, a grim expression on his face.

"Is something wrong?" she asked.

"Wrong? How could anything be wrong? I *like* owning a place that's about as popular as a small-pox ward."

"It's early in the day, Alex. You know that."

"Maybe so, but the place has never been what it used to be before that damned fire."

"No, I suppose not," she said. Alex had taken some ridicule for his part in the conflagration, but that had largely died down since the town council officially declared the fire an accident that easily could have started anywhere. They were right about that, of course, since virtually every town structure was built of wood and had at least one gasoline heater. And anyway, except for a few people, most of the population was either too transient or too focused on the gold fields to allow blame to fester. Even Alex thought of the fire as an unfortunate incident in which he had had no particular part.

"Maybe you ought to get out for a little while," she said. "Might help you get over your gloom. You could run an errand for me." She saw his face light up immediately. "I want you to take the money to the bank for the loan payment," she said, propping the broom in a corner behind the bar. "It's past due, and it's a little short, so you'll have to be ready to stand up to them. Just tell them I'll have the rest in a day or two."

Alex groaned. "You know I don't like having to beg."

"It's not begging, Alex. You will simply be explaining our situation."

"But I'm not good at it. Never have been. You know that. You're the one who always takes care of such things. When we were in Tennessee you always—"

"In Tennessee I talked to Ezra Byrne when we came up short of cash to pay our bill. A banker is different. They won't talk to women. Besides, I have to stay here to cook the lunch." She picked up an apron from behind the bar and tied it around her, then started for the kitchen. "By the way," she said, turning back to him, "I'll need more potatoes. Try to get me five pounds on credit at the Pikes Peak Grocery."

Alex groaned again, but he followed her into the back room, which served as both kitchen and bedroom, to dampen and comb his hair and part it sleekly in the middle. He put on his coat and his black felt hat, and by the time he was ready to leave, he was looking, Montana thought, as handsome as ever.

She handed him the packet of money for the loan payment and watched him leave. The two errands she had given him would take at least half an hour, and since he often stopped by the Central to drink with his friends when he was out, that would take even longer. For once she was actually counting on his going to the Central to give her extra time to talk to Harold Compton.

Alex would not have been happy about her having this meeting behind his back. But in the long run he would be grateful that he'd left business matters up to her, as always. Besides, if things worked out the way she hoped, the money from the option would mean he wouldn't have to explain about a late payment to the banker next time.

Montana took off her apron and went to the trunk for one of her good dresses. She was grateful that Diana had been able to save the trunk from the fire. After she was dressed, she smoothed her hair, then went to the bureau and pulled out the assay papers she'd gotten on the telluride samples Diana had brought in.

She herself had taken the samples to Jim Batteas's assay furnace. Jim, she'd heard from her customers, could provide either a "seller's assay" or a "buyer's assay," whichever happened to be needed. She had learned, also, that many a prospector had sold an option by putting out the word that he'd gotten a few good assays. She told Jim she was looking to sell an option on her claim, a signal that she needed a "seller's assay." The assay came back $150 a ton, enough to interest at least a few prospective buyers.

"There's gold-bearing telluride all right," Jim had assured her. "So I ain't tellin' no fib when I fill out the papers at one fifty. 'Course it's anybody's gamble how much of the rest of it will assay out at one fifty. But any buyer will know that's the gamble he's takin'."

"But if it really does assay at one fifty a ton, maybe I oughtn't to sell," Montana had said.

"The problem I see is it ain't oxidized telluride," Jim had told her. "It won't separate. You take it to a stamp mill, and the best you'll recover is twenty-five dollars for every ton o' rocks you bring in. The rest—say, one twenty-five—will stick to the telluride and be washed into the dump. But you want an option to sell, and the hundred and fifty I put on the papers ain't no lie. It just ain't the whole story."

Montana had thanked him, and she'd started spreading the word on the assay. That was only a few weeks ago, and last night Harold Compton, a representative of the Caxton Mining Syndicate, had come into the Golden Palace and made an appointment to talk about an option.

It was half an hour after Alex left before she saw Mr. Compton through the front window. She had begun to worry that there would not be enough time to talk before either Alex returned or some unexpected late-morning customers showed up in the saloon. But as Compton walked in the door, the saloon was empty, and she forced herself to relax. She stood behind the bar, pretending to be busy.

As he approached her, she glanced up casually. "Good morning, Mr. Compton." Her voice and smile were her most charming.

"I'm late," he said brusquely, "but I had some other claim owners to talk to. Some of them were businessmen. I had to get to them first before their day gets too busy. You know how that is."

"Oh, yes, Mr. Compton, I assure you, I do know how that is." Montana saw the look of uncertainty in Compton's face.

"Well, of course you're busy, too," he said. "But you're a woman, and—"

"And that makes it different for me, Mr. Compton?" She walked around the bar and showed him to a table.

"Well, naturally. The gentle sex, you know." He laughed uneasily. "You're so much more . . . understanding."

"Of course," Montana said, and smiled outwardly. She sat down across from him. "Now, I believe you said last night that you have something to discuss with me."

"Indeed," Compton said. "As I told you, I represent the Caxton Mining Syndicate in San Francisco. Our company is interested in exploring some of the Colorado gold fields, and I understand you're prepared to offer an option on your claim."

"That's right."

"I don't have to remind you, I'm sure, that while Eagleton District has made a good showing, your claim is unproven, so my offer will reflect that."

Montana studied Compton's face. He wasn't showing all his cards in this game, and she wasn't going to show hers, either. "But you do believe it has promise." She folded her hands in her lap, forcing herself to relax. "Otherwise you wouldn't be prepared to buy the option."

"Some promise, certainly." His shoulders stiffened slightly, and he cleared his throat. "I am prepared to offer reasonable terms."

"And I am prepared to accept reasonable terms." Montana once again gave him her most charming smile. "I would offer you the Sweet Ivy on a thirty-day option for a mere five thousand dollars down and one hundred and fifty thousand owing."

She saw Harold Compton blanch, and she immediately regretted her gamble. The $150,000 she had thrown out was more than twice the highest price paid to date for an unproved mine. She had planned to ask $50,000, with $2,000 down, hoping he'd settle for $2,000, or $1,000 at the least. She knew she'd never see more than the down payment, because he was bound to give up the option after the thirty-day period. But she had let her chagrin at his patronizing talk of the "gentle sex" rule her actions, and she had asked too much. Langdon had long ago taught her not to let her emotions rule when she was gambling. She wished she'd heeded his advice this time.

"I—ah—I'm afraid that's a bit high, madam," Compton said. "I'm authorized to offer ninety thousand dollars, with twenty-five hundred down."

Montana felt her heart thud in her chest. Two thousand five hundred dollars was more than enough. She should take it, she knew. There was no need to be greedy. But before she could stop herself, she was playing the game for all it was worth.

"That's out of the question, Mr. Compton." She hesitated for what seemed an interminably long moment, even to her. "Let us say one hundred thousand dollars, with three thousand down."

The confident look on Compton's face showed that he obviously had regained his composure. "Madam," he said, leaning forward slightly. "I understand that you've just suffered considerable loss from a fire." Montana said nothing, but her steady gaze never left his face. "You are, I understand, in desperate need of cash," he added.

"Then you have misunderstood, I'm afraid," she said evenly. "It was, however, my understanding that *you* wished to buy an option on a claim. I have given you my terms. You may take them if you wish."

Once again there was a long silence as they faced each other.

"Very well, madam," Compton said at last. "I believe we can do business."

He pulled a checkbook from his vest pocket. When he'd written the check for $3,000, Montana let him place it on the table. She wouldn't reach for it, wouldn't let him see how eager she was. Three thousand dollars was more money than she had ever dreamed of. There was but a remote possibility of ever receiving the remaining $97,000; that would come only if, after thirty days, Compton recommended that his firm buy the mine. Once he learned that what little gold was there was so difficult to extract, he'd give up the option, and she'd probably never be able to sell it again. But with a check for $3,000, she could pay the debt and have some left over—enough to launch the business again.

When Compton had put the check on the table, he seemed uncertain whether or not to shake her hand. He stood, letting his hands hang awkwardly at his sides. "We'd like to take over the Sweet Ivy as soon as possible," he said. "How long will it take you to give us possession?"

"I have some equipment at the mine," Montana said, standing to walk him to the door. "And an employee who's out there working. Can you give me two days to get things picked up?"

"Certainly," Compton said. He bowed formally, apparently deciding that would do in place of the more masculine handshake.

Montana watched him leave, then ran to the table to pick up the check. She pressed it to her bosom and had to sit down to keep from shaking.

Alex left the bank feeling disgruntled. The scene with Daniel Oxford, the banker, had been every bit as unpleasant as he'd expected. Oxford had complained that the payment had been either late or short too many times, and he wouldn't listen to Alex's assurances that all they needed was a little more time. If the late payments continued, he said, he'd seize the assets of the Golden Palace. That was almost laughable, since there were so few assets. Unfair, too. He and Montana were working as hard as they could to get the business going again. What more did Oxford expect?

The banker didn't seem to care how hard they'd been working, however. And there was something about him—the tone of his voice, the accusing look in his eyes—that made Alex think he was one of the old diehards in town who still blamed him for the fire. It made him damned uncomfortable, and now that he was finally out of Oxford's office, he definitely needed a drink. He walked away from the Baylor Avenue business district and headed for the new Central Dance Hall.

For a while after the fire some of the girls at the Central had treated him coolly. The reason, he supposed, was that two women had died in the blaze—Anna as well as Kate Sanders, who had gone back inside to rescue a caged bird she kept in her room. But for everyone who blamed him for the deaths, there was another who called him a hero for rescuing Lida Armstrong.

So far he'd been able to keep it a secret that he had "married" Lida before she got out of the hospital. She had put enough pressure on him that he finally gave in, but he had convinced her that telling no one was the best plan for now. "We'll announce it later, after the baby is born," he'd told her. "That way we can claim we were secretly married even earlier, and no one can pinpoint a date." It was a flimsy excuse, but so far it was working. No one except the doctor and maybe a few nurses knew she was pregnant, and he figured he could count on all of them not to spread around what they knew. And Lida had seemed content enough to go along with the secrecy once she was assured the marriage actually would take place.

Reverend Hopkins, the Methodist minister, had performed the ceremony in the hospital a few weeks after the fire and a few days before Lida had been moved to Denver, where, it was thought, her burns would receive better treatment. Although he had refused to alter the date of the marriage certificate, the reverend had agreed to keep the marriage quiet.

Alex had met with Lida only once since then. That was four months ago, when he'd gone to Denver for Montana to pick up a used cash register she'd seen advertised cheap. Seeing Lida in the hospital there had been a shock to him. After eight weeks he'd expected her to look better, but her face was a horrible, shriveled mass of scarred flesh, and her once plump body was thin and gaunt except for the bulge at her belly, where the seed he had planted continued to grow.

He was disappointed that she hadn't decided to get rid of the baby, and it was a mystery to him how she could carry the child, considering the horrors that racked her body. He could hardly bear to look at her, although he'd continued to deny it when she'd cried that she was ugly and said she knew he could never love her now.

At least he'd had the excuse of having to stay in Eagleton to run his business. She'd insisted on writing to him, though, and he'd had to give her a post office box number to which she could send the letters. He'd responded a few times, promising that, yes, as soon as she was well enough and the business was established again he'd bring her back to Eagleton. Over the last few weeks her letters had come less frequently. It was with a small pang of guilt that he realized it was probably because he had not answered many of hers.

It would be better for it to happen that way, though, better that they slowly grow apart. Of course she would be hurt, but in time she would want to divorce him. He only hoped it would be that easy. He could see no other way out of what could become a very sticky situation. It could get to be hell remembering which pretense he was supposed to keep up. As for the child, he didn't know what he would do about that. It hardly seemed a reality yet, and it was something he would worry about later. For now, he still needed that drink. He went to the bar and ordered a whiskey.

"That'll be two bits," the bartender said, waiting to be paid first. Everyone, it seemed, knew how tight things had gotten at the Golden Palace.

Alex handed him a quarter. The bartender poured the whiskey and set it in front of him. "Oh, I almost forgot," he said, pulling a folded piece of paper from his pocket. "You had a telephone call this morning."

Alex took the paper and glanced at it, noting that he was to call the Denver operator. Lida, no doubt. Since there was no telephone at the Golden Palace now, she'd called and left a message for him at the Central. He stuck it in his pocket and took his whiskey to a table.

The first sip was a warm caress to his insides. He took another drink and leaned back in the chair, starting to relax at last. He smiled at one of the new girls the Central had hired.

The girl walked toward him. "Hello," she said as she slid onto the chair next to him. She put her elbows on the table, rested her chin in her hands, and smiled at him. Her voice had a young, fresh sound.

"Well, hello," he said. "What's your name?"

"Wanda. What's yours?"

"Alex. Would you like a drink?"

She giggled. "I only drink lemonade."

"Well, then, lemonade it will be," Alex said, signaling to the bartender. "Now, tell me, Wanda," he said, glancing at the girl again, "what's a pretty girl like you doing at the Central?"

"Oh, I don't plan to be here forever," she said. "I'll have a place of my own someday. A nice place."

"I'm sure you will. You look like the kind who could do it."

"I do?"

"Uh-huh. You look like the kind of woman who knows what she wants and how to get it."

"Oh, Alex," she said, and giggled again.

"Say, I was just wondering," Alex said, glancing around. "Where do you girls who work here at the Central live?"

"We have nice new rooms upstairs. They built this place after a big fire burned up the other one. Did you know about that?"

"I heard something about it, yes. But tell me about your room. I'm thinking of adding on to my own place and hiring some taxi dancers, and I don't know what the rooms ought to look like. Could you maybe describe yours to me?"

Wanda launched into a detailed description of her room, but Alex was having such a difficult time understanding, it seemed he might have to see it for himself. She was on the verge of offering to show him when the telephone rang and the bartender called across the room to tell Alex it was for him— long distance from Denver.

Alex was annoyed. It had to be Lida, impatient because he hadn't responded to the first message. He picked up the receiver and waited for the operator to complete the connection. The voice he heard at last was not Lida's, but an unfamiliar male voice.

"Hello, Mr. Miller. I am Dr. Samuel Evans at St. Anthony's Hospital in Denver. You are Mrs. Lida Miller's husband?"

"Uh, yes, that's right." He turned his back to Wanda and spoke quietly into the telephone. "What is it?"

"Your wife went into labor early this morning, Mr. Miller."

Alex felt a knot forming in his stomach. Lida was delivering early. He was faced with the problem of what to do about the baby sooner than he'd expected.

"Mr. Miller? Mr. Miller, are you still there?"

"Yes, I'm still here," Alex answered.

"I'm afraid I have some bad news for you, sir."

"Yes?"

"It was a difficult birth, Mr. Miller." The doctor's voice had grown quiet. "Your wife was in a weakened condition as a result of her accident." He paused briefly. "I regret to have to tell you that Mrs. Miller died a few minutes ago."

Alex felt himself grow light-headed. "She died, you say? Lida's dead?"

"I am terribly sorry, Mr. Miller. But I am happy to tell you that the baby looks promising. A few weeks premature, of course, so it will need a little extra care for a while, but I can recommend a good nurse. You should be able to take the child back with you after the funeral."

"Funeral?"

"Mr. Miller, I know this is a great shock to you, and you have my deepest sympathy. I assure you the baby will be in the best of hands until you arrive. If I can be of any further assistance, please let me know."

"Yes. Yes, of course. Thank you." Alex continued to hold the receiver to his ear for several seconds after the connection was broken. Then he walked out of the Central, forgetting to tell Wanda good-bye. He was halfway back to the Golden Palace before he realized that he had neglected to ask whether the child was a boy or a girl.

"Alex, I have the most wonderful news!" Montana rushed to him as soon as he entered the Golden Palace. "I've found a way to pay off our loan." She'd expected him to respond with enthusiasm, but he only stared at her, looking slightly dazed. "Did you hear me, Alex?"

"What? Oh, yes. Yes, I did, and that is good news."

"Alex, are you all right?"

"I'm just dandy." He laughed, a nervous sound.

"Aren't you curious about how I did it?"

"Of course I am. But I won't be surprised at whatever it is. You're a very good businesswoman."

"I sold a thirty-day option to the Sweet Ivy for three thousand dollars with ninety-seven thousand owing." She let the words out in a rush, afraid of his reaction. He would not, she feared, be happy about even a remote possibility of losing the mine.

"My God! A hundred thousand dollars?"

"Well, we'll probably never see the entire amount—they won't be likely to buy the mine—but I did get the three thousand dollars. I've already paid off the debt." She laughed. "You should have seen Dan Oxford's face. And there's enough left over to get the Golden Palace back in good shape."

"Ivy, maybe we should leave." He looked oddly pale, and he had called her Ivy, something he rarely did now. Something was wrong.

"Leave?" she asked.

"Maybe now is the time to go on to something else," he said desperately. "We could leave soon. Start all over again."

"Of course we'll leave someday," she said. "But we'd have to sell the Golden Palace first. And it would be unwise to sell it now. Our best chance is to build the business back up again, and then it would bring more money." She had to look away when she said those words. She needed to believe that her real reason for wanting to stay was just as she had said and nothing more, nothing to do with the fact that she had changed . . . and that, if she left Colorado, even the remote chance of ever seeing Langdon again would be gone.

"I thought you were anxious to get back . . . to Susan and Elizabeth," Alex said in a haunted voice.

She turned her back to him and dropped her head. She had forgotten. For an awful moment she had forgotten. "Alex, I—"

His hands were on her shoulders, turning her slowly to face him. "Don't," he said. "Don't think about it. We'll go someplace new. Alaska, maybe. I hear it's even better than this. And we won't have to remember."

She gave him a troubled look. "We can't leave now, Alex. I just explained that—"

"God," he said, turning away from her. "I need a drink." He went to the bar and took a bottle from the shelf, then headed for the back room. She watched him go, still wondering what was troubling him.

That night he was too drunk to help in the saloon. He passed out early, and he was still asleep the next morning when she took the wagon to the mountains to tell Diana about the option.

When she reached the claim, Diana, clad in men's work clothes and a floppy old hat, was standing near the entrance to the shaft. She looked up when she heard the wagon. Montana waved to her, calling her name.

"Montana? What are you doing here?" Diana asked. "Is something wrong?" She dropped her pick and ore bucket and hurried toward the wagon.

"Nothing's wrong," Montana said. She took Diana's offered hand to climb out of the wagon.

"It's good to see you," Diana said. She seemed about to embrace her but instead simply clasped her shoulders. Montana, however, embraced her friend, touching her face to hers.

"It's good to see you, too, Diana."

Diana's face was flushed when she drew back. "What brings you out?"

"I've got good news. I want you to come back to the Golden Palace."

"What?"

"I need your help. I can't seem to run the place without you. And now I can pay you!"

"Why, that's wonderful, but—"

"I sold a thirty-day option on the claim. To the Caxton Mining Syndicate out of San Francisco. We have to get our equipment out today. They'll take over tomorrow."

Diana cocked her head warily. "You didn't let 'em cheat you, did you?"

"Three thousand dollars, Diana. Does that sound like I let 'em cheat me? And there's ninety-seven thousand owing if they decide to take the option."

Diana let out a whoop and grabbed Montana unabashedly. "By God, you didn't let 'em cheat you!" She laughed and tightened her arms around Montana, swinging her around. Then she suddenly seemed to realize what she was doing and let her go again, embarrassed. "I got to get some stuff out of the bottom," she said, looking at the ground. "You go on to the shack over there." She motioned toward the lean-to she'd built. "There's coffee on the stove. And you can stoke up the fire so you'll stay warm. It's still pretty cold up here. Even had a little dusting of spring snow last night."

"Diana, I don't need any coffee. I'll help you bring the equipment up."

"Oh, no, it's damp and dirty down there, and—"

"Let me help. Don't you think I know what you've been doing for me? You came out here to work this claim on an agreement to take half of what you found, but we both know you were wasting your time and spending your own money for supplies. You were loyal to me even when it cost you money. You could have gone somewhere else and taken a job."

"Doin' what? Tendin' bar? Not many wants to hire a woman for that. Tom McCrory was the only one I knew of. Even you just kinda inherited me. Most folks figure women, if they want a job, can teach school or run a whorehouse. I ain't educated for one nor suited for the other."

"You should have had your own business, Diana," Montana said. "It should have been you who had half interest in the Golden Palace, instead of Langdon."

Diana gave her a long look. "I ain't the one to take the place of Langdon Runnels," she said at last, then turned away toward the shaft. "Go on into the shack now."

As Diana started down the ladder into the mine, Montana said firmly, "I'll stand at the entrance. You hand me the equipment, and I'll load it into the wagon."

Diana gave her a resigned nod, then disappeared from sight. In a little while she emerged carrying another ore bucket and pick. "I got four crosscuts down there at about fifty feet," Diana said, "and there's stuff in all of 'em. It'll take me a while to get it."

Montana nodded and wordlessly took the equipment, carrying it to the wagon while Diana climbed into the hole again. In a little while she brought up lamps and more tools. The third time she descended into the shaft, many minutes passed, and she still had not emerged. Montana grew uneasy.

"Diana?" she called, bending over the shaft. She could see a lighted lantern at the bottom. "Diana, what are you doing down there?"

No answer. She called again, and this time she thought she heard a dull scraping sound, but still no response. Could there have been a cave-in? She knew that happened in mines sometimes, but she had heard no clamor from below. She called for Diana again, and when there was still no answer, she decided to descend the ladder. Lowering herself a few steps, she stopped to listen, hearing the scraping sound again. "Diana," she called, "answer me. Are you all right?"

"I'm all right," Diana said, her voice muffled. "I wanted to get some stuff outta this old crosscut down here that I ain't been in for a while, and it's all clogged up with rocks and stuff. I got to scraping around and noticed it's awful funny-looking."

"What do you mean?"

Diana didn't answer, but the scraping sounds continued. Montana waited, then took another step down, uneasily. By now the light at the bottom had disappeared. "Diana? What's happened? Where's the light?" For a moment it seemed to Montana as if the dark, narrow tunnel were closing in on her. She glanced toward the daylight at the top of the shaft, then into the black pit again.

At last she heard Diana's voice. "Montana! Do you think you can give me a hand?"

She almost wept with relief. "Yes," she said. "Yes. Just tell me what to do."

"Go back to the wagon and get me one of them big lanterns. There's matches in the lean-to. I want to have another look at this in better light. This lantern I have ain't big enough."

"What is it you're looking at?"

"I don't know for sure, but I think . . . I'll let you have a look for yourself when you get down here."

Montana climbed to the top and got the lantern and the matches. As she descended farther and farther down the ladder, she could see, in the light of the lantern, the jagged sides of the tunnel. There were crosscuts in the shaft, so narrow a small man would have trouble crawling into them. The closeness and the darkness were oppressive, but she made herself continue.

Now she could hear the scraping sounds more clearly, and she could see the glow of a lantern coming from one of the crosscuts. When she was level with it, she saw that it was strewn with rocks and debris. Diana was sitting inside, hunched over and poking at a rock with a rusty drill.

"Come look at this." She was so intent on what she was doing that she didn't even glance at Montana, and she spoke in a whisper, as if afraid the sound would carry through the thick granite walls.

Montana wormed her way into the crosscut, pushing the lantern along in front of her, until she had maneuvered herself to sit beside Diana.

"That!" Diana said. She moved the lantern closer to the walls and pointed to a discoloration in the rocky slab. "I'm pretty sure that's sylvanite."

"Sylvanite?" Montana asked, looking at the rock.

"That's what it's supposed to look like on the outside edge of a thick vein."

"You mean it's—"

"I don't know for sure. Let me keep diggin' so I can see which way this funny color goes."

"Diana, if it's gold, and the Caxton Syndicate has the option—"

"Don't go jumpin' to conclusions yet. Let's just see

what this looks like, then we'll decide what to do after we know more. But if this is the kind of vein I think it is, you sold yourself short for one hundred thousand dollars."

Montana climbed the ladder to find another pick. She went down again and, along with Diana, scraped and poked at the wall. They stayed there for more than an hour, sitting or lying flat on their stomachs and taking turns moving out of the crosscut periodically to stretch.

Finally Diana was satisfied that she knew the trend of the vein. She dragged toward her a bucket she had filled with samples of the ore she'd chipped off the rock wall. "Let's move out," she said. "We'll take these samples to Jim Batteas. We can trust him to keep his mouth shut if they're what I think they are."

Montana backed her way out, too excited to feel the stiffness in her shoulders and neck, too excited even to speak. When they reached the main shaft, Diana replaced the debris so the crosscut looked the way it had when they entered. "We got to keep it from looking suspicious," she said, whispering again. "And if this rock is what I think it is, we got to hope to God they don't decide to open it up again."

When they'd climbed to the top, Diana took the ore samples to her wagon. "You go on back to town," she said to Montana. "But don't mention this to anybody. Not even your brother. I'll follow along later tonight and take this stuff to Jim. Wait for me at the Palace."

Alex was busy behind the bar taking care of the usual handful of customers by the time Montana got to the saloon. He looked haggard, and he was disgruntled that she'd returned so late.

"What took you so long?" he asked. "Have trouble findin' the old bitch?"

"I found her, Alex. It just took us a while to get the tools out of the shaft."

"You look like the devil. You didn't climb down into the mine, did you?"

"Yes. I told you, we had to bring the equipment up."

He gave her a disapproving look. "I could use your help," he said crossly.

"I'll be there as soon as I change," she said.

The customers left early, as usual, migrating to the Central and the Nolton and the High Grade, all the old competitors of the Golden Palace, as well as to the bawdy new ones where they could find more excitement and bigger crowds. This time, though, Montana was eager for them to leave. If there was gold in the Sweet Ivy, Diana would wait until the last customer left before she came to tell her.

Alex went to bed early, still in his sour mood, and Diana came in shortly after he'd left for the back room. She laid the assay papers on a table and, without waiting for Montana to look at them, told her what they said.

"An average of three hundred and eighty dollars a ton all along that crosscut for about twenty-seven feet. By my estimate that vein won't be less than nine feet wide, and I figure it drops down at least a hundred."

"What does all that mean?" Montana asked.

"What it means," Diana said, "is there's at least three million dollars' worth of gold in just that one place."

14

Alex watched the woman move toward him, the soft fabric of her gown catching between her legs. Her breasts undulated in rhythm with the swaying of her hips. Two children clung to her, crying and calling out to him, and in her arms she carried Anna's charred body.

She moved ever closer, with her mouth formed into a large, perfect O, as if she would suck the very life from him. Soon she was hovering over him, and as he felt the first tug of tongue to pallet, he cried out. He flailed at her, trying to push her aside, trying to keep himself from being consumed by her.

"Alex! Alex, are you all right?" He opened his eyes to see someone standing over him. It took a while for him to focus and see that it was Montana.

He reached for her hand and held it, gasping for breath. He tried to press her palm against his face, to make sure that it was she and not the one who was trying to consume him. But the effort was too much for him, and he dropped her hand as his own fell limply at his side.

The more he looked at Montana, the stranger and more distorted her features became. He began to whimper and then cried out, a loud, anguished animal sound.

"It's all right," she said, and placed a damp cloth on his forehead. "It's just a bad dream."

He saw then that the distortion of her face was only shadows thrown by the one dim electric lamp hanging from the ceiling.

"What time is it?" he asked. His voice sounded strange to his own ears. His tongue felt thick and dry.

"It's seven o'clock," she said. "The saloon's already filling up. You've been asleep since noon."

He stared at her, not comprehending for a moment. And then he remembered. It had been late morning when he went to the little shack behind the High Grade Saloon for a pipe of opium. He'd remembered how it had helped him relax and forget things when he'd smoked it with Anna, how it had worked even better than liquor. He had expected the heavy, lethargic feeling afterward, and he had known he could sleep it off. He had not expected the nightmare. That had never happened before.

He shuddered, remembering how real it was—the woman sucking the life from him, and the words of Susan and Elizabeth when they cried out to him. Suddenly he felt bile rising in his throat, and his stomach began to churn. He tried to get out of bed, but the onslaught that came gushing forth from inside him forced him back.

Montana helped him clean himself and changed the bed linens, then insisted that he continue to rest. He felt weak and knew he had no other choice, but he couldn't relax, couldn't keep his legs from jerking convulsively on the mattress. The constant motion tired him. He felt the need for sleep, yet he was afraid to succumb because of the dreams.

He never should have taken to the pipe, he now realized. Instead he should have made himself a tonic. The cocaine powders Anna had taught him to use would, he believed, have opened up his mind, let him see things more clearly. But even now he shuddered at the thought of facing reality clearly. He preferred a retreat into numbness. Sinking back on the bed, he prayed for that numbness, but instead he felt worry and fear and another wave of nausea.

The day Montana had left him to mind the saloon while she went into the mountains to tell Diana to clear out of the mine, he had taken the time to steal away to the telegraph office. He had wired the doctor in Denver, explaining that he was too ill and distraught to attend his "wife's" funeral. If he had been a superstitious man, he would have thought that his saying it had made it so, that he had brought a curse upon himself.

It was no curse he was worried about, though. And while it saddened him to think of Lida dying, he knew that it was for the best. She would not have been happy going through life with a disfigured face, eventually she would have understood that they could never live together as man and wife. Yes, he was convinced that her death, under the circumstances, was for the best.

The problem was the baby. Damn Lida! At times he thought she'd done that on purpose to trap him into marrying her. And now that she was dead, it left him holding the bundle, literally. Just this morning a wire had arrived for him from Dr. Evans in Denver.

Fortunately, when it arrived, Montana and Diana were in the back with their heads together over some ledger or other. He had been sitting alone in front of the saloon, playing with a deck of cards.

He'd had a sinking feeling that something was amiss as soon as he saw the man from the telegraph office walk through the front door with the yellow envelope in his hand. His fears were confirmed when he read the message. He had destroyed the ugly yellow form immediately, but the words would not go away. They burned still in his brain:

PAUPER'S BURIAL FOR MRS. MILLER YESTERDAY STOP NURSE ARRIVING WITH BABY FRIDAY 2:15 FROM DENVER STOP SIGNED SAMUEL EVANS MD

When the baby arrived, how could he explain it to his dear sweet Ivy without hurting her? He thought of not meeting the train, but the nurse would ask for him, would identify him as the father. He thought of trying to convince everyone that he had agreed to take care of Lida's baby for her, but it would be a flimsy lie. He wasn't sure how many of the girls at the Central knew Lida was pregnant, but too many of them knew he had been seeing her. They would be able to fit the pieces of the story together, and eventually the truth would be out for Ivy to hear.

He could think of no solution, and that was when he had retreated to the opium den for a brief respite. Now the respite had ended, and he felt even worse.

The nervous twitching of his legs did not subside, and finally he threw back the covers and sought relief by standing. He dressed quickly and carelessly and walked into the saloon, disheveled and disoriented, still haunted by the ghosts of crying children and sucking women.

Montana intercepted him and tried to convince him to return to bed, but he refused. He made no attempt to take up his usual position at the roulette wheel. That seemed far too demanding. He could not even join in beery camaraderie with the customers as he usually did but instead sat alone at a table, drinking steadily. Montana came to him several times, looking worried, trying to convince him to go back to bed. He did his best to reassure her, but in the end he was forced to leave quite suddenly when a wave of nausea, even more violent than before, swept over him.

He did not remember going to bed but awakened there the next morning before dawn, fully clothed except for his boots and lying in a pool of sweat. Lavender light filtered in through the window. He could hear the even breathing of Montana and Diana as they slept in the other bed. The sound of the wind blowing through the pine trees outside the window made him shiver. He sat up to reach for the covers but decided against it and got up instead. He made his way to the stove in the corner that served for both heating and cooking. He opened the lid to the firebox, thinking he would stoke the fire that must have gone out during the night, but he saw that a new fire was blazing. He turned around and noticed that Diana was not in the bed after all. It was only Montana he'd heard breathing. Diana must have gotten up and started the fire, he thought. The woman never seemed to need sleep. She was always the last to bed and the first to rise.

When he had pulled on his boots and walked into the saloon, he saw that she was there, cleaning up after the night's business. She stopped her sweeping when he came in, and she looked at him in that way she had that made him feel as if she were seeing inside him and reading his thoughts. Without speaking to her, he retreated to the back room, got his coat, and left the Golden Palace, knowing that if he didn't, there would be no peace for him. He would not be able to escape the penetrating gaze of Diana Pollard, nor her silence that seemed to scream at him and set his nerves on edge.

A chilling blast of wind hit him in the face as soon as he opened the door. It was going to be a cold, gray day, one that would match his mood, he thought as he walked toward the edge of town. He had no idea where he was going; he wished only that he could keep walking until he had left Eagleton behind him forever, and with it the mess he now found himself in.

It was Providence, he later thought, that had led him to walk in the direction he had. If he had chosen another route, if he had not walked toward the Sisters of Mercy Hospital, he would not have found the answer to his problems that came to him like a sudden cry from heaven.

Filled with new confidence as a result of his romantic reasoning, he returned to the Golden Palace. He bathed and changed his clothes, and by 8:00 A.M. he was waiting outside the office of Sister Mary Frances in the small dark building behind the hospital. The building that housed the Sisters of Mercy Orphanage.

The nun who greeted him was not Sister Mary Frances but a diminutive, aging woman with eyes the color of a winter sky. She disappeared for a moment, then reemerged to escort him inside an office.

Sister Mary Frances's generous expanse seemed to overwhelm everything in the room, including her impeccably neat desk. She did not look up from her writing until Alex had stood there, clutching his hat in front of him and feeling uncomfortable, for several seconds. He sensed that she was enjoying making him wait.

"Mr. Miller?" she said, putting down her pen at last and looking up at him with the icy blue diamonds set in her fleshy face.

"Yes, ma'am."

"What is this matter you say you want to talk to me about?"

"I, uh, have a—a friend," Alex said, hating the way he had suddenly lost control of his tongue. "I have a friend who has a problem. And I reckon you're the only one can help her." Sister Mary Frances looked at him, saying nothing. Alex felt himself beginning to sweat. "It's a young woman," he said. His legs felt weak, and he moved toward a chair and sank onto it, even though Sister Mary Frances had not asked him to be seated. "She—the young woman I'm talking about—has had a child. Out of wedlock, I'm afraid, and—"

"We can't take every bastard that comes along, Mr. Miller. There simply isn't room. Young women who find themselves in such a predicament should turn to the fathers or to their own families."

"The young woman is—is dead, and the father is, uh, unknown."

"Indeed!"

"Yes," he said, hopeful that he had broken through her icy spirit.

"And how did you come to know of this unfortunate creature?"

"She, uh, contacted me before it happened. Before she died, I mean. Said if anything ever happened to her, I was to take the baby to you."

"Do I know this woman?"

"No!" Alex said a little too quickly. "Not—not well, I mean. She had heard of you, though. And the fine work you do, of course."

"If she died in our hospital, I would know her. I know everything that happens there."

"Oh, no. She was not in the hospital. She was . . . elsewhere."

"Elsewhere? Denver, perhaps? Could you possibly be referring to Miss Armstrong, the young woman whose bedroom you were in when you started the town fire?"

Her bluntness startled him, and he felt himself getting sick again. "Oh, no. Miss Armstrong is . . . doing well."

"I seem to recall she was pregnant."

"Not to my knowledge, Sister."

"Hmm. As I said, I am quite familiar with everything that goes on at the hospital, and I think I recall the doctor mentioning that she was expecting and that her weakened condition might make it difficult." She paused for a moment, her cold eyes cutting through him. "But perhaps I'm mistaken, Mr. Miller."

Alex managed a feeble smile and nodded uncomfortably.

"But back to this bastard child you mentioned. The mother obviously knew you well enough to trust you. In light of that, perhaps you and your sister could care for the infant."

"Oh, I'm afraid that would be impossible. You know the kind of business we're in. Hardly fitting for a child."

"Perhaps you're right," Sister Mary Frances said, leaning back in her chair.

Alex relaxed somewhat. The old battle-ax was beginning to come around.

"Perhaps, too, your sister would be jealous."

Alex felt momentarily disoriented, as if the nun had him trapped and was playing with him like a cat did a mouse. "I—I don't understand."

A corner of Sister Mary Frances's mouth twitched slightly. It could have been a smile. "According to what I've heard, you and your sister have a special . . . relationship."

Alex felt stunned, as if he had just been slammed into a wall. "My sister and I are very close, yes," he managed to say. "As many brothers and sisters are."

"Oh, but I understand your relationship is uncommonly close," Sister Mary Frances said. "Perhaps only Miss Armstrong realized just how close the two of you are."

So that was it. Lida had confided in the nun while she was in the hospital. She must have told her the rumor Anna had started. He hadn't thought she believed it in the end, and he certainly hadn't thought she would spread it. He had believed, in fact, that the rumor had died with Anna in the fire.

Sister Mary Frances leaned forward and rested her arms on her desk. "She was quite fond of you, you know. Spoke of you often. Even in her delirium."

"I don't know what you mean," he said weakly.

"I think you do, Mr. Miller." Alex drew back on his chair, as if he could escape her, but she kept him imprisoned with her silent gaze for what seemed an eternity. When she spoke again, her voice was grotesquely calm and soothing. "And now, Mr. Miller, about the child. It is in Denver?"

"Yes," he said, barely able to breathe.

"How did you propose to get it here?"

"The train," he said. "The doctor who cared for— for the mother, has made the arrangements. He's sending a nurse."

"I see. And when will the nurse arrive with the baby?"

"Friday. On the two-fifteen from Denver."

Sister Mary Frances nodded, then pushed back from her desk and stood up, going to the room's one window to stare out at the gray skies. "We are a Christian orphanage, Mr. Miller," she said with her back to him. "As Christians and as Catholics, we are obliged to follow our Lord's example and suffer the little children to come to us and to give succor to the needy." She turned to face him. "Even bastards, Mr. Miller." She paused again, letting her cold eyes cut through him. "Of course we will take the child."

Alex hardly dared believe that he had heard her correctly. But as he allowed himself to accept it, he felt overjoyed, as if a great weight had been lifted from him and he could move and breathe again. He smiled. "Thank you!" he said, standing and making an awkward gesture to shake hands with her, which she ignored.

"Of course, caring for a child requires money, Mr. Miller," she said, walking back to her desk. Alex sank onto his chair, following her with his eyes. "A great deal of money," she said, sitting down again.

"Well, I—"

"I know you will want to help all you can. I know you will understand, even if your sister does not."

Alex's mouth felt dry, and he tried to swallow, but it only made his throat hurt.

"And I assure you," Sister Mary Frances said, her eyes never leaving his face, "that if you help us, your sister need not know a thing."

Alex continued to stare at her mutely. "How—how much?" he asked at last.

"One hundred dollars a month."

Alex grew pale. "A hundred! But that's—I can't—"

"No one," Sister Mary Frances said, "need know of your generosity if you do not wish it so. And further, no one need know of the deep . . . *attachment* you and your sister have for each other, if you so wish." She had made her point.

Alex sat perfectly still, paralyzed. Some of the three-thousand-dollar option money remained after paying off their debt. He could make the first payment, but what would he do after that? At $100 a month, it would go all too fast. He thought of the $97,000 that would be coming to them should Harold Compton decide to exercise his option to buy the Sweet Ivy for the Caxton syndicate. That was a long shot, but it could be his salvation.

He wouldn't fritter away the money at $100 a month to this sanctimonious blackmailing witch, though. He and Ivy would take the money and leave this hellhole. They would go somewhere else and start over. And this time, he promised himself, this time he would make it work. It all hinged on their getting the money. Only a few more weeks, and they would know. He had to believe they would get it. He had to do everything he could to see to it that Compton took the option. But in the meantime, he had to pacify Sister Mary Frances.

"All right," he said. "I'll make the payments." He saw the self-satisfied smile on Sister Mary Frances's face and felt himself growing sick. He stood and hurriedly left the room.

Once he was outside the building, he shivered, both from the horror of his experience and from the cold March wind. His idea had seemed like such a perfect solution. He never could have guessed that it would turn out to be so messy. As he made his way through icy blasts, he decided to have a drink at the Central. Maybe he would find some good company there—someone who could help him get his mind off his problems.

Friday dawned as cold and gray as the rest of the week had been. A light snow had fallen the night before, giving the town the look of having grown a grizzled beard. By the time Sister Mary Frances left the orphanage to make her way down the hill to the train station that afternoon, the wind had blown away most of the snow.

She had wrapped herself in a woolen shawl as protection against the wind, and she had waited until she heard the whistle of the train as it rounded the mountain before she began her walk to the station. She didn't want a long wait in the depot where she might be noticed. What she was doing was best done quietly. She felt no remorse or guilt for the arrangement she had made with Alex Miller, and she refused to think of it as blackmail. She was firm in her conviction that people had to pay for their sins, and if the payment could benefit the work of God, then so be it. She had seen too many years of the righteous suffering while the sinful reaped riches and pleasure.

There were few passengers on the two-fifteen, and most of them were men—miners or mine owners. The nurse in her blue cape and white professional cap was easy to spot. Sister Mary Frances approached her quickly and, after a brief exchange, took the bundle and a slip of paper from her. She left the nurse waiting in the station for the return trip to Denver while she took the tiny bundle to its new home.

*   *   *

Alex was at the Central drinking and talking to the girls when the two-fifteen arrived. He ignored the sound of the whistle, just as he and everyone else in the town had come to do unless they were waiting for the train. Alex had made the first $100 payment and after that had, for the most part, succeeded in putting the whole affair out of his mind. He had an entire month to think of a way to make the next one. After a few drinks he had convinced himself that there was nothing to worry about anyway. Sister Mary Frances could never prove that the baby was his. And as for the ugly rumor about him and Montana, a nun would never spread that.

He left the Central at four o'clock to return to the Golden Palace to help prepare for the evening's business. Before he reached the front door, the old nun who had shown him into Sister Mary Frances's office approached him.

"Mr. Miller," she said. "I've been waiting for you. Sister Mary Frances said I was to give you this." The nun shoved a folded paper toward Alex, and when he took it she turned away, disappearing around the corner.

When Alex opened the note and read it, he knew he had been wrong to doubt that Sister Mary Frances had meant what she said.

The note read *The child arrived as scheduled. The name on her certificate of birth is Alexis Miller. I'm certain you will agree that it is best your sister does not know.*

15

The chill and snow flurries of the past two days had been encouraging to Montana. Each time even the slightest wind swept down the valley, she prayed the weather would worsen, that the mountains would be covered with a cold, wet blanket or swept by icy blasts. Maybe then Compton and his crew would have to stay out of the mountains and away from the Sweet Ivy, lessening their chances of stumbling upon the rich lode in the debris-filled fourth-level crosscut before the thirty days had elapsed. But the weather had remained, for the most part, uncommonly mild, with spring making only occasional flirtatious glances back at winter.

Montana headed down Baylor Avenue on her way to the bank, hoping she would not run into Harold Compton. She saw him in town now and then when he came in to buy supplies or to treat himself to dinner at the Portland Hotel or a night of relaxation. She avoided him as much as possible, however, for fear she would give herself away. And she fretted that even when he was in town, his crew was still at the Sweet Ivy, still gouging at her innards and, she imagined, getting closer and closer to the secret she harbored within her.

He had come into the Golden Palace twice, but she had managed to stay busy at the blackjack table while he played the roulette wheel with Alex. Alex, she had hoped, could be relaxed and friendly with him, since he had no inkling of the Sweet Ivy's worth. But even Alex seemed nervous around him and, contrary to what she had feared his attitude would be, eager for Compton to take the option to buy the Sweet Ivy.

Diana had reminded her again not to mention Sweet Ivy's secret to Alex. "Even if Compton don't buy the claim and you get it back, you can't let the word get out," Diana had warned her. "If you do, every bastard that's got a claim staked out there will file a suit against you saying the gold is his by rights of the law of apex."

Diana had explained to her that the law of apex meant that a vein belonged to the claim on which it surfaced or reached its apex. Neighboring claim owners would claim the vein surfaced or at least rose to its highest point on their property and would likely try to prove it in court. If one of them could prove it, then the entire vein would be his, even though it ran beyond the boundaries of his claim.

Together Diana and Montana had searched every square inch of ground within the boundaries of the Sweet Ivy claim, but no vein of gold surfaced. "They'll all sue," Diana had said. "They'll all do their damnedest to prove the vein rises to its apex on their property. And one of 'em just might be able to prove it does. What we got to do if we get the Sweet Ivy back is take the gold out at night in secret and try to save up enough money to fight the lawsuits when they hit."

Montana had agreed to the plan. Since that conversation, they had not spoken of the Sweet Ivy even to each other, except in the silent communication of a glance now and then.

It had not been an easy three weeks. Montana had tried to bury herself in the details of running the saloon and tried to comfort herself with the fact that even if the Sweet Ivy slipped from her grasp, she would have $97,000. With or without the Sweet Ivy, she knew that within a few days her life would change again.

Alex, it seemed, was already spending money as if they had the $97,000 in hand. She'd noticed an extra $100 withdrawal the last time she checked the account. That was foolish of him, of course, since as far as he knew $3,000 was all they'd ever get. But then, Alex had never been wise when it came to handling money. It seemed pointless to confront him now, though, since in one week they'd either have $97,000 or they'd have millions.

During the final week, she hardly left the Golden Palace. Too often thoughts of the Sweet Ivy and the gamble on gold she was taking led her to aching memories of Langdon, so she forced herself to stay busy to keep her mind off both. Two days before the option was to expire, she was particularly nervous. She sat at one of the tables early in the afternoon, attempting to work on the books, while Diana polished the same glasses over and over again and paced behind the bar.

Alex was serving drinks to customers at the tables. He was in a jovial mood, and Montana knew it to be the result of the tonic he occasionally made for himself, the way he had learned from Anna and Dovie. Alex sometimes grew careless when he'd had the tonic, and now he stumbled, and several mugs of beer he was carrying on a tray crashed and splattered on the floor.

"Can't you do anything right?" Montana screamed.

Alex looked at her, surprise and a flicker of embarrassment in his eyes. "Don't do this in front of the customers," he said quietly.

"Don't *you* do it in front of the customers," she retorted, hurrying toward him with a towel to mop up the mess. "How do you think it looks to slop beer and broken glass all over the place? Can't you see I'm trying to concentrate on the ledgers? I can't have you getting on my nerves like this."

Alex jerked off his apron and threw it to the floor where she knelt with the towel. "I'm not a damned waiter," he said. "I have as much right to run this place as you do, and I'll hire a waiter if I have to. Or a bookkeeper, if you're not up to the concentration."

Montana felt a knot in her stomach—a gathering of regret. She opened her mouth to speak to Alex, to apologize for her outburst, but he turned away and stalked out of the saloon.

He came back several hours later, even more keyed up. His hat was pushed back on his head, revealing a shock of thick blond hair. It might have given him a boyish look had it not been for the circles under his eyes. He was drunk, Montana thought, or else he'd had more of the cocaine powders.

He smiled at her. "Don't worry, my dear sister." His tone was mocking. "I know you're concerned, but I assure you that I'll be perfectly capable of serving your customers by the time the evenin' crowd of 'em get here." He walked away on unsteady legs, headed for the back room. When he saw Diana behind the bar, he stopped again and removed his hat, swinging it in an exaggerated sweep as he bowed toward her.

He disappeared into the back room, and Montana stood up to follow him, carefully avoiding Diana's eyes. Alex was at the kitchen pump, drawing water into a basin. Montana called his name, and he turned toward her.

"Alex, you're in no condition to work tonight. Why don't you just stay—"

"How would you know about my condition?" he asked, unbuttoning his shirt.

"Please, Alex, I—"

"You don't know a goddamned thing about me. Not lately, anyway. All you do is gripe at me, or else you have your nose in those damned ledgers, or you're scrubbing floors or you're at the blackjack table or you're out there in a low-cut dress showin' off your tits to the customers. Makes me wonder just what you been doin' behind my back to make this place so popular."

His words sickened her, and she turned her back to him to hide her humiliation and shame. She groped for the doorknob and would have fled had Alex not crossed the expanse between them in three long strides. He grasped her shoulders.

"Ivy, I—"

She dropped her head, unable, unwilling, to face him for a moment. But when at last she looked at him, she saw not regret in his eyes, but fear.

"I shouldn't have said that," he murmured. "I—I get a little crazy sometimes when I take too much of the powders. You know I didn't mean—"

"We've both said things we didn't mean today." Struggling to keep her voice from trembling, she made a small movement away from him, not wanting him to touch her.

"What's happening to us, Ivy?" he whispered. "What has this place done to us?" He dropped his hands and turned away from her.

"It's too late for that, Alex. We're here now, and we have to make the best—"

"Things have happened here," he said as if he hadn't heard her, "things that never should have happened." He looked into her eyes. "When we get the money, the ninety-seven thousand, we'll leave, like I said. We'll go someplace far away, and we'll start over."

"There's no guarantee we'll get the money, Alex, you know that," she said, hoping he wouldn't sense that she was equivocating. Just two more days. That was all. Just two more days and she would know whether or not they would be millionaires.

He seemed oddly agitated. "We could sell the Golden Palace and have enough money to leave."

"I've told you, Alex, now's not the time. And now's not the time to talk. We have customers out there. We'll talk later."

She felt sickened, knowing she could never tell him that mostly she didn't want to leave because of Langdon Runnels. She opened the door and left the room quickly, her heart racing as she crossed the saloon and took her place at the blackjack table.

It was several minutes before Alex emerged, wearing a clean shirt, his hair dampened and combed. He hadn't had time to recover from the effects of his powders, she was certain, but he had a role to play, just as she did. He had to run the roulette wheel tonight and for a few more nights at least. And then what? Return to Tennessee? Keep the Golden Palace? Her thoughts were a mass of confusion, and she couldn't sort through them yet. She would take things one at a time, and for the moment she had to concentrate on playing blackjack.

She was so intent on her game that she didn't see Harold Compton until he was standing in front of her table.

"Good evening, ma'am," he said.

When she raised her eyes and recognized him, she almost dropped a card. "Mr. Compton," she said, trying to recover, "what brings you into town?" She was aware that her voice sounded too high-pitched.

"Weather got a little cold," he said. "Besides, I needed a little diversion. Been at it pretty hard. Just a coupla days left on that option, you know."

"So there are, Mr. Compton." She glanced up at him again while she shuffled the cards. "Would you like to have a seat? Maybe try your hand at blackjack?"

"Not much in the mood for cards, but I'd be pleased if you'd have a drink with me."

Montana put the cards aside. "The drinks will be on the house, Mr. Compton. What will you have?" She signaled for Diana.

"Whiskey will do fine." He was still standing, looking down at her as he spoke.

"Won't you have a seat?" she asked in her most cordial tone.

"I was wondering if maybe there was someplace more private, where we could talk."

Montana felt as if a lead weight settled in her stomach. He wanted to talk. That meant he'd found something, and he wanted to take the option. "There's only the kitchen," she managed to say.

"The kitchen will do fine." He moved to help her out of her chair.

Diana had reached the table by that time and was waiting for their order. Montana knew she would be worried about Compton's sudden appearance, but outwardly she betrayed nothing.

"Mr. Compton would like a whiskey," Montana said. "And bring it to the kitchen, please. We have some business to discuss privately."

Diana nodded and turned away without speaking and without showing anything she must have felt.

Montana led the way toward the kitchen. "I'm afraid it's not very fancy," she said, walking toward the crude table, "but at least it's quieter."

Compton held one of the cane-bottom chairs for Montana to be seated, then sat down across from her. The room was dimly lit with the single electric bulb, and the only heat came from the wood-burning cookstove.

By the time they were seated, Diana entered the kitchen to set a glass of whiskey in front of Compton and a glass of buttermilk at Montana's place, then left without a word.

Compton picked up his whiskey and swallowed half of it at once. "Is that all you ever drink?" he asked, pointing to the buttermilk.

"It helps me keep my wits about me," she said.

"Wise woman." Compton wiped his mouth with the back of his hand. "I'm not ordinarily much of a drinking man myself, but, like I said, I been at it pretty hard out there at the Sweet Ivy."

"Yes, so you did." Montana, pretended to be interested in the froth on her buttermilk. "And how are things going out there?"

"Well, that's just what I wanted to talk to you about," Compton said. "The company I represent is in the same business you are. Gambling. Speculation, some people call it."

"I can see the similarity."

"There've been several gold mines found and developed here recently. That made Eagleton District seem like a reasonable venture."

"Yes, so you said." She began to relax. She could see where Compton was headed.

"Lotta worthless claims, too."

She took a sip of her buttermilk and glanced at him over the top of the glass. "Are you trying to tell me you haven't had any luck at the Sweet Ivy?"

"Oh, we've found a little gold, but barely enough to cover the three thousand dollars down payment, and it's cost us plenty to get it. We've been through three of those crosscuts and worked like the devil. I guess I'll start the crew on that old clogged-up fourth crosscut tomorrow."

Montana felt a tightness in her chest and was suddenly light-headed. Then Langdon's voice came to her out of nowhere, telling her not to let her opponent see in her face the cards she was holding in her hand. Carefully she set her glass on the table and waited. Her silence made the air heavy, but she didn't dare speak.

Compton took the last swallow of his whiskey and studied his glass, toying with it, twirling it around slowly on the table. "You know, ma'am," he said, still looking at the glass, "tomorrow's Friday, and there's a train outta here that could get me connections in Colorado Springs and then on to San Francisco by Sunday."

"You're wanting to go to San Francisco?" Montana asked, barely able to breathe.

"I was just thinking about the expense of another day's wages for that crew, just to dig through that last crosscut. You're a fair-and-square dealer. I'm sure you understand."

"What are you trying to say, Mr. Compton?"

"How about taking back my option and saving me those wages?" he asked, pulling the agreement from his inside vest pocket. "I sure would like to be on that train in the morning."

Montana tried to speak but found that she could not. Compton mistook her silence for reluctance.

"Besides the money the extra wages would cost me, I haven't seen my family in a month. You understand, don't you?"

She hesitated a moment longer, trying to appear reluctant, hoping she wasn't overplaying, praying her voice wouldn't betray her. "Well, Mr. Compton, I guess a couple of days doesn't make that much difference," she managed to say. She wondered whether she dared reach for the paper, lest she appear too eager. "All right," she said finally, "just toss the contract in one of the burners on the stove."

Compton's face erupted into a smile. "Thank you, madam," he said. He stood, confused again about whether or not he should shake her hand. At last he bowed rather formally and walked to the stove. He had just lifted the burner plate when Alex walked into the kitchen.

"So this is where you disappeared to," he said, his voice a bit too loud. He took a step toward Compton. "I saw you come in and didn't want you to get away before I could speak to you." He extended his hand for Compton to shake. "Don't you remember me?" Alex said. "I was runnin' the roulette wheel last time you were in. Alex Miller. Montana's brother."

Compton put down the burner lid to shake Alex's hand. He still held the option contract in his left hand. "Of course," he said. "You're working for your sister, I understand."

"I wouldn't put it quite that way," Alex said. "We're more like partners. I'm the silent partner, you might say. Just leave most of the business dealings up to my dear sister here." He gave her a forced smile.

"Oh, and she's admirably fair in the way she does business, too."

"That she is," Alex said. He glanced anxiously at Montana and back at Compton again.

"Alex, Mr. Compton was just about to leave. He—"

"Leave?" Alex said, "Why, you just got here. Montana, get the man some whiskey. We'll have a drink in here where it's quiet. Mr. Compton," he said, turning back to him, "tell me about the mine."

"As I was just telling your sister, Mr. Miller, we've explored three of the four crosscuts and found nothing. We've both agreed it's a waste of time, and your sister has graciously—"

"A waste of time? Mr. Compton, how can you be sure of that until you've looked through all of it? Montana, where's that whiskey?"

"Alex, can't you see—"

"The whiskey, Montana." His voice had an ugly edge to it, and she feared he would make a scene. She stood, uncertain what to do. Finally she turned to leave for another glass of whiskey.

"What's going on in there?" Diana asked when she saw Montana.

"You've got to help me get Alex out of there," she said, stepping behind the bar to pour the whiskey. "Think of something, quick."

When she returned and set the drink on the table, Alex was still talking, still trying to convince Compton of the importance of looking at every inch of the mine. Compton still held the contract in his hand. Within a few seconds there was knock at the door, and Diana stuck her head into the room.

"Excuse me," she said. "There's someone out here to see you, Alex."

"Tell 'em to wait. I'll be out in a minute," he said, waving her off.

"She says it can't wait."

"She?" He looked uncomfortable.

"I think you better get out here, Alex," Diana said. "This ain't somethin' Miss Montana's goin' to be able to handle."

Alex hesitated a moment, glancing first at Diana, then back at Compton. "I won't be a minute," he said. "Just wait for me." He turned and reluctantly left the room, looking over his shoulder as if to make sure Compton didn't escape.

Diana had managed it, Montana thought with gratitude, but whatever hoax she had cooked up wouldn't keep Alex out of the kitchen forever. She had to work fast and effectively.

"Mr. Compton, I apologize for what must be a very confusing situation for you. I had no idea my brother would suddenly take such an interest in the mine. He never has before, except for his first rush of excitement when we acquired it, but I can assure you that he will trust me to make the right—"

"I think your brother knows the truth about that mine."

"I beg your pardon?" Montana asked, barely able to speak.

"I think he knows as well as you and I that there's nothing there. Otherwise he wouldn't be so anxious for the ninety-seven thousand. He was trying to sell me a bill of goods, madam, which makes me appreciate your honesty and fair-mindedness all the more. And since the original agreement was between the two of us, I'm going to trust you'll let me off the hook."

He walked to the stove and lifted the burner lid. As he stuffed the contract inside, an orange tongue of flame licked out and consumed it. Montana felt as if she would faint.

"I hope you can pacify your brother," Compton said, lowering the burner lid.

"I'll do my best," Montana answered.

16

Montana showed Harold Compton out the back door, then walked from the kitchen into the saloon. Diana and Alex, she saw, were engaged in a heated argument next to the roulette wheel. They stopped their arguing as soon as they saw her, and both looked at her anxiously. Her eyes locked with Diana's briefly, and she gave her a slight smile and nod. Diana visibly relaxed and returned her smile before she walked abruptly away from Alex, toward the bar.

Montana glanced at Alex. He had seen the fleeting silent exchange between her and Diana, and it brought a tentative, hopeful smile to his lips. He made his way to her side.

"You did it, didn't you?" he asked hopefully. "You sold the claim. You got the ninety-seven thousand."

Montana felt Diana's eyes on her, and when she looked up, she saw her watching intently, sending her a silent message to be wary. Montana hesitated. Alex was her husband. He had a right to know. She could swear him to secrecy. Yet however adamantly he swore to keep the secret, could he manage it when he was drinking or when he felt the need to boast to his friends?

"Everything's all right, Alex," she said, stealing another quick glance at Diana.

"God, I was so afraid it was going to go bad. And I was fit to be tied when that damned bitch called me out, and then claimed she couldn't find the woman who said she—" He hesitated, and suddenly the realization came to him. "You put Diana up to that little trick, didn't you? To get me out of there."

"Alex, I—"

"Afraid I'd mess it up for us, I guess." For a moment she thought he was going to be angry, but he grinned and said, "Maybe I would have." His expression was boyish and quite charming. "I should have known you'd pull it off. You always do."

She tried to return his smile but found it difficult.

"Did you get the money?"

Montana felt the lead weight in her stomach again, and her throat seemed to be closing, making it impossible to speak. She had learned to live a life of deceit since coming to Colorado, but deceiving Alex was infinitely more difficult, despite the fact that she suspected he had deceived her many times. There was something of the old loyalty to him that would not die. And for good reason. How could she feel anything less than loyalty to him when he had never openly blamed her for her anger and negligence, which had been so destructive? "I—I don't have it yet," she managed to say.

"But he did agree to buy the claim, didn't he? We'll have the money soon."

"We'll have to talk about this later." She tried to move away from him toward a group of men beckoning her to the blackjack table.

"What's to talk about?" Alex asked, grabbing her arm. She turned to face him and saw that his smile had disappeared. "What's to talk about?" he said again. "Either you got the money or you didn't."

She stared at him, speechless, and she saw his face grow ashen.

"Oh, God," he said. "You didn't get it. You took back the option."

"Please, Alex. We'll talk about it later."

Alex's eyes were set in a fixed stare, and he seemed unable to speak for a moment. When he did, finally, he sounded incoherent. "No money and that goddamned sister suckin' the blood out of me like—"

"What do you mean?" Montana asked in a whisper, suddenly worried. "What sister? Are you talking about me? Who's sucking blood?"

Alex had turned away from her, walking as if in a daze toward the front door. She called his name, but he seemed not to hear. He kept walking.

Montana's first thought was to go after him, but she hesitated, not wanting to make more of a scene. She turned, instead, toward the roulette wheel to take over Alex's duties.

Sometime later she took a break and walked to the back room for a moment's rest. She was sitting at the kitchen table stirring sugar into a cup of thick black coffee from the pot that had been on the stove all day when Diana came in.

"Did you tell him?" she asked, closing the door behind her.

Montana looked up, surprised. Diana rarely left

her post at the bar. "No," she answered. "But I think I should."

"Why?"

Montana was even more surprised. Diana never questioned her judgment anymore. "He has a right to know what's going on. You saw how upset he was tonight. I think he's worried about something. The money, I think. He deserves some good news."

"If you want to keep the news good, then make sure as few people as possible know about it. Remember what I told you about them lawsuits."

"I remember. But if I can't trust my own . . . brother—"

"I guess that's something you have to decide," Diana said. With that she turned away and went back to the bar.

Within a few minutes Montana was back at work, too, but all night long she kept her eyes on the front door, watching for Alex to return. He still was not there by the time she closed the saloon at three in the morning.

It was after four before he came home, letting himself in though the back door. Having some time ago abandoned the crowded back room sleeping quarters, Diana was asleep on her pallet next to the bar. Montana was in bed, too, but she was not asleep. He was noisy when he came in, bumping into the table and the stove on his way to the bed. He must have known that his clumsiness would awaken her, but she didn't let him know that she was awake or that she knew he was drunk. He made it to his bed at last and fell across it, fully clothed. Within minutes he was asleep, and before dawn he was tossing and screaming in the throes of another of his nightmares.

He seemed to be beset with a horde of personal demons, all with women's names. He screamed in horror at faces that he said were bloated and oozing, and he tried to dodge objects thrown at him.

His cries awakened Diana. "What's wrong?" she asked, coming in from her pallet in the saloon.

"Another nightmare," Montana said. "He drinks too much. See what it does to him?"

Diana looked down at Alex, who now lay curled on his side, shaking convulsively. "It ain't the drink that's got him," she said.

Montana gave her a surprised look. "I never knew you to mince words, Diana. We both know he has a problem with liquor. Not that I think he's a drunkard," she added quickly, feeling she was being disloyal. "He just—"

"It ain't none of my business whether he's a drunkard or not," Diana said. "I'm just tellin' you that ain't what got him tonight."

"I wish you were right," Montana said. Her voice had a note of weariness in it as she pulled a quilt from her own bed to cover Alex. "But he was staggering when he came in. I could see that even in the shadows."

"Might've been staggerin', but I'd lay money he'd been to the opium dens again instead of the bar."

Montana was bent over Alex, tucking the quilt around him. She straightened slowly, looking at Diana. "Opium dens? You mean those little shacks in the alley?"

Diana didn't respond, but she kept her gaze locked with Montana's.

"No!" Montana said. "I don't believe it. It's only those—those lower-class girls from the parlor houses who do that. Alex knows what it can do to you. He would never—"

"I know how you feel about your brother, Montana. I know you've always took care of him. Protected him. Been kinda like a mama to him. And you been just as blind as any mama who can't see the truth about what her precious child is doin'." She seemed about to say something else, but she shook her head and turned toward the door again.

"That's not true," Montana said, going after her and following her into the saloon. "I know Alex has faults, but—"

"No. You don't know." Diana glanced at the door, as if to make sure it was closed and she was out of Alex's hearing range. "And I hate to be the one to tell you, 'cause the truth is gonna hurt you. But your brother's a woman chaser and a drunkard, and he's well on his way to being addicted to the opium pipe. Now, I reckon you'll fire me for tellin' you that, because I know blood's thicker than water, but I thought you ought to know the truth before you risk lettin' him ruin your chances with your mine. You tell him the truth about it, and he'll brag to some woman or say somethin' while he's drunk or on the pipe, and by this time tomorrow you'll have ever' claim holder within ten miles runnin' to slap a lawsuit on you, claimin' it's their gold."

"You don't know what you're talking about," Montana said. "He told me about being with that girl at the Central. But one mistake doesn't make him a woman chaser, and what you said about the opium can't be—"

"You got a good head on your shoulders, Montana. You're smart as any man or woman I ever seen. Except when it comes to your brother." She turned away and picked up her pallet. "I reckon after that,

I'd be better off going before you kick me out. But I hope you'll think about what I said."

Montana watched her with a mixture of anger and uncertainty. A part of her refused to believe that even Alex could be that weak. Yet another part of her knew he was. Diana wouldn't have said anything if she hadn't thought Alex could be dangerous to them. And she was right, of course. Diana always knew what to do, and Montana knew she couldn't let her get away now. She called her name just as she reached the door. Diana stopped but kept her back turned.

"There's no place you can go this time of night," Montana said. Diana turned around slowly, and Montana saw the anguish in her face. "Stay here," she said. "At least until morning." Diana hesitated for a moment before she walked back to the corner of the bar where she put her pallet every night. "Diana," Montana said again, "I know that pallet must be uncomfortable. I don't mind sharing the bed."

"No," Diana said without looking up. "I sleep just fine here."

Montana watched her lower herself onto the pallet, knowing she was too stubborn to relent. Finally she turned away and went to her own bed. She found she was restless, though, and completely unable to sleep. She thought of Alex and his nightmares and Diana's frightening accusations. Could what Diana said about Alex be true? she wondered. In the life she had lived in Tennessee as a farm wife, protected from all things worldly except for Alex's occasional nights of drinking and gambling, she had heard of opium only in books she'd read. It was something evil used by foreigners and the lower classes. She had certainly never even expected to see an opium den. Even after Langdon had shown her one on that first night so long ago, she had still equated them with outlandish debauchery and a sordid kind of life that would never be linked to her or Alex. It could not be true. Alex, though he had his weaknesses, could not be that weak, she told herself as she lay listening to his low, pathetic moans.

As for his being unfaithful to her, she could not judge him. Not when she herself was guilty of adultery. And not when she could not be truly sorry for what she had done but instead held the memory of that night close to her heart.

Her thoughts skipped back to Diana and how she had confronted her defiantly with the accusations about Alex. Diana and Alex had never liked each other. Alex had spoken out more than once about "the old bitch." But Diana had kept her mouth shut. She'd shown her feelings only in her cool attitude toward him, in the short, clipped way she spoke to him, or, even more eloquently, in the way she ignored him. Up to now, at least. Now she was not holding back, because there was so much at stake. Montana could not fully comprehend just how much was at stake. Diana had said there was millions in gold in the Sweet Ivy. The idea of that much wealth was beyond Montana's grasp.

Myriad thoughts and questions raced through her mind for the rest of the night. She still had not slept when morning came and she heard Diana stirring in the saloon. She got up, dressed quickly, started a fire in the stove to make coffee, then went out to meet Diana, who obviously had not slept either. Her eyes were red-rimmed and swollen, her face drawn and tired. She was sweeping out the saloon, and she glanced up when Montana entered from the kitchen. Montana hesitated, then spoke first.

"There'll be coffee in a minute."

Diana nodded. The silence between them was awkward. She put the broom aside, leaning it against the bar. "I was just sweeping up," she said. "There was nothin' else to do this early in the mornin', but I'll be leavin' in—"

"I don't want you to leave." Diana turned slowly to face Montana. She had grown oddly pale. "I'm going to need your help," Montana said. "I want you to hire a crew. Some that you know won't talk. We'll take it out at night, like you said. I want you to oversee the work, and we won't tell anyone. Not even Alex." Still Diana said nothing, but her eyes never left Montana. "I'll hire another bartender." Montana had begun to pace nervously as she worked out her plan. "Or let Alex do it. People won't think anything about your being gone for a while. You've done it before." She turned to face her. "How long do you think it will take before we have enough money to fight the lawsuits?"

Diana hesitated, as if she were still weighing whether or not she should stay. "If we're careful, we ought to be able to keep it a secret a month. Longer if we're lucky," she said at last.

"Will you stay? I don't know how to do this alone, Diana."

There was another pause before she answered. "I'll stay." She walked behind the bar and picked up one of the pads of paper she used to write down her grocery lists. "If we can keep it quiet for a month, it'll take at least a month after that, maybe two, for the lawsuits to reach the courts." She scribbled some figures on the pad. "We should have over a hundred thousand dollars by then. That's a start. You bank it in Colorado Springs so nobody here knows. The bank there will send somebody out to look at what you got, and my guess is the sky's the limit on your credit."

"Are you sure?"

"I'm sure. My bet is the Sweet Ivy will produce at least two thousand dollars a day. You're a damned millionaire!"

Montana felt her heart pounding. A profit of $2,000 a *year* was more than she had ever hoped for. To have that much in a day was beyond her comprehension. Shaking, she sat down at a table with Diana. "If it's worth that much, then surely there's enough to share with the other claim holders around there who might—"

"There won't be no sharin', Montana," Diana said. "If one of 'em wins the lawsuit, if he can prove the vein comes to its apex on his property, then the whole damned vein could be his. It's whole hog or none."

"Then if I bought the claims, paid the owners a fair price . . ."

"Might be cheaper in the long run," Diana agreed.

"I should hire someone to do the buying for me. So no one will know who's behind it and get suspicious."

Diana and Montana talked until the streets of Eagleton began to bustle with the business of the day. And then, long before the first noontime customer entered the Golden Palace, Diana left, taking with her a few cans of food and a bedroll in which she had wrapped her sparse wardrobe of two muslin dresses and a pair of coarsely woven men's trousers to wear while she worked the mine.

* * *

Alex spent most of the day in bed, recovering from what Diana had convinced Montana was opium, and he seemed in a particularly vile mood the following day.

"I'm sick of this place," he complained. "We're worse off than ever. You let our only chance slip through our fingers! How could you do that? I thought you were smarter than that."

"I'm sorry, Alex, I did the best I could." She was worried about the way he looked. The rigors of the recent night had taken their toll on him, and he was gaunt and pale and looked a good decade older than his thirty-seven years.

"Damn!" he exclaimed. "Damn! Why did it have to turn out like this? I can't take it anymore. I can't stay here and let—It's time we sell out and leave this place."

"That's out of the question."

"Of course it's not out of the question," he insisted. "We could get a few hundred dollars for the place, maybe even a thousand."

"A thousand is unlikely," she said. "We couldn't sell it for enough to get us started anywhere." She pretended to be busy washing glasses at the bar.

"God damn it!" He spat the words out as if they had a bitter taste.

Montana turned toward him and saw a look of terror on his face. "What's wrong with you?" she asked, making no attempt to hide her irritation. "Can't you see I'm trying to make the best of what we have?"

"And can't you see your best isn't good enough?"

Montana slammed a glass down so hard that it shattered. "Can *you* do any better? Half the time you're too sick to work. What do you do at night when you leave here and then come staggering home half out of your mind? What is it? Liquor? The opium pipe?"

Alex grew even paler. "My God, Montana—I—where'd you get that idea?"

Montana looked at him, trying to determine whether the look on his face was guilt or hurt. She waited for him to deny or confess to what she had just said. But he did neither. Instead his eyes went to her hand. She followed his gaze and saw the rivulets of blood seeping between her fingers, which still grasped the broken glass.

"My God," he said, and rushed toward her, taking her hand. "What have you done to yourself?"

"It's nothing, Alex. I wish you'd answer me about—"

"Let's go to the kitchen," he said, leading her away. "I'll wash and bandage that for you. You really ought to be more careful." He pumped water into a basin and thrust her hand in. "This place is not good for you," he said, watching the blood darken the water. "Not good for either of us."

"Alex, you're making a fuss over nothing. I've had worse—"

"I'm sorry," he said, reaching for a towel. I—I shouldn't have said what I did. I didn't mean it. I know you're doing all you can." He tore a strip from the towel and used it to bandage her hand. His own hands, scarred from the fire and still stiff, handled the bandages awkwardly. Their lives were becoming equally scarred, she thought, by the fires of their own private hells.

"Alex—"

"I used to have so much hope," he said, "before the fire." He was using the towel to wipe the blood from the front of her dress. "When the saloon was doing so . . ." He seemed distracted as his hand brushed over her breasts.

"There's still hope," she said. "Our business is beginning to pick up, haven't you noticed?"

"No, I hadn't noticed," Alex answered. He leaned forward to kiss her breasts, and she could feel his hot breath through the fabric of her dress. "Let's—"

"We can't," Montana protested. "We'll have customers in here soon. We can't afford to take any chances now. Not when we're beginning to make money again. I expect us to show a bigger profit this month than ever before."

Her words about bigger profits caught his attention. "You're sure?" he asked. "About the profits, I mean?"

"Quite sure," she answered. "You'll see when we make the next deposit."

Alex finished bandaging her hand and made no more protests when she returned to the front. She had decided not to press him further about the opium. The less she confronted him, the less likely she would be forced to talk about the Sweet Ivy.

Within a few minutes she was serving plates of beans and pork tenderloin to her lunchtime customers.

Alex was the model of perfection over the next few days. Evidently Montana's predictions about better profits had inspired him to work harder and longer hours. She had found a way, it seemed, to ease his fears. But she knew she had to deliver more than promises.

At the end of the first week she told Alex that she was going to Colorado Springs to order new tables for the saloon, assuring him that they needed to upgrade if they wanted to build the business and improve their profits. He insisted upon taking her to the train station, but she refused to allow it on the grounds that there was no one else to run the Golden Palace. Then, instead of taking the train, she hired a wagon to take her to the Sweet Ivy to meet Diana.

Diana, she soon saw, had hired several men. There were plenty of miners now who had found their way to Eagleton looking for work. President Grover Cleveland's decision to forsake bimetallism in favor of the gold standard had caused the silver mines to close down, providing a glut of out-of-work miners, so it wasn't hard to hire some who would be willing to keep their mouths shut.

The miners had worked hard, and Diana had the receipts for the sale of the gold they'd managed to bring out—$15,000 in the first week.

After they'd gone over the receipts, Montana spent the night with Diana in the shack she had built as protection; the rest of the crew slept in similar shacks. The next day she timed her return to Eagleton to coincide with the train from Colorado Springs.

She pretended to be busy with the saloon accounts after her return, and late on the second day she gave Alex a $500 deposit to take to the bank—a generous month's profit for the Golden Palace. Alex, who had been showing signs of nervousness as well as physical illness, took an immediate turn for the better. He didn't question how the deposits could have grown when there seemed to be no more than the usual number of customers. He just seemed happy that they had. He had no inkling of the secret account in Colorado Springs that held even more.

A few days later Montana told Alex that since she had not found just the right tables in Colorado Springs, she would have to go again. Alex did not seem to mind.

Over the next several weeks she made even more trips to Colorado Springs on the pretext of doctors' appointments and shopping trips, when in reality she was depositing money in the Colorado Springs Bank and searching for a lawyer who could help her with the anticipated lawsuits and who, in the meantime, would buy as many neighboring claims as possible in her name. Still Alex did not protest the trips. He trusted that Montana was telling the truth when she told him she was having trouble finding sturdy tables and chairs, or that she had developed a backache from sitting too long at the blackjack table and needed the care of a doctor in Colorado Springs. The five hundred dollars, it seemed, had gone a long way toward returning him to his old amiable self, and the next month's deposit of almost as much went even farther. He no longer mentioned leaving Eagleton.

He did, however, now that he was more relaxed, renew his interest in frequenting the Central. Only then did he begin to complain that Montana was spending too much time in Colorado Springs and was never there to help at the saloon. His motive was thinly veiled. Montana knew he wanted her there to run the Palace so he would have more time at the Central. It no longer bothered her to think that it was the young women who attracted him there.

In the end she solved the problem by telling him she thought it was time they hire some girls to replace Anna and Dovie, and she put Alex in charge of interviewing applicants.

17

The Golden Palace once again gave the appearance of prospering. Alex had found not two but three girls to dance with the customers, and Montana had hired a bartender to replace Diana. Alex, she noticed, had begun to seem more like his old self. He seemed less tense and nervous, and it was a relief to have him stop his talk of selling out and leaving, since she certainly couldn't afford to leave the Sweet Ivy now. The nightmares had stopped, too, leading her to hope that his visits to the opium dens had ceased. He had taken to spending less time at the Central and was content to stay at the Golden Palace, helping the new girls get settled in the room they had added on for them behind the kitchen. He had, in fact, taken a renewed interest in the Golden Palace in general. He was talking of remodeling even more extensively by adding a second floor for the hired help's bedrooms.

Montana advised against it, cautioning him not to spend too much or overextend their credit. Not, as

Alex assumed, because their income was limited, but because she didn't want anyone to become suspicious about all the money they were spending. For almost two months now she and Diana had succeeded in keeping the goings-on at the Sweet Ivy a secret, and she had ultimately found a lawyer, who had succeeded in buying up three of the claims near the Sweet Ivy.

Alex, because he never bothered to look at the ledgers, continued to believe that the modest increase in their Eagleton bank account was due to steady growth in profits of the Golden Palace, and so, it seemed, was everyone else. If they could keep the secret for another month or two, Bob Reed, the Colorado Springs lawyer she had hired, had calculated that she would have enough in reserve to fight the inevitable lawsuits. Part of keeping the secret called for Montana to continue business as usual in the saloon, and that meant running the gaming tables every night.

By early August the atmosphere inside the Golden Palace at night was close and steamy. Montana worked the blackjack table while outside rain slathered the earth and lightning tore the sky. The weather had been too bad all day for the miners to bring out ore. They couldn't even haul what was already out to the smelter. That meant the wagons would still be full in the morning, so even if the weather cleared, work couldn't start until the wagons were emptied.

Montana raked in the winnings from the previous game and picked up the cards to deal again, trying to concentrate on the game and not worry about losing a day's work at the mine. She was about to deal the first card when a hand, placed on her wrist, stopped her.

She knew the touch—the solid, hard feel of a wide palm and long, agile fingers grasping her wrist none too gently. Her first reaction was excitement that he had returned.

"Hello, Langdon," she said, looking up at him, her voice deceptively calm. When she saw his eyes, cold and angry, she was momentarily disconcerted. He was pulling her to her feet, but she managed to wrest her arm free so she could gather the playing cards. "Excuse me, gentlemen, I'll only be a minute," she said, smiling at her patrons.

"Would you like me to buy you a drink?" she asked, turning to Langdon, summoning up a voice as cold as his eyes had been. Without waiting for him to answer, she turned toward the bar, expecting him to follow her, but he stopped her again, grabbing her arm and turning her to face him.

"In the back," he said. "Where we can talk."

She studied his face. "Of course," she said, fighting to stay calm. She moved through the room at a leisurely pace, speaking to customers as she passed by. Once they were in the back room, she closed the door, and her smile evaporated. "What's this all about?" she asked.

"Suppose you tell *me* what it's all about."

"I don't know what you're talking about."

"You've gotten good at your little deceits, Montana, but don't try it with me. I taught you how to play the game. I know when you're bluffing."

"I have no idea what—"

"I said don't try it with me. I just had someone named Bob Reed offer me seventy thousand dollars for the Honesty. It's taken me all week to find out who was behind it."

Montana felt the blood drain from her face, and her heart began to pound in her chest. So Langdon had been the first to learn the truth. It wouldn't be long now before everyone knew.

"Langdon, I hope you understand that I instructed Mr. Reed to offer a fair—"

"Thought you'd swallow up the little fish so you'd have more resources against the big ones, did you? You're clever, Montana. You've come a long ways from the scared little housewife I had to teach how to play poker. How much is the Sweet Ivy worth? A couple million? More?"

She looked at him without answering and steadied herself against a chair to keep from shaking. He returned her gaze with a cold expression as he pulled a cheroot from his vest pocket and sniffed it before he clamped it between his teeth and lit it. Propping his foot on a chair, he leaned toward her, his elbow on his knee. "Whatever it's worth," he said, jabbing the cigar toward her to make his point, "you'll have a helluva time proving it doesn't apex on my claim."

"Langdon, I tried to tell you, I instructed Mr. Reed to offer a fair price for all—"

"I'm not one of your little fish," he said, straightening and moving toward her. She thought the movement looked menacing. "Seventy thousand dollars won't touch me. I can move that much out in a month."

She continued to stare at him, keeping her face expressionless. Was he lying? she wondered. Bluffing to get a bigger offer? "If you don't think the offer is fair," she said evenly, "then I reckon you're free to make a counter offer."

"I have a counter offer all right. Based on these." He pulled a paper from his pocket. "The last assay, showing an average of three hundred and twenty-five dollars a ton."

Montana glanced at the paper but didn't take it from him. "I've seen a seller's assay before, Langdon. I can have someone look at your claim, if you like, and I'll take a sample to an assayer."

"Cut it out, Montana. You know damned well that a buyer's assay is going to turn out at least three hundred."

"Gold that won't separate? That won't—"

"I'm not bluffing, Montana."

She studied his face in stony silence for a moment. "All right, what do you want?"

"I want to control Squaw Mountain."

This time she could not hide her shock. "What?"

"If the Sweet Ivy is worth all the trouble you're going to, there's no reason you can't share in the control. In fact, if the two of us join together, it'll be easier. If you're willing to cooperate."

"I don't know what you're talking about, and I have no interest in controlling anything."

"If you don't, then you're going to be plagued with lawsuits for a long time, and mine will be the first. And believe me, I've got the capital to make it a long and bloody battle."

"Don't try to manipulate me, Langdon," she said angrily.

"I'm not manipulating. I'm making you an offer. And to prove to you that I'm not bluffing, I want you to come to the Honesty. Bring whoever you want, whoever you trust, to look at my claim and see what it's worth."

So he wasn't bluffing. But he had left her feeling trapped. She had been trying to beat him at his own game, and she should have known he was better at it than she was.

"Join me as a partner," he said again.

He was pressuring her, intimidating, trying to get her to make a hasty decision, she knew. Langdon was good at this game. Maybe he wasn't telling her the truth. Maybe his claim was worthless after all. His cold, hard attitude seemed to have frozen out the warm, vulnerable side of him she had seen in the tent the night of the fire. Seen and dreamed of so many times since. Would it have been different if she had gone away with him as he had asked? Would they have been able to keep the warmth and passion of that night alive? It was too late to wonder about that now. She had expected—feared—that she would never see him again, but now that he had returned, it was obvious their relationship was going to be entirely professional. She met his gaze with a cool, hardened expression that rivaled his.

"All right," she said emotionlessly. "I'll look at your claim, and I'll bring someone with me. Someone who knows the business. We'll talk about a partnership after that."

Langdon hesitated, leading her to believe that he had expected her to accept his demands unquestioningly in spite of his offer to have his claim inspected. "You'd better make it soon," he said. "If I guessed your secret, you're not going to be able to keep it from anybody else much longer. We need to get a partnership formed quick if we're going to do it."

"I said we'll talk later," she said with as much firmness as she could manage. No matter how disappointing the circumstances, being near Langdon still had an unsettling effect on her. "I'll be at your claim tomorrow afternoon. With Diana."

"Diana Pollard?" He made no attempt to hide his

surprise. "You still have her working the Sweet Ivy?"

"Yes. She's the one who found the vein. I'm sure she'll be able to recognize anything that's in the Honesty."

"But she's a woman—"

"Yes, she is. And so am I. If you're superstitious about women in the mine, you should have thought of that before you proposed the partnership."

Langdon kept his eyes on her for several seconds, making her wonder what he was thinking. Then he turned away without making a reply until he reached the door. "Tomorrow afternoon," he said, glancing back at her. "Can you find the Honesty?"

"Yes," she said. "I've been there before, remember?"

With a slight nod he opened the door and left, giving no indication that he remembered that he had been the one who had taken her there, and that it had been the first time he had kissed her.

Langdon was waiting at the Honesty when Diana and Montana arrived. Montana had given Alex another excuse about going to Colorado Springs. This time she had said she was to talk to a beer supplier for the Golden Palace. Diana had been skeptical about Langdon's proposal, but she had agreed to go with Montana to have a look at the Honesty.

The sky was a clear, cloudless blue, and the sun was sinking into the horizon as they pulled up. A wagon, half-full of dull gray ore streaked with copperish orange, sat in front of a hoist shack. Langdon had sent his crew home early and now waited inside the shack for Montana and Diana.

Without a word Diana alighted from the wagon and went immediately to the ore. She picked up one of the samples, then another and another, examining them carefully.

"It's at least three hundred a ton," she said. "But let's see where it came from."

By that time Langdon had come outside. "This way," he said. "I'll lower you in the bucket." He led them to the mine opening, where a steel bucket, large enough to hold a man, was attached to a set of pulleys. Montana watched as Diana climbed inside the awkward contraption, then signaled for Langdon to lower her.

"All right, Langdon," Montana said as she watched Diana disappear into the shaft. "Tell me the rest of your story."

Langdon brought his cigar to his mouth in a slow, leisurely gesture and squinted at her through the smoke. "I've laid all my cards on the table, Montana. I don't know what you're getting at. Diana just told you that ore in the wagon is worth at least three hundred dollars a ton." She detected the same arrogant and slightly amused air about him that she'd noticed once before—when he'd first caught her posing as Montana McCrory in the Golden Palace saloon.

"Oh, I have no doubt that Diana is going to find a rich vein," Montana said, "but there's something you're not telling me. You need me for something that I can't see yet."

There was a moment of silence, and she saw his face change. "It seems to me I tried to tell you that the night of the fire," he said. All his arrogance was gone, and something in his expression made her want to go to him, to let him take her in his arms, to forget about the Honesty and the Sweet Ivy and everything else in the world except the two of them.

"I told you then, Langdon," she said, finding it

impossible to look at him now. She kept her voice low so that Diana could not possibly hear. "I am and always will be Alex's wife."

"So you did, Mrs. McCrory. Or is it Mrs. Barton who knows her lines so well?" His voice had grown cold again.

She faced him and tried to match his tone. "You have the advantage over me, Langdon, because you know the truth. I have always known that. Is that what's at the bottom of all of this? You want part of the Sweet Ivy, just as you asked for part of the Golden Palace, in exchange for your silence?"

"I taught you too well, Montana. You are too clever, too cynical, for your own good. I told you yesterday that I wasn't trying to manipulate you. This has nothing to do with knowing who you are. God knows I *don't* know who you are, and I doubt you do, either." His words cut through her like a knife, but before she could react, he continued. "What I'm doing is trying to protect myself, and if you get helped in the process, so be it. The point is, the odds against my surviving the lawsuits alone are damned poor. If I join with you, they get better."

"But why me? Why not some other claim holder?"

"Isn't that obvious? You're the one who's got the gold."

"I'm the one you can use."

"If you want to look at it that way, yes. But you'll be using me, too. Or we'll be helping each other. You could look at it that way."

They heard clanging on the ore bucket, Diana's signal that she was ready to be hoisted up. As she emerged from the shaft, Montana searched her face, looking for the confirmation she expected. She got it, not with a word but with a single nod. Diana refused Langdon's offer to help her out of the bucket but handed him the lantern she had used to light her way through the mine. Then she walked straight to Montana and showed her several samples of ore that she held in her open palm.

"It's high grade," she said. "As good as the Sweet Ivy. Probably the same vein runnin' straight through."

Montana took the samples from Diana and examined them. It was not so obviously high grade to her. It all looked like streaked gray rock. But if the looks of the ore meant nothing to her, Diana's words did.

"If it's the same vein, then that means all the ground in between's got that vein running through it, too, doesn't it?" Montana asked. "And that means whoever owns that ground can claim the vein apexes there, doesn't it?"

Diana cast an uneasy glance at Langdon before she answered. "You done the right thing buyin' up them claims," she said to Montana.

"I'll have a look at the Sweet Ivy tomorrow morning," Langdon said, "and if it looks the way I think it does, I'll be at the Golden Palace in the afternoon with the partnership papers for you and Alex to sign."

"Not so fast!" Montana said. "I haven't agreed to anything yet. And if I do, I want it specified that I am the controlling partner, since I now own three claims to your one."

"I'm afraid it's the other way around, madam. I now own four to your three. You see, I've been busy buying them up, too. But please don't concern yourself, Mrs. McCrory. I'm sure you'll have your lawyer look over the papers before you sign anything."

She looked at him, knowing she should have known better than to be as stunned as she was. "You can bet on that, Mr. Runnels," she said, and turned away toward the wagon.

Alex stirred the powders into two glasses of wine and handed one to Gladys, the youngest and prettiest of the three girls he and Montana had hired recently.

"I don't know if I should drink this or not," Gladys said as she sat on the edge of her bed. "The other time you gave it to me, I couldn't sleep for hours."

"I'm not giving it to you to make you sleep," Alex said, sitting beside her and leaning to kiss her neck. "It's a tonic. It's supposed to pep you up. That's what doctors give it to people for." He lowered his voice. "Remember the way it made you feel? Especially when we made love?" He nuzzled her neck again.

Gladys smiled almost shyly and sipped the tonic he had mixed for her. Alex returned her smile and raised his glass in a silent toast, then drank. When he had first offered Gladys the powders a week ago when Montana was on one of her trips to Colorado Springs, she'd claimed never to have tried them before. Alex had convinced her it was good for her and would counteract the sluggish feeling her daily dose of laudanum gave her. Alex had made a vow to himself to stick to the cocaine powders and to leave the opium alone, especially since he had begun to fear that he was showing the first signs of addiction. Cocaine was good for him, he was convinced, and some advertisements he had read even said it would help cure opium addiction. He'd even seen an advertisement in a magazine in which the pope had endorsed cocaine as an effective tonic.

"It's just that it's always so late by the time the customers leave," Gladys said, licking a little of the wine from her upper lip. "Then when we start this," she said, raising her glass, "it's even later. The next day all I want to do is sleep."

"And what's wrong with that?" Alex asked, reaching for her. He suddenly had the urge to dance with her, and he wanted to call in Nina and Roberta, the other two girls, as well. They could make it a party.

"What's wrong," Gladys said, giggling, "is that your sister wouldn't like it. She would hate for me to sleep all day." She turned to Alex and nuzzled his cheek. "But what she would hate worse is for you to be in here."

"What makes you say that?" Alex asked. Her remark had made him uneasy.

"You know why I say that," Gladys said. "You know because you never come in here unless she's gone off on one of her trips."

"My sister is very old-fashioned about some things. So I try to be careful not to offend her. You must be very careful, too. You must not ever mention what we do. I don't want to upset her. You understand, don't you?" Alex had begun to unlace her bodice.

"No, I don't understand," Gladys said. "Your sister has all these rules. I mean, about not having men in our rooms. It's really not fair, you know. Especially since she's always off on her own little flings."

"What do you mean by that?"

Gladys laughed. "Where is it she claims she goes? Colorado Springs, isn't it?"

"Of course that's where she goes. To buy things for the saloon."

"Don't you ever wonder why she goes so often? And how come we never see any of them tables or chairs or anything she buys?"

"I'm sure there's—there's a reason," Alex said

uneasily. Of course he had noticed that she'd been to Colorado Springs with unusual frequency lately, but he'd taken her word for it that she was looking for just the right bargain or seeing a doctor, as she had said once or twice. He had simply looked at it as an opportunity to get to know the girls better. Especially Gladys.

"Oh, there's a reason all right," Gladys said. "The reason is that she never makes it to Colorado Springs."

"What are you getting at?"

Gladys gave him a skeptical look. "Don't try to tell me you don't know."

"Don't know what?"

"That she don't go to Colorado Springs."

"Of course she does. She takes the train. She buys her tickets in advance. I've seen them myself."

"You may see a ticket, but she don't get on the train. At least not every time. She rents a wagon and rides off into the mountains." Gladys leaned toward him and said in a low, conspiratorial voice, "Ted Singer at the wagon yard told me about it. He says she has some old claim up there that she's suddenly showing a lot of interest in. *I* say it's a man."

"What?"

Gladys giggled again. "The widow McCrory won't let the girls in her saloon have a man in their room, 'cause she says she runs a respectable place. But the widow McCrory is gettin' herself fucked in some mountain cabin while she tries to keep the rest of us respectable."

Alex felt suddenly ill. "Who else knows about this?" he asked.

Gladys shrugged. "Ask Ted. He's the one told me. Say, what's wrong with you? You sick or something?"

Alex didn't answer. He got up from the bed and walked blindly toward the door.

"What's wrong?" Gladys called after him. "Was it what I said about your sister? My God, that ain't nothin' to get upset about. Ain't she human, too? Say, what is it with you?"

Her words were lost on Alex, and he slammed the door, leaving her alone in her room. He went to the back room and sat on one of the kitchen chairs, staring at Montana's bed, telling himself that what Gladys had said couldn't be true. But why else would Montana be going into the mountains? It couldn't have anything to do with the claim, as Gladys said Ted had suggested. Even the powerful Caxton Syndicate had found it worthless. And anyway, even if it wasn't, Montana didn't know anything about working a claim. It had to be that Gladys was right. She was meeting a man there. But who? Langdon Runnels? He had sensed an odd tension between them, but he couldn't believe his Ivy would ever let anything go beyond friendship. Besides, even their friendship had seemed strained when Langdon left.

Alex felt his heart pounding at a far too rapid rate, and he knew it was more than the cocaine powders affecting him. The strained relationship when Langdon left could have been the result of a lovers' quarrel, he realized. But they could have patched things up and be meeting secretly now. Behind his back. And he was making things easy by not protesting, because he had his own interests. What cheap, shallow interests they seemed when compared to his Ivy! But then, she had set it up for him, hadn't she? She had encouraged him to hire the girls and had given him the responsibility for them. She must have known what it would lead to. He had no doubt that she understood his weaknesses better than anyone.

All of the energy that he might have felt for love-making with Gladys was now suddenly transferred to anger with Ivy over her duplicity. He stood, picking up the chair and slamming it against the wall and watching it shatter into a dozen pieces. His anger soon dissolved into self-pitying tears, and he flung himself across the bed, sobbing until he fell asleep.

He awoke sometime during the night, shivering because the fire had gone out. He got up and tried to start it again, feeling miserable because his anger had given way to fear. Wrapped in a quilt, he stood by the fire rehearsing in his mind the words he would use to confront her the next day when she returned. Elizabeth and Susan. He would remind her of their shared past, their shared sorrows. Elizabeth and Susan. He would remind her how he had helped her through that awful time. He would remind her how she had needed him. How, in spite of the mistakes each had made, they needed each other. But when he thought of her with another man, he grew angry again. Angry and afraid.

He fell asleep, wrapped in the quilt and with his head on the table. He was still in that position when she awakened him the next morning. At first he couldn't remember why he was not in bed or why his back and neck felt so stiff, but he responded to the soft sound of her voice calling his name, and he accepted with gratitude the cup of hot coffee she thrust into his hands. Then he remembered.

"There's something important we have to talk about, Ivy," he said.

"Yes, she answered, "there is."

18

"*Nineteen lawsuits against* us so far," Langdon said. He shoved copies of the court documents across the table to Montana. The two of them, along with Alex and Diana, were in the back room of the Golden Palace. It had been eight months since Diana had first found gold in the Sweet Ivy and three months since they had formed the partnership. "The first one goes to court in two weeks," he added.

"Nineteen lawsuits!" Alex said, his face suddenly pale. "My God, Langdon, we'll never be able to stand up against that many."

Montana, Langdon noticed, seemed not to have heard Alex or noticed his nervousness. "I've had the lawyer buy up five more of the smaller claims," she said. Her eyes, green blazing with cold fire, met Langdon's. He could feel her excitement. There was danger in the risks they were taking, but she was feeding on the danger and growing stronger from it.

Alex turned toward her, alarmed. "You've bought

more? Good Lord, Iv—Montana. Now's not the time to *buy*. Not when we've got nineteen lawsuits to fight."

"It's all right, Alex," she said without looking at him.

"How'd you do it? Where'd you get the money?" he asked. "I thought we were saving to fight the lawsuits."

She turned to him and said with some impatience, "I borrowed most of it."

"How much?" Alex demanded. He looked as if he were about to be sick.

Langdon saw her hand move to cover his. "It's all right, Alex," she said again, quietly.

Langdon smiled inwardly at the irony of the moment. When he'd first met them more than two years ago, it had been Ivy who was cautioning Alex about the risks he was taking. But Ivy Barton was gone.

"How much?" Alex insisted.

"More than a million," Montana said.

"Oh, my God!"

Montana ignored Alex and turned to Langdon. "The bigger the partnership gets, the more collateral we have, and that means more power to bluff all those people suing us."

"I'm going to dissolve the partnership," Langdon said, testing her.

Her eyes widened slightly, and her mouth hardened. "You haven't asked for my consent to do that."

"You should read the partnership agreement more carefully," he said. "If you did, you'd see that I don't need your consent. Anyway, I've already spoken to Bob Reed. He's agreed to my plan."

"Bob doesn't speak for me unless I instruct him to," she said. Her voice was jagged, cutting ice.

Langdon was enjoying himself, watching the reaction of the tough woman he had helped create. "I think you'll agree when you hear the plan," he said. "We'll dissolve the partnership and form a public company. We'll call it the Honesty Gold Mining Company. We should be able to declare a pretty hefty dividend, and that'll shoot the price of the stock up."

Langdon saw Montana glance at Diana, and the two women exchanged a silent message he didn't understand. Montana had told him she'd given a share of the Sweet Ivy's gold to Diana in exchange for working the claim, and she'd insisted that Diana be present during the discussions. The woman, however, had said nothing during the meeting, and still she did not speak.

"How will the shares be divided?" Montana asked.

"The four of us will have controlling interest, of course. I'll have about eight hundred thousand shares, and you and Alex and Diana will have that many as well. You, of course, will own more than the other two."

"We'll all three have eight hundred thousand together, you mean."

"Of course."

"I see," Montana said. "But let me ask you something, if you don't mind. I read a little about stock companies when I had to deal with the Caxton Syndicate, and the way I understand it, companies like the one you're talking about have boards of directors. The board votes on everything, isn't that right? And the four of us are likely to be on the board?"

"That's right," Langdon said.

"And your vote carries more weight because you own more stock."

"Yes, but as I told you—"

"Ah, yes, as you told me, Alex and Diana and I together carry as much weight. But if you should, say, persuade one or the other to your side in the *unlikely* event of a disagreement with you, then it's obvious who would have the upper hand, don't you see?"

She was being condescending to nettle him, he thought, but he wasn't going to let her get by with it. He'd keep his head. "You're speculating on something you know is doubtful, Montana."

"Maybe. But I do believe it was you who taught me to consider all possibilities before I lay down my chips." She gave him her most gracious smile.

"So I did," Langdon said. "And you obviously learned well. But the important thing for now isn't who has controlling interest, but that once the company is formed, we'll have one of the richest enterprises in the state. That's going to scare the hell out of everybody that's got a lawsuit against us, and they're going to want to settle fast."

"The important thing—*always*," she said, leveling her gaze with his, "is who has control."

"The assets of the Sweet Ivy are about equal to the Honesty, and they sure as hell don't amount to three times as much. Let's keep this fair." He was having a hard time maintaining his calm.

"By all means, Langdon, let's keep it fair."

"I have no intention of cheating you, if that's what you're getting at," he said. "You can rest assured that we'll go over all of this with our lawyers, so that it will all be perfectly legal."

"Oh, you can rest assured of that," Montana said.

"Very well," Langdon snapped. He stood and gathered up the papers. Montana stopped him with a hand on his arm.

"There's one more thing," she said. He turned to look at her. "I'd like to make the name of the stock company the Sweet Ivy Gold Mining Company."

Langdon hesitated, surprised that she was still testing her power even in such a small way. "All right," he said, and managed a smile. "The Sweet Ivy it will be." He hoped that conceding that would gain him some advantage for what were sure to be the tougher battles later.

Within a week the Sweet Ivy Gold Mining Company had been formed as a stock company. Montana had met with the lawyers to iron out some of the details, and so had Langdon, but they had not encountered each other. Ever since the original partnership was formed, Langdon had hoped that the relationship would bring them together more often, and he cursed himself for having that hope. He should have stuck to his resolve to leave her alone with her miserable attachment to Alex. After all, he'd made his conquest, and that was all he'd set out to do. He had to forget that he'd fallen in love with her, had thought he could save her.

He knew that behind that tough exterior, there was still something that frightened her, something that kept her tied to Alex. But he also knew now that there was nothing he could do to save her. She had to do it herself. Or give up and die, the way his mother had.

The next time he saw her was in court, when the first lawsuit opened in Colorado Springs. She had come to town alone on the train; Diana and Alex had stayed to keep open the Golden Palace. Montana was still hanging on to the Palace as if afraid the Sweet

Ivy would slip from her hands, leaving her with the saloon as her sole means of support. Years of scrimping to get by had made her cautious in some respects.

He spotted her as soon as he walked into the courtroom. She was seated near the front, talking to Bob Reed while they waited for the proceedings to begin. The eyes of everyone in the room, it seemed, were on her. But that wasn't unusual. She had attracted attention since the first day of the trial. Women who owned gambling parlors and gold mines were not a common thing even in Colorado Springs, and that alone was enough to draw an audience. But the way she looked now made her even more alluring. On Bob Reed's advice she had purchased a new wardrobe. He'd told her that a show of wealth would further disarm her opponents in court, and Reed himself had taken her shopping and introduced her to dressmakers in town who catered not only to the wives of the newly rich, but to the European aristocracy that had been coming to Colorado Springs since the seventies, attracted by the gold and silver.

Montana was particularly lovely today in the brown velvet English-cut jacket suit she was wearing. Langdon sat next to her, and his own attorney, Richard Quinn, was next to him. Montana and Reed didn't break their huddle; Montana acknowledged his appearance with the briefest nod. Reed spoke to her for a moment longer before he got up to sit next to Quinn to discuss some of the aspects of the case.

The proceedings seemed long, drawn out, and dull, even when it was obvious to Langdon that the Sweet Ivy Company had the advantage. When they broke for the noon recess, he walked out of the courtroom with Montana and the two lawyers.

Reed had reserved a table for the four of them at the Antlers. He took Montana's arm solicitously and helped her into the carriage that would carry them to the hotel, and he sat beside her, leaving Langdon to sit across from them with Richard Quinn. Langdon didn't fail to note how often Reed purposely brushed against Montana while making the contact appear accidental.

The Antlers dining room was sumptuous, built with the benefits of the gold in the area. A liveried maître d' showed them to a private table, and within minutes a waiter appeared with an embossed menu. It was as fancy a place as any Langdon had seen in New Orleans, yet Montana looked as comfortable and poised as if she had been accustomed to such surroundings all her life. Reed leaned toward her as he made suggestions from the menu.

"The trial seems to be going well. I think we have them on the run," Quinn said, speaking to Langdon, and then he launched into some details of the case. Langdon tried to listen, but he was finding it difficult. Reed and Montana seemed to have forgotten that he and Quinn were there. Watching her with Reed filled him with an uncivilized urge to pull the man from his chair and hit him in the face. Montana was enjoying the attorney's company and blandishments far too much.

"What do you think, Reed?" Langdon asked, trying to force the man's attention away from Montana. "Are you sure things are really going as well as it seems?"

Reed looked perturbed. "Things are going very well," he said, brushing him off with a false smile before he turned back to Montana.

"Quinn here says it doesn't pay to get overconfident," Langdon said, trying again.

"It doesn't," Quinn agreed. "But there's no doubt we have them on the run. Just wait until the dividend is announced. That'll scare them even more."

"It was clever of you to think of the stock company move, Langdon," Montana said. He didn't mind that her voice still held no warmth. At least she'd finally noticed him. "I have to admit that it all seems to be working in our favor," she added. "Has Bob told you that the total number of your personal shares amounted to nine hundred and fifty-two thousand?"

"So I heard." Langdon wasn't at all certain he had heard the exact number, but he didn't like to think of Reed sharing details with her alone, no matter how innocuous.

"Since Alex and Diana and I also have nine hundred and fifty-two thousand together, that leaves five hundred and ninety-six thousand shares, I do believe," Montana said, drawing the words out in her Tennessee drawl.

"Counting the cards, are you?" Langdon asked. He liked the way she was smiling at him.

"Isn't that the way you taught me?"

Langdon acknowledged her remark with a nod and settled back on his seat, happy that he had at last gotten her attention.

"You might like to know that some of those shares have gone to Diana Pollard," Montana said. "Bob tells me that it was a general partnership that was drawn up. That means any debts owed by one of the partners become the debts of the partnership, isn't that right, Bob?"

Reed nodded, his eyes locked on her in a sickeningly admiring gaze.

"So," Montana continued, "since I owed Diana for

work she'd done, the best way to pay off that debt seemed to be to give her the shares. Then she purchased some of her own."

Langdon sat up straighter, his eyes never leaving hers. "How many, total?" he asked.

"Three hundred and seventy-five thousand," she said.

He was startled. That meant the three of them now had more than his total. It also meant Montana, in effect, had control of the Sweet Ivy Gold Mining Company. He had taught her well. Too well.

Diana worked behind the bar at the Golden Palace, drawing mugs of beer in an almost continuous foaming stream, the yeasty scent filling the saloon with a thick, heavy incense. Even with the extra girls Montana had hired to help, it was hard to keep up. Business at the Palace had more than doubled over the past three months, ever since word had gotten out of the fabulous strikes at the Sweet Ivy and the Honesty. Miners and prospectors had poured into town and into the Golden Palace. Even those who had been around for a while migrated to the Palace in hopes of catching a glimpse of the lucky lady, wishing some of her luck would rub off on them. If they were disappointed that during the past week she had been away from the Palace while she fought lawsuits in a Colorado Springs court, it didn't slow them down.

Diana found it ironic that now that Montana might not need the business, the crowds were heavier than ever. She understood Montana's cautious attitude that compelled her to keep the saloon open, though. There was no assurance that things would go well for her in court, and if she lost the Sweet Ivy, she'd need something to fall back on.

Despite the fact that they were busier than ever and needed all the help they could get, Alex was seldom there. Not that it mattered to Diana. She disliked him even more than she disliked most men, and preferred not to have him around. It didn't occur to her to care where he was during the days Montana was in Colorado Springs, but she was never surprised when he came home smelling of a whore or liquor. It did annoy her, though, that he was constantly getting calls from some woman on the new telephone Montana had installed recently. The woman had a raspy, distinctly unpleasant voice. Diana thought she knew the type—whores who burned out too soon and grew old before their time. She hadn't thought that was Alex's style, but it was none of her concern.

She missed Montana, and she didn't like to think of her being in Colorado Springs with Langdon Runnels. She was glad, though, that at least she was away from her brother. She knew that Alex often upset Montana, not only with his drinking and whoring, but in some other way, too, some way she could not quite understand. She brushed aside a niggling worry that Anna's filthy story could be true. Anna had come to her just before the fire and told her about seeing Montana and Alex together.

"They're sleeping together," Anna had said. "You know what that means, don't you?" she had asked, taunting her. "It means Alex is gettin' what you want. Don't try to hide it. I've seen the way you look at her." She had laughed then, her ugly, jeering laugh. "How long's it been, Diana? Long enough to get you good and horny? When you get horny enough, let me know. I like something different now and then."

It made Diana sick to think of the evil, twisted creature. She was glad she had died in the fire before she had a chance to hurt Montana with her lies.

On the third day of Montana's absence, Diana stepped out the front door of the Golden Palace on her way to the post office. She was surprised to see a nun standing a few yards from the door. She seemed nervous and was fiddling with something in her hand. Diana couldn't remember ever seeing one of the Sisters of Mercy on Myrtle Avenue. The street of saloons and brothels was definitely out of their usual territory. No wonder the sister was nervous.

The nun looked up anxiously, as if she were waiting for someone in the saloon, but when she saw that it was Diana coming out, she turned away. Diana recognized her as the woman they said was the head of the order. Sister Mary Frances, she thought she was called. What was she doing hanging around the Palace?

"Waitin' for somebody?" Diana asked, unable to contain her curiosity.

The nun seemed surprised that she had spoken to her. "I beg your pardon?" she said. The voice sounded vaguely familiar to Diana.

"Never mind. I just thought you looked like you was waitin' for somebody." Diana tried to move around her.

"Wait a minute!" the nun said. Diana turned to face her. "Actually I do have business with one of the proprietors of this saloon." She spat out the word *saloon* as if it were something putrid that had accidentally found its way to her lips.

"Montana McCrory, you mean?"

"Her brother," the nun said.

"He ain't a proprietor, and he ain't here. If you want to wait a while, he'll be back sooner or later, or maybe you can find him in the Central."

"I certainly won't be going to the Central," Sister Mary Frances said indignantly. "But if you will be so kind as to give Mr. Miller a message . . ."

"What message?" Diana asked. She was wary of the woman, but she was also curious to know what business she could possibly have with Alex.

"If you could deliver this," said Sister Mary Frances, extending a sealed envelope. "To Mr. Miller," she added.

Diana's took the envelope. When she had it in her hand, Sister Mary Frances wiped her own fingers with a quick swipe down the side of her habit and turned abruptly to walk away.

Diana stared at the envelope for a moment. Something about the old nun had bothered her. It was several seconds before she realized that it was her voice—the same voice that had been calling for Alex. What did she want with him? Whatever it was, it would do no good to give the letter to Alex. Alex would pay it no heed. He would throw it away, forget it, or wait for Montana to return to deal with it.

But Montana had no need for any more trouble, and Diana was certain that was what the letter would bring. The old nun probably wrote it to pound at them for running a place of sin or some such sanctimonious foolishness. Diana went back inside, lifted the burner plate on the stove, and pushed in a corner of the unopened envelope. Just as the paper caught fire, curiosity overcame her, and she pulled it out. She blew out the flame, then waved the envelope in the air to cool it and disperse the smoke. With a quick flick of her finger, she broke the seal and extracted a sheet of paper, slightly scorched along one edge. She read the letter, written in a heavy and precisely controlled penmanship.

> *Dear Mr. Miller,*
>
> *This is to assure you that your daughter, Alexis, now eight months old, is flourishing and receiving the best care possible. However, to assure that this care continues, it will be necessary for you to increase your monthly assistance above the $100 a month you have been providing. I suggest $200 a month. I am sure you and your sister will want to comply with this in order to guarantee your daughter's continued care and to keep her unfortunate origins unknown. In light of your recent good fortune in the gold fields, I am certain you will find no inconvenience with this. Since, as I am sure you agree, there is no reason for further discussion of this matter, I do not expect to hear from you except in the form of your monthly payment, which is due now.*
>
> *Yours in Christ, Sister M. F.*

Diana crumpled the letter in her hand and sank onto one of the chairs. Alex and Montana were being blackmailed by the goddamned devil so she would keep quiet about some bastard of Alex's.

Diana felt suddenly sick. She smoothed out the letter and read it again, trying to determine what the wording meant. " . . . *you and your sister will want to comply with this in order to keep her unfortunate origins unknown. . . .*" Was she linking the child to Montana, too? Was the ugly rumor true? Was Montana the mother?

Diana remembered that Montana had been frail and sickly right after the fire. She had thought it was just because she was overworked and had gone through the harrowing ordeal of losing the Palace and having to rebuild on a shoestring. Had it been something else? Had there been a baby growing inside her? Alex's baby? Diana knew she had stayed away long enough for Montana to have carried and delivered a baby. How had Montana kept the secret while she ran the saloon? Maybe she hadn't run it. Maybe she had gone into seclusion and let Alex run it, and that was why the business had gone down so bad. Now that she remembered it, Montana had mentioned that she had been ailing and in bed for a while. As much as Diana hated to think of it, she knew it could have been because she was pregnant. She must have kept it a secret somehow. Not showed herself, maybe. Then, when the baby was born, she had given it up to the orphanage. But the old nun must have heard rumors about Alex and Montana. Anna could have spread them farther than she had realized. Anyway, the nun had guessed the truth somehow, and now she was blackmailing Alex and Montana in exchange for her silence.

The more Diana spun out the fantastic story in her mind, the sicker and more paralyzed she became. She had concocted a truth that was too astonishing, too ugly and painful, to bear. With a great sorrowful moan, she flung herself across the table, her head buried in her arms, and wept bitterly.

In a few moments she raised her head, embarrassed with herself. But she was ashamed, too, over condemning Montana. It could not be all Montana's fault. It was probably mostly the fault of that goddamned Alex. And anyway, didn't she herself know the lengths that the desperate need for affection could lead a person to? She had no right to judge or condemn Montana. Instead she had to protect her. If she had somehow managed up to this point to keep people from knowing about the baby, it had to stay that way, even if it meant paying blackmail to Sister Mary Frances.

Diana gave a bitter smile as she thought of how chagrined the good sister would be if she had known that, considering the wealth of the Sweet Ivy, she could have demanded more than $200 a month. But $200 every month was more than many people who considered themselves well off would ever see, so she could feel smug about getting it. And Diana would see that she got it. If Alex had been the one making the payments, then that probably meant Montana knew nothing about them. Alex was irresponsible. He could get on one of his drunken binges and fail to meet the old nun's demands, then Montana would be vulnerable.

If the Sweet Ivy Company stayed intact, Diana knew she would be wealthy in her own right. In the meantime, she would use her savings to see that Sister Mary Francis got the first payment that would protect Montana. She would tell the old nun that Alex had handed over responsibility for the payments to her. If Alex kept up his payments as well, she would have to convince the good sister that was just evidence of his confused state—the result of too much liquor and opium.

Two days later, Langdon called the Colorado Mining Exchange and announced the $90,000 dividend that had been agreed upon earlier. Montana was surprised at how quickly it got the results he had predicted. By afternoon the price of the stock had soared. By early the next morning the plaintiffs were in a panic knowing they were up against a giant company more powerful than they had imagined. They threw in the towel and offered to settle. The Sweet Ivy Gold Mining Company had won the battle, intact and stronger than ever.

To celebrate, Bob planned an evening for all the stockholders at the Heinrich House, a casino on the outskirts of Colorado Springs owned by Eric Heinrich, a German count. Alex made the trip from Eagleton by train, but Diana chose not to attend.

The casino was as grand as its reputation. Glittering chandeliers hung from the ceilings, and carved rosewood panels graced the walls, over which were hung paintings of cavorting cherubs whose faces were said to be those of the count's lovers. Croupiers exuded charm along with their foreign accents, and men and women alike moved among the gaming tables.

Montana had been surrounded by people Bob had introduced to her, but she managed finally to move away from the crowds. She spotted Alex in the midst of the throng. He was in very good form, gambling and drinking with a group of men and women. She saw him offer the dice to one of the women to kiss for good luck before he threw them. The woman obliged him by touching them to her lips and then rubbed them slowly across the tops of her breasts while she smiled seductively. Her action brought a collective "Oooh" from the crowd around the table and then cheers when Alex won the throw. When Alex turned to the woman and kissed her hand and then the tops of her breasts, Montana turned away.

"Are you not enjoying yourself, Frau McCrory?" Montana turned to see an imposing gentleman of about fifty addressing her. He sported a large handle-bar mustache and a full beard, and he had a long-stemmed pipe clamped between his teeth. "Count Eric Heinrich," he said, bowing to her. He spoke in a heavy Teutonic accent.

"Count Heinrich," she said, acknowledging his greeting. "How did you know my name?" She had heard of the count but had never met him. He was said to be one of the early promoters of the gold fields around Colorado Springs, and he owned a mine of his own.

"You should not be surprised that I know who you are, madam," the count said. "You are all the talk of the Springs. Your lawsuit, your gold mining company, your dividend. And you are a casino owner, too, I hear, just as I am."

She laughed. "The Golden Palace is not as grand as this, I'm afraid."

"Ah, I see that you *can* smile," the count said. "And you are much more beautiful when you smile. Come, I insist that you have a good time. I will show you how. There are dozens of people waiting to meet you."

He pulled her into the crowd again, introducing her to more people, and she was showered with attention. Basil Ashcraft, a young grandee from London, was particularly attentive. He stayed by her side for an hour, bringing her champagne, encouraging her to try her luck at the tables.

"You must stand beside me at the roulette wheel," he said as he handed her yet another glass of champagne. "I'm certain you'll bring me luck."

"You have to bring your own luck," she said with a little laugh as she accepted the champagne. She had noticed that at the age of twenty his face still was not completely clear of its adolescent eruptions.

He looked at her a bit peevishly. "You don't want to stand by my side and bring me luck?"

"It's not that," she said. "I just—"

"Forgive me. I should have noticed. You must be tired."

"It's not so much that I'm tired. It's just the crowds. I'm afraid I'm not in the mood for them."

The young man brightened. "Of course," he said. "I understand. Come with me. We'll get some fresh air." He took her hand and led her across the floor to a door that opened onto a wide veranda.

Montana went along reluctantly, but once she was outside, the air did feel refreshing, and it was good to get away from the crush of people. She walked to the railing of the veranda and stared across a meadow at the peaceful scene of cattle grazing in the moonlight.

"A bit stuffy in there, wasn't it?" said young Ashcraft, walking up behind her.

"Yes," she said over her shoulder, "a little."

"But this is ever so much better."

"Yes, it is."

"I'm terribly glad you weren't in the mood for crowds tonight," he said, moving close to her. "I was a bit out of the mood myself, after I saw you."

Before she could respond, she felt an arm around her waist, then he had turned her around and was kissing her on the mouth. She struggled to free herself, but he held her close.

"There are rooms upstairs," he said with his mouth still close to hers. His hand was fumbling at the front of her dress.

"What are you doing?" she cried, trying to push him away.

"I knew what you meant when you said you wanted to get away," he said, persisting with his hands.

"No! No," she said, struggling. "You misunderstood. I—"

"So there you are, Montana!"

The voice came from somewhere on the darkened veranda, and as soon as he heard it, young Ashcraft dropped his hands from Montana and turned around.

Langdon Runnels stood silhouetted against the lights of the casino. "I've been looking all over for you."

"Langdon!" she said, both embarrassed and relieved to see him.

He walked toward them and offered his hand to Ashcraft. "My name is Langdon Runnels. I don't believe we've met."

Young Ashcraft cleared his throat. "Basil Ashcraft," he said, extending his hand awkwardly.

"Nice of you to keep the lady entertained while I was preoccupied," Langdon said.

"The lady is with me, sir," Ashcraft said defensively, as if he were spoiling for a fight. "She has been all evening."

Langdon took Montana's arm. "I know, and again I say thanks. If you'll excuse us . . ."

Ashcraft stared at Langdon, obviously sizing him up. "Yes, of course," he said finally, and with a nervous nod in Montana's direction he hurried into the casino.

Langdon turned to Montana and cocked an eyebrow. "Well, Mrs. McCrory, I'm afraid I interrupted your initiation into Colorado Springs high society."

19

Alex waited for one of the house servants he had hired to bring him the breakfast he had rung for, and as he waited he ran his hands over the sheets of his bed, which still smelled of heavy French perfume. The woman who had left the scent had slipped out before he awoke. It didn't bother him that she was gone. He would see her again eventually. If not, then he would find something else to amuse him. There was always plenty to do in Colorado Springs.

Alex had always known that money could change things for him, but he'd never guessed to what profound degree. It had now been more than a year since they'd struck it rich with the Sweet Ivy, and things were going well for him. Even Sister Mary Frances had stopped bothering him. He had gotten lax about his payments, but she hadn't seemed to notice. If he didn't know better, he would think someone was making them for him. But no one knew about the child except him, he was sure. More likely Sister

Mary Frances had, in the end, done what was best for the child and sent her away someplace where she'd be better off. Gotten her a nice family. It had occurred to him once or twice to inquire, but then he'd thought better of it. In later years the child wouldn't want to be reminded that she was a bastard, and it was best to sever the ties now. Staying out of her life was probably the kindest, most thoughtful thing he could do.

It also left him free to enjoy his new wealth. He had bought clothes and carriages and horses and even a house—a mansion on Wood Avenue that a British earl sold when he decided to return to England. He was about to resell it himself, as soon as the new one was built. He felt at home in Colorado Springs. Poor, rough men who had suddenly become wealthy were not new to the Springs, so he was not looked upon with disdain for his lack of old money or breeding or education.

He and Montana were constantly in demand at parties in Colorado Springs, which, even more than Denver, was the social center of the state. Alex enjoyed the glittering society of "Little London" with all its trappings of European aristocracy, but Montana shunned it most of the time, preferring to stay in Eagleton at the Golden Palace.

She had built the Palace up bigger than ever. Sparkling glass chandeliers even grander than those in the Nolton hung from the high ceiling of the new building. There were new rosewood panels on the walls, similar to those in the Heinrich House casino, and they matched the heavily carved rosewood bar. Paintings of pastoral scenes hung in gilded frames above the paneling. Upstairs were the rooms for the staff of fourteen, which included dancing girls, croupiers, a cook, and a bartender. Montana had also had suites of rooms designed for herself and another suite for him, although he was seldom there to occupy it.

She never complained about the time he spent in Colorado Springs, and it seemed to Alex that his life couldn't be better. He had even allowed himself to hope that Montana was happy with their new life as well, that she would forget all about Tennessee.

The last time she'd come to the Springs to meet with some of the other mine owners, she'd sounded like she might have leaving on her mind. He'd quickly reminded her that there was trouble brewing with the mine workers union, even though he wasn't clear on just what the union trouble was. He knew he had to think of a way to convince her to stay, though. He was more certain than ever that he could never go back and face those graves again. The graves were the reason he'd left. The reason he'd sold the farm at the first excuse he could find.

Maybe he hadn't been much of a father. Maybe he hadn't always measured up. But he'd loved the girls, and he'd suffered when they died more than Ivy knew. More than anyone could ever know.

Their deaths had haunted him for years. Finally, after he'd come to Colorado, he'd learned to keep the memory at bay most of the time. It was only rarely now that it would reopen unexpectedly like a rotting sore, leaving him sick and frightened and desperate for some means of closing up the putridity again.

He wouldn't go back to that old sickness. He would stay in Colorado even if it meant sending Ivy back to Tennessee without him.

The more he thought about that idea, the more he liked it. Ivy had never wanted to leave Byrneville. He could give her something she wanted now—have a house built for her, a home near the children's graves. He could even make the arrangements for her to travel back there to look around for a site. There was no point in buying two tickets to Tennessee, though. She was quite capable of taking care of things without him.

Diana had stopped by the Golden Palace as she often did to discuss Sweet Ivy business with Montana. Today she had wanted to look over some assay reports, so she sat at Montana's desk, going over the reports while Montana met at a private table in the saloon with Maxwell Hayes, the union organizer.

The union was demanding three dollars a day for eight hours of work. Most of the other mine owners said they had to work their miners nine hours a day for three dollars to make a profit. Montana told Diana she was going to propose a compromise for the miners who worked for the Sweet Ivy Company mines, and that was what this meeting was about.

While Diana sat at Montana's desk, the telephone jangled insistently. Since the remodeling, the old black box on the wall had been replaced by a long-necked model that stood on Montana's desk in a spacious office next to the kitchen. Montana had a full-time clerk now, Frank Neff, who helped her keep the books on both the Golden Palace and the Sweet Ivy Company. He usually took care of answering the telephone, intercepting the clamoring bell with ardent dispatch. Mr. Neff had not yet come in, however.

Absorbed in the latest assay reports from the mine, Diana had let the telephone ring three times before she finally picked up the bell-shaped receiver and placed it to her ear. She felt a chill of recognition when she heard the voice at the other end of the line asking for Montana.

"Your sister is busy now, Alex."

"She can't be too goddamned busy to talk to me," Alex insisted. "Go get her and tell her I'm on the line. She won't like it if I tell her you refused."

"She's busy," Diana said. "She'll call you back." With that she hung up the phone and imagined, with pleasure, Alex seething with anger.

When Montana came into the office, she asked her about the meeting with Maxwell Hayes.

"We've worked out a compromise," Montana said. "The Sweet Ivy mines will pay three twenty-five for nine hours' work, and night shift miners will work eight hours for the same amount."

"The other mine owners are going to hit the ceiling and yell traitor even louder," Diana said.

"They will at first," Montana said. "But I think they'll come around. I think they'll see the value of compromise. Especially if it keeps the miners from striking."

They talked for several minutes longer before Diana remembered to give her Alex's message. She felt a secret stab of chagrin when she saw how eager Montana was to talk to him.

Diana waited outside in the noisy saloon while Montana rang up the operator for the long-distance call. When, after several minutes, Montana still had not emerged from the office, Diana began to worry. She walked to the door and tapped on it softly. The door swung open under the pressure of her hand, and she saw Montana seated at the desk, an aura of sadness about her.

"Are you all right?" she asked, wondering what the bastard had done to upset her.

Montana glanced at her. "We're going back," she said. Her voice sounded strangely detached.

"Back?"

"To Tennessee. Alex says he's made the arrangements."

"I see," Diana said. She felt a weight on her chest. She had heard Montana and her brother speak of Tennessee enough to know that was where they had called home before they'd both moved to Kansas City, where Montana had married Tom McCrory. It must have been there, Diana thought, that Montana had been known as Ivy, the name she had heard Alex call her once or twice. Diana had noticed that Montana didn't like him calling her that, but she had never protested the name Sweet Ivy for the mine.

"I should have gone long ago," Montana said, more to herself than to Diana.

Diana knew something was wrong, and before she could stop herself, she voiced her worst fear. "It's not just a visit—you're going to stay."

Montana said nothing for a long moment. "I belong there, Diana. You won't understand, I know, but—"

"I understand that you belong here," Diana said. "With—" She had almost said "with me," but she had caught herself in time. "With your businesses," she said. "The Golden Palace, the Sweet Ivy."

"They can run themselves without me. I have enough money to hire competent managers."

"What about this union matter?"

"It's taken care of. I told you. We reached a compromise."

"If the other mine owners don't go for it, it ain't settled."

"It will be all right. I'm sure of it. It's a reasonable compromise for both sides."

"But this is your home now, Montana. I—we need you here."

"Oh, Diana," Montana said, getting up and moving to embrace her. "I have just been trying to tell you that you don't need me here."

Diana stiffened in her embrace and fought back tears. "When are you leaving?" she asked, pushing her away and pretending to be busy straightening papers on the desk.

"In a week. Alex already has the train reservations. I never thought he wanted to go back, but he actually seemed excited." She hesitated, and Diana saw the troubled, frightened look on her face. "Diana," she said, her voice trembling, "I think it's time I tell you this. It's about Alex and me. We—"

"Will you sell the Golden Palace?" Diana interrupted, her voice a little too shrill. She didn't want to hear any confessions, and she turned her eyes so she would not have to look at Montana. But when Montana didn't answer right away, Diana glanced at her, concerned. She was even more concerned when she saw her stricken look. The confused words she spoke troubled her still more.

"I have no right to sell what is not—I mean, I don't know—" She stood up abruptly and hurried toward the door.

"It's that damned brother of yours, ain't it?" Diana called after her. "He's upset you."

There was no answer.

Diana made plans to leave Eagleton the next day for a two-week stay in Denver. She didn't want to be around for the final good-bye. Before she left, she made her way to the Sisters of Mercy Orphanage.

Two-year-old Alexis recognized her as soon as she entered and extended her chubby arms, prattling the nonsense that made Diana's heart sing.

"Nonny Di," the child said, running toward her.

"Yes, it's Aunty Di," said Sister Augusta, the young nun who cared for the children. She pretended not to see the stick of licorice Diana handed Alexis.

Diana was the only person who visited Alexis regularly, and it had taken some doing to arrange it. Sister Mary Frances had forbidden it at first, claiming Diana was an unsavory influence. But Diana had increased the monthly payment, and Sister Mary Frances had relented, as long as she or one of the other nuns was present during the visit to make sure Diana did or said nothing to corrupt the child. Initially, Diana had tried to convince Sister Mary Frances that Alex had given her responsibility for delivering the payments, but since Alex had kept up his $100 each month for a brief time, the nun had caught on quickly. Eventually Alex, in his typical irresponsible manner, had stopped his payments altogether. Now it no longer seemed to matter to either of the two women who was providing the money. Diana knew that as long as no one confronted Alex about the payments, he would not concern himself. She was not about to confront him. Alexis had given her a reason to keep things just the way they were.

Alexis was a beautiful child with golden-blond hair and pale skin and eyes the color of blue China silk. She had taken after her father in looks, without a doubt.

"Nonny Di," Alexis said again, kissing Diana with lips sticky from the candy she had just given her.

"And look at what else Aunty Di has brought you," she said, reaching into a bag and bringing out a rag doll she had bought at the N.O. Johnson Department Store.

Alexis took the doll and held it in front of her, giggling at its funny embroidered face. Her bubbling laughter made Diana and the young nun laugh too. "Lexy's baby," she said, and planted a wet, sticky kiss on the doll's yellow yarn curls. "Kiss Lexy's baby," she insisted, shoving the doll first at Diana and then at Sister Augusta.

Diana stayed with Alexis for the two hours allotted her and then left, dreading the emptiness she always felt when her visit was over. In spite of the money she now had from her share of Sweet Ivy stock, Alexis and Montana were the only true bright spots in her life. It had saddened her at first to think that Montana had never visited the child, but gradually she had constructed the reason in her mind. Montana would never neglect little Alexis out of selfishness or cruelty. Whatever her faults, Montana was neither of those. It had to be partly out of shame. And Diana understood shame. It also had to be to protect the child. It wouldn't do for the little girl to ever suspect the truth about her parentage.

She could not blame Montana for her sin. It was, she was certain, her brother's fault. He had seduced his sister, just as he had tried to seduce practically every other woman he met. Alex and Montana seemed to have grown apart recently, though, and Diana had thought that Montana's feelings for him had changed. She wondered now, though, if she'd been wrong since the two of them were going away together.

The thought of it worried her. And saddened her.

For a while, after Alex had moved to Colorado Springs, leaving Montana in Eagleton, Diana had allowed herself to dream. She had dreamed of Montana and Alexis moving with her into the house she had built at the edge of town. It would be a fine house for a child and a happy family. Alexis would never want for anything, and they would make certain she had a proper Sunday school upbringing. She would never even be allowed to get near Myrtle Avenue and the saloons and parlor houses. They could buy her a pony, maybe, and they could teach her to ride and to cook, and Montana would teach her to sew. They need never talk about who Alexis's parents were. She could be brought up thinking they had died.

Diana pulled her shawl more tightly around her shoulders as she made her way to the train station, forcing herself not to think of those things, willing herself not to dream.

Langdon had spent a good part of the day at the mines, inspecting the new hoist that had been installed at the Honesty, then riding over to the Sweet Ivy to look at the new equipment there. By the time he had finished, it was too late to catch the last train from Eagleton back to Colorado Springs. He decided to get a room at the Portland Hotel and go back on the first train the next morning.

His visits to Eagleton had been rare since the stock company was formed, but he had ridden the train in a few times on his way to the mines. Each time he came to town he had seen the new Golden Palace rising and heard talk of the fancy new interior, but he had never given in to the temptation to go see it or Montana. It had been hard enough to see her at the board meetings until he resigned from the board three months ago. During those meetings they had managed to keep their encounters brief and confine their discussions to business matters. It was the way they both preferred it. At least he pretended he preferred it.

He'd tried to keep her out of his thoughts in between those encounters by staying busy, and there was plenty in the way of social life to keep him entertained in Colorado Springs. Money had opened up even more opportunities than he had cultivated earlier. It had opened up opportunities to make more money as well, and he found himself looking for chances to test his luck as well as his imagination and wits.

He was on the verge of a new venture now, one that would take him away from Colorado. He had to get out of Colorado, because none of the other things—not work, not women, not society balls or parties—could keep Montana out of his thoughts. He had never figured out the hold Alex had on her, but maybe it didn't matter. What mattered was that Montana could not be his.

After he ate his supper, it was still early in the evening, so he decided to make the rounds of the gambling parlors and saloons. He had not intended to go to the Golden Palace, but he could hear the noise coming from it several blocks down the street, and he could see the diffuse yellow glow from the electric lights shining through tall arched windows in front. It looked, he thought, at long last, golden. He found himself following the sound of the crowd and the glimmering lights like a man drawn by the call of a siren. He would just have a look, just enough to satisfy his curiosity. He would not stay long. He would not make any attempt to see her, and if he did, he would keep up his guard.

When he stepped inside, the warmth of the ornate room enveloped him like a blanket. His eyes scanned the crowd as, in spite of himself, he searched for Montana. There were several women in the room, young and beautiful, all of them laughing, dancing, and drinking with the customers, but none of them was Montana. His eyes went to the bar, where a tall man with a long, carefully groomed mustache had replaced the dour-faced Diana, but still he did not see Montana.

Behind him a croupier with a French accent was calling out numbers on a roulette wheel. Langdon walked to the wheel and placed a bet. He played for several minutes and had lost a hundred dollars before he moved on toward a blackjack table. He had just placed his bet when he saw her. She apparently had just entered from the back, but she had already attracted attention. Langdon watched her as she stood like a queen surrounded by her court, benevolently bestowing her smile and attention on each courtier in turn.

In a moment she moved toward one of the tables. She had not seen him, and he did nothing to attract her attention, but he watched her, thinking how, even more than her expensive velvet gown and elaborate hairstyle, her maturity was making her more beautiful. Her face had become more sculptured and her manner more regal and confident.

He left while her back was to him, and he moved on to another saloon. By three in the morning, when most of the saloons and gambling parlors were closing their doors, she still had not left his thoughts.

Soon he would be leaving Eagleton for good, and he knew he had to see her one more time. He made his way, once again, down the street toward the Palace, which still glimmered in the quiet darkness.

There was no sound of a crowd, but he found the front door still unlocked. He opened it and stepped inside. She was alone in the large room, standing at the cash register behind the bar, tallying the night's take. She had not seen him or heard him enter, and for a moment he watched her again, seeing her as he had so often when they had owned the Palace together.

"Still worried you're not making a profit?"

She sucked in her breath, and her hand went to her breast as she whirled to face him. Then she recognized him, and he saw her face change. Her voice, when she spoke, was charged with tension. "What are you doing here?"

"Is that any way to greet an old friend?"

"I didn't expect to see you so far away from Little London," she said, not without rancor.

"We miss you in the Springs," he said. "You make yourself even more socially desirable by hiding out here in the hinterlands."

She gave a short, cynical laugh and went back to her tally sheet. "I can assure you, that's not my intent."

"I would think you would want to be with your— with Alex." He watched her closely to gauge her reaction and saw her face blanch and her hands tremble slightly.

"I don't care for the Springs—all that social whirl," she said. "Alex does, of course. I expect you've heard he's building a house there."

"I've heard. And I've seen it. It's going to be one of the biggest mansions in town. Have you seen it?"

"Not in several months." She wrote something on the tally sheet. "The frame had only begun to take shape the last time I stopped by."

"So it will be Alex's house. Not yours as well." He wondered if she knew about all the women Alex had in Colorado Springs. He was certain she did, and in spite of it, she continued to remain loyal.

"I will have rooms there, of course," she said.

"You're still playing the game."

She glanced up at him, a green flame flickering in her eyes. "You know as well as I do, Langdon, that this was no game. It was a way to survive."

"*Was*," he said. "And you've survived very well. You don't have to play the game anymore."

"What Alex and I do or do not do is none of your business, Mr. Runnels." She slammed the cash register drawer closed and picked up her tally sheet.

"You're right, Mrs. McCrory," he said. "We established that long ago." He contrived his cocky smile and tipped his hat. "I bid you good night."

He had moved only a few steps toward the door when she called him back. "Langdon, wait!"

He turned slowly to face her.

"It's . . . been a long time. I shouldn't have been so rude. I should have offered you a drink."

"Buttermilk? Isn't that what you always have before you go to bed?"

She laughed a little uneasily. "Yes, but we have some of that brandy you used to like." She had already taken two glasses down from the shelf. She led the way to one of the tables and poured brandy for both of them. "About the—the game, as you call it—"

"You're right. It's none of my business."

"But it is. You've been a part of it. And it's time it

ended. But neither of us has known how to do it. Alex says it's sure to cause a scandal whether people believe us or not, and I'm afraid he's right."

"Are you afraid of a scandal?"

"I plan to avoid a scandal," she said. He noticed that she had not answered his question.

He picked up his glass and offered a toast. "To your plan, whatever it is."

She smiled slightly, touched her glass to his, and tasted the brandy. He saw the grimace that played across her face and knew that in spite of her sophistication, she still had not grown used to strong drink. Still was partly Ivy Barton.

"What are you doing in Eagleton?" she asked.

"I came to look at the new hoist on the Honesty. You've heard about it, I'm sure."

"Of course. We authorized the purchase at the last board meeting."

"I wanted to see it in operation," he said. "I'm thinking of investing in the company that manufactures it."

She offered to pour more brandy, but he declined with a wave of his hand. "You're getting into several other investments, I hear. Even sold off some of the Sweet Ivy stock at quite a profit to pay for them," she said.

"I want to keep my money working for me."

"You always were clever, Langdon, and you always knew the right time to get in and out of a business."

He had not missed her barb. "My getting out of the Golden Palace had nothing to do with business, if you remember."

Her eyes met his, and he saw something, some acknowledgment of the truth, flicker there for a moment before she lowered them again. "Whatever your reason, it doesn't matter now. You've done well enough without the Golden Palace."

"And so have you. Why do you hang on to it?"

"I'm not sure," she said, still without looking at him. "Maybe it's because of her. The real—the first Montana. I still feel as if it's hers in a way, and I keep asking myself what she would want."

"You do too much of that, Montana—too much trying to do what others would want you to do."

Her eyes met his again, and she smiled. "Maybe you're right," she said. "Maybe I'll sell the Golden Palace. I've been thinking of it." Her face was a stiff mask, and he knew she was hiding something again.

"And leave Eagleton?" he asked. "To go to the Springs and Alex's house?"

"We're not certain what we will do," she said, avoiding his eyes. She laughed, and the sound had a false ring. "Money, as you know, offers a lot of choices."

"Indeed it does." He stood and picked up his hat. "And I'll be exercising one of those choices soon. One of the reasons I came was to say good-bye," he said.

"Good-bye?" she asked, surprised.

"Yes," he said. "I'm going to Texas. They're beginning to explore for oil there. I've invested in a company to—"

"Texas? But—"

"Will you miss me?" he asked, grinning, teasing her, because it was easier to fall into his old ways than to say good-bye.

She stood and faced him. "Of course I'll miss you," she said. "We've been . . . friends—and—we've been through a lot together." She turned her back to him. "I wish you good luck." She moved toward the bar.

There was a long silence while he watched her walk away from him. "Montana," he said suddenly, without knowing he was going to say it. "Come with me."

She turned to face him.

"I asked you to come with me once before. You said you couldn't because Alex needed you. He doesn't need you now. Come with me."

"Langdon, I can't. I—"

"You can," he said, walking toward her. "You said you loved me once. Has that changed?"

She lowered her eyes, but he caught her chin and forced her to look at him. "Tell me the truth."

"No," she whispered. "Nothing's changed."

He moved his hand to the back of her neck, pulling her to him and slanting his mouth across hers. He felt her resist, but he wouldn't let her go. Finally her arms went around him, her hands caressed his back, and she returned his kiss for a moment, shyly, before she tried to pull away. He held her, refusing to let her go, his mouth close to her ear. "Come with me," he said.

"No." Her voice was little more than a murmur. "No." But her protests died as he lifted her in his arms and walked toward the stairs. The door to her suite was open, and he carried her inside, kicking the door closed behind him.

He put her gently on the bed, and for a moment she seemed to want to leave. "Langdon—" She rose slightly, beginning a protest. He pushed her back, kissed her again, and felt her relax. With his mouth still on hers, he slipped the low-cut top of her dress off her shoulders and touched her bare back, felt her shiver, felt her shoulder blades bunch together. Her bosom was thrust forward with the involuntarily movement, and he moved his hand slowly to the front to caress a breast. He heard the sound of her breath like a small protest when he took it into his mouth, then felt her arch toward him, felt the flutter of a hand at the front of his shirt.

She sat up and pulled at the buttons recklessly, fingers trembling, until she could slip her hands inside and let them roam the expanse of his chest, his shoulders, his back.

"So warm," she whispered, her palms still moving over him. Then she was on her knees, kissing him, trying to balance herself on the springy mattress while she forced his shirt off his shoulders. His hands were busy with hooks and buttons and crinoline strings. Finally he took her down again, gently, and slipped it all off, a piece at a time, over her hips until she was naked. Her flesh was cool, and he covered her with his half-naked body to warm her.

She raised her knees and opened her legs and let him lie between them.

"Langdon," she whispered, but he kissed her again before she could say more. First her mouth, then her neck, her breasts, her belly.

"God in heaven, Langdon!"

He felt her tremble, felt her pulling herself up, helping him remove his trousers. Then he was on top of her again, and she was guiding him with her hand to invade her flesh.

He felt again the wild mix of emotions and passions when she stirred beside him just as the first sunlight touched them. She opened her eyes slowly, moved an arm lazily, seductively, over him, and she clung to him a moment, not speaking. He could feel his heart beating recklessly against his chest.

He kissed the top of her head, and she stayed near him a moment longer before she pushed away. He tried to pull her back, but she resisted. She stood, pulling a wrapper around her naked body as she walked to the washstand to pour water from a porcelain pitcher into a matching bowl.

"You're beautiful," he said, lying on his back with his hands behind his head, watching her. She didn't answer, but she turned to face him, and a faint smile flickered across her mouth. The hint of sadness in it worried him. "I love you, Montana," he said.

She turned her back to him again and said, almost in a whisper, "Let's not pretend, Langdon."

He felt as if her words had mortally wounded him. He got out of bed and reached for his trousers. "I haven't been pretending," he said. "Have you?"

When she didn't answer, he went to her and grasped her shoulders, turning her around and forcing her to look at him. "Were you pretending?" he demanded.

Her eyes held his for a moment before she spoke. "No," she said, pulling away from him. "But that doesn't matter."

"What in hell does matter? You admitted to me that you—"

"I'll always love Alex," she said, turning suddenly to face him again. "Not as I love you." She hesitated and seemed near tears. "But in a way that you may never understand."

"Don't be a fool, Montana."

"I'm no fool," she said defiantly, all trace of tears gone now. "I know he's had other women. But who am I to cast stones? I've shared your bed more than once."

"But if we love each other—and I do love you, Montana. I want you. By God, I want children with you." He saw her blanch.

"I can't—"

He waited for her to say more but saw that she could not. "You had children once," he said. "Are you telling me you can't have more? It doesn't matter," he said before she could answer. "We could adopt or—"

"Stop it!" she cried. "Stop talking that way."

"No," he said. "No, I won't stop. I love you. I want you. I know you love me, and we both know you don't love Alex."

"It's not that simple."

"Of course it's that simple. Leave him."

"No. I can't."

"What holds you to him, Montana? What dark and evil thing holds you to him?"

She turned away from him again and dropped her face into her hands.

"Tell me," he said, turning her to face him.

"*He* holds me to him!" she said, unable to keep the tears back now. "He was there when I—when I needed him. When I thought I couldn't bear my own shame. When I—"

"My God, what are you talking about?" He grasped her shoulders to keep her from collapsing with her sobs. When he tried to draw her to him, she pulled away. She continued to cry, leaving him feeling helpless, but she wouldn't let him touch her. "Tell me," he pleaded. "Tell me what's wrong."

"I've used you, Langdon," she said at last. "Maybe I should feel shame for that, too."

"Used me? How?" His voice was edged with mockery and anger, but he knew it only disguised his pain.

"By making love to you." She faced him now with a stiff, refractory manner, but he saw that her hands were trembling. "You must never think that I did it without love, but you must also know that I did it for my own selfish purposes."

"What do you mean?"

"I knew it might be the last time I saw you again, and I couldn't bear—"

"It doesn't have to be the last time. I want you to come with me."

"Alex and I are going away. He's taking me back to Tennessee."

"Did he say that? He's building that big house in Colorado Springs. He'd never leave that for—"

"The house was a mistake. Alex has never been wise when it comes to investments. But he can sell it, of course. He told me himself, he wants to go back to Tennessee."

"Don't be a fool, Montana. Think of what you're doing."

"I know what I'm doing. Alex and I belong in Tennessee."

"You belong here," he said. "Not in Tennessee. Those children's graves you told me about once, they're just that, graves. You can't tie yourself to them. You can't bring anyone back by standing over their graves. You have to live your own life."

"Stop it! Stop it!" she cried. "You don't know. You can never know. You can never understand!"

I know, he thought. *I know all too well about it being too late to bring someone back.* Aloud he uttered a grim laugh. It was all he could manage. He was too angry for the hurt she made him feel. "You don't give a damn whether I really understand or not, do you?" He turned away from her, picked up his hat, and started for the door. "Well, maybe I had that coming. I started out just trying to seduce you. But you trapped me somehow. Made me fall in love with you. I guess it's not the first time the student has bested the teacher."

He pushed the door open but turned back to look at her. "You damn near bested me one other time, when you tried to buy the Honesty out from under me. In fact, you've kept me on my toes ever since I first gave you a deck of cards and taught you the difference between an ace and a joker. You've kept this game interesting up to the very end," he said, clamping his hat on his head. Without looking back, he slammed the door and started down the stairs.

She always made him angry when she clung so stubbornly to Alex, and when he was reminded of how he could no more free her of him than he could free his mother of his father's tyranny. His anger was also a flashing sword he had to use to keep back the painful reminder that Montana had, for a moment, made his soul sing, but that once again the music had stopped.

20

 Montana was in Colorado Springs shopping for a new traveling suit to make the trip back to Tennessee when she got the news about the strike. Bob Reed had come to Alex's house to warn her.

"I don't understand how it could have happened," Montana said. "I thought that contract I signed with the Western Federation of Miners would serve as an example for the other mine owners."

"You know the mine owners never liked that idea."

"I knew they were angry at first because I dealt with the union, but I thought they'd finally seen it was a reasonable compromise."

"Nobody's being reasonable, I'm afraid."

"I'll cancel my trip, of course," she said.

"That's unnecessary," Bob said, reaching for her hand and holding it in a protective gesture. "It would be better for you to leave for a little while. It's dangerous to go back to Eagleton."

"Dangerous?"

"Tempers are running high, and they're running irrational. The strikers could be after you just because you're a mine owner, and even some mine owners could be laying for you because of that contract you signed."

"Laying for me?"

"With guns, Montana, or dynamite. It's getting bloody. The super at the Lucky Lady got blown up yesterday."

She was sickened, unable to speak for a moment. "Oh, Lord, no, not Clay Tuttle," she whispered. "I hadn't heard—"

"Some of the union men set a trap in the mine shaft. They were aiming for scabs."

"Union men setting traps? Scabs? Bob, what happened? Everything was peaceful when I left Eagleton last week. I thought—"

"That's just it. You left. And so did Max Hayes. Everything went to hell after that. Hayes went down to Leadville on some union business, and he left some idiot named Theodore Zentner in charge of the WFM bunch in Eagleton. Some of the mine owners—Lem Bailey, Ira Griffith—they were still balking, still wanting to hold out for the old nine-hour, three-dollar day. They sent some spies into a miners' meeting. Seems Zentner found out about 'em, and he and some of his men roughed 'em up a little. Then Bailey and Griffith went after Zentner, and, well, it just went downhill from there."

"Has anybody gotten in touch with Maxwell?" Montana asked. "We've got to get him out there. Maybe he can stop it before it gets any bloodier."

"I don't know, but it may be already too late to stop it. Both sides are wanting blood."

Montana stood, gathering up her wrap and gloves. "Get in touch with Alex for me. Tell him we're postponing the trip to Tennessee. I'm going back to Eagleton."

"You'll be lucky to get a seat on the train," Bob said, standing, too, and putting a restraining hand on her arm. "They're all full of militiamen."

She paused. "The militia?"

"I told you, Montana, it's getting bloody. The governor's getting involved.

"Why hasn't it been in the papers? Why haven't I heard?"

"It'll be in the press today, probably, but I wanted you to know ahead of time."

"I'm going to be on that train, Bob. I'm going back to Eagleton."

"Not alone, you're not," he said, following her when he saw he could not stop her. "I'm going with you."

"Then you'd better hurry."

When they arrived, they found the town in turmoil. An angry crowd had gathered near the depot. Uniformed militiamen were everywhere, trying in vain to control the chaos. Bob helped her from the train and tried to shield her from the crowd while he led her toward the Golden Palace, but Montana held back, hoping to hear what was being said.

"What's happened?" she asked, trying to attract the attention of anyone who would listen. A man dressed in miner's clothing turned to her.

"Explosion at the depot up at Freedom!" he shouted, pointing up the mountain toward the small village that had sprung up around the Freedom mine.

"Oh, dear God! Was anyone hurt?"

"Hell, yes, they was hurt. Body parts strewed all over the place."

Montana felt the blood drain from her face. "Who—"

Her voice was too weak to be heard above the din, but the miner went on talking.

"Damned union did it. After scabs, they say. Scabs, they call us! Don't they know we got a right to work? Got families to feed, damn it!"

He was bumped by someone behind him, then he turned away and disappeared into the crowd. Someone shouted, "Run the damned union out! Shoot the sons of bitches." There were more shouts and angry protests. Fear rose in Montana like bile. She turned to Bob, ready to go with him to the shelter of the Golden Palace, but as she turned, she saw Diana a few yards away, standing near a wagon. She was helping someone up to the wagon bed. When the man was up on his platform, he waved his arms and shouted until at last the crowd grew quieter.

"Listen to me! This is all wrong!" he shouted. "The dynamite at the Lucky Lady was wrong, and the explosion at union headquarters. There's wrong on both sides, and it's got to stop!"

"He's a union man!" someone in the crowd shouted.

"Yes," replied the man on the wagon. "I'm a union man. And I abhor this killing. Sane men on both sides have got to work together so it comes out fair to all of us."

"Shoot the son of a bitch!" a heckler shouted.

At that, someone hit the heckler in the mouth with a powerful right hook. Another—it looked like a militiaman—fired a shot into the air. Suddenly there were shouts and more gunfire.

Montana was frozen with terror, her eyes fixed on the wagon. She saw Diana in a blur and in the next instant heard another shot and saw Diana slump forward and fall to the ground.

Montana screamed and tried to make her way through the crowd to the wagon, but hands from behind caught her and pulled her back. Bob Reed's arms encircled her, and he lifted her off her feet, forcing his way out of the crowd, carrying her in his arms. Montana tried in vain to make him hear her pleas to find Diana, but it wasn't until they were well away from the crowd that he set her down.

"I've got to go back," she said. "Diana's in there. She—"

"It won't do any good," he said, holding her wrist to restrain her. "Look, there's the sheriff with the militiamen. Leave it to them."

"But I've got to find her!"

"You'll find her!" he said. "Later." He was forcing her toward the Golden Palace, but Montana pulled away from him and ran through the angry crowd to the wagon.

She found Diana on the ground, bleeding from a wound that seemed to encompass an entire side of her chest. A few people stood around her, trying to keep the crowd from pressing in too close. Someone held her head in his lap.

Montana screamed her name. Diana's eyes met hers, and she tried to answer, but nothing came from her lips except a bloody foam. Montana dropped to her knees and reached for Diana's hand. It was cold and almost lifeless. She called her name again, but Diana had slipped into unconsciousness.

"Get a doctor!" Montana cried.

"He's on his way," someone said. It was only minutes, but it seemed an eternity before he arrived, being led through the crowd by some of the militiamen.

Montana stayed beside Diana while the doctor took her pulse and listened to her chest with a stethoscope. He turned around then and motioned for two men to bring a stretcher. When he straightened and glanced at Montana, she saw the truth in his eyes. "I'll try to make her as comfortable as I can," he said. Montana tried to speak but couldn't. "Come along with us to the hospital," the doctor said. "She'll need someone who cares."

Montana had not been in the hospital since the fire two years ago. Being there brought back memories of Alex, his burned hands, and the woman whose room he'd been in. It reminded her of Langdon, too, who had stayed with her through the night. A faint moan from Diana brought her back to the present, and she turned to her.

"Montana," she whispered, "I—"

"Don't try to talk, Diana. Please, save your strength. You've got to pull through this."

Montana had to wait outside an examining room while the doctor and the nurses cleaned and bandaged Diana's wound. When the doctor emerged at last, his expression was grave.

"Her wound is very serious," he said. "The bullet punctured a lung. I've given her morphine for the pain, but I'm afraid there's nothing more I can do."

Montana had guessed the truth, but she didn't want to hear the doctor admit it. She turned away from him, fighting tears.

"You can see her now if you like," the doctor said softly to her back. "Having a friend with her will do more for her than I can now."

Montana nodded and took a moment longer to collect herself before she went to Diana's room.

Her eyes were closed and her face a pale mask. Montana was afraid for a moment that it was already too late, but her eyes opened slowly and a faint smile crossed her lips. "You're still here," Diana said. Her voice was only a whisper.

"I'm still here," she acknowledged. "Why aren't you still in Denver?"

"Trouble . . . came back . . . Tennessee?" The words were barely audible.

"I canceled the trip when I heard about this." Montana was suddenly overcome with guilt. "Oh, Lord, Diana, I never should have even gone to the Springs. Maybe if I'd stayed, I could have stopped this."

"Knew you'd be back anyway. Even if this hadn't happened. Because of—of the baby."

"Because of what?" Montana was alarmed. Diana sounded delirious.

"It's all right," Diana said. "I know. But not even the sisters know it's yours." Diana was interrupted by a coughing spasm, and Montana, frightened, tried to comfort her. She urged her not to speak, but Diana seemed intent on telling her something. "Just thinks she's Alex's," she managed to gasp finally.

"Diana, I don't know what—"

"Please," Diana insisted, misinterpreting her protest. "Doesn't matter. I know about . . . mistakes." She grasped Montana's hand and held it tightly. "I have never loved a man. Never loved anyone, except—except you. Oh, God!" She turned her head away. "Didn't mean to tell you that. Thought you could see that I understand. I don't feel wrong to love you. That's why I understand if you don't feel wrong to love your brother. But the baby. You had to hide the baby."

Montana felt disoriented. Diana had never loved a man . . . but she loved her? She wasn't sure what that meant. She'd heard stories, of course, but she couldn't fully comprehend that Diana would fit the role, or that she herself would. And why did Diana think she was hiding a child? "Please, Diana," she pleaded again. "I don't understand—"

"I've seen her," Diana said. She seemed intent upon explaining something. "Little Alexis. Seen her almost every day for the past year . . . love her like she was my own daughter." She chuckled, and it turned into another coughing spasm.

The cough and the blood it produced frightened Montana, and she urged Diana again not to talk. But again Diana ignored her.

"Used to daydream that we could live together, the three of us." Her voice was growing noticeably weaker. "Oh, Montana—" The last was hardly more than a gasp. Her eyes were closed, and blood flecks moistened the corners of her mouth. Montana screamed her name, but there was no response. She put her face close to Diana's and could feel her slight breathing. Pulling away a little, she saw Diana's eyes flutter, then open. She raised her head a few inches to brush Montana's lips with her own, and then she lay back peacefully.

"You can't die, damn you!" Montana knew, even before she uttered those words, that Diana was dead. She had felt the passing of her spirit and had been engulfed in the enormous calm that followed the transition with such totality and brevity. But the calm had given way almost immediately to anger.

How could her one friend in the world leave her? And how could she leave her with so many questions about a child that she claimed was born of incest— hers and Alex's? How dare she die and not explain about her own love!

Montana's sudden anger was just as quickly replaced by deep anguish, and she threw herself across Diana's body and embraced her, crying softly. Finally a nurse entered the room and pulled her away. The nurse led her to the hallway, where she found Bob waiting.

He took her arm. "Let me get you out of this. There's still time to catch the last train back to the Springs."

"No. I can't go," she said. "I have to stay." Her voice sounded to her own ears as if it were coming from a great distance away.

"You have to leave, Montana. They could kill you, too, just like they did Miss Pollard. They're going to run the union out after what's happened now, and there's nothing you can do about it. They're going to remember that you tried to deal with the union, and that's not going to make it easy for you." He grasped her arm firmly. "I'll get you back to safety."

"No," she said again. "No, I can't let the others handle it. Not now. Not after this."

"Montana, please—"

"I've got to do what I can to stop the bloodshed." She glanced toward the hospital room where Diana's body lay. "I want to do it for her."

"It's too late for her, Montana. But it's not too late for you." Bob put his arm around her. "Let me take you back to the Springs," he said gently.

"I don't want to go back to the Springs!"

"All right. We don't have to go all the way back. We'll both stay at the Palace tonight if you like. We can talk in the morning. Things will look different, seem clearer, then. But I want you out of here early."

Montana allowed him to take her to her suite at the Golden Palace. Then he left her, telling her he'd be in the room next to hers if she should need him.

Alone in her bedroom, Montana found sleep impossible. It was not the bloody strike that occupied her mind, but Alex's child—Alexis, Diana had called her. If Diana thought she was a child of incest, then she must have heard the rumor, too. But where was her real mother? Did the baby look like Alex? Did Alex see the child regularly? Diana had said she was two years old now. That most likely meant her mother was the poor, unfortunate girl who had been burned in the fire. But, Montana realized, she could be the daughter of any number of women.

She remembered that Alex had mentioned that the young woman from the fire had died sometime back. Lida—was that her name? If she was the mother, then that meant, of course, that the child had to have a place to live. Had Alex been too concerned about how it would hurt her to suggest the child come live with them? How it must have hurt him not to be able to have the child in his home! She remembered how he had loved their girls and how often he had mentioned wanting another one, and she felt a moment of guilt for the cotton-soaked camphor. It was only that she had been so afraid. But it didn't matter now. Now they would have a child anyway. They would take her—Alexis—to Tennessee, away from rumors and gossip. They would be happy again. A family.

She got up from her bed and began to dress, thinking

she would go to the Sisters of Mercy and ask to see the child. But she turned back to her bed, tearing her clothes off in dismay, knowing that it would be a futile effort. She would have to wake someone to get inside, and they would surely turn her away at such a late hour.

She wondered if Alex had told the sisters who the mother was. Or if they, like Diana, thought it was she? The possibility that the rumor had spread that far left her even more unsettled and restless.

She sat up, staring into the darkness of her gilded bedroom, groping with another question that had now begun to haunt her. Why had Alex been so eager to live in Colorado Springs if the child was here? He loved children. He would want to be near his own. She knew him well enough to know that.

But did she? Had she ever really thought that Alex would be unfaithful to her with so many women? No more than she'd ever thought that she would be unfaithful to him. But he did love children. She couldn't forget that, and she knew that the truth had to be that he had never told her about Alexis because he didn't want to hurt her.

As the hours passed, Montana could come to no absolute conclusions about what should be done about anything she had learned, except that she knew she had to see the child. By the time the first light had turned the sky to amber gold, and before anyone else in the Golden Palace was out of bed, she stood at the door of the Sisters of Mercy.

The aging nun who opened the door was obviously flustered to see Montana McCrory standing in front of her. She could only stare at her at first, unable to speak.

"May I come in please?" Montana said.

The nun flushed and stepped aside. "Of course, Mrs. McCrory. But if you will wait in the vestibule, please, I will tell Sister."

In a few minutes she returned and motioned for Montana to follow her. She led her into Sister Mary Frances's office. Sister Mary Frances glanced up from the work at her desk, then dismissed the other nun with a wave of her hand.

"So you've come," Sister Mary Frances said.

The nun's eyes glowing from her fleshy face were too wise, too knowing, but Montana refused to let her uneasiness show. "I have come to see Alex's child," she said.

Sister Mary Frances showed no surprise at her request, and she answered without emotion. "I'm afraid that's not possible."

"Not possible? I don't understand." Montana struggled to keep a cold, self-assured edge to her voice.

"We must protect the children. I'm sure you can understand that."

"I have a right to see her. She is—"

"You have a right?" Sister Mary Frances's voice was sharp and authoritative, overriding Montana's. "What right do you have? Are you her mother?"

Montana stared at her, uncertain whether the question was rhetorical or accusing. "What right do you have to ask that?" she asked finally. She couldn't keep her voice from shaking.

"You cannot be unaware of the talk of your brother and you."

"That is gossip!" Montana said angrily. "Ugly gossip. You must know that. Up until a few weeks ago I had hardly left this town. If I had borne a child, you and everyone else here would have known."

"Gossip does not concern me, Mrs. McCrory. The child is my concern."

"Then don't use it against me. Especially when you know there is no truth in it."

"I am using nothing against you, and I am not casting stones. I don't know whether the gossip about you and your brother is true or not." The nun held her eyes for a moment, as if considering something. "I'm no fool," she said at length. "I knew the child was not yours. I knew the young woman who bore it. Your brother was the fool, and I let him think what he would about what I do or don't know."

"Then you must—"

"I must protect the children. We cannot always allow even the closest relatives to see them. It serves only to upset them. You can well imagine, I'm sure, the harm that might do."

"No, I can't imagine. I can't imagine why you would allow Diana Pollard to see her and not me."

"It is Miss Pollard who sees to the child's welfare."

"What?"

"Miss Pollard provides support."

"You mean she bribed you."

"No, Mrs. McCrory. I mean she provides support. It takes money to run an orphanage. Miss Pollard realizes that. At first she tried to make me think she was only the messenger who was bringing your brother's money for him. But I knew differently. Your brother provided money because, quite frankly, I insisted that he do so in exchange for a home for his bastard child. When he stopped, Miss Pollard provided help without my request. You, however, did not seem to have Miss Pollard's sensitivity."

"I didn't know that my brother's child was here until Diana—until yesterday. Had I known, I would certainly—"

"You didn't know your *brother's* child was here, Mrs. McCrory?" Sister Mary Frances stood suddenly. "What possible difference should that have made? You knew there were *children* here, did you not?" She slammed the desk with the palm of her hand. "You knew there was an orphanage here with the need to feed and clothe and care for those children. Whether they were brought into this world by your brother or not, they have needs. You and all the others seem to have forgotten that. You may as well have left them to die."

Montana could not speak, and her heart was pounding so hard that there was a pain in her chest. Tears burned her eyes as she looked at Sister Mary Frances. "No," she said at last, her voice barely a whisper. "No, I didn't want the children to die."

Sister Mary Frances was oblivious of her emotions. "But you, just like all the others, want no responsibility," she continued. "You want to visit them now and then, like animals in a zoo. To bring them trinkets and false hopes, only to have your visits dwindle along with their hopes for a chance to live on the outside. I can't allow that."

"You are mistaken," Montana said, her voice trembling. "You don't understand."

"I understand all too well." She spat the words out.

"But if you allowed Diana—"

"I did not *allow* Miss Pollard to do anything. One of the sisters broke the rules and let her in behind my back. You can be certain that the sister was punished, but by the time I knew what was happening, Alexis had grown attached to the woman, and I thought it best not to interfere."

Montana stared at her, thinking that what she had left unsaid was that she did not want to offend Diana since she was providing the money. And Diana had, no doubt, been generous. Yet despite the woman's harsh, condemning attitude, Montana could not feel contempt for her. She recognized a sisterhood with her in her ruthless battle to survive and to protect the children. Seeing her now, rigid behind the desk with her cold, flinty eyes locked defiantly on hers, Montana suddenly knew what she had to do.

"Sister," she said, "there is something we must discuss."

"We have nothing to discuss, Mrs. McCrory."

"Diana Pollard is dead," Montana said flatly.

Sister Mary Frances grew visibly pale. She seemed about to speak, then appeared unable.

"She was killed yesterday in the rioting."

Sister Mary Frances stared at her a moment longer, then turned and walked to the window. She stood there for several seconds, her hands folded behind her back, as she stared out at the town at the bottom of the hill. "It is greed that has done this. Greed on both sides. I heard the shouting and the shots all the way up here," she said, sounding as if she were speaking to herself. "But I didn't go to the hospital yesterday. I had no idea—" She hesitated a moment, then turned slowly to face Montana. "Perhaps you're right," she said abruptly. "We do need to talk." She sat down at her desk, and her gaze pierced Montana. "Why has your brother not come here about this matter?"

"My . . . brother is out of town. He doesn't know about any of this."

"Miss Pollard told you about Alexis?"

"Yes."

"And you knew nothing about her until then?"

"No."

"So now you have come to resume the support Miss Pollard has provided." Sister Mary Frances said the last like a judgment. She obviously did not expect to be contradicted.

"I have come," Montana said, straightening, "to take the child away from here."

Sister Mary Frances stared at Montana, her eyes cold with scorn. "I cannot allow that, of course," she said.

"I am willing to pay handsomely."

"We do not *sell* children, Mrs. McCrory."

"But you do arrange adoptions."

"Of course, but only to families we deem fitting. You have no husband, Mrs. McCrory, and you are a saloon keeper. For all the gold in your Sweet Ivy, and for all the countless dollars your fancy Golden Palace provides you, you are still a saloon keeper. You surely know that does not provide the proper atmosphere to raise a child."

Montana stood. "I would like to see her now," she said.

"Mrs. McCrory, I have just told you, I won't allow—"

"You have just told me that the orphanage is in need of funds. I am willing to provide those funds, Sister, in such a manner that you will have a perpetual income if you are clever enough. You have also said that because I have no husband and because I

am a saloon keeper, I am unfit. Let me assure you
that you have no reason for concern. I *have* a husband, Sister. I have been secretly married for some
time. And I will soon be rid of my saloon."

There was a silence. Sister Mary Frances shifted
her weight on her chair. "I would want to meet your
husband, to make certain he is . . . fit, and I would
want to investigate carefully this financial arrangement you spoke of."

"You will meet my husband, in time, Sister. But I
can give you all the details you want today, right now,
about the financial arrangement."

By the time Montana finished telling Sister Mary
Frances her proposal, the nun was stunned, but she
knew Montana had won the game, and she had reluctantly agreed to expedite the necessary papers for the
adoption of Alexis Miller. Sister Mary Frances had
also agreed, with considerable reservation, to allow
Montana to see the child. She was led into the nurs-
ery by the elderly nun who had first greeted her.

"We have the little ones in here," she said. "With
Sister Augusta." As she reached for the door to push
it open, Montana felt sweat break out on her forehead, and she knew her hands were trembling. Five
children were in the room. They appeared to range in
age from two to five years. Two of the older children,
both boys, played with a toy wooden train, while a little girl sat dressing and undressing a doll with a
painted china face. Two more of the youngest children, a boy and a girl, tugged at a wooden rocking
horse. A nun sat at a desk in the corner and glanced
up when the door opened.

Montana felt unable to speak, unable even to
move. Alex's child was one of the two girls, but

which? The golden-haired child who played so con-
tentedly with the doll? She certainly could be his. But
the little girl who was now squabbling with the boy
over who should ride the horse was also as blond and
fair as Alex. For a moment she saw Elizabeth on the
floor with the doll. Her hair would darken as she
grew older, but she would always be the quiet one,
content to play alone. Susan, whose blond hair fell
about her face in unruly curls, was never content.
She might have argued with a playmate, might have
lured her sister away to the creek.

Montana's hand flew to her throat to control an
involuntary gasp. The nun who had escorted her mistook its meaning for concern over the childish quarrel.

"Oh, don't worry," she said with a little laugh.
"Sister Augusta will see that the quarrel stops."
Montana watched as the nun who had been seated at
a desk in the corner walked toward the two squabbling children and pulled them apart, scolding them
and swatting each soundly on the bottom. Both
began to cry loudly. The two older boys ignored
them and continued to play with their train, but the
little girl put aside her doll and toddled to the crying
children and tried to give one of them a comforting
kiss.

Sister Augusta, satisfied that she had put a stop to
the squabble, now moved toward Montana and the
other nun with a questioning look on her face.

"Sister Augusta," the older nun said, "this is Mrs.
McCrory."

"How do you do, Mrs. McCrory," Sister Augusta
said politely.

"Sister Mary Frances has given her permission to
see little Alexis."

Sister Augusta's eyes widened, and she continued to stare a moment longer. "Very well," she said at last. "But beware. At this age they don't take well to strangers."

"Yes, I remember," Montana said before she realized it.

Both nuns gave her a curious look, then the older one smiled. "She's there," she said. "That's little Alexis." The nun pointed at the little girl who had just been spanked and was now seated on the floor beside her equally miserable playmate.

Montana walked cautiously toward Alexis and knelt beside her. Alexis stopped crying and stared at her curiously, as did her playmate. Montana reached a hand toward Alexis's plump fist and called her name. The child continued to stare at her a few seconds longer, then she jumped up and ran to Sister Augusta, trying to hide herself in the protective folds of her habit.

"I want my nonny Di," she cried. "I want my nonny Di."

"Aunty Diana isn't here," Sister Agusta said. "She'll be around later."

Alexis would have to be told about Diana, Montana thought, but not now. Not for a very long time. There was enough for her to get used to now. Enough for both of them. Montana settled herself on the floor beside the wooden horse and waited until Alexis stopped her crying and peeked tentatively around the nun's skirts. Montana smiled at her. Alexis hid her face, but she did not cry again. She stole one more glance at Montana, and Montana smiled again, waiting for Alexis to make a move toward her. She had begun the long process of getting acquainted.

*   *   *

Montana got back to the Golden Palace only a few minutes before Bob Reed came downstairs, ready to accompany her to Colorado Springs. He found her seated at her desk.

"I'm not going," she said to him when he urged her to get her things before they missed the train.

"You're not going? Why not? I thought we agreed—"

"We agreed to nothing, Bob. I told you last night I had to do what I could to end the strike."

"There's nothing you *can* do. You're going to have to leave this to—"

"There's plenty I can do. I want you to send a wire to Maxwell Hayes for me. Tell him to get back here as soon as he can. I want to set up a meeting with him and the mine owners."

"You're out of your mind! You know the mine owners won't go for that. Anyway, they've already set up their own meeting, without Hayes. Friday at the Antlers in the Springs."

She glanced up suddenly from her writing. "Friday? That's only two days away. Why wasn't I told about it?"

"Maybe everyone thought you were in Tennessee. But even if they didn't, I don't know why you'd be surprised at being left out."

"Well, I'll show them," she said, going back to her work. "I won't be left out. I *will* go with you to Colorado Springs. I'll leave as soon as Diana's funeral is over, and I'll be at that meeting." She glanced at Bob again and said pointedly, "I still want you to get hold of Maxwell for me."

"Montana, please. Don't try bringing Max Hayes in on this. It won't do any good. You're not going to push something down the other mine owners' throats the way you pushed that compromise through the Sweet Ivy board. The owners have already made up their minds to—"

"I'm going to change their minds."

"Good God! You're just going to make matters worse. You're already in trouble with the other mine owners, you know that."

"I don't care what kind of trouble I'm in," she said, slamming her open palm against the desk. "I want this violence stopped!"

There was a short silence as their gazes met. "All right," Bob said. "I'll do what I can. But how am I going to find Hayes?" He sounded annoyed. "All I know is that he's in Leadville inspecting some mine or organizing another union or something."

"Send a wire to the mine. To the sheriff. I don't care how you do it. Just get him to that meeting."

"Don't expect miracles from me," he said curtly. "It may already be too late."

"What do you mean?" she asked, alarmed.

"The mine owners have deputized an army of more than a hundred men to—"

"What!" Montana was suddenly on her feet.

"They saw it as the only way to settle this thing."

"What do you mean, 'deputized'? Only the sheriff has a right to do that."

"They're acting as citizens who, in an emergency—"

"They've taken the law into their own hands, you mean!" Montana felt as if her entire soul had gone queasy. "They've bought themselves an army. Where'd they get them? From the prison in Canyon

City? Off the back streets of Denver?"

"Montana, if you will just—"

"We've already got the state militia here, and there's already been enough bloodshed. Now this *army* you're talking about could get out of control and shoot every militiaman as well as union man on sight." She was pacing the room nervously. "And the union and militia will both retaliate. It will be a bloody civil war! Besides, it's illegal, Bob, you know that."

"Yes, I know it, but don't put the blame on me. You could have stopped it. Instead of preparing to run off to Tennessee—"

"I've made a lot of mistakes in my life," she fired back angrily. "Trying to run off to Tennessee was just one of them."

"Montana," Bob said, suddenly contrite, "I didn't mean—"

"Don't think I'm being a martyr," she said with a wave of her hand. "I'm not. I'm not taking all the blame for everything that's happened, either. I offered a compromise. I thought it would work. It didn't. Now I'm trying again."

"Don't get your hopes up. Even the governor couldn't stop the mine owners from deputizing their own army."

"The governor?"

"He threatened to send in more militia, but it looks like they called his bluff. That's when they organized their army."

Montana turned away from Bob, rubbing her hands together in a nervous gesture. "We've got to get the governor at the meeting," she said.

"That would only inflame everyone more. You know how the mine owners hate Governor Waite and his populist ideas. If he showed up, he'd just negotiate for the strikers."

"If we're going to end this, we've got to have him there, too," she said, turning to face him again. "I'll send the wire myself."

By Thursday word reached town that the mine owners' hired brigade was camped within thirty miles of Eagleton. Everyone in Eagleton was edgy, including the small crowd that gathered at the cemetery for the simple graveside service for Diana. Word had gotten out among the striking miners that Diana was to be buried, and many of them came down from their headquarters on Squaw Mountain to attend. Some of them had been customers of the Golden Palace and had known her first as the bartender and later as a tough but fair employer at the Sweet Ivy. They stood around the grave, facing Montana and the others who attended, while the service was read.

"She was a generous woman who, before her life came to its untimely end, had acquired great wealth, but who never wanted more than love," the minister said, reading the words Montana had written for him. "Those who have come here today to honor her could give her no greater honor than to render love and to work for peace among their fellow men."

His words had no apparent effect. Miners turned away without speaking to Montana or the others, going back to their camp to await the next turn of events. Montana returned to the Golden Palace, which she had ordered closed for the day in honor of Diana.

Within a few hours of the funeral, the hired brigade had halted within three miles of the miners' camp, and the state militia had positioned itself between the strikers on Squaw Mountain and the advancing army. They remained there all night and into the next morning as Montana prepared to leave for the Colorado Springs meeting.

Bob got up early to accompany her, and he looked haggard. "I managed to find Hayes, and I contacted the governor. The other mine owners agreed to the meeting, but I can't say they're any too happy about it. I had to call in some political favors, and I can assure you, this was not the way I had in mind to use those favors."

"You're very resourceful, Bob," Montana assured him. "No one can say you don't earn your fee when you work for me."

Bob gave a cynical snort and escorted her out the door to his waiting carriage and then to the train station.

The atmosphere in the meeting room was strained and fueled with tension. Maxwell Hayes was allowed in only long enough to state his case, then he was banished to the hallway. He agreed to stay in the hallway if the governor was granted the right to speak for the striking miners.

"I think you'll agree," the governor said, "that a working man deserves a decent wage."

"Why should we agree to anything?" Lem Bailey asked. "Why should we agree to pay a passel of god-damned murderers?"

"They're not all murderers," the governor argued. "The situation has gotten out of hand by indiscretions on both sides, and for that reason I think it wise that neither side seek prosecution for criminal acts."

The room erupted into angry shouts until finally Montana stood and walked to the head of the table. The mine owners, always uncomfortable at the presence of a woman in their midst, quieted themselves in grudging deference to her sex.

"The governor is right on one count," she said. "Every man deserves a decent wage. The Sweet Ivy Gold Mining Company hasn't lost any profits with three twenty-five for nine hours. I don't see that the three dollars for eight hours will be any different. I say we all agree to the three-dollar, eight-hour day."

"You caved in a long time ago," Ira Griffith said. "But if we all give in to their bloody demands, it will only get worse from now on. It'll be like giving the damn union permission to kill and maim to get their way."

"The union isn't by itself in killing and maiming," she said. "What about those miners blown up on the train? Who's responsible for that?"

"Don't make no difference who's responsible," another owner said. "You offered the miners a fair compromise, and it didn't stop nothing. I say we join together and run 'em out."

"We can run them out," Montana said, "but they'll be back. Maybe under another name, but they'll be back. And I disagree with the governor on one point. We can't let them get away with violence. We have to see that the guilty parties are prosecuted. But that goes for both sides."

"I ain't caving in," Ira Griffith said. "The Sweet Ivy Company may be the biggest in the district, but we outnumber you."

"Ah, hell, how easy do you think it's going to be to hire for a nine-hour day once the Sweet Ivy goes to eight?" Lem Bailey asked. "The lady's got us by the balls—if you'll excuse the expression, ma'am."

The meeting lasted for four hours. By the time it ended, the mine owners had agreed to the three-dollar, eight-hour day, and they had agreed to allow the state militia, rather than the hired brigade, to take the strikers' arms.

An angry crowd of mine owner supporters, fueled by fears that the strikers were about to wreak havoc on the town, had gathered outside the meeting place. While Lem Bailey stood on the steps to announce that a victory had been won because the strikers would be disarmed and the Springs would be saved from pillage, Hayes and the governor prepared to return to Eagleton to announce victory for the strikers.

"You were brilliant," Bob said to Montana after the meeting. "You're as tough as any man when it comes to business. But of course I knew that. I've seen you in action before, against Runnels." He laughed. "He'll be amused when he hears what you've done."

Montana's eyes widened. "You know how to get in touch with him?"

"Of course. He's still a stockholder, you know. And remember, you'll have to go through the motions of notifying him and all the others of a vote to sign a contract for the three-dollar, eight-hour day. Naturally, with your controlling interest, it's only a formality, but—"

"Have you heard from him?"

"Only a forwarding address. But let's forget about Runnels and stockholders and votes and unions. Let's celebrate tonight. We'll have dinner at the Antlers and then—"

"Thank you, Bob, but I don't think so. I'm going to spend the night at Alex's house, and I want to catch the first train back to Eagleton tomorrow, so I'm going to bed early."

She didn't tell him that she wanted time alone to think. She would have to decide on the best timing to resign from the board of the Sweet Ivy so she could leave Eagleton with Alex for Tennessee as they'd planned. There, no one had ever known them as brother and sister, so there would be no scandal for Alexis. Alex might have not wanted the child around before, but surely that was not the case now. He obviously was ready to give up the fast life. Otherwise he wouldn't have agreed to go back to Tennessee. And if he had kept Alexis a secret to protect himself from his wife's anger, he would soon see that was no longer necessary.

Bob looked at her, not attempting to hide his disappointment. "All right," he said with a resigned laugh. "I know better than to try to change your mind. But let me remind you, all work and no play makes you a dull girl."

"I suppose you're right," she said with a laugh of her own, "but I have a lot on my mind right now."

"What do you mean?"

"I'm afraid I'm about to stir up more business for you."

"Dare I ask what?"

"It's about the Golden Palace. I'm getting rid of it."

Bob's eyes lit up with surprise and delight. "Wonderful! It's about time you moved into the Springs and started a new life."

Montana smiled. "It will be a new life all right. And there's something I'll have to tell you about Alex and me."

"Oh, no," Bob said. "This sounds ominous. That brother of yours hasn't gotten himself into trouble, has he?"

"Not the kind of trouble you're thinking of. But we'll discuss it later. I have to talk to Alex first."

"I'm always at your service, Montana. I think you know that, don't you? And I hope you know that I would like to make the arrangement permanent. I mean—what I'm trying to say, Montana, is that I've fallen in love—"

"I know what you're trying to say, Bob," Montana said quietly. "But I think it's best unsaid."

"It's Runnels, isn't it?" he asked.

"No," Montana said. "Of course not. I—"

"Don't try to hide it. I could see it when the two of you were together. Even when you were arguing at board meetings. But he's gone, Montana. Please accept that, and please accept that he wouldn't have left if he loved you as I do. Give me a chance to try—"

"It's not Langdon," she said, her heart pounding. "It's something else entirely. I'll explain everything later. But, please, give me some time."

Bob held her eyes with his for a moment before he stood. "Whatever you wish," he said. "But allow me to give you a bit of advice. Don't waste your life on someone who cares nothing for you when you can have someone who loves you beyond words."

21

Alex had thought it best he put in an appearance in Eagleton now that the trouble was coming to an end. It wouldn't look good if he stayed away completely, so he'd called ahead to let Montana know he was coming.

To his surprise, Montana did not meet him at the train station. Instead, she had left instructions with the driver of a freight wagon to pick him up and deliver him to the Golden Palace. The driver, a man he recognized as a frequent patron of the Palace, said she'd told him she had an appointment she had to keep.

Alex was peeved not only because Montana had failed to meet him, but because she had sent so ignoble a vehicle to convey him. He would admit that it wasn't easy to find a carriage for hire in Eagleton, but it certainly wouldn't be impossible. He was sure Montana would be waiting for him at the Golden Palace. He needed to talk to her about rescheduling her trip to Tennessee.

When he walked inside the Palace, he saw that it

was crowded with militiamen and miners as well. He had learned on his way out that the militia had been instructed to remain in town for a few more days to make certain no more trouble erupted. He looked around for Montana, and as he walked across the saloon, the new bartender signaled to him.

"Mr. Miller," he said, "there's somebody waiting for you in the office."

Alex gave him a nod of thanks and started for the office, expecting to see Montana waiting there for him. It wasn't Montana who sat at the desk however, but someone in a militia uniform, seated with his back to the door. He couldn't imagine why a militiaman was waiting to see him—until the man turned around. Alex's chest tightened when he recognized the face. Bill Mott stared back at him, a self-satisfied grin on his ugly face. While Alex watched, Mott pulled a gun from his belt and aimed it at his chest.

Montana had known she wouldn't be able to meet Alex at the train, because visiting hours at the Sisters of Mercy Orphanage coincided with his arrival. Soon, though, she wouldn't have to worry about visiting hours. She had just told Sister Mary Frances that Alex was not her brother, but her husband. She had produced the marriage license bearing her real name, and she had told her the story of Montana McCrory. The nun had been shocked, but the financial arrangement Montana proposed was enough to buy her silence.

Montana had now only to tell Alex. Whatever his reasons for keeping his daughter a secret these past years, whether shame, embarrassment, or inconvenience, he had to face up to it now.

She arrived at the saloon only a few minutes behind him, and she scanned the room, searching for him in the crowd just as he had for her. When she didn't see him, she assumed he was upstairs resting after his trip. Before she reached the stairs, though, the bartender signaled her to go to the office. She assumed that meant Alex was waiting there for her. When she opened the door she saw him. He was pressed against the wall, a look of terror on his face. A militiaman stood in front of him with a gun to his head. She sucked in her breath and started to scream, but the sound froze in her throat when the man turned suddenly and pointed the gun at her. Alex, who might have used the opportunity to wrest the gun from the man's hand, instead slumped to the floor in fright.

"It's you," Montana said, barely able even to whisper.

"Yeah," Mott said, keeping the gun trained on her while he reached down and grabbed Alex by the collar and pulled him to his feet. He shoved Alex toward her, forcing them to stand together so he could keep the gun on both of them. "Yeah, it's me. It took me a while, but I found you." He laughed. "Who woulda thought it would be my patriotic duty that brought me to you?"

"What do you want?" Montana demanded.

"I think you know what I want," Mott said. "I want what's rightfully mine. What I won in that poker game three years ago."

"You got what you won. A worthless piece of paper," Montana said.

"Goddamn you! Don't try to cheat me again," he said waving the gun in her face. "You thought you could hide from me by pretendin' to be somebody else, but it didn't work. I heard about this place as soon as I hit town with the troops. People talked about the fancy woman that runs it and her no-'count brother named Alex. The name got me curious. I ain't never forgot it was Alex that cheated me. And when I started askin' questions, I found out the description of the no-'count matched the same no-'count I was lookin' for. Your brother, huh?" He laughed again. "Now, that's a good one!" His expression changed to a smirk. "I found out more than who your brother was, though. I found out about the gold mine. The goddamned Sweet Ivy. Sweet Ivy!" he said, his laughter causing flecks of foamy moisture to appear in the corners of his mouth. "Ever'body in the state's heard o' that. The name Ivy shoulda rung a bell with me. But it didn't. Not until I got here and started puttin' two and two together."

Montana felt her throat tighten as he waved the gun carelessly. "I don't know what you expect to gain by this," she said.

"I'll tell you what I expect to gain," Mott answered, leering at her and making another threatening gesture with the gun. "Several million dollars in gold mine shares, that's what. Whatever you got is rightfully mine, because you cheated me out of my winnings."

"You're crazy," Montana said. "Nobody cheated you. You got what—"

Mott turned toward Alex, grabbing him and forcing his mouth open with the barrel of the gun. With the gun inside Alex's mouth, he turned to Montana. "I want the shares!" he said.

Alex grunted, motioning with his head toward the safe, indicating with frightened eyes that he wanted her to give Mott whatever he wanted.

"Your little 'brother' here claims he don't know the combination to the safe," Mott said. He clicked back the hammer of the gun and laughed at the look on Alex's face. Alex's mouth gaped open to make room for the gun barrel, and his eyes were frightened and pleading.

"All right," Montana said in a voice she didn't recognize. "All right. I'll get whatever you want." She moved cautiously toward the safe, trying to clear her head of terror so she would remember the numbers to the combination. With trembling fingers she turned the dial. She fumbled and had to try it twice more before the safe finally opened and she could reach inside. She pulled out a stack of papers and placed them on the desk. "They're in Alex's name," she said. "He'll have to sign them."

"Do it!" Mott said, taking the gun from Alex's mouth. He moved toward Montana, pulling her toward him and holding the gun close to her temple.

Montana watched while Alex sat at the desk and signed the stocks with his unsteady hand, then shoved the pile toward Mott.

Mott picked them up, holding them in an untidy bundle in one hand while his other hand still held the gun. He picked up a carpetbag in which Montana kept business papers, dumped the papers on the floor, then stuffed the stock certificates inside. "All right," he said, backing toward the door. "I didn't steal a goddamned thing here, and you know it. All I did was take what was rightfully mine. But in case you get any ideas about goin' to the police or claimin' I got these stocks any way except by payin' for 'em legal, you're gonna find the goddamned lid blowed off your pretty little story, and you'll go to jail for stealin' this fuckin' saloon."

Montana felt a quiet shift in her bloodstream as the man moved toward the door. It would be over soon, and once he was gone she would be able to think more clearly.

"Don't get any ideas about comin' after me," Mott

said as if he had read her thoughts. "Stay right where
you are for thirty minutes. I'll be on the next troop
train out of here by then. If I see you on the streets or
if I see a law officer anywhere near me, your story is
as good as blowed to hell."

When he had gone, Alex slumped farther onto the
chair. "Oh, my God," he breathed. Montana could
see that he was trembling. She grasped the edge of
the desk to stop her own shaking.

"Are you all right?" she asked.

"Yes," he said, his voice barely audible. "Yes, I
think so." His gaze held hers. "That bastard. He had
no right. What are we going to do?"

Montana didn't answer.

"At least he didn't get everything," Alex said. He
sounded near tears. "It was smart of you not to give
him all the stock. Just what was in my name." He
laughed nervously. "That leaves me busted. But he
didn't know about the stock we had in your name. At
least we've still got that. He didn't know it was worth
millions." He laughed again. "And you're smart
enough to get the rest of it back from him somehow.
You'll find a way. I know you will," he said, still not
able to control his shaking. "Until then, until I get
back what's in my name, we'll stick together, won't
we? You and me. We'll stay together."

"I know about Alexis," Montana said as if she
hadn't heard him.

He stared at her, his face bloodless.

"Why didn't you tell me?"

"Oh, my God, Ivy, I—"

"She's Lida's child, isn't she?"

Alex put his head on the desk, burying his face in
his arms.

"And you haven't visited her in two years. That's the part I don't understand, Alex."

"Can't you?" he asked, looking up at her while tears streamed down his face. "I didn't want to hurt you." He stood and walked to the window, sobbing.

"You didn't want to hurt *me*?" she demanded. "Why didn't you think of your little girl and how she might be hurting?"

"Don't say that!" he said, whirling to face her. "Don't make me feel I don't measure up. I saw the child once. Nobody knew, except the old nun. I couldn't go back, though. I couldn't look at her without thinking of Susan and Elizabeth. Without seeing the way they looked that day." He sobbed even harder. "I hear their voices still."

"Alex—"

"You never thought I measured up, did you? And neither did they. They laughed at me. Because I couldn't swim. I can still hear them crying for me to help them, and I couldn't. I couldn't swim. I—"

"Alex, what are you saying?"

"Oh, my God," he said, turning away from her again, his body shaking with sobs.

"What did you say?" she asked, her voice oddly calm. "You *saw* them go to the river? You saw them drowning?"

"Why weren't you there, Ivy? Why weren't you there? You never would have let them go—"

"*You* could have stopped them. But you didn't, did you? You never tried to discipline them." Anger rose in her throat like bile. "You gave them permission to go to the river, and all this time you made me think it was my fault because I had left them alone!"

Alex collapsed onto a chair, his face in his hands.

"If you only knew. If you only knew the pain I've suffered because—"

"The pain *you've* suffered?" she cried. She felt as if the blood had drained from her body. "You didn't accept any pain, any more than you've ever accepted any other responsibility. You gave it to me. You'd have let it destroy me."

He looked at her, his eyes reddened, his face swollen. "No, Ivy, I never meant—"

"You used that against me. To control me! Is that why you wanted to go back to Tennessee? To regain control?"

"I never wanted control, only your happiness. I was sending you back to Tennessee to find a place to build a house. It's what you always wanted. To be near their graves—"

"*Sending* me back? Is that what you said? Sending me back? You weren't going with me?"

"I couldn't face the graves—"

"But I could. You'd see to that. So I could continue to take the blame. And all those little ways you had of reminding me of the girls and of their death. I was a fool. I couldn't see what you were doing, but I can see it now. You didn't want me to forget, did you? Because as long as I took the blame, you didn't have to."

"Ivy—"

She turned away from him and ran through the crowded saloon all the way up the stairs and into her room. She opened her closet, pulled out an armload of dresses, and stuffed them into a bag she took from the top shelf.

Alex burst into the room. "What are you doing?" he asked, terrified.

"I'm leaving, and I'm taking Alexis with me. We'll divorce as soon as the adoption is final."

"No!" he cried. "No, you can't. Not now. My stock is gone. I need you, Ivy. You can't—"

"I can, and I will. I should have done this a long time ago, but I let you deceive me. But, worst of all, I deceived myself. But now I'm through with all this deceit."

"You can't leave me!" he cried again. "You don't know what I've done for you. You don't—"

She interrupted him with a bitter laugh.

"I've killed for you, Ivy."

"What!"

"Anna. You don't think it was an accident, do you? I knew what she was saying about us. She was in Lida's room that day of the fire. I could have saved her, but I didn't. I blocked her way, so she couldn't get out. I couldn't let her ruin you."

She looked at him in horror. "You never give up, do you, Alex? You tell me you *murder* someone, and you expect me to be pleased? To believe you did it for *me?*" She shuddered and turned away from him, throwing more clothes into her bag.

"Ivy, I swear I—"

"I suppose it doesn't matter anymore, Alex. It's too late for Anna, and I know now that whatever you do, you do for yourself. Not for me."

"I need you now," he said pathetically. "I need you! All my shares are gone. What will I do? I don't know anything about running the Golden Palace. I—"

"You won't need to worry about running the Golden Palace," she said without looking at him. "I've given it away to charity, just the way Mrs. McCrory wanted it."

"You what?"

"I've given it to Sister Mary Frances for the orphanage." She laughed, turning to face him. "Isn't that a twist of irony? Sister Mary Frances owning a saloon! Maybe she'll give you a job."

She saw then that his face was pale and stricken, and she felt a surge of pity. "I'm sorry, Alex," she said. "I'm truly sorry." She let her eyes linger on him for a moment. "I tried to love you. I really did. And I'll always feel something for you. Fondness, maybe. Maybe only pity, I don't know." She suddenly remembered Bob Reed's words. *"Don't waste your life on someone who cares nothing for you when you can have someone who loves you beyond words."*

"Don't worry about your shares, Alex," she said simply. "I'll have Mott arrested, of course, for stealing them."

"He'll ruin us. He'll tell everybody about us."

"Who will believe a common thief? And how can it hurt us now, anyway? We have all the money we'll ever want." She picked up her bag and started for the door. "Good-bye, Alex," she said without turning around.

"Where will you go?"

She heard the desperation in his voice, and she stopped, but still she did not turn around as she answered. "To Texas."

"Texas? But why? There's nothing for you there."

"I'm gambling that there is," she said. She opened the door and stepped into the hallway.

Alex followed her and watched her descend the stairs. "Come back, Ivy," he called. "Please come back!" She walked through the saloon, never looking back. "Ivy!" he called again. "Oh, my dear, sweet Ivy . . ."

* * *

Montana had forgotten how fretful a two-year-old could be, especially traveling. Not that she had ever gone farther than Nashville with Susan and Elizabeth. Alexis was either hungry or in need of changing or wanting to be read to or otherwise entertained a good part of the three days on the train ride to Beaumont, Texas. At first she cried for Sister Augusta, but Montana found her attention easy to divert, and soon she would be babbling happily about the scenery passing by the window or asking endless questions about everything from the train's whistle to bits of debris she found on the floor.

Montana was grateful for her rambunctious energy. It kept her from thinking too much about her upcoming meeting with Langdon. She had gotten his address in Beaumont from Bob Reed and had thought at first that she would send him a telegram telling him when she would arrive. But at the last minute she'd lost her courage.

How could she tell him in a wire about Alexis? Could he accept that the two of them came together now, as a package, so to speak? Of course he'd said he wanted children, but how would he feel about Alex's child? She would have to tell him, of course. She would tell him everything. She was through with deceit. But she wanted to tell him everything face to face. It was best to see Langdon's eyes when he first learned about Alexis. It was best not to give him time to prepare a facade.

By the time they left Houston, she couldn't keep her hands from trembling. She longed to see him, to be in his arms again, but she knew she'd done a foolish thing. Of course she should have told him she was coming, even if she didn't mention Alexis. No one liked surprise visits. And if he'd changed his mind about wanting her with him . . . at least he would have had time to think of a way to tell her graciously.

It was too late to change all that now, though. The train was rushing her on toward her uncertain destiny.

In a short time she sensed the train slowing, and the conductor made his way through the cars, announcing Beaumont as the next stop. She glanced out the window and saw nothing at first but a flat stretch of land clogged with undergrowth. In a little while a few weathered buildings came into view. The train stopped in front of a high platform. The station looked deserted.

Montana gathered up her wrap and traveling bag and took Alexis into her arms, then made her way down the aisle to the door. Once before a train journey had brought tremendous changes in her life. Would this one do the same? Or would she and Alexis soon be on another train? Going back to Colorado was impossible, she knew. She had passed the point of no return. Whatever happened in Beaumont, she would not be going back to Colorado.

The air was thick with moisture from the Gulf, creating a haze that partially obscured the few buildings that dotted the green plain behind the station. A wagon lumbered down one of the dirt streets in the distance, but otherwise the town looked as deserted as the train station. And it looked even shabbier than Eagleton had the first time she had seen it. Langdon had come here to look for oil—a commodity he said would be as valuable as gold someday. He was being foolish, of course. Black, sticky oil could never be as valuable as gold. And even if it were, it was obvious no one had had much luck finding it here. But then, Langdon Runnels had always liked a gamble.

She put Alexis down and took her hand to lead her

toward the building. She would inquire inside for directions to the address where Bob had said Langdon had an office. She halted, uncertain now whether or not that was the thing to do. It was growing late. Langdon would no longer be in his office. Maybe she should find a room first. Alexis looked up at her with a questioning expression.

But then Montana saw the figure approaching them. The walk, the swing of the shoulders, the cocky way he tilted his head, were all blessedly familiar to her. It was as if she were seeing him walking across the prairie to her again, with the stranded train behind him. Still holding Alexis's hand, she took several steps toward him, then stopped, uncertain again. But he moved ever closer, carrying a misshapen package in his arms.

As he drew nearer, she saw his smile, heard him call her name. She ran toward him, and in the next moment she was in his arms.

He kissed her, and she forgot everything else until she felt Alexis tugging at her skirts. She knelt beside her and looked up at Langdon. "This is . . . Alexis," she said breathlessly, her pulse dancing erratically in her throat.

"I know."

"You—you know? But how—"

"Bob Reed sent a wire. That's how I knew to meet the train."

Her eyes brimmed at Langdon's easy acceptance, and her heart was warmed at the thought of Bob's noble resignation. Then she thought she saw a moist glimmer in Langdon's eyes just before he knelt to help Alexis unwrap the package he had handed her.

Inside was a miniature violin.

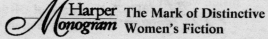

COMING NEXT MONTH

SILVER SHADOWS by Marianne Willman

In this dramatic western of love and betrayal, Marianne Willman, author of *Yesterday's Shadows*, continues the saga of the Howards. Intent on revenge for wrongs done to his family, half-Cheyenne Grayson Howard unexpectedly finds love with a beautiful widow.

THE WAY IT SHOULD HAVE BEEN by Georgia Bockoven

From the author of *A Marriage Of Convenience* comes a story of drama, courage, and tenderness. Carly is reasonably happy with a stable marriage and three wonderful children. Then David comes back to town. Now a famous author, David had left twenty years before when Carly married his best friend. He'd never stopped loving Carly, nor forgiven her for leaving him. Yet, Carly did what she had to do. It was the only way to keep the secret she must hide—at all costs.

THE HEART'S LEGACY by Barbara Keller

When Céline Morand married the man she'd dreamed of for years, she thought the demands of love and duty were the same. But an unexpected trip to the lush plantation of her husband's cousin in Louisiana ends Céline's naiveté and opens her heart to a man she can't have.

LADY OF LOCHABAR by Jeanette Ramirez

In this beautiful, heartbreaking love story, Maggie Macdonald is but seven years old when Simon Campbell saves her life after his father's army has massacred her entire family. As fate would have it, they meet ten years later and enter into a forbidden love.

OUT OF THE PAST by Shirl Jensen

When Debbie Dillion moves to Texas to pick up the pieces of her life, she finds her dream house waiting for her. But soon Debbie wonders if she has walked into a living nightmare, where someone is willing to do anything to hide the past—even commit murder.

WHEN DESTINY CALLS by Suzanne Elizabeth

A delightful time-travel romance about a modern-day police officer, Kristen Ford, who would go to any distance—even to the rugged mountains of Nevada in the 1890s—to find her soul mate.

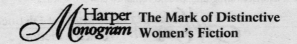

Harper Monogram The Mark of Distinctive Women's Fiction

ANALISE

Analise Caldwell was the reigning belle of New Orleans. Disguised as a Confederate soldier, Union major Mark Schaeffer captured the Rebel beauty's heart as part of his mission. Stunned by his deception, Analise swore never to yield to the caresses of this Yankee spy...until he delivered an ultimatum.

ROSEWOOD

Millicent Hayes had lived all her life amid the lush woodland of Emmetsville, Texas. Bound by her duty to her crippled brother, the dark-haired innocent had never known desire...until a handsome stranger moved in next door.

BONDS OF LOVE

Katherine Devereaux was a willful, defiant beauty who had yet to meet her match in any man—until the winds of war swept the Union innocent into the arms of Confederate Captain Matthew Hampton.

LIGHT AND SHADOW

The day nobleman Jason Somerville broke into her rooms and swept her away to his ancestral estate, Carolyn Mabry began living a dangerous charade. Posing as her twin sister, Jason's wife, Carolyn thought she was helping her gentle twin. Instead she found herself drawn to the man she had so seductively deceived.

CRYSTAL HEART

A seductive beauty, Lady Lettice Kenton swore never to give her heart to any man—until she met the rugged American rebel Charles Murdock. Together on a ship bound for America, they shared a perfect passion, but danger awaited them on the shores of Boston Harbor.